BIG MOTHER 40

BIG MOTHER 40

By

Marc Liebman

Fireship Press
www.FireshipPress.com

BIG MOTHER 40 : BY MARC LIEBMAN

ISBN-13:978-1-61179-231-7: Paperback
ISBN 978-1-61179-232-4: ebook

BISAC Subject Headings:
FIC014000FICTION / Historical
FIC032000FICTION / War & Military
FIC0012000FICTION / Action

Edited by Dorrie Obrien
Cover Work: Christine Horner

Address all correspondence to:
Fireship Press, LLC
P.O. Box 68412
Tucson, AZ 85737

Or visit our website at:
www.FireshipPress.com

Table of Contents

Table of Contents

Acknowledgements

In writing BIG MOTHER 40, I had several goals besides telling a good story that readers would enjoy. First, I wanted to be historically accurate even though the story is fiction. Yes, I did change some call signs and may have some squadrons in the wrong air wing. If I did, my apologies.

Second, as Dorrie O'Brien, the editor who helped me polish the book, often pointed out, you could write a textbook on the command relationships and while that may be interesting to some, trying to explain the intricacies of them doesn't belong in a novel unless it affects the plot. So, we compromised – they're in the book but simplified enough so they are both believable and understandable.

Third, the flying scenes had to be technically accurate. Yes, I took some liberties with the performance of the H-3, but you would have to go into a NATOPS manual – that's the Navy's version of a pilot operating handbook – for the H-3 to find them. There were many writing and rewriting sessions where I had my H-3 NATOPS manual open on my lap. Besides being an excellent reference, it brought back many memories as well as a reminder of how much time I spent studying it.

Fourth, is using side numbers and call signs correctly. Again, within the confines of a novel, I tried to be true to how Naval Aviators and military pilots talk on the radio.

Sometimes we use the word "zero," sometimes it comes out "Oh." "Niner" is the phonetically correct radio term for the number "nine" and it is often used both ways. I deliberately stayed away from aviator slang such as "triple sticks" for an airplane with a side number of 111 or "double nickel" for airplanes or helicopters with 55 in their side numbers.

Fifth and last, is that I wanted to convey the importance of authentication procedures in rescues and special operations. So, you want to get in and out as soon as possible and most important, make sure that the person you are about to pick up is a good guy and you are not flying into a trap. Early in each deployment, we gave the intelligence folks four questions and answers that they could ask if we were shot down and about to be rescued. One of the lessons learned is that when you make multiple attempts, you run out of questions so one had to improvise by asking the survivor questions that only he would know the answer.

Since this is my first published novel, there are way too many people to thank and I don't want to turn this into an Oscar acceptance speech. However, I do want to thank Michael James, the COO of Fireship Press for his faith and willingness to invest in a book called BIG MOTHER 40 written by a newcomer. Without his leadership and commitment, this book would still be a dream and ones and zeros on my laptop. Then there is Chris Paige of the Fireship team who spent time getting this book to print. I also want to thank Barbara Marriott, fellow author and wife of another Naval Aviator and helicopter pilot for making the introduction to Fireship.

Marc Liebman

My most important thanks go to Betty, my lovely, understanding wife of 42+ years who put up with the long hours I spent in what I refer to as my "garrett" working on the book and what will, I hope, become sequels. My mother, may she rest in peace, kept encouraging me to write and keep writing knowing that some day it would pan out. Mom, thanks and that day has come.

I hope you enjoy reading BIG MOTHER 40 as much as I enjoyed creating it.

Marc Liebman

September, 2012

RULES TO LIVE BY
IN SPECIAL OPS FLYING
a.k.a. DICTA HAMAN

> Always assume the bad guys are smarter than you.

> You'll live longer by being sneaky and stealthy than if you are brave and bold.

> Be unpredictable. Predictability gets you killed.

> Always have one more viable alternative than the bad guys.

> Expect the unexpected. That's why you have so many alternatives worked out.

> Don't be afraid to ask for all the help you need, and then use it wisely.

> The best way to demonstrate your skill in the cockpit is by completing the mission and bringing everyone home alive and the machine undamaged.

> Plan your own missions. Don't ever let anyone plan it for you unless they will be sitting in the cockpit with you.

> Build your own intelligence picture to augment/clarify what the spooks tell you.

> Complacency is as dangerous as the enemy and just as deadly.

> Teamwork keeps you alive; individuality gets you killed.

> Dying is an individual event and is to be avoided whenever possible.

Indochina

Ho Chi Minh Trail and Sea Infiltration Routes

Vietnam War theatre, c. 1965–70

CHINA

Ha Giang

Chinese buffer zone (50 km)

Lang Son

Dien Bien Phu

Hanoi

Haiphong

Gulf of Tonkin

Ninh Binh

Thanh Hoa

Black River

Red River

HAINAN ISLAND

Vinh

Ha Tinh

L A O S

Mekong

Ho Chi Minh Trail

B-52s from Guam and Okinawa

Vientiane

Dong Hoi

Udon Thani

Nakhon Phanom

DMZ

Khe Sanh

Quang Tri

Hue

Da Nang

THAILAND

Ubon Ratchathani

Ho Chi Minh Trail

Chu Lai

My Lai

Nakhon Ratchasima

Dak To

Phu Cat

Pleiku

Qui Nhon

B-52s from Thailand

Tonle Sap

Mekong

CENTRAL HIGHLANDS

U-Tapao

CAMBODIA

Nha Trang

Cam Ranh

Phuoc Long

Loc Ninh

Gulf of Thailand

Phnom Penh

Phan Rang

Tan Son Nhut

Kâmpóng Saôm

Saigon

Bien Hoa

Communist supply route

Major North Vietnamese air base

Can Tho

Mekong Delta

SOUTH CHINA SEA

Major U.S. air base

U.S. corps headquarters

U.S. aircraft carrier group

0   50   100 mi
0   50   100 150 km

© 2005 Encyclopædia Britannica, Inc.

Location of Venom Base in Northwest North

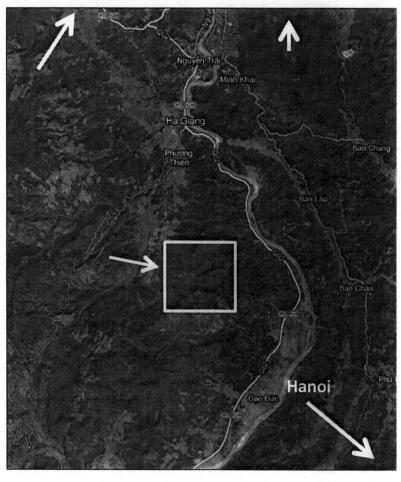

Chapter 1
ANGER AND EARLY BATTLES

JANUARY, 1968, OUTSIDE LENINGRAD, USSR

Colonel Alexei Koniev of the Soviet Air Defense Forces relished the stinging, needle-like pain from the icy rain pelting his face. It was, in his mind, the perfect weather for a funeral: bleak, dark, and cold. Just like death itself.

For the second time in ten days, he was standing alone by a gravesite. Last week it had been his wife's. Today it was his seventeen years old daughter's.

Both were dead because his country didn't have enough antibiotics. They were both dead because of incompetent doctors who either didn't care or know how fast complications from the flu that turned to pneumonia could kill a young girl with asthma.

There were no more tears to be shed. They, like the rest of his family, were gone. Alexei no longer cried; he retched. Three things were left in his life—his career in the air defense artillery, loneliness, and the never-ending sense of loss. And what were any of them worth?

MARCH, 1968, 2 MONTHS LATER, A-SHAU VALLEY WEST OF HUE ON THE LAOTIAN BORDER, REPUBLIC OF SOUTH VIETNAM

Captain Nguyen Thai of the North Vietnamese Army stared through the circle of his East German binoculars at bare-headed American soldiers tossing dirt into growing mounds that would become fighting positions. He judged the distance between them and his men—hidden in a clump of trees about fifty meters behind him—to be about seventy-five meters. Each man in his company waited for the order that would send all two hundred fifty of them creeping in darkness through the meter-high, razor-sharp elephant grass. They hoped a mortar barrage would let them get close enough to toss grenades into the machine-gun pits and then overwhelm the American defenders inside their defensive perimeter.

1

Thai was sure his head was well below the small rise, when he pulled out his map to mark what he assumed would be M-60 machine gun positions that would be targets for his two mortars. He was laying on his back, which gave him a chance to study the shape of the few cumulous clouds, when a flash froze him in place. He scanned the sky.

He sensed the North American F-100 jets' presence before he saw or heard them, but by then it was too late. Thai recognized the jets as they flew low and parallel to the tree line, which meant one thing: napalm. Time slowed as he watched two silver canisters tumble from the first F-100's wings and, despite the fading shriek of the jets' engines, he heard the pop as the tanks exploded just above the treetops. Thai tried to roll under an exposed root just as the air was sucked out of his lungs. He wondered what the odd odor was, and then realized he was smelling his clothes and flesh burn.

WEDNESDAY, 2 YEARS, 3 MONTHS LATER, JUNE 9, 1971, 0700 LOCAL TIME, ALONG THE HO CHI MINH TRAIL BORDER ABOUT 40 MILES WEST OF DONG HA, THE NORTHERNMOST TOWN IN SOUTH VIETNAM

Dawn doesn't come easy in the jungle, and the lack of early morning light makes people think it is earlier than it is. The pungent smell of a cooking fire alerted Marty Cabot's stomach to tell his brain to shift into wake-up gear and get some breakfast, but an unfamiliar weight pressing into his abdomen kept him from moving. He tilted his head up and saw the blue and black bands of a krait coiled on his belly.

The krait sensed its warm bed stir and raised its oval head to sample the air with its forked tongue, while it stared at the dirty face with six days' growth of beard. It slithered off after deciding the source of the heat was not a meal. When the deadly foot-long snake was about three feet away, Marty pulled his Kukri, a Gurkha knife, from the sheath on the side of his pack and with a short stroke chopped off the snake's head.

The silent beheading brought smiles from the other seven members of his team, one of whom gutted the snake and put the carcass in a plastic bag to save it as a potential meal. No one spoke since they, too, smelled pungent mung bean paste mixed with rice and other spices heating in leaves, which would become *banh chung* for the NVA soldiers about one hundred and fifty meters away on the other side of the clearing that was supposed to be their primary pick-up point.

After Marty motioned to two of his men to go down the trail to see if their claymores had been disarmed, he low-crawled to the center of the even-sided, triangular shaped ravine where he could study the grass-covered meadow, whose shape and size matched the picture in his pack.

As he scanned the tree line on the far side, he could see tendrils of smoke and an occasional North Vietnamese soldier.

It was decision time. Were the Vietnamese passing through, or were they waiting to ambush the helicopter coming to pick them up? He munched on his next to last D-ration candy bar while observing the Vietnamese soldiers prepare their breakfast.

Today was "hunger day" for the SEALs, whose call sign for this mission was Gringo Six, because it was the day they ate the last of their rations. If they had to stay in North Vietnam longer, they would have to live off what they could find in the jungle. They'd already begun to prepare for that possibility by collecting wild fruit—mostly pomelos—and now the dead snake.

Gentle pressure on his leg told Marty to slide back from his perch. A team member told him in hushed tones that their claymores were untouched, and the extra grenade they'd set to explode if anyone had cut the trip wires was also undisturbed.

They'd arrived at the LZ a day earlier after spending three days counting trucks pass between the lines of porters pushing bicycles with saddle bags filled with supplies on the Ho Chi Minh Trail. Movement continued day and night along the section they watched, though the southward flow stopped to allow small convoys with wounded soldiers to pass on their way north. The most important find was a refueling station which, if the drums of fuel were set on fire, would slow the movement of trucks until it was replenished.

Decision time. Move or stay? If they moved, they'd have to contact the Air Force EC-121s, which flew orbits over Laos with the call sign of Billiard Ball, to tell Big Mother 40 to pick them up at their first alternate pick-up point, Kneissl 200, instead of the primary one labeled "alpha."

Marty looked at his map and confirmed that Kneissl 200 was about two kilometers away from their present position before taking up his perch again to watch the North Vietnamese soldiers. They had time before they had to notify Billiard Ball if they wanted to change the pick-up time and location.

He was studying the map and was about to make the call on whether they should move to Kneissl 200 or to stay, when a team member tapped his foot. Looking up, the hand signals told him what the suddenly quiet jungle said—many NVA were approaching their position from their front and to the right, and a battle was about to begin.

Marty folded the map as he reviewed their plan to escape from the deep wedge-shaped ravine that had its ten-yard wide base a few yards inside the tree line and narrowed into the tip of a triangle with a base farther into in the jungle about eight yards down the hillside. Water erosion dug it about four to five feet deep in places, which made it an excellent defensive position, but no one in Gringo Six had any intention of making their last stand there. As he gathered the team, Marty figured they had ten minutes to deploy to their pre-selected positions before the shit hit the fan.

One fire team of two SEALs would protect each side of the triangle while the fourth team, equipped with one of the Stoner light machine guns, set up farther along the ridge and on the flank of the ravine. The second Stoner team in the triangle would swap with one of the other teams to gain fire superiority, which would let them disengage and escape.

Marty positioned himself just off to one side of the point of the triangle and nearest the approaching enemy. When he spotted two NVA soldiers attempting to scout their position, Marty made sure the safety on the suppressed Smith and Wesson Model 39 semi-automatic pistol chambered in 9mm was off as he slid it through the foliage and aimed it at the NVA soldiers, who were less than twenty yards away.

The first soldier who fell with two red holes in his face caused the second to pause before he, too, started to fall face flat on the wet earth. A third crawled up, touched the soldiers and looked up, trying to find the shooter, when Marty squeezed the trigger two more times. The third NVA soldier crumpled to the ground on top of one his comrades, not knowing where the shooter was located.

The clatter of several PKM light machine guns which broke the sudden quiet and sent bullets whizzing well over his head were meant to pin his team down as the attack began. Marty was sure four were spraying bullets at their position below the top of the ravine, which meant, according to his knowledge of North Vietnamese People's Army organizations, that there was at least a platoon in front of them. If they followed their traditional doctrine, the series of attacks from the front and the flank would to try to flush them out into the clearing, which would make it easy for the NVA soldiers on the other side to pick them off.

The intermittent machine gun fire went on for about five minutes, providing cover to allow the NVA to get close so they could rush the SEALs' position and overwhelm them with superior numbers. Marty was wondering why the rounds weren't chewing up the dirt at the edge of the ravine when the first Claymore went off and the steel balls made three distinct noises as they ripped through the leaves, smacked into tree trunks, and thudded into NVA soldiers.

The second Claymore banged off with the same result as the first with the added clang of the spoon coming off when the trip line for the Claymore was released by its explosion. A few seconds later, the grenade went off. The explosions and the screams from the mine's victims told the SEALs that the attackers were about thirty yards from their position.

The gaps between the bursts from the PKMs became shorter and then began to taper off when there was a yell and the thrashing of men running through the jungle which set off a ripple of their remaining six Claymores. After the singing of the mine's ball bearings died down, the surviving NVA soldiers charged.

Marty dropped the first two men he saw with short three-round bursts from his M-16. As much as he hated and mistrusted the light automatic rifle, because of its reputation for jamming in the middle of a firefight, Gringo Six carried them for two reasons. One, because it fired the same 5.56mm cartridge as the Stoners, and two, each man could carry three hundred and sixty rounds, along with a spare one hundred-round box magazine for the Stoners.

Pausing between targets, Marty could hear the Stoner on the left side of the triangle's base ripping off short aimed bursts. With only a dozen thirty-round clips per man, the SEALs used discipline and aimed their fire; they didn't have the ammo supply to spray and pray. They had to get fire supremacy in a hurry and then disengage.

When the SEALs didn't see any new targets and the PKMs stopped firing, Marty tapped the Stoner team leader in the ravine on the shoulder, then pointed to the position where the second Stoner was hidden and had, according to their plan, still not fired a shot. A nod, and the two men reached the second position just as the second rush came. All four men left in the triangular shaped ravine were firing continuously when the leader of the fire team on the other side of the ravine looked at Marty, who gave him the signal to bug out. Marty and his teammate kept up a steady stream of accurate bursts while the two men joined the four others about thirty yards farther up the hill and away from the NVA.

The PKMs started increasing their rate of fire, but the shooting was still well above the edge of the ravine. Lying on his back, reloading, it suddenly struck Marty why the soldiers were firing the PKMs high. "Get two grenades ready." He pointed toward the clearing behind them four times to give his fire team the direction to toss grenades, then mouthed *one, two, three*, and both men tossed their first grenades simultaneously, following quickly with their seconds.

Screams from wounded men in the elephant grass confirmed what he suspected. One of the Stoners started spraying the elephant grass, the other started shooting, killing men in the jungle approaching the right side of the ravine, giving Marty and his fire teammate cover to scramble out and join the rest of the team as they poured bullets into the NVA soldiers swarming over their former position.

Big Mother 40

The SEALs kept up a steady stream of accurate fire for another two minutes before clambering down a steep slope they'd scouted the day before in case they needed to get out of the area. On the way down the trail, one of the SEALs, Thomas, at the tail end of the line yelled, "Shit, I'm hit!"

Chief Jenkins and two other SEALs ran back up the trail. While one man kept firing, the Chief and the other looped their arms under the fallen man's armpits and hauled him down to the others, who scanned the jungle for NVA while the team's medic tended to Thomas.

Sixty minutes later, Marty called a halt and the team deployed in a rough circle around its leader.

"Ammo check."

The reports from the seven other members told him that they'd expended about forty percent of their ammunition for the M-16s and all their Claymores. For the Stoners, they had three one hundred-round boxes left for each.

Satisfied with the report because he had guessed that they were down to less than fifty percent, he pulled out his map. "We need to call in and tell Big Mother 40 that Kneissl 200 is the new pick-up point and we'll be there for a dawn pick up."

The radioman nodded and began getting the radio ready.

Chief Chris Jenkins, Gringo Six's number two, cradled his M-16 in one arm while he levered himself into a sitting position on the muddy jungle floor next to his team leader. "What the hell happened back there?"

"I think some of their scouts stumbled on us and then they moved on us from two directions, figuring the first to make contact would fix our position and keep us occupied to burn up ammo. While they were doing that, they'd hit us from another direction and then from the back." Marty used a twig to draw their position and the direction of the attack in the soft earth. "The PKMs firing well over our heads gave it away. The bastards were making sure they didn't hit their own guys in the elephant grass."

"Got it. Good news is there were a bunch of bodies in the ravine and in the grass. My guess is there was the better part of a company coming at us in that ravine and we got maybe thirty."

"Yeah, but that was way too close. They almost got us all."

"Boss, Billiard Ball is on the line. This airplane's call sign is Billiard Ball Zero Nine." The radioman handed Marty the handset.

6

Marc Liebman

Josh Haman was about to put the last piece of bacon in his mouth when the bartender asked, "Are you Navy Lieutenant Haman?"

"Yes." Josh looked at his watch. It was a little after 9:00 a.m. in the officers' club at Nakhon Phanom Air Base in Thailand, where the bar was open twenty-two hours a day. You could order breakfast with the alcoholic beverage of your choice at 6:00 a.m.

"Sir, you have a call." The Thai bartender handed him the black dial phone and moved to the other end of the bar.

"Lieutenant Haman here."

"Sir, this is the command center. You have a message here and this is not a secure line. We are sending a driver over to pick you up."

"Thank you. I'll be waiting." After he hung up, the tab for both meals appeared on the bar out of nowhere and Josh tossed several bills on the table that more than covered the cost.

"What's up?" Lieutenant (junior grade) William E. Braxton III, AKA "Call me Bill," Josh's co-pilot for the last three months, struggled with the zipper that was caught on the Nomex fabric of his flight suit.

"Got a message in the command center. Do you know where the guys are?"

"Yeah, either at the BEQ or the enlisted club. I can get them on the phone. Why?"

"You never know. We may need to go get a team that's in trouble."

The dark blue van with yellow lettering on the door was waiting for them by the time they came out of the club; two or three minutes later it dropped them at the front door of the operations center. After presenting their identification cards and signing the log, the two Naval aviators were led to a darkened and soundproofed room that had its own cipher lock. Their guide introduced Josh to the communications center's senior non-commissioned officer, who handed Josh a sheet of yellow paper with the hand written text of the message from Gringo Six.

"Sergeant, do you have radio contact with Billiard Ball?"

"Yes, sir."

"Can I talk to them?"

"Sir, the operations officer would need to approve that. But I think that can be arranged. I'll go get him."

Two minutes later, Josh slipped on a headset with ear phones that were bulky, bulbous dark blue sound suppressors and adjusted the boom mike.

"Sir, this is the mike switch. The EC-121's call sign is Billiard Ball Zero Nine. They got on station about oh-six-hundred and then had a call from Gringo Six. Sir, when we talk to Billiard Ball, our call sign is Dome. Today, we're Dome Five Five. When the communicator on board Billiard Ball Zero Nine acknowledges your call and knows the topic, he'll route you to the operator who talked to Gringo Six. The back end of the airplane is full of guys who are monitoring different frequencies. Everything is encrypted, so it'll take a few seconds for everything to sync when you key the mike."

"Thanks, Sergeant." Josh waited for a few seconds and then keyed the mike and waited until he had a clear side tone before speaking. "Billiard Ball Zero Nine, this is Dome Five Five, over."

"Dome Five Five, this is Billiard Ball Zero Niner, over."

Josh could hear the noise from the four big, supercharged eighteen-cylinder radial piston engines and the hum from the four-bladed props, even with the distortion from the encryption. The stillness of the soundproofed corner of communications area made it easy to concentrate on the conversation, unlike in the noisy, vibrating environment of a helicopter. "Billiard Ball Zero Niner, understand you had talked to Gringo Six. Can you provide more details, over?"

"Stand by." The circuit went silent and Josh figured that another operator was about to come on the line.

"Dome Five Five, who's asking?"

"Big Mother Four Zero's aircraft commander, over."

"Roger, Gringo Six asked for next usual time pick-up at landing zone Kneissl 200 for eight. One wounded. Steep narrow mogul run. Copy?"

"Billiard Ball Zero Niner, did he say anything else, over?"

"Dome Five Five, he added that surfer boy is swimming with the sharks. May be late. It didn't make sense to us and we thought it was gibberish to confuse the NVA because they were using their PRC-90 survival radio. That was all that was said, over."

"Thanks. Dome Five Five out." Josh took off the headset and handed it to the sergeant. "Thanks. That was very helpful."

"I guess we've got work to do, so I'll get the guys together," Braxton said, leaning against the edge of a table behind the Air Force sergeant's desk.

"Next 'usual time' is dawn and they're about an hour and half from here at the most. That means we'll take off around oh four hundred. Let's get everyone up to speed and then get some sleep. It may be a long day."

When Marty Cabot sat down and leaned against the tree; he was so tired his bones ached. Besides the NVA, he was fighting mental fatigue, his brain dulled by physical exertion and the post adrenaline crash that follows firefights. Marty sat there with his head resting against the trunk, knowing it was going to be another night of fitful sleep and no real rest for his weary body and brain. No one on the team was going to close their eyes for more than two hours until they were on Big Mother 40, headed to Thailand. Yesterday was the easy day, because it was over.

The NVA seemed to be everywhere on this mission. Gringo Six had been playing a deadly game of hide since seek the day after they were inserted on the eastern edge of Ho Chi Minh Trail, about one hundred kilometers north of the DMZ near where Highway 18 crossed into Laos.

In four productive days they had found, photographed, and mapped two large truck parks and refueling stations set up so a convoy could pull in among the drums and diesel fuel would be pumped by hand into the vehicle's tank from a fifty-five-gallon drum. The SEALs watched the NVA soldiers empty one and then roll another into place in a practiced drill. The second facility, near the Laotian border, had a large garage in a metal shed that was under a camouflage net.

The team, at this point in the mission, was tired of running, tired of hiding, and tired of avoiding contact with the NVA. Marty and each of the other seven men on the team knew that stealth was more important than winning a firefight like the one they'd just had.

His watch glowed 2223, about an hour after he'd gave Billiard Ball a status report.

"We've been here for thirty minutes," Chief Jenkins said, kneeling beside him. "We gave Thomas some blood and we're ready to go. Bad news, we'll have to carry him on a stretcher. We got the bleeding stopped but he's got to keep the weight off his leg. Round went into his thigh and probably messed up the bone a bit."

It was dark with the stars and moon hidden by clouds when Big Mother 40 flew over the glistening Mekong River that separated Thailand and Laos well south of Nakhon Phanom with a full crew: AMS2 Derek Van der Jagt, Aviation Avionics Technician Third Class John Vance, and Aviation Electrician's Mate Second Class Nicholas Kostas. An hour later, light was beginning to appear on the horizon as the helicopter crossed the line on the map that said they were leaving Laos and entering North Vietnam.

"Josh, turn about twenty degrees to the left to oh-seven-five and that should take us right to Kneissl. It is about twenty minutes from where we are now. Radio's set."

"Billiard Ball Six Four, Big Mother 40 is in Indian country."

"Big Mother 40, roger that. Be advised Billiard Ball Six Four has four helo Sandys about ten minutes away, and two A-6 Intruders, call sign Green Lizard Five Oh Six and Five Oh Eight, on a road reconnaissance in your area, if you need help, over."

"Big Mother 40 copies."

In the growing light, the trees one hundred feet below the helicopter were changing from a dull, black, indistinguishable blur to individual trees that made up the lush green canopy. Josh pushed the intercom button. "When we are ten minutes out, give Marty a call."

"That's about now." Bill took a deep breath—the fun part of the pick-up was about to begin. "Gringo Six, Big Mother 40, do you copy?" He waited about ten seconds for an answer and hearing none, keyed the mike again, repeating his call.

Chief Jenkins twisted the soft plastic ear piece to ensure it was seated properly and that the plug was firmly in the socket before he turned the radio on. Before keying the mike, he reminded himself to use the zero one identifier to tell the guys in the helo that Marty was not the speaker. "Big Mother 40, this is Gringo Six Zero One, we're ready. All clear."

"That was not Marty." Josh pulled the intercom switch back before Bill could answer the call. "Gringo Six Zero One, authenticate."

"Big Mother 40, surf's up, beach boy is with a wounded swimmer. Copy?"

Braxton looked at Josh. "What the fuck does that mean?"

"He's telling me that Marty is with the wounded guy and I'm guessing they may or may not all be at the LZ. We'll find out soon. Do you see the LZ?"

"Two o'clock, about a mile."

"Got it." Josh kept the helo at a hundred knots as they passed over the clearing and then rolled the helicopter into a sixty degree right bank so he could keep it in sight as he circled for a landing. The landing zone was big enough.

"Do the landing checklist. Doesn't look like much wind. Am going to land to the east."

"Already done, gear going down." When he saw the indicators switch to down, Bill keyed the mike. "Gear down and locked. We're ready for the pick up."

As the helo was flaring to a stop prior to touchdown, two figures carrying their M-16s by the handle ran from the jungle. As they got on board, Van der Jagt handed one a set of sound suppressors that had a mike and earphones.

"Sir, Chief Jenkins. Marty and the rest of them are okay, but they are carrying Petty Officer Thomas on a stretcher. He's got a nasty thigh wound. My guess is that they are about two to three hours behind me. He sent the two of us ahead to let you know."

"Where does he want us to pick him up? We're not going to leave him behind. We don't have the gas for a search, it is way too dangerous to fly around and wait for him, and we can't sit here for that long. It'll draw the NVA like shit draws flies."

"Sir, he said you'd figure something out."

"His confidence in me is inspiring. Let's get out of here." Josh looked over his left shoulder and saw Van der Jagt close the personnel door. He pulled up on the collective and Big Mother lifted straight up. He lowered the nose a degree or two about fifty feet off the elephant grass and began a climbing turn as the helicopter accelerated.

"Chief, does Marty have a radio, and do you know about where he is at the moment?"

"Yes, he has one of our two radios. I don't know where he is, but I can show you the direction we came to the LZ."

"That's a start. Bill, take us west as if we were going back to Nakhom Phanom while I talk to the chief." Two clicks acknowledged while Josh loosened his straps so he could turn in his seat to face the chief. "Did you pass any small clearings that could be used?"

"I think we passed a couple of small ones, but it was hard to see in the dark. We didn't stop to look."

Josh held out their map and photo of the landing zone. "Which route did you take to Kneissl?"

The chief studied the map for a few seconds. "We came in this way."

"Are you sure?"

"Yes, sir."

"Okay. Take us back to Kneissl, Bill, and take us over it heading one seven zero at about sixty knots."

Big Mother 40

Braxton clicked twice and made a shallow bank to turn the helicopter to a heading that would take them over Kneissl and down the route Jenkins had shown them.

"All the guys have their load-bearing harnesses with the crotch straps on?"

"Everyone except Thomas."

"Do we have to lift him in a litter?"

"No sir, we've got his thigh tightly bandaged and the leg splinted. The bleeding has stopped but he can't stand on his left leg. He's also sedated."

"Okay, everyone listen up. Here's the plan: We're going to come back around and fly down the route the SEALs took to Kneissl, looking for a hole in the jungle big enough to get the jungle penetrator down to the ground and pull them up. I hope Lieutenant Cabot has the radio on. When we find him, we'll direct him to the nearest hole and hoist them out. Van der Jagt, I'm going to tell them we're going to lift them out two at a time. That's three hoists. It means we're going to be in a high hover for a long time. I expect we're going to take some small arms fire."

Josh pointed to his chest and took back the controls. "I've got it," he said to Bill on the intercom before keying the mike to talk on the radio. "Gringo Six, you listening?"

"We're up."

Josh could tell the speaker was struggling to control his breathing. "Mark me on top." Two clicks. He slowed the helicopter to fifty knots by pulling back on the cyclic and lowering the collective.

"You just passed me about two hundred meters to the right."

Josh counted to three, then wracked Big Mother 40 into a seventy-degree bank to the left for ninety degrees and then back to the left for two hundred and seventy so he could roll out a on a reciprocal heading he hoped would bring him over the top of Gringo Six.

"On top NOW!"

"Boss, there's a small clearing about a hundred meters to the west that looks to be about fifteen to twenty feet in diameter."

"Gringo Six, there's a clearing about a hundred meters to the west. Meet me there in less than ten. Am going to hover over it and drop the penetrator with a smoke just before you get there. Hook up with your torso harnesses and then sit on the spokes. Copy."

"Copy. Moving now."

"Bill, dial up full power and we'll see if this beast will hover at a hundred feet out-of-ground effect. I think it will be marginal, but I'm willing to drop down to about ninety-six percent rather than going away and dumping some fuel."

"Got it."

"Billiard Ball Six Four, this is Big Mother 40, over."

"Big Mother 40, Billiard Ball Six Four, we've been monitoring your transmissions, go."

"Billiard Ball Six Four, we're going in to pick up Gringo Six and we'd like some help because we suspect it will be a hot pick-up. We'll get just one shot at getting them out before all hell breaks loose."

"Billiard Ball Six Four copies. Will direct the Green Lizard Intruders and two Sandys. Have two Jolly Green helos covering the morning strike, but can divert if needed. Squawk forty-sixteen and ident, over."

Bill gave Josh a thumbs up after he spun the new IFF frequency into the transponder and pushed the Ident button.

"Big Mother 40, radar contact. The cavalry is on the way. ETA plus ten for the Sandys, less than three for the Green Lizards, which have less than ten minutes of play time. Copy?"

"Penetrator's rigged and I have smoke ready to drop as soon as you're in a hover," Van der Jagt said.

"We're going to ease into the hover to make sure we have the power to do it. Assuming we don't have to dump fuel, you can direct me in."

"Yes, sir, agreed."

Josh eased back on the cyclic and raised the collective to slow the HH-3A. He guessed they were down to about nineteen thousand pounds, including about twenty-five hundred pounds of fuel, which, according to a quick look at the performance tables, meant the helicopter might have just enough power to do the job. Emphasize *might*, because the charts don't account for the age and hours on the engine or the efficiency and age of the rotor system. The wild card was that they didn't know how much power the seventy percent humidity and eighty-eight degree Fahrenheit temperature would rob from the engines.

Bill called out the rotor RPM. "Ten knots, down to ninety-nine percent."

"I've got the clearing fifty feet ahead. Easy," Van der Jagt called out.

Josh flexed his fingers and then eased forward on the cyclic and added a bit more power on the collective. The helicopter crept forward.

"Ninety-eight percent and steady."

"Ten feet. Tossing the smoke now."

Josh eased back on the cyclic and added more power to hover.

"Ninety-seven percent."

"Steady hover. Penetrator is on the ground. Two men hooking up."

The clatter from an M-60 and the green tracers passing by the nose of the helicopter told Josh the pick-up was not going to go unnoticed.

"This is Green Lizard Five Zero Six. Both Green Lizard Oh Six and Oh Eight have a visual on Big Mother 40. We can see the source of the ground fire. Oh Six is rolling in hot followed by Oh Eight."

Josh heard a series of pings and a hole opened in his side window, followed by a smack into the wing of his armor-plated seat; he winced. He had to focus on keeping the helicopter in a steady hover over the clearing, about twenty feet above the treetops and about one hundred and ten feet, according to the radar altimeter, above the jungle floor.

"First two SEALs approaching the helicopter." The words were followed by the distinct humming sound the mini-gun that shot out the cargo door on the starboard side made when it was fired. The first long burst was followed by three more.

"We've got the first two in the helicopter. Steady. Steady hover. Penetrator is going back down."

Josh could sense the scurrying around going on in the cabin as Thomas was moved to a position where they could take care of him. The M-60 and an M-16 began firing out the passenger door and Van der Jagt's mini-gun was humming away. Good news was that the expenditure of ammunition was making them lighter.

"Down to ninety-six percent and steady. We're getting heavier due to the extra people. No caution lights."

Josh lost count of the loud thwacks that said bullets were finding the boron epoxy armor and the pings made by rounds going through the fuselage's thin aluminum skin. He pushed back into the seat, trying to make himself small and have only his legs and arms out beyond the wings of the armored seat. They had to just sit there in a hover and take it and hope the NVA didn't hit something vital, like him, or put a hole in the transmission, which would seize in less than thirty seconds if it lost all its oil.

"Green Lizard Five Oh Six and Five Oh Eight are Winchester and at bingo fuel. Understand Sandys will be here in less than two minutes. Good luck, Big Mother 40."

"Steady. Steady. Last two survivors are on the penetrator."

The thrum of the mini-gun was clear in the background. Josh thought he could hear the tinkle of the brass piling up at the gunner's feet.

"Penetrator coming up."

Josh had to sit there and wait until Van der Jagt said the two SEALs were clear of the trees because he didn't have any spare power to climb vertically. More pings. More smacks. Three holes opened in the upper windscreen and then went through the eyebrow window; as he stole a long glance at all the instruments, Josh wondered if the bullets had hit something important, like an engine or hydraulic line, after leaving the cockpit.

"Survivors well clear of the trees." Van der Jagt's voice was muffled by the mask he wore to limit wind and rotor noise. The hum of the mini-gun was noticeable in the background.

Josh counted to three and eased the cyclic forward; as he increased power, the helicopter would settle. How much he did not know, but he didn't want to drag Marty and the other SEAL through the treetops.

"Survivors almost to the helicopter."

Another hole in the windscreen showered him with glass, making it obvious that the NVA were aiming at the pilots. More thwacks as the helicopter began to accelerate.

"Everyone's on board and okay. Let's get the hell—!" The last few words were drowned out by the sound of the mini-gun.

Chapter 2
FIRST DATES AND ASSIGNMENTS

Despite the ankle-length poncho impregnated with rubber, the bottom of newly promoted Colonel Nguyen Thai's uniform trousers and new boots were soaking wet by the time he got from the pedi-cab to the doors of the nondescript gray structure that, in a different era, had been the French Army in Indochina's headquarters. Since the steps leading up to the entrance were almost fifty feet above the street level, he stopped to look around to see how the war had affected downtown Hanoi. He was surprised at how little had changed since he'd left for the south in early 1971 for his second tour, other than that there were fewer young men on the streets. He was glad to be back in his home town now, after being wounded in a battle along the Ho Chi Minh Trail.

Thai had made the trip from Army Central Hospital 201 in Haiphong the night before; he'd had the truck driver, who'd been on his way to the Xuan Mai Military Barracks, drop him off at a small hotel. He wanted to be in the city center rather than spend a night near a location he was sure was high on the Americans' target list. To him, the higher cost, which would not be reimbursed, was insignificant compared to spending one precious night just a little farther away from the war.

He shook the water off the poncho in the shelter of the portico of the French-built building before rolling it up. Entering the rotunda, Thai saw a small desk near the center, manned by two soldiers, one of them a corporal, and a waist-high wooden banister preventing access to the elevators, which he assumed weren't working, due to a lack of either parts or trained maintenance technicians.

"General Chung's office," Colonel Thai said, and handed the corporal his identity card. If needed, he had a copy of the teletype message in his shirt pocket that ordered him to this building to prove that he had an appointment.

17

Big Mother 40

The young soldier looked up and came to attention. Thai guessed he was still in Hanoi by family connections. He saw the reaction in the teenage corporal's eyes as he took in Thai's ruined face, while the private stared where the wall joined the ceiling at the far end of the room. *They ought to see what the rest of my body looks like,* he thought.

The young man's stare took him back to the A-Shau Valley in 1968. The sight of the two silver canisters from an American Air Force F-100 tumbling toward his unit's position was still vivid in his mind. Despite his scars, he was lucky that the jellied liquid had only burned his back, right arm, right side and the right half of his face.

After six months in agony in an underground hospital, Thai had begun the slow trek north from the field hospital whose entrance was, he guessed, about four kilometers or so inside Cambodia. He was placed on a stretcher and carried to a pick-up point on the Ho Chi Minh Trail where he, along with another hundred or so wounded, lay out in the open, waiting for the empty trucks to arrive that would take them on the five-hundred kilometer journey back along the twisting and turning trail north to recover in a hospital outside Hai Duong, a small town about halfway between the port of Haiphong and Hanoi.

Soldiers and porters moving south, along with an occasional truck carrying food and other supplies as well as ammunition; and returning trucks carried the wounded who could be moved north on a journey that would take weeks because the southward movement was given priority. Together, they made the trail look like a path of army ants. The road was often bombed and under repair and the overused trucks broke down under the strain. Trucks that broke down or were damaged by bombs and couldn't be repaired were scavenged for parts and left to rust.

His burned skin had kept cracking and his body had weakened as it fought infection. He'd been given occasional doses of morphine and antibiotics and nothing else. Thai had turned down the painkillers and had lain on his cot, enduring the pain as he waited for his body to heal. It wasn't until six months later that he was returned to duty and sent back to South Vietnam as a major in command of the 716th Special Reconnaissance Battalion. The two-hundred-fifty-man unit was tasked with tracking American Army reconnaissance teams being inserted into Laos and Cambodia to reconnoiter the trail and call in air strikes.

Rather than react and chase the American and South Vietnamese patrols, Major Thai trained his battalion on how to find and drive the Americans into traps where the small, four-to-eight-man teams could be annihilated before they could be rescued. He tried several different tactics, some were successful and some failed; but after about six months his unit had a string of eight actions in which the American team was flushed out shortly after they were inserted and forced to run before they could accomplish their mission, or taken prisoner, or annihilated. His success was noted and he became Lieutenant Colonel Thai and tasked with training another similar unit, the 623rd.

The tactics he devised were as traditional as they were simple:

- Flood the suspected area with platoons that were at least fifty men strong;

- Once contact was made, pin the Americans down to keep them from disengaging;

- Maneuver to get on one of their flanks;

- Maintain contact to keep the pressure on until the Americans were out of ammunition and surrendered, or were overrun and killed or captured; and,

- Do it fast before the Americans could call in an air strike or a rescue helicopter.

Thai didn't realize the Americans had changed tactics until his battalion had run into an eight-man team prepared to fight a short, pitched battle. He often replayed the events of that June day in 1971, trying to figure out what went wrong and how he could avoid future defeats like that. They'd been in trouble from the moment the first Claymore mine had exploded, decimating the leading squad. The second and third squads went off the trail and charged, setting off more of the deadly Claymores: Three squads ceased to exist within seconds of each other.

Thai had rushed forward to take command because the company commander was killed and he was afraid that the platoon commanders would hesitate to keep pressuring the Americans to force them to use ammunition. Once he found the company's command element, he sent a runner back to his executive officer with orders to take another platoon out to the right of where they thought the ambush was and to try to get behind the Americans. He ordered a reserve platoon to go forward to gain fire supremacy with their PKM machine guns and AK-47s.

That had been a terrible mistake. The Americans had been waiting there for several days and were well prepared to stop him. Thai had been hit twice, once in the arm and once in the shoulder, and his left leg took several shrapnel wounds from grenades in the side; but he, unlike most of his men, survived. Each time they made contact, the Americans escaped and his troops were further decimated. Of the three hundred men with him that night, fifty carried thirty wounded comrades back to their base and twenty were left to bury the rest. After exploring the American positions, they found no evidence that any of the Americans had been wounded or killed; it was clear from the piles of shell casings they'd been up against eight well-armed and prepared soldiers.

Later, Thai learned through reading radio intercepts that the team had an unusual call sign: Gringo Six. He could not get the name out of his mind.

The corporal dropped his eyes and used his finger to search a list of names and then found a note. His companion decided to focus his attention elsewhere in the empty rotunda rather than look at the colonel's scarred face.

"General Chung's office is on the second floor, in room two oh one, Colonel. He is expecting you." Both soldiers saluted.

"Thank you, Corporal Trang." Thai returned the salute.

Another soldier at the top of the stairs armed with a Makarov pistol ushered Thai into a small conference room and placed a glass of mineral water on a table next to a chair. Thai took that as a suggestion as to where General Chung wanted him to sit.

"Good morning, Colonel Thai." The voice was strange: lilting and high-pitched, even for a Vietnamese. He guessed the short man weighed, soaking wet, at most fifty-five kilos. But shaking his hand was like putting your hand in a vise. "An old friend of yours, General Tran Van Dong, will be joining us in a few minutes."

"Yes, sir, and good morning sir." Thai didn't know what to say. General Dong had sent him south to take command of the 716th and then the 623rd. Since he hadn't heard from the general after his return from the battle in which two companies were decimated and his subsequent assignment to an infantry officer training unit just outside Haiphong, he figured he was no longer well regarded and was, as the French Catholics would say, in purgatory. This was all right with him, because the longer he stayed out of the meat grinder in the south, the greater were his chances of surviving this war. As he often did when he thought he might live through the war, Thai wondered what he would do. He could, he hoped, take advantage of the expensive French education his parents had provided him.

"I hear you have recovered from your wounds." General Chung smiled as he spoke.

"Yes, sir. I am both healthy and fit."

"You come highly recommended for the assignment we'll be discussing soon. From what I read, you are an excellent battlefield commander, trusted and respected by your comrades above and below you in rank. And, despite getting a degree from the Sorbonne, you are politically reliable."

"Thank you, sir." What the hell was the remark about the French school and politically reliable supposed to mean? Had Chung not seen his medical records or looked at his face?

"I understand you speak Russian."

"Yes. With my father's encouragement, I studied Russian history and learned the language, but have not had many chances to speak it since the war began." Thai thought Chung must know that his father, a university professor, had become a Communist when he was at the Sorbonne in the thirties, had been an ardent admirer of Stalin and Lenin, and had come back to Indochina right after World War II to fight the French. He had been, for God's sake, a close friend of Ho Chi Minh. Now both he and his mother were gone. Disease, more than old age, had taken them when they were in their sixties.

"That is going to change. We have a special job for you."

The door opened without a knock and the weathered face of General Tran Van Dong appeared. "Ah, the right room."

He opened the door wider and Thai saw that his boots were wet, which meant he didn't work in this building, either. Why was Dong here? The last time Thai had seen him was when he'd left to go south to take over the 716th.

Colonel Thai stood up and came to attention before shaking hands with his former superior officer.

"Please, sit down, we are among friends," Dong said in a pleasant voice.

Were they? Thai had known the general for most of his career. He was one of the instructors at the officers' academy, then Thai's first battalion commander, and then again his division commanding officer. But where had Dong been since? Other than the chance meeting they'd had as Thai was heading south, he'd not seen or talked to the general in at least two years.

Back then, as he was recovering from his wounds, Thai was working at army headquarters helping analyze the latest intelligence on American reconnaissance teams that operated along the trail, particularly in the area just south of the DMZ where it went into Cambodia, when General Dong had come in the room. They'd talked briefly, and Dong had ended the conversation saying that he was confident that Thai would do well and he wished him good luck. So Thai would not call Dong a friend. They knew each other because they'd worked together, but in the end, Dong was

Thai's superior officer who could order him into hopeless situations where he could die.

"I am sorry I am late. General Chung, what have you told Colonel Thai?"

"Only that he has been chosen for a special project and I have confirmed that he is fit." General Chung pulled a folder out of his briefcase. He slid the sheet of paper across the table to General Dong, who glanced at it and then pushed it aside as if to say "I have already figured that out from the officer and my own sources."

Thai sat mute, feeling like an outsider looking in, wondering why two generals wanted to tell him about his new orders rather than just send him a piece of paper. He crossed his legs as Dong pulled a folder out of his own briefcase.

"General Chung, I assume this room is very secure."

"It is. There should be no one in the rooms on either side of us and the guards at either end of the hall will prevent anyone from passing by."

"Excellent." General Dong took a deep breath. "So let us begin."

"Colonel Thai," General Chung began by pulling another sheet of paper from his briefcase, "you have been selected for a very special, Top Secret assignment. It is based on your experience and combat record for creating units that can excel at difficult missions. You are also one of our leading experts at tracking, finding, and annihilating enemy special forces teams." The general paused for a second. "Our country is in the process of building a secret missile base northwest of Hanoi located under the route the American Air Force jets take to attack us from Thailand. This base will be equipped with the latest surface-to-air missiles from our Russian comrades and have its own firing control radars."

Thai forced himself to be impassive and unemotional, but he couldn't help wondering, *Why me?* Both generals knew that he didn't know a damned thing about missiles.

"The base will be home to Soviet Anti-Aircraft Defense Force experts who will operate the new missiles. We will have our own officers assigned to work with them. This base will also need protection because, in the end, it will be found and attacked. So we are creating a combined regiment of anti-aircraft batteries and infantry to defend the base and a detachment of our officers who will learn how to use the missiles. These men will have already been trained by the Russians and will have used older versions of their Divina missiles in the defense of our country. You will be the base commander and responsible for the defense of the base and will report directly to me. Our Soviet comrades in arms are there to run the intercepts and shoot the missiles. I would like you to leave as soon as possible, so please contact my office to arrange for transportation. They will provide you with copies of the officers' personnel files and training records, as well."

The general looked down at his paper on which Thai could see had many handwritten notes. "The Russian missiles and our anti-aircraft batteries will get information from and be tied into our air defense network but will operate and fire independently. The Russians want to try out some new tactics and are sending one of their top experts to test out some new theories that can increase the kill ratio. Our country has agreed to build this base for this experiment."

"General, I am honored by the assignment and will do my best to carry out my orders." Questions raced through his mind. "If I may, I would like to ask a few questions."

Generals Dong and Chung nodded.

"Where are the men located now?"

"Most of the infantry is already at the base. You should have four companies of about two hundred fifty men each."

"Sir, how many anti-aircraft guns will we have? Will they be S-60s?"

"Yes. Four batteries of four S-60 57mm guns each will be sent up there as soon as the base can accommodate them. Once you determine the base is ready, then the S-60s will be sent."

"How many Russians will be there?"

"We are not sure yet, but they have asked if they can send their special forces, the Spetznaz, along with the officers. We are thinking about twenty to operate the missiles and maybe another twenty Spetznaz."

Thai hesitated, but he knew he needed to ask the next question, even though asking it might lead to a change of orders to some division in the south. "Who will be in overall command of the base?"

Both generals looked at each other, which told Thai that neither had a good, clear, and simple answer. General Chung pushed a sealed envelope across the table. "You are responsible for protection and operation of the base. It is in your written orders along with the notification that promotes you to full colonel. Both documents are in this envelope. The senior Soviet officer will be responsible for shooting the missiles. That is all we can tell you."

Big Mother 40

The cold gray sky reflected his mood and told him more snow was coming to the Zhukov Command Academy of Air Defense, located on the Volga River about a hundred miles northwest of Moscow. The low temperatures meant spring was still a long way off. The wind battering the window outside his small office, cluttered with Soviet Air Defense Force missile systems' manuals, was a hard reminder that winter was still around. The side of his messy desk sat against one of the dull gray concrete walls adorned only by the obligatory pictures of Lenin and Breshnev. The desk and to a large extent the small room was dominated by the only real picture, a large black-and-white photo of a young girl and her mother.

Today was the fourth anniversary of his wife's death from pneumonia. He and Valentina had been married for twenty-four years. The coming Monday would be the anniversary of their child's, Alexandra's, death. Fewer tears came with each anniversary, but even though the pain lessened with time, it still hurt.

When he heard a knock on the door, he placed the framed picture on the bookcase behind him. It had been taken in happier times when he'd been stationed in East Germany. "Come in."

Colonel Alexei Koniev stood up when he saw the towering figure of General Dimitri Poliakov, the head of the school where he was a senior instructor, teaching air defense system tactics and doctrine. The school was the older man's last assignment, and the respected World War II veteran had stayed on active duty in the army he loved as long as he could. Poliakov, the father of the Soviet surface-to-air missile systems tactical doctrine, was a very, very large man, almost two-and-a-quarter-meters tall, and Koniev guessed a taut, muscled one hundred and twenty-five kilograms. "Alexei, am I interrupting something?"

"No, sir. I was just reading and grading some of my students' papers."

"You looked very thoughtful. Were you thinking of Valentina and Alexandra?"

Alexei realized that his moist eyes had given him away. Poliakov had rescued him from the bottle and despair by installing him in the school to dry out and share his innovative ideas. "It is the fourth anniversary of Valentina's death, and next week is the anniversary of Alexandra's passing. It is a hard time of the year for me."

"I am sorry. I should have remembered the dates. It is hard to lose a wife, much less a wife and child just a week apart."

"Life must go on." And they wouldn't have died if their great socialist republic provided competent doctors who could stay sober so they could use their knowledge to treat their patients, or sufficient medicines for its citizens.

"I have something that may cheer you up. It will let you put some of your more interesting theories into practice." The general was referring to Koniev's top secret study called "Ambushing Attacking Aircraft with Dispersed Missile Sites."

"What do I have to do?" The only place they were shooting Soviet surface-to-air missiles at enemy aircraft was in North Vietnam. Koniev was one of the favored few who saw the reports coming out of that embattled country. He was careful not to voice his opinion that the optimistic analyses overstated the effectiveness of the missiles. When asked, he offered no comment other than saying they made interesting reading.

"The General Staff wants you to test your theories in North Vietnam. They, as I do, think you are the perfect man for the job. This is a two-year assignment. You will be told more if you agree to go."

"When would I leave?" It wasn't like Koniev had a choice.

"Soon. We will send you to language school to learn Vietnamese. We cannot assume that our allies will speak Russian. Then off you go to Hanoi where you will be further briefed. The plan has you in Hanoi by the first week of April." The general stopped for a few seconds. "You should get a star out of this."

"Thank you for your confidence, General, but you know I am not after promotions." Koniev looked up at the General, who was leaning with both hands on the back of the chair in front of his desk. "How big is the detachment and who will I be working for in Vietnam?"

"From what I understand, we'll be sending about four to eight officers who have been trained here, about a dozen technicians to maintain the missiles, and a platoon of our special forces—you know, the Spetznaz—to protect the stuff we don't want our Vietnamese friends to have. I don't know any other details. My guess is that our Vietnamese allies will provide security and you will be responsible for shooting the latest generation Divina missiles."

"Sir, I'll go."

"Excellent. I will notify the general staff, who will be pleased. Do not discuss this with anyone. We will tell your colleagues you have been picked for a new assignment."

Big Mother 40

"See those two girls over there?" Jack D'Onofrio nodded with his head in the direction of one of the small nooks well away from the bar and dance floor. As usual, the club was filled with attractive, available women and Naval Aviators and Naval Flight Officers looking to score. On the rare occasions women had to buy their own drinks, they were half price.

"Where?"

"My ten o'clock." Jack had his back against the bar. "Two girls, one has long dark hair, dark complexion and is your type. She's sitting next to a sandy blonde. Both are at least eights."

"Tally ho."

"Standard bet." Standard bet meant ten dollars was on the line; the challenge was to get to 'first base,' i.e., buying a girl a drink. "It doubles if you get the dark-haired one onto the dance floor, triples if she leaves with you, and I pay you fifty if you get her into bed on the first date." Josh was ahead of the game because the last two times they'd made this bet, Jack hadn't even gotten to sit down and Josh had collected twenty bucks, which he'd spent on a dinner for both of them.

Josh put down his beer. He'd been back in the states for almost four months as an HH-3A Sea King replacement pilot instructor but was bored, so he'd volunteered for a second tour with HC-7 and was awaiting his official orders. D'Onofrio was one of his students, about three-quarters of the way through the training syllabus, and already had orders to HC-7.

The two of them, both from the Northeast, had become running buddies. Jack was from a traditional New York Italian family and had grown up in Queens. He was 5'8" on a good day, broad-shouldered, and built like a bowling ball. Josh was just under six feet, lean but not skinny, muscled, but not muscular. Josh had moved around the world because his dad had been in the Air Force before he retired and settled in Sudbury, outside Boston. Both were competitive. Josh was an excellent ski racer, good enough to be considered for the U.S. National team. Jack's build made him ideal for wrestling, which he never pursued beyond high school because college sports took too much time away from chasing girls.

"Okay, you're on." Josh finished his beer before taking a $10 bill out of his wallet and slapping it into his friend's hand. *Well, here goes nothing.* She'd probably think he was just another horny Naval aviator and after a few seconds turn him down cold.

"Hi, my name is Josh. I'd like to talk." It was the best he could do at the moment. He was addressing both of them, but looking at the dark-haired girl whose hair, now that he was closer and could see it, shimmered in the reflected light. She had large, black, oval eyes that sparkled.

"This is Carla," the girl whose hair shimmered said, "and I'm Natalie." There was a definite pause but he could feel the tension relax a smidgen. "Please, take a seat."

"Before I do, what are you drinking?" he asked.

"At the moment, nothing. We're between drinks."

And, Josh thought, I don't have a drink or a clue what you are drinking, if anything. Was this a hint to offer to buy them a drink? "Can I get you a refill of whatever both of you are drinking?"

"Maybe later. You're going to be disappointed. Carla had a Seven Up and I'm drinking a Coke and haven't finished this one." Natalie held up the glass: it was three quarters empty.

"Do you want another?" Why would he be disappointed? She was gorgeous and he was already ten bucks ahead.

"Not yet." Another pause. "Does Josh have a last name? Tell me something about you that might interest me."

Game on. She was either toying with him or interested. Could go either way, but he liked her expressive eyes. If he didn't interest her in the next thirty seconds, he was going down in flames and would lost ten dollars in the process. "Last name is Haman. Turned twenty-five this past summer, I fly helicopters, am a native Vermonter and an Air Force brat who grew up in Central Europe whose favorite sports are skiing and sailing. I love Italian, Chinese, and Mexican food, in that order. Now it's your turn."

"Not bad. You're assuming that I am going to say anything."

"I am." He smiled as he looked at the very attractive face on the other side of the table. "One has to have high expectations."

"And your intentions are?"

"Strictly honorable."

Natalie laughed. "I don't believe that for a minute. If you weren't interested in getting me into bed as fast as you can, you'd be a disgrace to Naval aviation."

"Guilty as charged, but one has to start with honorable intentions." It sounded hollow but Josh felt it to be true.

"I'll accept that for the moment. I'm a junior at San Diego State, majoring in dietary science. Grew up here in San Diego. Parents immigrated after World War Two, which explains my last name, which is Vishinski and… I used to play soccer. Favorite foods, well, let's just say I'll try almost anything."

Josh shifted to speaking in Russian. "So how is your Russian?"

Natalie's eyes registered a smile before she responded in Russian. "Excellent, but my father hates the Russians and prefers to speak Ukrainian or Romanian. How's your Ukrainian?"

"Non-existent." Josh shifted back to English, enjoying the challenge. "Do you speak Ukrainian and Romanian, too?"

Carla stood up. "If you're going to keep up this foreign language thing, I'm going to walk around unless you want to speak and swear in Spanish or Polish. Natalie, I'll be back to check on you to make sure Mr. Josh Haman's intentions stay honorable."

Natalie smiled as she looked up at Carla and nodded, then she turned back to Josh and thought, *God, those ice blue eyes are intense.* "Sort of…. I'm not sure whether or not the Ukrainian my father uses can be used in polite company. He and my mother speak Romanian when they don't want me to understand what they're talking about." She stopped for a second, before asking. "How'd you learn Russian?"

"In school. I figured I ought to learn the language and culture of our primary enemy. I grew up less than a hundred miles from the Wall that divided Germany. My dad had assignments in Bitburg and Spangdahlem, but most of the time he was based in Wiesbaden."

"My father has lots of Russian émigré friends, and Russian and English are their common languages. Soooo, when they're around, everyone is more comfortable speaking Russian. I still get dragged in every so often to help translate, even though my dad's English is pretty good. My mother's is not." Natalie took a tiny sip of the remaining Coke. "You grew up in Germany? Do you speak German, too?"

"Yes. We had a German housekeeper who refused to speak to me in English. Plus, I spent five years in a German *kinderschüle* because there were no American schools nearby, so yes, I speak German pretty well, along with French."

"What was your major?"

"Girls, skiing, cars, and oh, by the way, getting grades just good enough so I could keep my ROTC scholarship. In that order, but I did manage to graduate with a mechanical engineering degree from Norwich University, in Vermont."

"Brothers or sisters?"

Wow, the questions keep coming. She was interested in him, or maybe this was a test? He liked it; he liked her. "Two brothers. One flies Hueys for the Army's 101st Airborne Division and just left for Vietnam, and the other is in high school. How about you?"

"I'm an only child."

Natalie turned down his second request to dance, which raised his curiosity because it was unusual. He decided to ask why later; most girls he met liked to get out on the dance floor.

Natalie put up the palm of her hand as Carla approached the table. "Carla, give us fifteen more minutes. I know we've got to go." She turned back to Josh. "We've got classes in the morning."

Josh looked at his watch and was stunned to see it was past eleven. "I'd like to have dinner with you this weekend, either Friday or Saturday. You pick the cuisine and I'll pick the place." What he wanted to do was go out Friday and then have the option for Saturday and maybe Sunday. Or have the weekend to call another flame on short notice.

"Okay, Friday." Natalie was thinking that maybe they could get past the first date without him trying to get her into bed as another conquest. And if, like some other guys, he stood her up, she'd have the whole weekend to herself. "I'd like that. Just the two of us, and we can continue the conversation. Let me give you my address and phone number." She dug two scraps of paper out of her purse and scribbled a phone number and an address on them before sliding the pen and second piece of paper to Josh. "I need a number where I can reach you in case I have to cancel."

"Okay. Pick you up at seven on Friday."

"Super. By now Carla should be waiting for me by the door. She's my ride home." Natalie bent down and then had to use the table to keep from falling as she stood up before she got two aluminum forearm crutches in position. Josh pulled the table back to make it easier and she swung herself in full view."Are you sure you still want to go out with me?" she asked, looking right into his eyes.

Josh saw her left leg ended above the hemline of her mid-thigh skirt. "Absolutely. I'll be at your front door at seven."

WEDNESDAY, 7 DAYS LATER, JANUARY 19, 1972, 0600 LOCAL TIME, ABOUT 100 KILOMETERS NNW OF HANOI AND NEAR THE MOUNTAINS 50 KILOMETERS SOUTH OF HA GIANG

Colonel Thai sat in the passenger seat of the lead vehicle, a Soviet-made GAZ-69 four-wheel-drive light truck that left the capital on Highway 2 at 2 a.m., so the seven-vehicle convoy could get to the coarse gravel road before daylight. Behind him, four blacked-out, Soviet-made ten-wheeled trucks carried food and steel reinforcing rods under their canvas covers. He found out at a stop where they pulled off the road to avoid low-flying American aircraft that the last two vehicles were packed with cases of dynamite made in France. *So now,* he mused, *the French are selling us explosives rather than killing us.*

Leaving in the dark had the advantage that traffic was nonexistent in the countryside, which let them drive down the center of the road, but it also made them sitting ducks for any prowling U.S. aircraft, and Colonel Thai worried that the Americans would scream down at any moment and pummel them with bombs.

At first, the trucks maintained hundred meter spacing as they trundled along at seventy-five kilometers per hour along the French-built road. About an hour outside Hanoi, the drivers slowed to forty-five kph when the macadam surface turned to gravel mixed with tar and then just to gravel and potholes.

Thai leaned back in his seat, trying not to disturb the driver of the four wheel drive truck as he picked his way among the potholes. When he'd tossed his pack and duffel bag into the back of the truck, he'd noted that the small vehicle was filled with cases of grenades and one thousand round boxes of Chinese-made ammunition for their AK-47s and light machine guns. Other boxes held empty magazines that would ultimately be loaded with thirty cartridges from the boxes by the soldiers in his regiment.

The leather briefcase at his feet contained his notes from the personnel records of the four infantry companies and antiaircraft battery commanders who would make up his new regiment, his formal orders, and a timeline when the missiles, additional communications equipment, and the anti-aircraft guns were supposed to arrive. When the base was operational, the battery commanders would control sixteen S-60 guns that would be deployed around the base.

General Chung's words, "Once you make your assessment of what you need to protect the base, ask, and we will provide it," rang in his head through the night. He'd also been told that Soviet technicians would come in about five months when the missiles and radar equipment arrived, making it early May.

He'd been surprised to learn during his formal briefing by General Chung's chief of staff that there was a team of six NVA engineers at the site managing a large company of North Koreans. The Koreans, he was told, were experts in tunneling. When he asked if they were a potential security risk, General Chung said, "No. All they know is that they are someplace in Vietnam. From the reports I gather that they are A, very

Marc Liebman

good at what they do; B, happy because they are out of the cold North Korean winter; and C, are being fed better than at home."

The driver pointed out a dirt road that led off into the distance. "That's the road to Lang Tuc, which goes to the last village we pass before we turn into the hills about ten kilometers from here. By now the convoy commander has radioed ahead, so they'll know to put the submerged bridge at Sông Hông River in place for us. Once we are on the other side of the river, the bridge will be hidden again," the driver said. The Sông Hông River was often called by its French name, the Claire River. The Americans called it the Red River.

By the time dawn began to break, the trucks had spent thirty minutes inching up a narrow gravel road made from rock taken from the caves and then crushed, before each parked in its own revetment. Trees above him blocked out the rising sun, and at over 1000 meters above sea level, the air was moist but much cooler.

Thai was led to a cave that had been set up as a briefing room, where he was introduced to each of the officers in his command. Maps had been tacked to wooden frames so that Thai could see the base's facilities and defenses. He listened to each officer, comparing his notes from his personnel file to his first impression as he began the process of determining whether or not the officer was a combat leader or someone with a soft job away from the real fighting in the south.

He planned to turn the infantry companies into hunters. His plan called for two of each company's four platoons to be out hunting and patrolling its sector, the third would remain to guard its base, and the fourth would be held in reserve as a rapid reaction force should they find an intruder.

Colonel Thai looked at his watch as he stood up to face his company commanders. "Thank you for the information. Excellent briefing." Turning, Thai tapped a square marked on one of the maps indicating a watch tower on the peak of a nearby ridge. "Let us start my tour here."

It took an hour along a maintained trail to get to the small clearing where the workers had cut down small trees and brush to slow the jungle's attempts to reclaim the ground. The uphill climb along a cleared trail that was wide enough for soldiers to walk two abreast was the most exercise he'd had in weeks, other than his daily Tai Chi workout, which he used to clear his mind as well as build muscle control and strength. Nothing had been done to damage the leafy canopy that blocked out the sun and hid the base from the prying eyes of American photo interpreters.

"I think you will be pleased, sir, when you get to the platform," his executive officer, Major Loi, said, motioning to the wooden boards nailed to a large tree. Above him, enough branches were left to conceal the platform from a plane, but it's position still gave the occupants a clear view of the valley and sky.

Thai used the time it took for the rest of the officers to get to the platform to catch his breath while he enjoyed the bird's-eye view of the terrain his command controlled. As he stood waiting for the others, his leg muscles had time to recover. Glancing at his watch and seeing it was now almost lunch time, he realized he had been running on adrenaline and had not slept since the night before he left.

"The platform is about five meters by five meters, so about twenty-five square meters, Colonel. It is lashed to four trees in such a way that it allows movement so it will not be ripped from its mounts when the trees move in a gale during the typhoon season. There are four other platforms just like this one on each corner of the valley. Each one is always occupied by a team of four lookouts who are connected to our command center by telephone. We have radios, but do not use them because we fear the Americans are listening," Loi explained.

"Excellent." Thai took up a pair of binoculars from the small table that contained a Russian-made field phone and handset and scanned the narrow valley, now covered with a thin layer of mist.

Loi stepped to his side. "Sir, the platforms give us an excellent view from all sides. Even if you know where to look, you can't see them. The netting as well as the natural tree cover hides any reflection from the binoculars."

Colonel Thai turned around. "This is excellent. I am pleased."

After a hike along the ridge to inspect a 57mm anti-aircraft gun battery, they returned to the area around the caves that was the nerve center of the base. Thai needed a break before joining the officers for dinner. Rather than remaining aloof during the meal, Thai asked and answered questions, trying not to make his questions sound like orders that required a response.

The conversation confirmed what he suspected. All came from families well connected in the Party and had been educated in the country's best schools. This also explained their rank despite none having been, as they said in the People's Army, "to the South." It was also a warning sign because displeasure with his leadership would get to people of influence, and then he would be walking back down the trail to the hell in the south that was consuming so many of his country's young men.

"Comrades," Colonel Thai said, "I am impressed by what I have seen so far. But our preparations are far from finished and our training has just begun. This base is supposed to be operational by the end of May when Soviet air defense artillery officers arrive with new versions of their missiles and new tactics. The purpose of this base is to test new tactics that will increase the number of American airplanes that are shot down. I have been ordered to keep this base hidden for as long as possible, which should explain the unusual steps the army is taking to build this facility. Our role here is to prevent any attacks from the ground, and if possible, from the air. Please note, I used the word prevent. To do that, we must become hunters who know their prey and the land as well as their hands." He looked around the table. "By the end of March our regiment will know every ravine, stream, tree, trail, and rock in this base. Each of you will know it well, but so will your platoon leaders, sergeants, and privates." Thai took a sip of the mineral water from the glass in front of him before putting it down on the table with a noticeable *thunk* designed to emphasize what he just said—and what he was about to say. "We will be hunters and know our ground. That is number one.

"Number two is that this unit, which has been designated the 133rd Special Operations Regiment, will operate in the field twenty-four hours a day, every day. Each anti-aircraft battery will always have one of its guns manned. We will sting the enemy any time they come near us. We will sting with the missiles and we will sting with our rifles. This is why I have approval to rename the base. As of this moment, we are now Venom Base. Venom is also our call sign.

"And number three, we will know our enemy and their tactics. I brought intelligence that you will study on how American Army Special Forces, U.S. Navy SEALs, and the CIA operate. Do not underestimate them. The enemy soldiers we might encounter here will be their very best, and I know from personal experience that they are very, very good. And since we are at war, we must be ready to defend the base, because eventually Venom will be found and attacked. It is not a question of *if*, but *when*, and we must be prepared so that we can survive the attack and our Soviet comrades can keep shooting down American planes."

Thai stopped for a moment to let what he'd said sink in before continuing.

"Each company commander will be asked to assign a lieutenant, a sergeant, and four privates to create a regimental intelligence section. Their role will be to evaluate information as we collect it and provide it to all company commanders. Our lives will depend on how good they are at piecing together the puzzle of what the enemy may be doing on the ground around this base."

Thai stopped speaking. He was sure they'd been told that they would come up here, set up a base, go out on a few patrols, and sit out the war in relative safety.

"So let me sum up what I expect: We will provide defense by being hunters. No one enters our operating area, which is about six kilometers in every direction from where we are standing, without our knowing who it is, when they got here, and if they are a threat." Another pause. "Any questions?"

None.

"Good. Here's how we start: I want the base divided up into four logical sectors. One company will be assigned to each sector. Once they know their area, they will then teach the other three companies about their sector. We will rotate every month. Each company will have two platoons patrolling, one guarding its bivouac area, and one ready as a quick reaction force. We will practice tracking, movement, and ambushes at first, just to learn how, and then we will practice with live ammunition."

Another sip of water. "I have been up since before midnight. I am going to take a quick nap and in two hours be back in the command center cave. By then, I expect you to have divided the base up into four sectors and can provide highlights of the geography of each sector. And you will have selected the men for our intelligence team." What Thai wanted to say, but couldn't, was, "I don't want political officers in the intelligence group because I don't trust them. They see military tactics in terms of party loyalty and how it furthers the Party's and their own agendas, not how to win battles with the minimum number of men killed and wounded, because in most cases, they're not on the front lines getting shot at." He nodded and left the silent group of seven officers.

Thai regretted that he didn't remember his orderly's name when the private, who was stationed outside his hooch, stuck his head in the door. Thai was just pulling on his boots. "Sir, Major Trung to see you."

Ah, the political officer has arrived. Thai had wondered where he was. As much as he dislike political officers and the roles they played, Thai wanted to meet the man whose absence was noticed when he arrived. The thump of boots on the steps told Thai that someone approached. "Come in."

Major Trung's furtive glances around the room told Thai that the man responsible for making everyone adhere to the Party line was very uncomfortable in his commanding officer's presence. Thai wondered if the Major were afraid that he might send him into battle, or require him to do more than lecture his regiment and parrot Party propaganda.

"I can come back later, sir."

"No, this is a good time. What can I do for you?"

"I came to introduce myself. I am sorry I was not available when you arrived."

Because, Thai thought, *you were still in bed when I arrived, and because you are so beloved by the men in this regiment that no one made sure you were awake.* From reading the personnel files he knew Trung's father was a member of the Politburo. He had gotten Trung this assignment thinking it would keep his son out of harm's way—and advance his career.

"Quite all right, Major. I was not expecting anything special."

"Sir, if I may say so, it is an honor to serve you. Your record speaks for itself."

So his father had given him information on Thai. Another warning sign. Thai remembered about the power of the Party. He wondered how much Trung had shared with the other officers. Based on the reactions and behaviors of the men during their briefing that morning, Trung hadn't shared anything other than that Thai was a seasoned soldier and an excellent leader who had success against the Americans. He may have phrased it in such a way to suggest that Thai would be able to keep them from getting killed.

"I spent an interesting morning and early afternoon taking a partial tour of the base, Major. Later this afternoon, I would like to meet the Koreans." The less Thai told him at this point, the better. According to the unit's organizational chart, the man reported to Thai, but with Trung's connections, every fart Thai made could be reported to the Party's leadership, or the army's, or both.

"Excellent. I am good friends with the Korean's Political Officer, who speaks passable Vietnamese. My Korean is non-existent."

Typical for a Party appointee: the man lacked the skills necessary for his responsibilities.

"I should be able to meet with the Koreans at say, nineteen-thirty this afternoon which should be after dinner."

"Excellent. I will set that up."

"Very good. See you at their camp, then."

The tone in Colonel Thai's voice suggested that the meeting was over. Scheduling and arranging the meeting would give Major Trung something to do; Thai did not want him at the meeting with the company commanders. If, in spite of this assignment, he showed up to the meeting, Thai would know that Major Trung had established relationships with at least one officer.

"Thank you, sir." Major Trung saluted and left Colonel Thai to finish dressing.

Big Mother 40

Natalie eased down the steps on the walkway from her parents' house to the street, putting the crutches onto the concrete step below before swinging her leg through in a deliberate, practiced motion. A little hop in the middle while she was swinging the forearm crutches forward made it obvious to anyone who cared to watch that she was in a hurry.

"You're glowing and smiling." Carla Glowaski waited until her best friend tossed her backpack and aluminum crutches into the back seat of her silver VW Beetle convertible. "It must have been a great weekend. I didn't hear a peep from you."

"It was." Natalie turned to her friend and grinned. "You owe me five bucks. Josh didn't cancel or stand me up. In reality, you owe me ten because we had a second date."

"I'll pay up after I hear all the details. So, what happened?"

"Not a whole lot."

"Oh, bullshit. I've known you since we were both freshmen in high school and newbies who just made the drill team. A lot happened or you would have called. So, again, what happened over the weekend?" For emphasis, Carla revved the engine to the redline before shifting to make her point and show her feigned annoyance.

"We went out to dinner and then went to see *Diamonds Are Forever* on Friday night, which was fun. Other than hold my hand in the theater, he didn't try anything. We agreed to go sailing and Josh picked me up late Saturday morning. He's got a twenty-two foot boat called an Ensign he keeps at the yacht basin over at the North Island Naval Air Station."

"Sounds like fun."

"I'd never been sailing before. Anyway, we went down toward Imperial Beach for a bit and then anchored off the Silver Strand State Park for lunch. You'd like sailing because it is so quiet. The only the sound you hear is the water rushing by the boat and the sails flapping. If we go again, I can ask Josh if you can go out with us. There's plenty of room for four in the cockpit.... Anyway, we came back in around four and went to his house."

"Where does he live?"

"He's got a three-bedroom house in Oceanside, near the north end of La Jolla. It doesn't look like much from the street, but the back of the house opens up on a large deck with a fabulous view of the ocean." Natalie brushed her hair out of her face. "After giving me a tour, he poured me a glass of wine and ushered me to a chair on the deck. Then I went inside to go to the bathroom while he was working on the salad. He had a flank steak already marinating so I offered to help, and then we started kissing."

"Is this when you tell me you had sex with him?"

"No, Carla, we didn't have sex. We made love, love with a capital L. He got me so turned on.... It was one orgasm after another. And, before you ask, he wasn't the least bit turned off by my stump. He caressed it just like he did my right leg. In fact, he found a few areas where my stump is very sensitive that I didn't know about. Then he held me in his arms for about an hour or so and stroked me all over while we talked and then we did it again. I just exploded. It has never been like that for me before."

"Oh, wow. Then what?"

"We had dinner and he dropped me off at eleven."

"What about Sunday?"

"He picked me up about ten-ish, but he got into a discussion with my dad about some Russian army machine gun and they talked in Russian for about an hour. We went sailing again and did it on the boat. Oh, my God, was that wonderful."

"Is there a bed in the cabin?"

"No, I just sat on his lap facing him. My leg was draped over the side and I used it to pull myself toward him. And we made EL OHH VEE EEE! God, was it great! By the time I got home last night, it was all I could do to keep my eyes open. I didn't do any studying at all."

"Are you in love?"

"Not yet, but when Josh Haman is around, I am going to be in heat."

TUESDAY, NEXT DAY, FEBRUARY 1, 1972, 0730 LOCAL TIME, VENOM BASE

Colonel Thai sat at the wooden desk he'd made in the shelter he used as a combination of living quarters, private mess, and office. The raised wooden floor and frame with waist-high walls kept the contents of the building off the moist, sodden ground, and the corrugated metal roof that extended well over the sides kept him dry. Wall-to-ceiling screens kept most of the bugs out. The bad news, as he found out, was the building was impossible to heat and the damp, cool winter weather in the highlands made his joints ache.

Each company had its own complex of similar structures. Major Minh and the company political officers threatened to report his requirement of having the officers and men share their quarters and meals to the Party. As officers, they wanted a separate mess and quarters. It was a request from his officers that Thai decided to turn down, but delayed his "no" for a day. He believed officers should live and eat with their men in the field.

Thai had his men build similar buildings around the base so the platoons had places to stay between patrols. Platoons in reserve spent two days every week on the special training range, which had been built in the western-most section of the base. Live fire exercises were held there, where the platoon set up ambushes, fired their weapons, and responded to commands, first from Thai and then from their officers.

To increase the tempo and realism of his training plan, he had platoons hunt each other in cat-and-mouse games that built up their jungle warfare skills. The competition was healthy and he went out in the field with them to increase his fitness; when he'd been assigned to this job he was still not a hundred percent recovered from his wounds from the battle almost a year ago, despite what he told the doctors and the generals.

Thai's adjutant, a skinny captain with a pockmarked face from a fishing village near Haiphong, knocked on the thin wood door. "Excuse me, sir, the Koreans are ready for you."

"Let's honor them with our presence then, Captain Dai."

Colonel Thai wasn't surprised to see the two hundred-odd Koreans arrayed in a precise military formation. Right after he'd arrived in January and inspected the caves for the first time, he'd learned the "civilian volunteers" were a company of engineers from the Korean People's Army. Colonel Thai saluted the Korean Peoples' Army commander, Lieutenant Colonel Hyun Kim, who, he'd learned, was a mining engineer and an expert in building tunnels to hide everything from infantry to surface-to-air missiles to tanks.

"Colonel Thai, please honor my men by going through the ranks before we begin our formal inspection of the caves. Our work here is almost done."

"My pleasure, Colonel Kim. Please, lead the way."

This was the first time he'd seen the Koreans in anything but muddy, dirty fatigues since he'd been at Venom. It was obvious that each man had taken the time to make sure he had a clean and pressed uniform. None of them had weapons, but Thai was sure that each could use an AK-47.

All the Koreans spoke Vietnamese very well, and when he met with Kim each week they presented their report in Vietnamese. On a few occasions, they would discuss among themselves a problem they'd encountered excavating a cave or building a road bed on the muddy jungle floor in Korean and come up with an answer. When they came to an agreement, one would tell him in Vietnamese what they had discussed before apologizing for not being fluent enough in Vietnamese. Thai found the Koreans to be pleasant, polite, and very efficient.

As they blasted their way deeper into the mountains, the noise from the explosions became more muted. Rock removed from the caves was fed into a U.S.-made crusher. It turned large chunks into gravel about two centimeters in diameter that was used to build the road network, then stands for the missile trailers, and last, mixed into concrete for the missile launcher pads.

Thai was amazed at the detailed planning that went into every operation the Koreans undertook. Each tree cut down was studied beforehand to determine its impact on the overall jungle canopy as well as how much lumber it could provide. Now that they were almost done, one could walk or drive throughout the base camp area on dry gravel roads that drained well during heavy rains so each of the concrete missile launcher hard stands and the missile storage shed did not flood.

"Colonel Kim, please thank your men for all their hard work. I know their work here is not yet finished, but on behalf of my country, I want to make sure that they know how much we appreciate their effort."

"Thank you, Colonel, and I will." Lieutenant Colonel Kim saluted. Both men were about the same height and build, but Thai guessed Kim was in his late forties, which made him more than a decade older than Thai. Every day, rain or shine, the North Korean officer spent an hour doing Tae Kwon Do katas outside the quarters he shared with his officers. "May I dismiss the men who will not be in the inspection party? They can go back to work while we finish our tour."

"Yes, please tell them to carry on." Thai stood at attention while Kim did an about-face and said a few words before barking an order. The men cheered and the formation dissolved as several officers gathered behind their commander.

"Let us start with the new command center," Kim said to Thai.

Each time Colonel Thai went into one of the new tunnels, he marveled at how large and open they were, in stark contrast to those in the south, which were claustrophobic. In the underground hospital in Cambodia where he had been taken, when he was able to stand, the ceiling was just a few centimeters above his head. Worse, they often caved in without notice, even though they were about ten meters underground.

When the B-52s carpet-bombed an area, engineers would spend the next few days repairing the damage. Collapsed tunnels weren't excavated unless they contained something valuable such as ammunition, food, or medicine. If they couldn't see an arm or a leg or get to comrades in a few minutes, the men were left buried where the tunnels collapsed.

Lieutenant Colonel Kim stopped inside the tunnel, a meter or so from the gravel path. "The entrance to each tunnel turns ninety degrees at about five meters after the entrance and then proceeds for another five meters so that if a bomb goes off right outside the entrance, there is little or no blast damage. Each tunnel is connected to the other so that there are multiple entrances and exits. The two tunnels not connected to the others are the one where the Russians are going to have their communications equipment and the one for the senior Russian officer."

Thai had wondered why the Russians were going to be allowed to have a separate communications center and had asked General Chung's chief of staff during their meeting in Hanoi, who had answered with a curt, "That is the way it was designed and will not change." Thai believed there was more that Chung hadn't told him and had let the subject drop; he'd find out, eventually.

Kim waited until they were deeper into the tunnel that housed their generators, which Thai could see were ready for use after Kim flipped a switch. "There are two separate tunnels so that a fire in one will not damage the other. The next tunnel has the generators and this one contains the fuel tanks, which is pumped in through the pipe on the floor to the generators. The nozzle to fill the tanks is just inside the entrance."

Thai walked up to one of the pumps and looked up to see how high the pipes went before they disappeared into the rock behind the metal tanks.

Kim waited until it was clear Thai was ready to continue. "Each personnel tunnel has a spine, which is what we are walking down now, with rooms about ten meters long and five meters wide off to each side. The rooms are separated by about five meters of solid rock so there is little, if any, danger of collapse. One of the things that surprised us was that we did not find any major faults. The rock here is very stable and should provide excellent protection."

Thai stopped to look around. The bright lights made it easy to see up and down the tunnels, which were about three meters high. The rock was scarred from the drilling and blasting, but he was surprised at how little debris remained. Colonel Thai didn't want to tell Kim that he didn't want his men in here if they were attacked. He didn't want to fight and die in holes like the Japanese. He wanted them out in the field, hunting the attackers. He believed if they were dispersed, it would be harder for bombs to kill them. If the attackers were airplanes, then his S-60 anti-aircraft batteries should be firing and the Russians had better be shooting their missiles to keep the bombers away.

"In each barracks tunnel, there is an enclave with running water, bathrooms, and showers that drain through a hole bored through the rock into a thing called a septic tank outside the cave downhill from the cave complex. There it will degrade as it empties into the jungle. This will make a healthier living environment for your men."

Kim turned and led Thai down the spine to the end of the tunnel and then back out to the entrance. They followed this process three more times before the Korean stopped at the entrance of a tunnel set apart from the rest. "This is the complex for the Russians. It will have its own generators because it will have a lot of electrical equipment."

"I would like to see what you have done so far."

Kim nodded and headed into the cave.

SATURDAY, 4 DAYS LATER, FEBRUARY 5, 1972, 2020 LOCAL TIME, SAN DIEGO, CA

Josh watched Natalie's eyes sparkle as she sipped on her refilled glass of ice-cold white Zinfandel. She pulled her leg crosswise on the couch to create some space between them because she wanted to talk. "Why did you join the Navy rather than the Air Force?"

"That's the same question my dad asked."

"That's logical; your dad was an Air Force pilot."

"The Navy guaranteed me pilot training, assuming I passed the physical and mental tests; the Air Force wouldn't. The Air Force recruiter said we'd be assigned after the initial ground school, based on the Air Force's needs. I could get commissioned and then be sent to navigator school or something else, and I wanted to be a pilot. My dad always said if you fly in the military, you want to have control of the airplane, not be a passenger. Plus, I like the sea and wanted to fly off aircraft carriers."

"I've been to the Miramar O Club several times before and you're the first Jewish guy in the Navy I've met."

"Doesn't surprise me. I've not met any others since I was commissioned." It had never bothered him being the only Jew on the block, so to speak. Josh took it as a fact of life and never gave it much thought. "My dad would have preferred it if I had gone into the Air Force rather than the Navy because, I think, old feelings die hard. Back in nineteen thirty-eight, when he applied for the Naval Aviation Cadet program, he was turned down, even though he had all the required qualifications, plus over a hundred hours of flying experience, and

41

passed the physical and mental exams. He found out later from a friend who was accepted that the Navy in those days wasn't taking Jews."

"How'd they know? Haman isn't a common Jewish name."

Josh grinned. "He was wearing a Star of David that his father had worn during World War One and had given him for good luck. It's the same one I wear with my dog tags."

"Is there anti-Semitism in the Navy? Where my dad grew up, in what's now Moldavia, anti-Semitism was unofficially sponsored by the government and harassing Jews was viewed by many Moldavians as a sport. Stalin kept telling the people that Jews were the enemies of communism, which was absurd because most of his early comrades, Trotsky, Kamenev, Zinoviev, to name a few, were all Jews. It wasn't until Stalin accepted the fact that a war with the Germans was coming and the government had to draft everyone into the army it could find that Stalin stopped the pogroms."

"Well, I've seen ignorance, but not anti-Semitism."

"Like what?"

"When I arrived in Pensacola, I was like every other brand new ensign, assigned a room in the BOQ where each officer shared a living room, but had his own bedroom and bath. My roommate was a guy by the name of Tim Ferguson from Tupelo, Mississippi. He'd been there a week, waiting for ground school to start, and was looking for a sports car. When I walked into the living room, the coffee table was covered with brochures for Corvettes, Camaros, and Mustangs. I think he even had ones for Pontiac GTOs and an Olds 4-4-2."

"No foreign cars?"

"No. Just American cars with big engines. Anyway, we started talking about cars; and as he told me about each car he test drove he said that if he decided to buy it, he would Jew the dealer down in price." Josh took a long swig from his wine as he replayed the conversations in his mind. "The first time I heard him say it, I ignored it, thinking it was a mistake. But he kept using it as a verb. After a few days, it began to bother me."

"What did you do?"

"Well, he was intrigued by my Porsche, so I let him drive it on the way to dinner one evening. When we were finished eating, I asked him why did he keep using the word Jew as a verb. Tim said they used it that way all the time back home. Then he asked me why I asked the question."

"And you said?"

"I said, 'I find it offensive because I'm Jewish.' Tim looked at me as if I were someone from another planet and said, 'You don't look Jewish.' I asked what was I supposed to look like and he said, 'First, you don't wear thick glasses,' and then he went on to describe someone who looked like Fagin, the character in Dickens' novel, *Oliver Twist*. Then Tim said, 'I've never met a Jew before, and I'm sorry.' And from that day on, he never used the phrase in front of me again. But he did bring me with him when he negotiated the purchase of a two year old Corvette and kept asking me if it was a good deal. How the hell was I supposed to know? So I told him if that's the car you want, buy it if you can afford it."

"What happened to him?"

"He flunked out during pre-flight."

Chapter 3

INTRODUCING THE NEWBIE TO
"THE PEARL OF THE ORIENT"

SUNDAY, 1 MONTH LATER, MARCH 5, 1972, 1324 LOCAL TIME, 7TH AIR
FORCE INTELLIGENCE CENTER, TAN SON NHUT AB, SOUTH VIETNAM

"Captain Johnson, come look at this." The Air Force photo
interpreter was adjusting the two rows of 8"x10" photos laid out on table
so that one could see the timing in the white box at the bottom that had
the mission number, date and the photo number. Grayson then checked
parts of the image on each one with a four-power loupe to make sure he
had the photos he wanted.

"What do you have, Grayson?"

"Sir, please look at these two sequences. The first one comes from
last night's Buffalo Hunter drone mission that went back and forth along
Route Two, north of Viet Tri. The first row is a sequence as the bird flew
northwest over Route Two and southeast of the town of Phu Tho, thirty
to forty kilometers from Viet Tri. What you see is a battery of six S-60
anti-aircraft guns being towed by trucks. We see the convoy first here,
just southeast of Phu Tho." The photo interpreter reached up and pulled a
map closer so Johnson could see. "Then we see the same convoy again
here, just north of Phu Tho based on the planned drone's track. We know
it is the same group of trucks because we can read the numbers on the
side." He pulled the second row of photos down. "Based on my
calculations from the data from the drone, the trucks are making about
thirty-five miles an hour, which is about right for the road conditions,
time of day, et cetera."

"Where are you going with this?"

"Sir, if you look at the third pass when the bird is heading northeast
again before it begins its turn to the south to come home, the convoy is
nowhere to be found. I've looked at past photos as well as all the images
in the string and the trucks and guns have just disappeared."

"What are you suggesting?"

45

"I think the gooks are putting in some kind of flak trap someplace in this area. These guns are a big threat to the Jolly Green helos and Sandys coming down the Red River Valley to make rescues."

"They could just be hiding them before they move on tomorrow night. The last photos are just before dawn."

"No, sir, I don't think so. It would take too long to camouflage them. Plus, if they were trying to hide them, they would already have branches tied to the tops of the trucks while they were on the road. They don't, so I believe they turned off someplace into one of these valleys."

"Okay. Your hunches have been right before. Write it up, mark the photos and the maps, and I'll pass it up the chain to Seventh Air Force's intelligence officer with a recommendation that they do further analysis. These are obviously going someplace, and the question is where, and to protect what? They should be able put two and two together. Good work, Grayson."

MONDAY, NEXT DAY, MARCH 6, 1972, 2022 LOCAL TIME, CAT ROOM, O'CLUB, NAVAL AIR STATION CUBI POINT, SUBIC BAY, CLOSE TO MANILA, LUZON ISLAND, THE PHILIPPINES

"Welcome to Cubi's Cat Room." Josh opened the door to the new arrival Lieutenant Junior Grade Jack D'Onofrio. "This is the place I told you about, and it makes the wildest fraternity house look tame. How about a beer, or do you want something stronger?"

"Whatever you're having."

"San Miguel beer. It's brewed right here in the Philippines. The local water makes it taste special."

"Beer's fine." Jack looked around. They'd just entered a rectangular building built from cinderblocks; the polished mahogany bar was the sole furniture-like structure in it. It ran the length of the long south wall. Behind the bar were latched, polished cabinets that were opened only when a bartender needed a bottle.

Josh signaled the bartender, who held the necks of two bottles of San Miguel in his left hand and then popped off the caps with a church key in his right. In one smooth move, he filled two plastic cups set on the counter with the golden liquid, leaving a half-inch-thick head. Satisfied, the bartender slid the two clear cups across the bar to Josh, who put a dollar bill on the table, which amounted to a fifty percent tip.

After handing one to Jack, he held it up. "Cheers!"

"Cheers. To good times and good friends." Jack responded by touching his cup to his friend's.

Josh waved his cup of beer around to his side. "Everything in the Cat Room is served in a plastic or paper cup. It's open to four in the morning, then they clean it out with hoses, and it opens again at eight for those who like to drink their breakfast."

Before the new arrival could reply, their conversation was interrupted by a cheer from a crowd at one end of the room, clustered around a device that Jack couldn't see in the dim light. At the other end of the room was a Filipino band on a platform behind tall stands of Plexiglas. The music was loud but not deafening.

Jack was in sensory overload, trying to catch up; he'd been at Hickam AFB in Honolulu just seventeen hours earlier, waiting for his plane. He'd arrived on the third airlift flight of the day from Hawaii, which deposited him on the tarmac at Clark Air Base, ninety miles north of Manila. Josh had been waiting in the air-conditioned arrival lounge, along with seven others who needed a ride to Cubi in the Navy's gray-and-white shuttle helicopter the squadron used for logistics runs and training.

"Are there any single women around here?"

"Yes, and they come in four categories: teachers and nurses, flight attendants, dependent wives, and locals who have access to the base. Knowledge of their marital state is optional and depends on whether or not they tell you the truth. The ones looking for male companionship are not down here in the Cat Room. If we come to the club tomorrow night, the ones looking will be in the main bar in the club. Most women don't come down here unless they're attached to someone."

"Oh." A noisy cheer again rose from the far end of the room. "What's that all about?"

Josh pointed with the top of his plastic glass of beer. "Come and you'll see why this place is called the Cat Room."

As they got closer, both saw a guy get into what looked like a cockpit. A bystander helped strap him in, while on the other side another young aviator stood behind a small panel with his hands raised high over his head. Once the aviator settled in the cockpit, another arm handed him a drink, which he drained in a couple of swallows before returning the empty plastic cup to the hand of the outstretched arm.

A few feet in front the cockpit, another aviator twirled two fingers over his head and the seated aviator saluted, at which point the officer with his hands over his head punched a button on the console and the cockpit shot off down the track and into the swimming pool. The aviator in the mock cockpit remembered his Dilbert Dunker training and unstrapped, pushed himself out of the seat and swam to the ladder on the side of the pool where, smiling, he climbed back into the Cat Room.

"The object is to catch the wire at the end of the cat track, and if you do, you get your name on the board on the wall over there." Josh's voice was one level below shouting into Jack's ear. "If you don't, you get wet. Note the little deflector just in front of the wire to make it interesting. They adjust the speed depending on who you are. Cost for this little ride is a buck, but it includes the mandatory stinger which you drink before you go."

"Oh." It was all Jack could say. He watched another aviator get wet, and then a well-endowed young American woman, whose bra could easily be seen through her wet white blouse, wanted to try again. She was enthusiastically encouraged by cheers from the gallery as she French-kissed one of the young officers helping her into the mock cockpit.

"I'm bushed. I'll take a taxi back to the BOQ. Tomorrow's gonna be a busy day."

"Yeah, it will be." Josh tossed his empty plastic cup into one of several large plastic trash barrels up against the walls of the Cat Room. "We have the official exchange tour and a tour of the naval base. Maybe some beach time, and if we get bored, a little sailing. Oh, and you have to check in and meet the support detachment Officer-in-Charge. If you're lucky, you'll get in a quick familiarization flight. After dinner, if you're up to it, I'll continue your education with a beer in Olongapo, the Pearl of the Orient."

"What's in Olangapo?"

"You'll see. It is an essential part of the education of each Naval Officer deployed to WESTPAC. Consider it one part fun, one part education, and one part on-the-job-training about what the men in your division might be doing in their spare time."

"I've heard stories about Po City."

"Whatever you've heard, I doubt it would even begin to describe the place. It needs to be experienced to be understood. Only those who have been know; and only those who have partaken really know! A visit to the Pearl of the Orient is an essential part of every Naval officer's professional development. If you are too tired, we can go tomorrow or the next day. No rush, it's not going anywhere."

"Okay, after I have been here a day or two is probably better." Jack seemed unconvinced.

"Oh, I forgot to tell you, the regular support detachment O-in-C is in Atsugi this week, along with the admin officer for a meeting with the CO, so you'll have to meet his new, but very temporary officer-in-charge at oh eight thirty, who'll check you in and outline the training plan and assign you to a detachment."

"Who's that?"

"Me." Josh let that sink in for a few seconds. "I'll go back to the Q with you. I've seen all this before and I've got a letter to write."

"Natalie?"

"Yup. I try to write. Well, what I do is record about twenty, thirty minutes or more on a tape of what I did during the day, along with how much I miss her and send it out every other day."

"So Carla and the RAG rumor mill got it right. You didn't end it when you left."

"Nope. We both want to keep it going. She's agreed to meet me in Hawaii in about four months when I get my magic carpet flight."

"So this is getting very serious?"

"Not getting, it *is very* serious."

"Another rumor confirmed. I was at a RAG function after you left and the wives were saying Josh the Bachelor is no more. I was wondering if you'd figured it out."

"Figure out what?"

"That the two of you are in love. Anyone who has seen you two together would know it in an instant."

"It's that obvious?"

"Yes, it is." Jack gave his friend a condescending pat on the back. "How the mighty have fallen."

"Shit."

Chapter 4

ARRIVALS

D'Onofrio saw his roommate staring off into space in the office assigned to whoever was acting operations officer. In front of him was a battered and scratched gray metal desk that looked like a support structure for message boards, helicopter maintenance records, and reports printed by computers on green-and-white striped paper. There were three neat piles of what Jack instantly recognized as messages in the only clear area.

"What are you so down about?"

"Read this." The single sheet of paper crackled as Josh handed his co-pilot the message that was sitting alone on the desk. "Big Mother 12 is way overdue and presumed lost. The crew, led by Big Tom Bridges, and the eight SEALs aboard have been declared missing in action. They went feet dry about twenty-three fifteen and that's the last we heard from them."

"Thirteen guys?"

"Yeah. Big Bill wanted the mission. That sortie could have been assigned to us, except we had to stay at Phu Bai. Remember? We had to flush out the tail rotor gear box because the chip light came on when we went there to pick up mail and some parts that got delivered there by mistake. So, since we weren't around, Big Bill got the mission. If you remember, I didn't like the recommended route and wanted to modify it, but Big Bill thought it was okay, so I said good luck, go for it."

Jack didn't say anything. The mix of CSAR missions, logistics runs, sleep, helping the maintenance guys, and paperwork precluded much interaction among the six crews that made up and flew DET 110's four helicopters. As he handed the message back, he could see Josh's eyes were brimming with tears. "What happens next?"

51

"Couple of things. One, I need to go tell the boss. I just picked up the messages and started going through them. Twelve should have reported in earlier this a.m., but if they went to Thailand, it could take a half a day before a routine message gets to us back here in PI. The longer it goes, the more worried I am that something bad's happened. Once I tell Lieutenant Commander Montemayor, it's officially his problem. Two, some poor bastard will be appointed to pack their personnel effects. If we were still on the *Ranger*, that would be you, since you're the most junior officer and this is an ugly, typical 'Slo Joe' task that the boss will assign to someone. Lucky for you, we're here in PI and you'll escape that morbid job. Three, when we get out to the Gulf, I'm going to see if I can do a post-mortem to see if we can figure out what happened."

THURSDAY, NEXT DAY, APRIL 6, 1972, 1522 LOCAL TIME, GIA LAM AIR BASE JUST OUTSIDE HANOI, NORTH VIETNAM

The last two thousand kilometers of the two-day trip from the military airfield outside Moscow on the Aeroflot four-engine turbo-prop dulled the senses as it droned and vibrated on and on. Each passenger was thankful that the noisy, unpressurized cabin was heated, for winter hadn't left the southern Siberian town of Novosibirsk where the nine men had spent several cold, uncomfortable hours in their summer uniforms while the plane was refueled for the leg to Beijing.

Koniev and the four captains who'd "volunteered" for two-year tours in North Vietnam had been lumped together in a class at the Military Institute of Foreign Languages. All four were recent graduates of the Marshal of the Soviet Union Govorov Air Defense Radio Engineering Academy outside Moscow. According to what Koniev had been told, they were among the best and brightest junior anti-air warfare officers his country had to offer.

Also with them were four intelligence officers who had likewise "volunteered."

All nine were cooped up in the forward end of the cabin between the cargo pallets and the cockpit. The four intelligence officers were there to operate the crypto logic equipment, to code and decode messages from the embassy in Hanoi, and to ensure that their Vietnamese comrades were not to use or be trained in their equipment. The four demonstrated proper military courtesy but kept to themselves. Their army uniforms had black collar tabs denoting they were members of the "technical corps," but to Koniev they smelled like either KGB or GRU.

Koniev tried every position he could to get comfortable in the canvas bucket seats that lined the cabin and which had, by now, bruised any part of his body that came in contact with their aluminum frames. Four pallets of equipment were lashed to the floor; one was sealed and inspected each day by the intelligence officers.

Koniev and his four captains from the Air Defense Artillery checked the other three pallets before each takeoff to make sure that no one tampered with the black boxes that would be installed in each missile to let them use frequencies the American's had not yet heard. The new missile controllers would let them launch the S-75s, more commonly known by its NATO designation SA-2 Guideline, in a passive mode to a point in space where either the missile automatically turned on its terminal seeker or was activated by the ground station. Koniev's theory was that by launching the missile with the tracking and guidance radar off, the only way the American pilots could detect missiles would be if they saw them coming, and by the time their radar warning systems detected the terminal seeker, it would be too late.

In his last formal briefing at Soviet Army headquarters in Moscow, Koniev had been assured that the equipment on the plane was compatible with the missiles on the freighters in Haiphong Harbor. Knowing the problems he'd had in East Germany during exercises, when about thirty to forty percent of the missiles they shot didn't follow commands from the missile control van, he doubted the generals knew what they were talking about. If they didn't match, he planned to fire the missiles in their traditional modes and the generals could blame the manufacturers. Whether they matched or not wasn't their problem, it was now his, and he'd be the scapegoat if they didn't work.

For the umpteenth time, Koniev walked up and down the cabin in the narrow gap between the fuselage and the pallets and peered out each of the small cabin windows. Something else was in the air and it took him a few seconds to recognize the growing warmth and humidity that was now causing condensation to form on the skin of the cabin.

"Colonel Koniev?" Turning around, Koniev saw the navigator emerging from the cockpit. "Please tell your men we will begin our descent for landing in about fifteen minutes. We will drop from our present altitude of thirty-five hundred meters to sea level in a very short period of time. So they must be strapped in and make sure they have their puke bags handy in case they get sick."

Koniev sensed that the navigator was leaving something out. "And?"

"There are American military aircraft all over Vietnam. We have been informed that there have been air raids near Hanoi and Haiphong this morning. We hope they will not shoot us down because, as you know, we are an unarmed, civilian Aeroflot flight." They both laughed because the sole non-military aspect of Aeroflot Flight 1412 was the blue-and-white markings on the side of the airplane.

As the airplane began a steep descending turn, Koniev ran his hand through the gray-brown stubble of his crew cut and was surprised to find his scalp damp. For a moment he wondered why, and then he remembered he was less than a thousand kilometers north of the equator. By the time they landed, he could smell the sweat showing through his uniform.

Once they'd landed, a tubby colonel entered through the passenger door. "Good afternoon, Colonel Koniev. I am Colonel Boris Rokossovsky from the Soviet Military Mission. I hope you had a pleasant flight."

"Good afternoon." The two officers shook hands after saluting, and Koniev noticed that Rokossovsky, who was also sweating through his summer uniform, had the collar tabs showing that he was a member of the Soviet Army. "We got here and that is the important thing."

"We should have you cleared through customs and immigration in a few minutes." Rokossovsky looked around the cabin, counting noses. "Then I will take you straight to your hotel so you can clean up. If you don't mind, General Nikishev and I would like to have dinner with you tonight. Then, in the morning, we will start the scheduled briefings."

"Excellent. When do we leave for the base?"

"We should be able to arrange for transport in two or three days, at most a week. Even though there is a war going on, things here in Vietnam often happen at a slower pace than back home in Russia."

Koniev wondered what Rokossovsky meant by his comment about pace. Was it a warning? Warnings, when they came at all, were rarely direct. A man could go mad, wondering what constituted warnings, what was misdirection, and what was mere information.

Smiling, Rokossovsky, continued. "Your officers will be housed in the same hotel and we will have officers from the embassy entertain them tonight. They will also participate in some of your briefings and have some of their own. The special equipment you brought will be stored at the embassy warehouse until you are ready to leave."

Which was a polite way of saying the intelligence officers would be met by the local GRU officers. Koniev suspected the missile officers would be told little that was new to them.

"Welcome to our country, Colonel." The Vietnamese customs officer spoke in Russian as he handed Koniev his passport, now with the proper stamps.

"Thank you. I am delighted to be here." Koniev responded in Vietnamese, and the officer smiled.

Marc Liebman

"Your Vietnamese is very good. We welcome your help against the Americans and their lackeys in the south." The Vietnamese again spoke in Russian and saluted.

"Your Russian is excellent as well." Koniev returned the salute and stepped out into the humidity and sunshine where the stale air of the airplane was replaced by a humid, dank smell that was foreign to his nose.

While he waited for the customs officials to finish their work, Koniev looked around the ramp and noted that his Aeroflot plane was parked by itself. A couple of hundred meters away, an oil-streaked Air France DC-6 that showed its age with faded and, in some places, missing paint was next to the passenger terminal. Nearby was a Lockheed Constellation with British Overseas Airways markings and other, smaller planes with Chinese, Laotian, and Cambodian markings that looked like Russian Ilyushin-14s. All had their national flags displayed on their rudders.

When he got his new passport, which allowed him to travel outside the Soviet Union and Warsaw Pact nations, the blood-red document with the gold hammer and sickle on the cover encouraged him to he let his mind wonder what would happen if he bought a ticket for either a BOAC or Air France flight and showed them his passport. The first question they would ask would be, "Colonel Koniev, why do you want to go to Singapore?" That was a pleasant way of asking if he were defecting, and the next step was a jail cell in Hanoi from which he'd bet even money that he would exit either on a stretcher with a bullet in the back of his head or in handcuffs on his way to the Lubyanka where he would be tortured and then shot.

Koniev pushed the thought of defection out of his mind as he took a deep breath to purge his brain of his very un-Soviet Army officer thoughts. He knew he would smell this air for the next two years unless he was in a wooden box two meters under the earth.

The windowless conference room in which the three Soviet officer sat was supposed to be air conditioned, but one would never know it because the ancient fan just stirred the musty air. Koniev was sure it was close to 35°C when he picked up three ice cubes from the melting contents of a battered ice bucket and dropped them into a glass. The ice was followed by the contents of a bottle of mineral water he'd taken from a tray at the end of the table.

"Colonel Koniev, just for the record, this is a secure conference room and nothing that we share in this meeting can be discussed with anyone else. Do you understand?" General Nikishev had a pitcher of water next to his chair and stared into the newcomer's eyes as he spoke.

"Yes, sir, I do."

"Good. How much do you know about the set-up here?"

"I studied the reports sent to the school on the effectiveness of our missiles against the American fighter bombers in preparation for this mission, and I have a pretty good understanding of their tactics and jamming equipment. Other than I am being sent to a new base where I am to test the tactics I outlined in a paper, I know very little."

"At least our security is better than the Americans." General Nikishev smiled to let his comment sink in. "First, the base is about a hundred-fifty kilometers north northwest of here, right under what the Americans call Route Packs Five and Six, which were on the maps we sent to General Poliakov at the Zhukov Academy. Our Vietnamese comrades call the new base Venom because they think it will kill Americans like a cobra. Your missiles are its poison. Second, underground telephone cables link the base with the Vietnamese air defense system. This gives you a direct line to the senior Soviet Army advisor on duty at their air defense command centers. A major or lieutenant colonel and a Zhukov graduate are always on duty and will answer the phone. Some may have been your students. We will use that line to call you; or, if you need anything from the Soviet Union, you can call the embassy and speak to Colonel Rokosovssky or myself."

By telling him their rank, the General was informing Koniev that the Soviet officer would be junior to him and would have to follow his orders. Since he'd accepted this job, he'd wondered how many Soviet Army and Air Force officers and men were here. The unconfirmed rumors, discussed in hushed tones among close friends outside the school buildings in the large courtyards, estimated that there were several thousand, which would explain why a General was head of the mission. Koniev wondered if the Soviet Army advisors were under his command or the General's? Konev's gut told him to stay in listening mode and maybe ask a few questions later when had heard more.

"Excellent, General. Where will the radars be positioned?"

"Here is a chart with the exact location of each of the P-12 surveillance radars." The general didn't unfold the map as he passed it to Koniev, who placed it by his right hand as the start of what he hoped would be a pile of more documents. "The radars are the latest versions we have and their control vans are already in place, so you will be able to see and use anything that our comrades-in-arms can see. They just finished testing two S-75 fire-control radars in camouflaged positions on the ridge tops at the base."

"Can they be seen from the air?" Koniev asked, unsure how much effort was being made to hide the base. In his past experience, everything was pretty much out in the open in the standard six-point star arrangement with the launchers out at the tip and the radars and control van in the center.

"No, we are sure of that. Colonel Rokossovsky flew over them two days ago, and neither he nor anyone else on board could see the radars or any of the missile launchers under the netting. You will find that our Vietnamese comrades are experts at camouflage."

On cue, Rokossovsky slid several 20 x 25 centimeter black-and-white photos across the conference table, which Koniev studied, one by one, for several seconds before putting them in a neat pile off to his right.

That was good news. Rokossovsky might not be a chair-bound colonel after all. No one in Moscow had told him about the pudgy Rokossovsky, but General Poliakov had had nothing but good things to say about Nikishev, who was a Frunze graduate and a World War II tank commander. He had also introduced him to some of his friends who knew Nikishev well and who said he was a very a good soldier who didn't tolerate incompetence. Nonetheless, why was the general here? The Vietnamese were not fighting a conventional war with tanks and infantry, and Nikishev had admitted last night at dinner that he knew very little about guided missiles. Koniev wondered if he were being tested by Nikishev, or if the general really didn't know. He thought that was unlikely, because many of his countrymen were here to support the North Vietnamese air defense system, which relied on the SA-2 missile. Koniev pushed both questions to the back of his mind with a mental note to find out the truth later.

"Have either of you been to this new base?"

The gaunt Nikishev wheezed as if he were struggling for breath. Nikishev nodded toward Rokossovsky, who answered. "We wanted to wait until it was operational before we visited. Right now there isn't much to see, though the reports are that construction of the base is ahead of schedule, which is a pleasant surprise."

Koniev took the answer to mean it was dangerous and they hadn't wanted to take the risk because the Soviet Union was not at war with the Americans. Soviet advisors who had visited the school after tours in Vietnam said many of their friends and some pilots had already been killed in the war even though the government would not admit it. Relatives of those killed were told their son or husband died on an exercise in a foreign country. Koniev had seen some of the uncensored letters smuggled out of Vietnam; these just added to his distrust of whatever his government told him. He thought it best not say anything as he did not know what the two officers' instructions from Moscow were, nor what they were told about him.

Nikishev changed the subject. "We have a small eighteen-man Spetznaz platoon at the site. They will help provide security for the cryptographic equipment and whatever else you want them to do. You may, as much as they will not like the thought, think of them as your bodyguards."

"I understand." Koniev thought for a moment and then debated on how to ask the obvious question. "My orders say I am to take command of the base. My assumption is that I am responsible for the missile operations and our Vietnamese comrades will provide the soldiers to defend the base." Soviet doctrine suggested that an S-75 Divina battery operating by itself should have at least an infantry company for protection. Eighteen Spetnaz, no matter how good they were, weren't enough to protect six missile launchers, a command-and-control van, and the communications equipment.

"Excellent question, Colonel. You will be the senior Russian Army officer and in command of all the Soviet Army personnel assigned to the base. You are there for the sole purpose of testing your theories by shooting down American planes. How you do that is up to you, and in that capacity you report to me. The Vietnamese get to watch, but not control the new versions of the missiles. You are not responsible for the decision as to whether or not we give them the equipment. That will come to me from Moscow. Is that clear?"

"Yes, sir, that confirms my written orders." Nikishev hadn't answered Koniev's question. Reality at the base would be different from what was perceived in Hanoi and believed in Moscow. "Who is the Vietnamese base commander?"

"A Colonel Nguyen Thai. We have been told that he is a very experienced infantry officer who has four infantry companies in his command for a total of about a thousand men, and sixteen S-60 anti-aircraft guns in pairs deployed around the base. The batteries add about another one twenty to one hundred fifty men."

Koniev wondered why the Vietnamese had assigned such a large ground force at the site. Were they expecting some kind of commando attack? Were the Americans that bold? "What is his chain of command?"

Nikishev coughed before he spoke, sending small puffs of smoke out of his mouth. "He reports to General Tran Van Dong, who commands the Northwest Sector of the Peoples' Air Defense Forces. Neither Van Dong or General Ngo Dinh, who is the Commander of the Peoples Air Defense Force, selected Thai. Our sources tell us he was hand-picked by General Chung, who is on the general staff and is very familiar with his combat record." The general struggled to take a deep breath. "If you are asking who is in overall command, Colonel, it is neither of you; it will be a shared command. You are responsible for missile operations and he is responsible for protection of the base. The two of you are going to have to figure out how to work together. We have been told you can be quite diplomatic, having worked with our East German and Chinese comrades."

That was a recipe for a disaster; someone had to be in charge. Koniev took a long drink from his glass rather than respond, thinking, *No one is in charge.* "When do the new missiles arrive?"

"Seventy-two new missiles in the first shipment are sitting on a ship in Haiphong Harbor where we know the Americans won't attack it. We're waiting for you to let us know that the base is ready. Neither Colonel Rokossovsky nor I are qualified to make that decision. You are the expert and we will rely on you to tell us when the base is ready for them."

"How long will it take to get the missiles off the ships and up there?"

"That depends on the Americans. As I said earlier, the S-75 Divina radars to support missile launches are already in place and tested but have not been turned on. The Vietnamese can get the modified missiles off the ship in two days, working around the clock, once we get it to the pier. Then we have to get them up to the base. The plan was to send them up six at a time in small convoys at night and hope the Americans don't figure this out and try to stop the shipments. Unless we are very lucky, we expect to lose one or two convoys to the Americans."

"When can I have my men inspect what has arrived?"

"Whenever you are ready." Colonel Rokossovsky spoke while General Nikishev coughed. "I can order the missiles unloaded at any time."

"Please do that now, Colonel. I will have two of my officers remain here to inspect the missiles as they are unloaded, and one each will accompany the last two convoys of six. Once I get to the base, I will call to set up a shipping schedule. If my men have any questions, they can call me on the secure phone."

"Yes, Colonel. I will ask the Vietnamese to get the ship alongside a pier as soon as possible."

"How soon can I get to Venom?"

"You can leave when you are ready. We thought you might want to spend a few days in Hanoi before you go. The base is very primitive."

"I don't mind living in the field, so I'd like to leave as soon as we can arrange transport." Koniev didn't want to stay in Hanoi. It was time to see whether or not his theories were real or just the work of an academic.

General Nikishev didn't respond. Instead, he pulled a sheet from one of the three piles of paper arrayed in a line on the polished rosewood table. "Do you know what this is?"

Koniev picked up the sheet and studied the groupings of numbers and letters for a few seconds. "No, sir."

"This is an extract of what the American Air Force and Navy calls an 'air tasking' order. Each group of lines is a segment from a strike plan that assigns the target, weapons to be carried by each plane, time on target, IFF codes, frequencies, number of aircraft and call signs, as well as other useful information for coordinating the mission."

"Where did we get this?" Koniev couldn't help himself and suspected someone from the GRU must trust Nikishev a lot. The fact that Nikishev was showing him this document said someone very high up on the General's staff had already approved this conversation. Whoever that was had been able to get the KGB as well as GRU to agree on the importance of sharing this intelligence.

"We'll get to that in a minute. Do you understand the significance?"

"Yes. Assuming the information is accurate, it tells us where the Americans are going to strike, when they will be there, and what route they are taking. It makes it easier to shoot them down." A light went off in Koniev's head when he remembered the stories celebrating the North Korean's seizure of an American spy ship. If they got the machines, all they would need were the code keys. And, if the GRU had smart mathematicians, they could continue to break the codes. So, it was possible. Now, what was the name of the American ship?

Koniev blinked back to the present when General Nikishev picked up two more sheets from another pile. "We get these messages several times a week from Moscow, and we will pass them on to you if we get them ahead of a planned strike. When they are sent to you, your cryptographic officers will be alerted and you will have the room cleared so you alone will watch the decoded information come off the secure tele-printer. No one else at the base is to see them. Understood?"

Koniev nodded. This explained why the four crypto-logic experts were on the airplane. They were there to decrypt these messages. But maintaining secrecy would be very hard to do. All the cryptographers had to do was delay calling him and they'd see the message. Didn't anyone in this country trust anyone else? If the intelligence officers weren't cleared for this, it must be very, very secret. He'd see if it were a fantasy or reality.

"One more thing. As the date of the information passes, destroy the messages. There are to be no files kept of these messages, none whatsoever. Burn them. Understood?"

"Yes, sir."

"Our experts in Moscow also send us other information like this." Nikishev picked another piece of paper from the third pile. "This is an American Navy operations plan for a mission to insert a reconnaissance team inside this country."

"How accurate is this?" It had crossed Koniev's mind that this could be an American deception operation, but didn't want to suggest it.

"I am told it is very accurate. I do not know the source." Koniev nodded and General Nikishev continued. "First, we verified all the information in the tasking orders with spies stationed near American air bases in Thailand and Vietnam as well as our intelligence gathering ships in the Gulf of Tonkin. Second, the tasking order you are holding was for a mission attempted just a few days ago; an American helicopter with the call sign 'Big Mother 12' was shot down.

"Interesting." Koniev had just realized that his life could depend on Colonel Thai's skills as an infantry officer; they hadn't told him back in Russia that the American Spetznaz were conducting raids in North Vietnam. He made a mental note to practice with the AK-47 when he got to Venom.

"It gets better. Our analysts are convinced that Gringo Six and Sierra Six are call signs of the same American SEAL team. We don't know the pattern of when they use each call sign, but we are eighty percent sure it is the same team. They are the only two American teams who use the brand names of skis to designate their landing zones. The reason we know that is because one of our GRU officers is a former Soviet cross-country skier who competed in the Olympics and he pointed it out. This SEAL team is very hard to track and we believe Colonel Thai has an interest in them because they wounded him and mauled one of his battalions back in June of last year. We know that from our intercepts of messages from the Americans and our Vietnamese allies and we believe that the good Colonel Thai does not. We do not want him to find out that Gringo Six and Sierra Six are probably the same SEAL team because he will tell his superiors that we are decoding their messages. That is something that we do not want our socialist comrades to know. Understand?"

Big Mother 40

"You promised that during dinner you would tell me why we're celebrating." Jack tilted the top of a brown bottle of San Miguel beer toward his friend. "The last time you said we were celebrating, it was at the East End Club in Olongapo the second day I was in PI. You disappeared, leaving me to the tender mercies of two young local women, and the next thing I know, it's early morning. When I left, the owner says my bill had been paid and they had instructions to, after giving me a good-bye blow job, drop me off at the front gate in time to make our oh-seven-thirty muster."

"That's what friends are for." Josh raised his cold San Miguel beer and, smiling, took a long swig. "From what I recall, you showed up having had your dick either in a girl's mouth or vagina all night long. I believe the correct description is that you had your brains fucked out. And you said you had a wonderful time and enjoyed the experience."

D'Onofrio just looked at his friend and smiled. Memories flooded back of the nights he'd spent in the Pearl of the Orient at the East End Club that preferred serving young officers. The girls at the door checked ID cards, but once inside, anything could be had, from booze to sex anyway you wanted it.

"We'll leave out the part where you went back several times before we left to repeat the experience on your own nickel. And that doesn't include the enjoyment you get of tossing quarters into the Shit River and watching Filipino kids diving to catch them in the filthy water."

Josh stopped talking when he heard a commotion behind them at the bar. They were sitting at one of the tables in the stepped dining room that overlooked the dance floor and bandstand. Past the floor-to-ceiling window was a large, Olympic-sized swimming pool which could be seen from all of the tables except those where the view was blocked by the band.

After Josh tossed a couple of dollar bills on the table, they joined a crowd of men gathered around one end of the small bar. Some were in uniform, others dressed in the O'Club "uniform" of slacks and a golf shirt, because blue jeans, t-shirts and shorts were not allowed in the "formal" part of the club. Between the heads, Josh could see a large man he recognized as the CO of one of the fighter squadrons in Air Wing Nine on the *America*, which was tied up at the pier at Cubi for a week's break between line periods in the Gulf.

"Whaddaya mean I have to stop drinking?" the large man roared. It was well known among the Cubi regulars that the CO was an All-American lineman at Notre Dame; he had a reputation for being a noisy, belligerent drunk who often passed out for a few moments, fell down, and then got up and continued drinking. His behavior was overlooked because he was an outstanding leader.

"Sir, you are setting a bad example for your younger officers." The man speaking was a lieutenant commander in summer whites. A tag saying Cubi Point Naval Air Station COMMAND DUTY OFFICER hung from the button hole of the pocket beneath a couple rows of ribbons. The star on his shoulder boards said he was a line officer, but he was not wearing the gold wings of a Naval Aviator or Naval Flight Officer.

"Bullshit, I am enjoying the company of my fellow officers here at the bar. We are celebrating another line period in which we didn't lose a man or plane and got two MiGs."

"Sir, there have been complaints about your foul language and behavior. The club manager wants you to leave."

"Lieutenant Commander." The CO lurched as he leaned forward to get eyeball-to-eyeball with the CDO. "Go tell the club manager that we pay his salary by buying booze and food. If he wants us to come back, he needs to leave us the fuck alone."

"Sir, with all due respect, I must to ask you to leave." The lieutenant commander was now flanked by two enlisted men in their Cracker Jack whites, wearing the blue armbands with MP in white letters, who were ready to draw their billy clubs.

The CO leered at the younger, more junior officer for a few seconds, and then searched for something at the end of the bar. Finding a squeeze ketchup bottle, he wrote VF-41 on the front of the CDO's whites.

"CDO, your uniform is soiled. It needs washing." He then picked up the lieutenant commander, cradled him in his massive arms as he would a large child, and marched down the steps to the swimming pool. To the cheers of his officers, he tossed the CDO in the water.

Josh grabbed a stunned Jack by the arm. "Let's go back to the BOQ before the shit hits the fan."

TUESDAY, SAME DAY, APRIL 10, 1972, 1202 LOCAL TIME, HA GIANG, NORTH VIETNAM

"Bolt Three-two, Ratchet zero-five approaching the initial point." The pilot in the gray McDonnell Douglas RF-101 flexed the fingers on his left hand and then dropped them down onto the two throttles on the left side of the cockpit. Once again he went through each item on the checklist, touching each switch to make sure it was in the right position so that all he had to do was open the red cover on one and flick the toggle up to start the cameras.

Big Mother 40

Satisfied, the pilot trimmed the nose down, pushed the throttles to the detent, and then to the left and up again. The muffled *whump*, the increasing airspeed that followed, the being pushed back into the ejection seat, and the read outs on the gauges on the left side of the instrument panel all satisfied him that the afterburners on the two engines had lit as advertised.

"Ratchet Zero Five, Bold Three Two is starting the music."

"Ratchet Zero Five, this is Cowboy Six Eight. You're clear. No bogeys."

The pilot of Ratchet Zero Five clicked the mike switch twice to show he knew the jammers were on the air and the two F-4s escorting him believed the sky was clear of MiGs. He glanced down at his map for the last time on the photo run to make sure that he was right where he was supposed to be at five thousand feet. Up ahead, he could see the railroad line that disappeared over the horizon toward the Peoples' Republic of China.

This was his 32nd mission in the fast RF-101, and the twenty-six year old loved the job. The pilot wanted to fly the unarmed reconnaissance airplanes because, as a kid growing up, he'd read about the P-38s and Spitfires that the pilots flew alone all over Europe, perfecting the art of taking pictures from fast moving airplanes.

A quick glance at the airspeed indicator told him that he was ripping through the air at near .98 Mach or about six hundred knots, which would make him a tough target to hit. As soon as the Claire River disappeared under the nose, he reached down and flipped the camera switch up; he was rewarded by humming sounds of different tones that said the high-resolution cameras in the forward station and the two twelve-inch cameras in the after station under his seat had begun taking pictures.

When he within about two miles of Ha Giang's rail yard, the anti-aircraft guns started. The first sets of tracers that reached out looked as if they were right on target; but then, as their paths converged, it became clear that the bullets, which he recognized as 57mms, were going to pass well behind the airplane. The explosions from the shells rocked the speeding airplane, but so far none were close enough to do damage, and in seconds he was planning to break hard to the left to make his escape back over Laos and find the waiting tanker before heading back to base in southern Thailand.

He did not see the six-round burst that passed over the top of the fighter. It was followed by a more accurate one in which the first round passed about a hundred feet in front of the airplane. Before he could move the controls, the second round entered the cockpit and exploded, while the third round in the burst entered the fuselage just above the engines and detonated in the half empty fuel tank.

Chapter 5

FUNERALS

The crew of Big Mother 22 followed the route dictated by the operational planners at CINCPAC and COMMACV and plotted the waypoints on a strip chart made from a Defense Mapping Agency Tactical Pilotage chart. They'd launched about an hour before from the modified World War II-vintage USS *Oklahoma City*, which had been turned into a guided missile cruiser in the 1960s. The seaplane handling area on the stern was now a roomy helicopter pad.

The mission started when Big Mother 22 picked up a six-man SEAL team at Da Nang and flew to the light cruiser, steaming about forty-fifty miles southeast of Haiphong. Two minutes before the helicopter went feet dry, the co-pilot pushed the "ident" button to give their position to the crew on the E-2 Hawkeye orbiting between the Gulf of Tonkin Yankee Station and the *Oklahoma City*. At that point, the crew turned off its IFF and radar altimeter and switched the HF and UHF radios into the standby position. The loss of the identifying data on Big Mother 22's blip was the signal for the controller in the belly of the E-2 orbiting at twenty-five thousand feet to try to follow the helo from the radar reflections from its rotor blades.

After crossing the beach between Ha Long and Cam Pha at about one in the morning, Big Mother 22 headed northwest on a zig-zag route toward an LZ south of Ha Giang that had them following ridges and avoiding known villages. Rather than staying just below the ridge lines and flying closer to the treetops, slowly at forty-sixty knots to mask the noise of the helicopter, the crew of Big Mother 22 stayed five hundred feet above the top of the ridgeline and flew fast.

Forty kilometers ahead of Big Mother 22's track, the phone jangled twice before being picked up. "Thai." He looked at his watch: 0213.

"Sir, an American helicopter is approaching."

67

"Have Major Loi meet me in the command center at once." Colonel Thai had gradually learned a little more about his assigned executive officer. Like Thai, Loi had been wounded in the south and been sent north to recuperate, then ordered to join the new regiment assigned to protect Venom.

By the time Thai reached the command center, the two sergeants on duty had plotted the course of the American helicopter and calculated when it would pass over Venom. He smiled when the captain on watch pointed out which S-60 battery would be in the best position to bring down the helicopter.

"Are the guns manned and ready?"

"Yes, sir. All four batteries are ready to fire if they see the helicopter."

Based on the route of the helicopter, only those in the battery with the call sign Krait in the southeast part of the base would have a shot. The two observers moved off to one side to give Thai and Loi a clear view of the black sky so they could see the tracers and maybe even the helicopter. The silence was broken twenty-five meters above the jungle floor by the occasional rustling of the leaves.

Thai sensed the helicopter before he saw or heard it. The overcast sky made the helicopter almost invisible until its black shape was silhouetted against the lighter charcoal-gray clouds. "Major, Krait can fire as soon as the helicopter is in range."

When Loi didn't answer, Thai turned to see him on the phone, giving the batteries instructions not to fire all at once. It was a good tactic to minimize the number of guns used in case the helicopter escaped and the crew survived to report back.

The tracers from first burst of six shells passed underneath and behind the helicopter, which Thai easily identified as an American Navy Sea King. The helicopter turned in a steep bank away from the ridgeline toward Thai when the second burst of six shells reached out. They saw the flash as the first shell passed through the rotor blades and went off in the cockpit. The second hit somewhere in the rotor head, and the next two exploded in the tumbling debris.

WEDNESDAY, NEXT DAY, APRIL 12, 1972, 1743 LOCAL TIME, ELECTRONIC INTELLIGENCE ANALYSIS CENTER, NAVAL AIR STATION, AGANA, GUAM

Lieutenant Commander Greg Winston started his Navy career as an enlisted man riding in the bellies of World War II patrol bombers converted to electronic intelligence roles. Now he was the old man of the squadron, and at the age of 42, Winston was only thinking of retiring. His hearing was going bad from having sat for way too many hours in noisy, poorly heated and insulated cabins and it was getting to be time to pass the torch.

Winston's ability to pick out electronic signals from atmospheric noise depended on his hearing, and if that went away, so did his value to the Navy. But still, time and time again, Winston would play back tapes that the squadron's newest aircraft had recorded and find a valuable nugget that none of the younger men heard, or even saw on a scope. Experience still counted for something. After listening to this particular tape at least ten times, he was now sure of what he'd found.

Sheets of carbon paper separated the three preprinted forms that he fed, with practiced ease, into the typewriter. The original would go with the original tape to NICPAC, one would generate the message alerting NICPAC to conduct a more detailed analysis of the inbound tape, and one would go into the squadron's archives with a copy of the tape.

His thick fingers adjusted the roller on the battered, gray IBM Selectric typewriter so that it was centered in the space where he was about to enter in his analysis. Winston made one last check of the ball to make sure it was the OCR version which enabled radiomen to automate the encryption process and pecked out addresses from memory. Satisfied they were correct, he flexed his fingers and began typing.

UNCLAS: DATA

> 1. TS/SI: RECORDED PULSES ON E BAND FREQUENCIES—440.1, 448.3 AND 446.7—NEVER BEFORE USED IN THIS THEATER.

> 2. TS/SI: EMISSIONS WERE VERY SHORT IN LENGTH, GENERALLY LESS THAN 10-15 SECONDS. PATTERN WAS SIMILAR TO OPERATOR TESTING INSTALLATION.

> 3. TS/SI: HIGH EMITTER PULSE RATE SUGGESTS TARGET TRACKING RADAR.

UNCLAS: EMITTER LOCATION

> 1. TS/SI: EMITTERS WERE NOT ON THE AIR LONG ENOUGH TO ALERT AIRCRAFT OPERATORS OR TO ACCURATELY CALCULATE BEARING FROM THE AIRCRAFT TO THE EMITTER SITE.

> 2. TS/SI: BASED ON THE TRACK OF THE AIRCRAFT, TIME THE EMITTERS WERE RECORDED, SUSPECT LOCATION OF THE

ANTENNA IS IN MOUNTAINS, 75-100 NAUTICAL MILES NORTHWEST OF HANOI. LOCATION IS IN MOUNTAINOUS AREA OF NORTH VIETNAM NOT NORMALLY ASSOCIATED WITH SA-2 MISSILE LAUNCH COMPLEXES.

UNCLAS: ANALYSIS

1. TS/SI: SIGNAL STRENGTH SUGGESTS THAT AIRCRAFT COLLECTING THE SIGNAL WAS OUTSIDE THE DETECTION RANGE OF THE EMITTER.

2. TS/SI: FREQUENCIES DETECTED ARE NORMALLY IN RANGE ASSOCIATED WITH FAN SONG A/B/C FIRE CONTROL RADARS FOR SA-2 GUIDELINE MISSILES AND COULD BE NEW "WAR RESERVE" FREQUENCIES TO COMPLICATE DETECTION AND COUNTERMEASURES OR A NEW VERSION OF THE RADAR.

3. TS/SI: IF MISSILES ARE LOCATED IN GENERAL AREA OF EMITTERS, THEY ARE WELL POSITIONED TO ATTACK AIRCRAFT APPROACHING TARGETS IN HANOI AREA FROM THE WEST AND NORTH WEST 75-100 NAUTICAL MILES EARLIER THAN CURRENTLY ESTIMATED CAPABILTY.

THURSDAY, NEXT DAY, APRIL 13, 1972,
0610 LOCAL TIME, VENOM BASE

Alexei Koniev ignored the two Soviet officers for a few seconds as he twisted his torso to ease the stiffness in his back and joints. He had been riding in a small truck since 0200 in the morning. Stretching also gave him time to look over the group to try to figure out who, in the growing light, was Colonel Thai. Koniev had been welcoming the coming sunrise when they'd turned off on the gravel road and the jungle canopy turned the dawn back into night.

Now that he could see it, the jungle reminded him of the lush, hardwood forests around his parents' home near Vytegra, where he'd played during the summers. Even there, first light came later and darkness came quicker in the dense woods east of Leningrad.

It was not until he put on his hat that one of the Vietnamese officers started toward him and he saw the four silver stars in a diamond pattern, along with the two gold stripes, of a Vietnamese colonel. Koniev, at 190 centimeters in height, was almost a head taller than the man who held out his hand. "Good morning, Colonel Thai, I am Alexei Koniev." He held out his own hand and hoped his Vietnamese was understandable.

Thai shook his hand with two vigorous pumps. "Good morning, Colonel Koniev. Welcome to Venom. We are glad you are here." Thai spoke Russian without hesitating.

Where did he learn Russian? Koniev thought the Vietnamese officer's Russian was far better than his Vietnamese. "I am glad to be here." Koniev again spoke Vietnamese.

"Colonel, after you have had a chance to freshen up, may I suggest that we have breakfast?" Again, Russian from the Vietnamese officer.

Koniev tried to decide whether the Vietnamese officer was being hospitable or just trying to establish that they were equals. Did he want to meet alone or with his officers? "Colonel Thai, I would be happy to join you. Can you give me about thirty minutes?"

"Excellent. I will send my orderly to lead you to my quarters." Thai touched the brim of his hat, more of a signal that the conversation was over than a salute, which would have been acknowledgement that Koniev was senior to him. Or was the gesture meant for his officers?

The walk from his tunnel quarters to the wooden structure that was Colonel Thai's office and residence took less than five minutes. Koniev climbed the four steps to the floor that was at least a meter off the ground. Coarse planking went up the sides to about the height of his chest and was topped by a shelf, above which screens went to the roof. Outside, planks nailed together looked like shutters that could be lowered. The roof was corrugated metal of some kind that extended way out over the side of the building.

Inside, he saw doors to two rooms and none of the walls went all the way to the roof. The one he was standing in was an office with a large conference table, also made out of wood that had been sanded down to make it smooth. Koniev could see into the room that served as a bedroom and Koniev guessed the one behind the closed door was a bathroom.

Thai motioned to the table and Koniev, who had changed from his sweat-soaked summer uniform to a set of camouflaged utilities and a soft field cap, decided not to sit at the head of the table. Thai sat on the other side of the table and waited for the orderly to pour some tea. A nod of his head and the private closed the door to the building as he left.

"Sugar?"

Koniev took the small glass jar with coarse off-white crystals from the scarred hand. He wondered how much of Thai's body had been burned, how long it took him to recover and how had it affected his judgment? "Thank you." He dropped two small scoops into the hot liquid.

"I thought it best that the two of us of meet first so I could tell you about this base." Thai was speaking Russian. "How much have you been told?"

"Not much. I think an overview from you would be very helpful." Koniev responded in Vietnamese. "Colonel, I would like to improve my Vietnamese, so if you don't mind, let's speak in Vietnamese. If I don't understand, I'll either ask you to explain or ask you in Russian."

"Very well." Thai thought that was unusual for a Russian; most of the Soviet officers he'd met had been arrogant and condescending and insisted on speaking Russian.

Koniev nodded as if to say "Go on," after Thai spoke a few sentences with deliberate diction as he began to tell him about Venom. Koniev raised his hand every few minutes to signal that he had a question, but between the map that Colonel Thai brought to the table and the discussion, Koniev was able to create a mental picture of the base's layout.

Koniev sat back to signal he wanted to change topics. "Colonel, why were you picked for command of Venom?"

Thai chuckled. "I don't know. Perhaps it was fate. I was the commander of a base that was training officers how to hunt American Special Forces teams when I was summoned to army headquarters. They confirmed I could speak Russian and the next thing I knew I was in front of two generals telling me about this place." Thai took a sip of tea, thinking it was his turn to ask a question. "From what I hear, you are one of the Soviet Army's leading experts in S-75 Divina tactics. Is that true?"

It was Koniev's chance to laugh. "I am not sure about that. I wrote a paper that described how, if we changed tactics and made a small modification to the missile, we can minimize the amount of telemetry, limit the time the American pilots have to react and as a result, should shoot down more planes." Koniev thought about the events that led to his coming to Vietnam. "In January, the general commanding our air defense academy walked into my office and asked me if I wanted to put my theories to work."

"So we both used to be school teachers?" Thai tipped his cup in a salute to the Soviet officer opposite him.

"Yes, I guess that is true." Koniev returned the salute with his cup. Time would tell, but Koniev's instincts suggested that he could work with this man. "Colonel, in order for me to get a much better understanding of this base, I need to see it. Can you give me a tour?"

"It will take several days to see it all."

"I'm not going anyplace soon."

Thai laughed. "We will do one company sector a day and I know just the place to start." He got up and picked up a field phone and spoke in rapid-fire Vietnamese that Koniev could not follow. "Colonel, my orderly will take you back to your quarters and then at ten hundred hours or so, we'll climb up to an observation post in the trees that that will give you an unobstructed view of the valley. And then we will walk to the command post for the company assigned to defend this sector and along the way, we will see your control van and one of the radars."

"Excellent. I could use the exercise."

FRIDAY, NEXT DAY, APRIL 14, 1972, 0946 LOCAL TIME, CAM RANH BAY, 180 MILES NORTH OF SAIGON, SOUTH VIETNAM

"Mancuso. This is a secure line." The SEAL who'd answered the phone was wearing a faded olive-drab t-shirt and torn fatigues that were cut into Bermuda shorts. The name tag on his desk in the private office was the only indication that he was a captain. His orders that brought him back to Vietnam for his third tour said he was to assume command of all Navy Special Warfare Forces in Vietnam.

"Captain, Major General Cruz here. I've got a tasker for you. Commac-V, along with Seventh Air Force are hot to trot about this one." The fact that Cruz, who was both a friend and a Marine major general, had used both their ranks instead of his first name meant this call had a serious subject.

"Yes, sir, so what do they want us to do that is so important?" Mancuso knew Hector Cruz was the chief of staff for operations for the Army four-star who was running the war in Vietnam, a.k.a. COMMACV, pronounced "Com-Mac-V."

"The Air Force is convinced that SAMs are coming in from China via a railroad. There's a railroad junction near Ha Giang where they think they are hidden before being shipped to the missile sites around Hanoi. Ha Giang, if you don't know, is a little town in northwest North Vietnam a few miles south of the PRC border. They want your guys to eyeball the rail yard from a few hundred yards away to get pictures of the suspected hidden storage area to prove their theory."

"Why don't they run a couple of photo birds up there and get some pictures, or dump a few bombs on it and see what happens?"

"They tried both. After several strikes on the rail yard, they didn't get any fires or secondary explosions that would indicate missiles or any kind of munitions. They've sent in a couple of photo birds three times and lost a plane a couple of days ago."

"Let me make sure I understand what you're telling me. The Air Force bombs the yard, nothing blows up, and they don't believe their own damage assessment, so they want *my* guys to go in and look for rail sidings where the North Vietnamese are hiding missiles."

"That's it."

"It doesn't make any sense. They ought to go look at all the photos of Haiphong's piers taken while and after the missiles were offloaded from Soviet freighters. The SAMs are out in the open because the idiots in DC won't let us bomb the piers. Anyway, that's how the missiles are coming into Vietnam, and it doesn't take a rocket scientist to figure it out. What am I missing?"

"Tony, your problem is that you're applying logic to the situation. It is complicated because the Air Force general who runs intelligence at Seventh Air Force is an old war horse from World War II and Korea, and he has his boss convinced that the only way they can get so many missiles into the country is by railroad. He discounts the Navy's analysis which is, as you know, supported by imagery as well as other information. Anyway, Commac-V, at least for the moment, has bought this Air Force guy's theory."

"Why my SEALs?"

"Three reasons. First, Commac-V doesn't trust the CIA's teams of locals. Second, the Army's long-range reconnaissance teams are focused on Cambodia. They claim they don't have anybody to send. And third, and what I think is the real reason, your teams are the only ones who seem to get in and out of North Vietnam without much drama."

"Thank you, sir. I'll pass that compliment along to my teams and their taxi drivers."

"You're welcome. Anyway, we need a plan ASAP. How soon can you put one together?"

Mancuso sipped from his steaming mug of coffee which gave him a few seconds to answer. "Give me seventy-two hours and I'll bring it to you."

"Great. I'll have my chief of staff get back to you with a time and date in about four days. Keep in mind, no one around here wants to take on this Air Force guy. I think he's full of shit, but to placate him and either prove him right or wrong, Commac-V wants your guys to go have a look-see and end the discussion one way or the other."

"Yes, sir. I am going to assume that anyone in the room will have both the necessary clearances and a bona fide need to know about the mission. As a precaution, we won't leave any of the material behind. Just tell us when and where. Just let us know when to come down. We'll be ready, sir."

"Good. You know CINCPAC and Commac-V will have to approve it."

"Yes, sir, I understand." Mancuso knew why the general mentioned the approval process. "Sir, between now and the time of the op, assuming it is approved, no, and I repeat, *no* messages on the proposed mission tasking are to be sent out. Everything must be sent by courier or we don't plan, much less go. If Seventh Air Force wants us to do this mission, they must play by my rules or we're out. If I find out that they violated these rules during the planning process, we don't go. Before we go, both CINCPAC and Commac-V agree *in writing* to move heaven and earth to get my guys out if we find out after the team has been inserted that some idiot sent a message about the mission."

"I know how strongly you feel. I'll pass the request along. I gather by your statement that you still believe there's a leak?"

"Yes, sir, I do. More so than ever before. And, for the record, sir, it is not a *request* that no messages be sent, it *is* a requirement."

"I know that." General Cruz paused for a few seconds. "What makes you even more convinced?"

"Sir, if you remember, we tested our theory several times back in 'seventy-one that there was a leak, and each time the NVA walked right into the ambushes. In one, Marty Cabot and an augmented team went in a few days ahead of the dates in the message to give them time to prepare the traps. In a short, quick battle, they decimated the better part of a battalion. In another, they set up an ambush using Claymore mines along a route from the Ho Chi Minh Trail into South Vietnam. When about three hundred men were in the killing zone, they set off the Claymores. They took pictures of over two hundred bodies lying along the trail. The NVA spent two more weeks looking for additional Claymores they'd left as booby traps."

"Agreed, they proved that the NVA was getting info on where your teams were going. But, it doesn't give us the source of the leak. What do you have that is new?"

"Last year after those three operations, we ran a very successful op around Route 19 in North Vietnam, but my guys were hunted from the time they arrived until we got them out five days later. The bad guys knew we were going to be in the area. I had one of the SEALs on Commac-V's staff do some rooting around and he found several messages from one of Commac-V's minions requesting a sneak-and-peek along Route 19 at a specific time, and they discussed the locations they wanted us to reconnoiter. None of us knew about the messages before my guys went in. The team leader, Marty Cabot, and I both believe that the NVA knew where they were operating and were waiting when my guys arrived in North Vietnam. The NVA didn't know which LZ needed a welcoming committee, which gave our guys a day's head start. Nonetheless, it was pretty close."

"Are you one hundred percent sure they were compromised?"

"Yes, sir, I am. I have copies of the messages that went back and forth. If you want to talk to Lieutenant Cabot, he's back in-country on his second tour and he can brief you firsthand, because he set a couple of the traps using message traffic with mission details as the bait."

"Like you, I don't believe in coincidences." The general paused for a few seconds. "Tony, I'll make a phone call to a classmate of mine in Hawaii who's a two-star on CINCPAC's staff and will pass on your position on the no messages issue and strongest possible recommendation that they implement the restrictions you suggest. He's been very interested in this subject and has the horsepower to get your requirement approved. However, I'm warning you that some idiot here at Commac-V will try to get his way. If CINCPAC says okay, no messages, then no one around better violate the policy, or Commac-V will relieve and charge him faster than a bullet leaving a gun. Just between you, me, and the gatepost, keeping sensitive stuff out of messages is just good operational security."

"Good. Thank you, sir." Mancuso waited a few seconds to see if the general was going to say anything before changing the subject. "Sir, do you know about the helo that we believe was shot down in North Vietnam a few days ago?"

"I do, but what's your take on what happened?"

"Everything about Big Mother 22's mission was in the message that went from a Navy liaison officer on Commac-V's staff to CINCPAC. We were copied, as well as Commander Task Force 77. All we know is an E-2 held them in radar contact until they were well into North Vietnam, and they never came out. My gut tells me that the NVA knew their route and shot them down. An HC-7 crew of five, plus six of my guys are missing, and I have to write eleven letters that start with *Dear Mr. and Mrs. Jones, I have the sad duty to inform you that ...*"

"That's tough." Both men knew that in the close-knit SEAL community, losses like this were hard to take. The general had known Mancuso since they served together during the Korean War. He knew Mancuso had lots of evidence that strongly suggested a security leak, but what he didn't have was the smoking gun that proved, beyond a shadow of a doubt, that there was a traitor, nor could he point in the general direction of the possible source.

Cruz paused. "I don't know if anyone has told you, but you are not the only one who smells a rat. I've been told by my friend at CINCPAC that, as we speak, there are guys in both DC and Honolulu looking for a traitor because there have been too many 'coincidences' over the past few years, not only here in Vietnam, but all over the world. How hard are they chasing this down, I don't know. The bad news is that this rumor has been around for a couple of years, and he suspects that the folks in the fairytale world of DC have convinced themselves that there is no leak. More I don't know, because we're not cleared for that kind of stuff. But, for us poor grunts out here in the field, we need to proceed as if the leak has not been plugged."

"Agreed. Sir, that is good to know."

Cruz hesitated, and then decided to offer a suggestion. "When you get here, be sensitive to the fact that everyone around the headquarters thinks the message system is secure, so try not to stomp on their toes on this subject."

"Yes, sir. I will take your advice."

"One more thing to keep under your hat." Again a long pause. "The jet jockey commander who insisted that Big Mother 22 follow his planned route and sent all the messages is on his way home looking for a new career. The guidance he got was that he was supposed to suggest a route, not dictate one."

Mancuso was smiling as he was listening. "Sir, thank you for telling me."

"The bastard will have to live with the consequences of his actions for the rest of his life. I hope has nightmares about it every night."

It was well after 8 p.m. when Josh and Jack left HC-7's spaces at the Cubi Point Naval Air Station. They were tired, sweaty, and hungry, and decided, on the walk back, that they would just go into the bar and have a beer and a burger before calling it a night. The helo was ready to deploy and it was now a question of waiting for a ship to take them back to the Gulf of Tonkin and whichever carrier was hosting Detachment 110.

"Josh, I have to ask a question that's been bugging me since we flew that first mission together about a month ago." Jack had waited until the small bar in the NAS Cubi BOQ was almost empty. Most of the other patrons had left for their rooms, an evening in Olongapo, or other hangouts on the combined Naval Base and Naval Air Station.

"Fire away." Josh plunked down his brown bottle of San Miguel. It was empty and he signaled for another.

"Do you ever get scared?"

Josh turned to look his friend in the eye. "Yes, every time we go flying. My gut is churning when we launch on a mission where I know we may get shot at. Sometimes I want to throw up or take a shit." He tossed a dollar bill on the counter to cover what he planned to be his last beer. "Then, when I know I am about to get shot at, I can feel the fear and panic rising, but I don't let it win. Instead. I focus on the job at hand and then I'm too busy to be scared. When we're out of harm's way, that's when my knees shake."

"How do you deal with it?"

"By not letting it dictate what I do. If you are not scared, then you are not normal and shouldn't be flying anything. much less flying in combat. I've already accepted I could die, but that keeps me focused because I'll be dammed if I will make it easy for the bastards to kill me." Josh took a long pull on the bottle. "I'm also not afraid to talk about it with others. You don't lose any macho if you admit you're scared. I talk about my experience as I type a diary. Every week, the pages are sent to my dad; so in a way, every day I sit down to type. I'm talking to my dad. And after my first tour my dad more or less forced me to sit down and talk. He's a World War II and Korean War veteran; we emptied a few beers while we shared our experiences flying in combat. Plus, Natalie and I have talked about it, not in as much detail because it would scare the shit out of her, but just to help me deal with it."

"You're not worried about breaching security by what's in the diary?"

"No. My dad promised not to read the pages unless I get killed. He's putting the letters in a bank vault and I'll collect them when I get home. If the bad guys are reading my mail, then we've got a whole other set of problems."

"But what happens when the shit hits the fan? Do you ever think about getting killed? Doesn't it cross your mind?"

"I think about it before and after missions. Once the action starts, I am way too busy trying to keep from buying the farm to dwell on it. If the golden BB gets me, it gets me. which means that it was my time to die." Josh paused for a moment to collect his thoughts and to let what he just said sink in. He wasn't sure if he was telling himself or Jack, or both. "Do you remember the rules I handed out at the RAG to all the guys who had orders to HC-7?"

"You mean the 'Dicta Haman'?"

"Yup. I'm always trying to abide by them and look for more to add. So far, they've kept me and my crews alive and unhurt, and I intend to keep that record intact."

"I'm all for that."

Chapter 6
SUNDAY, 9 DAYS LATER

Koniev's boots crunched noticeably on the gravel that extended fifteen meters out from the raised concrete missile pads. Colonel Thai was conducting him around the launch area, explaining the strategy behind the set up. The self-propelled cranes were hidden under the trees and camouflage netting, positioned on individual gravel parking pads next to two trailers, each with a spare missile on a pad nearby. Unlike the shoddy work he'd seen in Eastern Europe and his native country, the Koreans' cleaned out the brush so twigs and branches around the pads wouldn't hurtle through the air when the missiles blasted off.

"The waving of the tree branches will look from an airplane as if they are blown by the wind. The trees should contain the smoke, which will make it harder to spot the launch site from the air." Colonel Thai then proudly described the mechanism that enabled them to pull back the jungle canopy just before a missile was fired and then allow the trees to quickly spring back into position.

After the tour, Koniev returned to the base.

The ever-present humidity made the rock walls shine in Koniev's quarters, which were in a separate, small tunnel. A secure rotary dial telephone on a separate table in the main room linked the base to the Soviet embassy and Thai's command center. The Koreans had added walls from rough planks to create a separate living area where he had a cot, a small refrigerator, and Soviet army field stove which he used to heat cups of tea. Washed clothes were draped on three crude sawhorses along one wall. Koniev had learned after a few tries that nothing ever got dry; they were just not as wet.

Since accepting this assignment, Koniev had begun each day with a vigorous workout. At first this had left him with aching muscles and joints, but after a few days he began to feel renewed and energized. It had kept him motivated to keep going, and now that he was in Vietnam he was glad he was in good shape and felt better than he had in years. It certainly wasn't the new diet of Vietnamese food.

Koniev tacked a detailed map of the base on a plank frame leaned against another wall, with the precise locations of each missile launcher, S-60 anti-aircraft position, hut, trail, and prepared fighting positions. Four, green, locking storage cabinets the Vietnamese were kind enough to provide stood in a neat row, creating a small divider against the back of which he had built a desk from empty ammo boxes and a couple of planks. Koniev assumed that the Vietnamese had the combinations, so every time he left the tunnel for more than an hour he lodged a small piece of paper under the drawer which held the encrypted messages. If opened, the piece would fall to the ground unnoticed, or so he hoped.

Full AK-47 magazines held down the corners of a map of North Vietnam on the table that dominated the open area, marked with the routes and altitudes U.S. Air Force airplanes took from their Thailand bases to targets in the Hanoi area. Thai had provided him with the version of the AK-47 called the AKMS that had a folding metal stock; it was never more than an arm's length or a few steps from where he was working. Whenever he ventured out of the cave, Koniev carried the assault rifle and wore a canvas harness that contained six spare magazines in three pouches in the front. Whenever he wasn't wearing the harness, it was draped over one of the chairs in the command center.

He did this for two reasons. One, it sent a message to his Vietnamese comrades that he knew they were at war and he was ready to do his part to defend the base. And two, it made him feel like a soldier again. When he'd first started carrying the AK with a loaded magazine, it gave him comfort and sent his psyche a clear message that he was where he should be: at the pointy edge of the sword doing battle with the enemy.

Laid out before him was not a theoretical classroom problem such as he had often dealt with in East Germany and in the anti-aircraft artillery school, but a real war in which, if he succeeded, the enemies of his allies would die. Venom was his own lab where he could test his theories which didn't fit the rigid Red Army air defense doctrine.

As Koniev estimated the intercept geometry based on the typical routes of the American planes, he settled on two goals for each missile engagement:

1. Shorten the warning the American pilots received by shortening the time of flight for each missile; and,

2. Minimize the chances the Americans had to locate the launchers and destroy the base.

The tinny jangling of the secure phone echoing off the walls of the cave was a new, unfamiliar sound. He strode over to the table and picked up the receiver. "Koniev."

"Good afternoon, Colonel. How are you enjoying your camping trip?" The deep bass voice of Boris Rokossovsky was clear despite the metallic overtone from the encryption equipment.

"We are ready to shoot down planes, but we need the new missile controllers." Koniev vacillated between pegging the former infantry officer as a political player, one who would always find a way to be close enough to the action to claim he was there but never near enough to risk getting shot, and being a leader who wanted to be with his men where the action was and sharing the same dangers. There was something odd about Rokossovsky that he just couldn't figure out.

"Excellent. You should have them soon."

"You found the missing equipment?"

"Not exactly. Is there anyone there with you?"

"No."

"We think our allies borrowed the missile control computers you brought on the plane to see if they can figure out what is so different. That will be very difficult and probably beyond their capabilities. So they will return some or all of them with an excuse as to why one or more of them were damaged. Or, they don't know these are different models and they will try to use them; then the missiles will fail their pre-flight tests, and our advisors will get a call. In either case, we should get most, if not all of them back. In the meantime, a new shipment arrives by air tomorrow and will be trucked to Venom with the first missiles."

"Thank you." Koniev wondered whether the missing computers had been stolen or someone from the embassy had given them to the North Vietnamese. He didn't know how Rokossovsky justified the replacements, but his guess was that he himself would be blamed for the losses. He wasn't going to cover Rokossovsky's ass.

Rokossovsky continued, "You will, however, have to adjust your records so that you have the correct serial numbers."

"When will they be here?" Koniev had already decided that he was going to show what he'd brought on the plane and then list the replacements. If anyone asked, he was covered.

"Thai will have the convoy schedule. The plan is to send two convoys each night until the base has its full complement of two for each of the six launchers and twenty-four spares, and then we will replace them as they are fired."

"Thank you." Koniev hung up.

Big Mother 40

Four hours later, Koniev was sitting on the damp ground with the butt of the folding stock of his AK-47 resting between his heels and his back against a large tree. Despite his efforts at improving his fitness, every step of the last four hours had reminded him that he'd spent too much time during the past two years drinking vodka.

The Vietnamese officer had concluded the tour with exercises in which Colonel Thai's soldiers showed how easily they could annihilate the patrolling Spetznaz. They had run two different scenarios. In one the NVA platoon was given a head start and the Spetznaz was supposed to find the NVA and set up an ambush. Each time they approached, the NVA had heard the Spetnaz coming and ambushed them instead. In the second, the Spetznaz were supposed to set up and ambush an advancing NVA platoon. But the NVA identified the ambush site and turned the tables by flanking and attacking the Spetznaz. If any of the battles had been real, the Spetznaz would have been wiped out.

Koniev used the massive tree trunk to help push his weary body upright before addressing the Spetznaz.

"This exercise proves that we are not masters of the jungle. Colonel Thai and I believe that the best way to improve your jungle fighting skills is to assign a four-man team to each of his companies. That way you will learn how to operate in the jungle as well as get to know each sector of this base as well as our comrades do. The Spetznaz officers will join Colonel Thai's regimental command staff to learn more about his jungle warfare tactics, which were just demonstrated, and rotate with the companies in the field at Colonel Thai's discretion.

"Second, there are hand-to-hand combat techniques you can teach our Vietnamese comrades, which will give you the opportunity to share your skills."

Koniev looked at Colonel Thai, who nodded.

"And last, we are going to combine our messes. We—that means all of us—will eat together from now on. It will improve their Russian and our Vietnamese." Koniev waited for a question, and hearing none, spoke. "Dismissed."

THURSDAY, 4 DAYS LATER, APRIL 27, 1972, 2210 LOCAL TIME, USS *FOX* IN THE GULF OF TONKIN

As Josh tightened the grease and sweat-stained lap belts and shoulder harness, he smelled the familiar mix of raw jet fuel, spilled hydraulic fluid and residue from the special molybdenum disulfide grease ingrained in the fabric. "Moly-D" had great lubricating properties but generated hydrochloric acid when mixed with salt air or water and heated by friction. As a result, every ten flight hours, the plane captain was required to pump fresh grease into the fittings to lubricate the helicopter's dynamic components, which slung grease everywhere.

"They don't give you much time to get comfortable out here." Jack bent forward as he wedged his lower back into the seat cushion and pulled the lap belts tight. "This is my first takeoff from the back of a destroyer and it's a night mission. You'd think I'd get to do it during the day first and then a few times for practice before doing it on a live mission."

"Not to worry." Josh held up his hands before stuffing his grease-stained pre-flighting gloves into one of the leg pockets of his olive-drab flight suit. They were replaced by a clean pair of tight-fitting Nomex and leather gloves he pulled on and then held up. "You're in good hands."

"You've banged into my head and everyone else's at the RAG that night take-offs in a loaded helicopter from small ships like destroyers in the Gulf are really hairy ... as in dangerous ... as in crashing ... as in—"

"Everything we do out here is dangerous. Much of it isn't in NATOPS and in many ways it's a crap shoot. And yeah, if you go by the book, we violate NATOPS almost on every mission. NATOPS is a guide, it is not the be all and end all on flying because there is no way you can envision every situation and come up with a set of procedures. We're over gross weight, wind isn't always perfect, and we fly aircraft that have been battle damaged without sending them back to maintenance depots. When we get back, you can pull all the gear out of the back and decide what you want to leave behind to bring our weight down. You won't be the first 2P to do it..." Josh paused for a few seconds. "I did it when I first got here..."

"I may just take you up on that."

"Please do. If nothing else, it'll be a good check to see if we have stuff that we don't need. Just keep in mind, the HH-3A wasn't designed for the missions we're flying. We just have to adapt, know what the helo can do and pay attention to detail." Josh flexed his fingers in the tight-fitting gloves. "Consider yourself lucky that they didn't bundle you off to two weeks of fun in the jungle before sending you out on a det."

"I was scheduled to go this Monday, but you drafted me as a replacement pilot, remember? After this line period, I get to go to jungle survival school and spend another few days in a simulated POW camp getting the shit beat out of me. Again! SERE school in the states was bad enough. Now I have to go to JEST." Annoyed at the thought of going to the Jungle Escape and Survival Training school in the Philippines, Jack tugged on the shoulder belts and then tested them against the shoulder harness lock. "I am not looking forward to it. Basic survival school was enough for me."

"Look at it this way: people spend millions to get to spend two weeks camping in a jungle paradise; we get to do it on the taxpayer's nickel. Where else can you spend a few days being chased through the jungle by Negrito tribesmen and then finish the experience with seven days in a simulated POW camp where the guards look, sound, and treat you just like the NVA would?"

"Can't wait." Jack flipped through the two-inch thick book of plastic sleeves that contained checklists, performance charts, and emergency procedures from the pocket NATOPS guide, and slid it into the plastic holder to protect them from greasy fingers. "Ready with the pre-start checklist."

The call and response of going through the pre-start, start, and engagement checklists took the two of them less than five minutes to get both engines started and the rotors engaged. In an emergency, one pilot could get it done in less than a minute, but Josh wanted to take their time to make sure that everything was checked and Jack was comfortable.

He had to take advantage of translational lift, which increased the available lift generated by the rotor by about twenty-five percent in the overloaded helicopter. It began at about ten knots ground speed and peaked at about forty knots. An aircraft carrier plowing through the water at fifteen knots gave the crew the speed of the ship plus any available wind, so once the rotors were engaged, the helicopter on the large carrier deck was already in translational lift.

But from the small deck of a large destroyer like the *Fox*, Josh had neither the room for a rolling takeoff nor lots of wind over the deck. The helicopter's nose was positioned thirty degrees to the port side, which diminished the headwind component made by the ambient wind and the ship's speed by about half, so he had to get the overloaded HH-3A into translational lift as soon as possible or they would wind up in the snake- and shark-infested Gulf of Tonkin. The Gulf's thin, hot humid air reduced the available engine power, which made take-offs from the confined helo pads on the back of destroyers even riskier.

Before manning the helicopter, Josh had brought Jack over to the side of the flight deck and pointed to the wake. "Looks like the *Fox* is making about twenty knots, so we should have about ten knots of headwind."

All Jack had seen was white foaming water disappearing into inky blackness. Gauging the speed of a boat by its water trail must be one of those things you learned, he decided. He wondered if it were an essential skill for a pilot or optional.

At takeoff, the HH-3A, with all her equipment, ammunition, forty-five hundred pounds—about seven hundred and fifty gallons—of jet fuel and crew of five, was about two thousand pounds over its designed maximum takeoff weight. To get it off the deck, they'd spool up the engines so the rotor RPM was at the maximum safe speed of one hundred four percent. Then Josh would pull up on the collective, dropping the rotor rpm down to between ninety-four to ninety-five percent as he traded rotor speed for lift to get the helo off the deck. Josh had to be careful because generators would start going off-line below ninety-two percent and the hydraulic pumps stopped working below eighty-eight percent. If that happened, he would lose control of the helicopter and they would die.

"Take-off check list complete," Jack announced and saw a visible nod from Josh before he keyed the mike. "Big Mother 40 is ready for take-off."

"Cleared for take off. Wind thirty degrees port at fifteen." The radio call came from a radar operator in the ship's combat information center. At the same time, the small light forward of the missile launcher changed from red to green.

Jack answered with two clicks of the radio mike and worried if he'd be able to remember details of Josh's thorough briefing before they walked out on deck. If not done perfectly, the take-off would result in a semi-controlled water landing that could capsize the helicopter, trapping all on board on its trip to the bottom.

They heard Aviation Machinist Mate Second Class Derek Van der Jagt's familiar voice over the intercom. "Ready in the back."

"Signal them to remove the chocks and chains." Josh flexed the fingers of both hands as he held the cyclic in his right and the collective in his left.

"Roger." Jack held his fists out in front of him and then separated them, motioning outward with his thumbs pointing to the sides of the aircraft. "Four chains. Two chocks." Jack confirmed what both saw as the flight deck crewmen held them up so they were visible in the dull red light of the flight deck. He hoped no one heard the fear in his voice and the anxiety churning his stomach on this first night mission.

"Clear aft." Van der Jagt's report told both pilots he had stuck his head far enough out of the cargo door to make sure the tail wheel and rotor were clear.

Josh didn't want to drift back because the top of the aft five-inch gun mount was five feet higher than the helo deck on the first level. Take-offs from the first level on the missile destroyer gave Josh about ten feet more altitude than they would have if the landing pad were on the main deck.

Big Mother 40

The enlisted man designated as the Landing Signal Enlisted twirled his flashlight over his head and then ran for cover. Jack noted that the reflective striping on the bright yellow grease-stained floatation vest flickered in the red light.

"Back me up on the throttles. Here we go." It was Josh's way of reminding Jack that he had forgotten to put his hand on the throttles that hung just forward of the circuit breaker panel mounted in the cockpit's ceiling. If something went wrong, he could quickly shove them all the way forward and then use the emergency throttles mounted on the window frame to maximize the power generated from the two 1,450-horsepower turbo-shaft engines.

Big Mother groaned noticeably as the blades coned and bit into the moist air as Josh pulled the collective almost all the way up.

"Ninety-eight percent ... Ninety-six percent ..." Jack focused on the engine instruments as well as the triple tachometer which showed power turbine speed for each engine as well as rotor RPM.

"Wheels off the deck." Van der Jagt had his head out the cargo door.

By the time the words were out of his mouth, Josh was sliding the heavy helicopter over the edge and diving toward the water. Nose down, he lowered the collective ever so slightly.

"Ninety-four percent. Thirty feet, twenty-five knots. Radar altimeter is working."

Jack barely remembered making the call as they plunged from the dull red light into what looked like a black hole. But he did remember Josh's caution about how calm seas didn't usually provide a good signal return for the radar altimeter. If it flickered a lot, he needed to let the pilot know because then they had to judge their height above the water without any help from their instruments. The barometric altimeter could be off by as much as twenty feet, which at night, coupled the lack of depth perception, meant a mistake in gauging their height above the sea would at best get them all wet, at worst, kill them.

Jack remembered Josh telling him in the RAG that the best way to simulate a moonless night at sea was to walk into a closet, turn out the light, close the door behind you and wrap a towel around your head and eyes. He had doubted it because their night hops then were off San Diego, and there was always the ambient light from the coast that was still visible twenty to thirty miles at sea. Here in the Gulf of Tonkin, the description was an understatement.

"Twenty feet, thirty knots. Ninety-four percent."

He could feel Josh begin to raise the nose and increase the collective a little bit to get the last amount of power from the engines. The texture from the small ripples in the Gulf was barely visible, but it was enough to allow the radar altimeter to work. The airspeed indicator crept up and the needle on the radar altimeter holding steady at twenty feet told Jack that Josh's smooth touch won the bet of getting into translational lift.

"Ninety-seven percent, forty knots, and twenty feet," Jack announced and realized that he had been holding his breath.

"I'm going to droop down another two percent to see if we can get some more altitude." Josh eased up on the collective and the rotor RPM dropped, but the helicopter climbed to thirty feet where he relaxed by flexing his fingers so that he didn't squeeze the controls with a death grip and lose his feel for the helicopter.

After a few minutes, Josh repeated the process of milking the collective by dropping the rotor rpm, letting the helicopter accelerate and gain both altitude and rotor speed. When he got it up to a hundred feet above the glassy Gulf and seventy knots, the TACAN said they were five miles from the *Fox*.

"Here, you fly and see if you can get us up to five hundred feet without putting us in the water." Josh held up both his hands and pulled his feet off the rudder pedals as Jack took over.

Jack was too focused on flying the climbing helicopter to see the deep breaths Josh was taking to relieve his tension.

"Let's fly three-three-five at ninety knots for about forty-five minutes." Josh put the chart down he'd been studying. "That should take us close to our orbit for tonight. Van der Jagt, go ahead and do your security check."

Jack waited until he had steadied up on the heading and was level at five hundred feet on both altimeters and doing ninety knots before keying the mike. "I heard from a very reliable source that you told some commander from CTF 77 on your last tour to take his mission plan and stuff it. What was that all about?"

"I can guess who your source is and I will have a large piece of his ass when we get back to the *Fox*." Josh could hear the laughter over the noise in the cabin. "What I am about to tell you is ground truth, so in the future you can tell fact from fiction. We were on temp duty to help the SEALS out and this commander from the CTF 77 staff comes and says: 'Here's where I want to put the SEALS, and here's the route I want you to fly on the way in and out.' I looked at it and it took us over a bunch of known flak traps and didn't allow us to take advantage of terrain to mask the noise and make it harder for the bad guys to spot us. So I said, in my most humble gentle junior officer voice, I said, 'Commander, I will be happy to fly the mission, get the SEALS where they need to be on time, and when required go back and pick them up, but I want to plan the ingress and egress routes as well as the launch and pick-up times.'"

Josh paused for a second to look up and enter frequency and held up his hand. "Red Crown, Big Mother 40 will be on station in approximately ten minutes." After he spoke, he pushed the Ident button on the transponder and watched it glow yellow for a few seconds.

"So then what happened?"

"The commander who was the air operations officer and whose name is Sturm, said, 'Lieutenant, you will fly this route because that is what you are being ordered to do. Based on our intelligence and my analysis of the threats, you shouldn't have any problems.' To which I replied, 'Commander, with all due respect, I know from experience where all the flak traps are located and this route takes us through most of them, any one of which will blow us out of the sky.' I pointed them all out, one at a time. He asked if I was refusing to fly the mission and I said, No, I'd be happy to fly it, but I want to take a different route in and out."

"What pissed him off?"

"I think two things. First, I wasn't interested in getting shot down and getting all of us killed, and second that I wasn't going to fly it unless I planned it. At which time, he told me I was relieved and confined to my quarters until charges could be brought against me."

"Then what?"

"He went to another crew, which agreed to fly the route ... and they were never heard from again. The HAC was a ring-knocker and it wasn't in his genes to question the knowledge or expertise of a superior officer, even if that superior officer was a jet driver who had never flown this type of mission before."

They both paused to listen to the strike frequency for a few seconds.

"I want to make one thing clear. I never refused to fly the mission. All I wanted to do was change the routes, and that's where Sturm and I got into it. I found out later this was his pet project and he'd spent a week or more planning it. Based on the route and timing, I am pretty sure where they got bagged. We lost six SEALS and a crew of five. The senior SEAL raised such a shit storm that Sturm was relieved and told to return to the States by someone with more stars than his boss, and I got out of hack."

"That's it?

"More or less. Commac-V still wanted to put a recon team in that area, so I mapped a way in and a different one out. The SEALS were on the ground for about five days, didn't find what they were looking for, and we never saw a round either on the way in or the way out."

"That's not quite the story I heard."

"Really. What did you hear?"

"That there were some very ugly words exchanged between you and Sturm after the crew was reported missing."

"I did share some thoughts about his ancestry, number of legal parents, and IQ rather bluntly. Just so you know, I went through the training command and the RAG with both the pilots who went down and flew a couple missions out here with them. One of the few good things our boss Nagano did was insist that we fly as crews. That's why we pair folks up at Cubi and unless something ugly happens or they rotate out, the crew stays together."

"That's how I wound up with this motley crew?"

"Yup." Josh turned to his co-pilot and smiled. "You were handpicked and are now stuck with us."

"Go on with the story."

"As I was saying, I knew everyone on board, and it was a waste of good men. I told Sturm that their ghosts would haunt him to his dying day because their lives were wasted. That's one of the things that sent him off the deep end. When this war is over, if I can, I am going to find where they went down and send their dog tags or something from the helo to Sturm."

SUNDAY, 10 DAYS LATER, MAY 7, 1972, 1725 LOCAL TIME, COMMANDER'S OFFICE, 355TH TACTICAL FIGHTER WING, TAHKLIT AIR FORCE BASE, THAILAND

Gus Thomes was still sweating as he shifted in his swivel chair. The 45 year-old colonel worked out daily to keep his stocky frame from getting pudgy and postpone the day Father Time told him he could no longer fly fighters. On his arrival in the unit, he had told his squadron commanders that when the wing flew, he would fly. His assistant made sure he rotated among the 355th's three squadrons and attended strike planning briefings just like any of the other hundred and twenty odd pilots in the wing.

The cause of the Command Pilot's unease was that he'd rather fly a combat mission into the heart of Hanoi than talk to a general, even one he knew. Thomes stared at the red phone, dreading the moment when the light would start blinking, signaling an incoming call.

This was his third war, and he accepted as fate that in each he would fly Republic Aviation-built airplanes. The Long Island-based company started supplying fighters to the U.S. Army Air Corps in 1939 with the

Big Mother 40

Alexander Seversky designed P-43 Lancer, then the P-47 Thunderbolt, then the F-84 Thunderjet series, and now the F-105 Thunderchief.

When he arrived in Northern France in December, 1944 as a replacement pilot, he was disappointed that his P-47 squadron was ground attack specialists and for months he rarely saw, much less dueled with Focke-Wulfs and Messerschmitts.

In a duel with a flak battery while flying his seventeenth mission late in the Battle of the Bulge, he got pissed off when a 20mm round exploded in the cockpit, peppering him with shrapnel from the shell as well as fragments of glass and instruments. Rather than taking his damaged Thunderbolt home, he spent the next ten minutes in a blood-spattered cockpit putting all four mounts in the battery of quad 20mm guns out of action, which won him a Distinguished Service Cross as well as a Purple Heart.

Missions in the F-84 Thunderjet in Korea were replays of those over France, except he was in a rugged jet airplane that didn't have a chance against the faster MiG-15s flown by the Chinese. Although he never saw a MiG on a mission, he knew in the underpowered Thunderjet, if he were attacked, he would be defensive in a dogfight. To give himself the best chance to survive a battle with a MiG, he would have to get down near the ground and force a slow-turning fight, but that made him an easier target for enemy gunners.

Thomes, now divorced and just another lieutenant colonel instructor in the Republic F-105 Thunderchief, had been contemplating retirement when he got a call to see if he was interested in taking over the 355th. The friend on the phone asked him if he wanted the job, not *telling* him, and if he accepted, by the time he arrived in Thailand, he would be a bird colonel. Now, three months later, he was waiting for a call from that man who was his squadron commander in Korea.

He took a long sip from the glass of ice water that was on a coaster with the wing's crest and was about to review his notes on the yellow pad in the center of his cluttered desk when the red phone began making its annoying noise.

"Thomes."

"Good evening, Gus. What's on your mind?"

"General, we've got a problem that I need your permission to solve."

"Just so I understand, Gus, you're asking for permission rather than begging for forgiveness. That's a switch. What's going on? I've noticed the wing has had more losses than usual, but that can happen. No need to apologize; we all go through bad streaks."

Thomes ignored the friendly facetious attempt at humor. "Boss, it's not the losses, it's how we're losing the planes and the pilots."

"You know as well as I do, if you go down in North Vietnam, the chances of getting picked up are above sixty percent. That's not bad, considering what we're up against."

"Sir, I know and accept that, and so do my pilots. Again, it's not the losses, it's how and why."

The General knew Thomes well enough that when he pushed back, there was more to the story and he should listen. Whether he could help or not was another discussion. The losses were probably eating Thomes up because he'd probably trained many of the pilots in his wing and felt responsible, maybe even guilty. "Okay, what's going on?"

"Boss, in the past week, we've lost one near Hanoi to SAMs and another eight on the way out. Here's the interesting part, of the eight that were shot down on the way home, all were in northwestern North Vietnam. We're a hundred percent sure that all were shot down by SAMs and the six guys who got out were captured immediately. And, here's the most interesting part, we didn't know we were being targeted until the missiles were right on top of the formation, which is when our radar warning systems went off. By then, it was too late to do anything except wait for the explosion and hope you weren't the one targeted."

Thomes leaned forward as he looked at the ringed map that represented a thirty-mile radius centered on twelve Xs. "I flew over to Korat and talked to Walt and his guys in the 388th who lost four the same way in the same area. We know about where the twelve went down and if you plotted the range rings from each shoot down, you'd come to two conclusions: One is that the gooks have some sort of missile base in the area and two, they are using a new version of the missile that doesn't set off our radar warning gear until it's way too late."

"Are you sure of this?"

"Yes, sir. I'm positive because I saw it myself on the last mission."

"What do you want to do?"

"Go hunting with some Wild Weasels to find this site, and when we find the bastards, blow them to shit."

"Neither Thirteenth or Seventh Air Force will ever let you go freelancing over North Vietnam."

"The Navy does it all the time. They call it armed reconnaissance."

"We don't do things that way, you know that. It has to be a mission tasked by Seventh Air Force or Thirteenth Air Force. Then, depending on the mission and the sequence they decide they need, the mission planners assign squadrons to provide planes and crews. Those assignments are in the air tasking order. You don't get to make the assignments. You just make sure you have the planes and pilots ready to fly whatever missions they are assigned."

"Sir, that's the problem. We follow the same route at the same time because it is more convenient to do it the same way each day. As a result, we're taking losses that are, to be frank, unacceptable. We didn't lose guys this fast in World War II or Korea. If we did, we'd figure out what was wrong, change tactics, and hammer the bad guys. Back in the good old days, faced with this sort of a problem, the wing commander would be asked what's the plan to put the bad guys out of action." Thomes bit his lip.

"Colonel, you're out of line."

"With all due respect, General, sir, this is bullshit and you know it. It is one thing to ask my pilots to risk their asses over North Vietnam, but it is another to know about a new threat and not do anything about it. If we keep taking losses like this and no one addresses this missile base, some pilots may start tossing their wings on the table."

"Are you telling me that some of your pilots may refuse to fly?"

"Yes, General, I am." Thomes harsh tone matched that of the caller.

"That's mutiny and will get all of you a life sentence in Leavenworth."

"No, General, it won't. Two reasons. One, we're all volunteers and if a man who's been flying his share of missions drops his wings on the table and said he has had enough, there isn't a goddamn thing the Air Force or you can do about it except send him home. The only decision is whether or not he finishes his commitment flying a desk or gets an immediate honorable discharge. Second, if you tried to court-martial them, the facts would come out and everyone in the chain of command will look stupid and may get charged with dereliction of duty. And in fact, if you pull that kind of move, I'll personally request a general courts martial which will get public and ugly."

"Are you threatening me?"

"No, General, I am not. I'm just laying out the facts as they are. How you deal with them is up to you."

MONDAY, NEXT DAY, MAY 8, 1972,
1113 LOCAL TIME, WEST OF HANOI

"Rocket Three Three, Rocket Three One. Take the lead."

"Rocket Three One. Roger, Three has the lead."

With that acknowledgement, Gus Thomes pulled the throttle back in his F-105 and looked to the left to make sure his wingman, who was also the wing administrative officer, was also slowing as they began the dance to move back out of the four-plane formation. Since they were in a modified combat spread in which the four airplanes were flying with about a thousand feet of lateral and five hundred of vertical separation, it was easier than if they were flying with the usual twenty-foot vertical and twenty-foot lateral distance.

Thomes was flying with eleven other F-105Ds of the 333rd Tactical Fighter Squadron of the wing, and the group was returning through Route Pack Six after bombing a rail yard west of Hanoi. The 334th also attacked the yard while the 335th helped the supporting Wild Weasels by hitting several SAM sites south of Hanoi.

It had almost been a milk run, if there were such a thing on trips to Hanoi: no MiGs, a few SAMs, and a lot of flak. Most important, there were no beepers, which signaled that someone had had to eject, and none of the F-105s were damaged. The 333rd was now about five miles behind of the 334th and 335th. Both were cruising at 20,000 feet toward the tankers waiting for them over Northern Laos when he made the radio call.

To create even more distance between the two airplanes and those in the 333rd, Bill pulled the throttle back about five percent more and looked to his left to make sure his wingman was staying with him as they decelerated below four hundred knots and rolled into a thirty-degree descending right turn. In combat, speed is life, and both pilots were playing with fire even though they had their wing-mounted jamming pods in standby.

Seeing nothing, Bill rolled the airplane to the right, hoping that their wounded duck act would trigger a reaction from the North Vietnamese. A tone from the RAW's gear exploded in his ears, telling him that a missile was tracking his aircraft. He tightened the turn to sixty degrees of bank and shoved the throttle up to the detent to get maximum power without the afterburner.

"SAM! SAM! Two at three o'clock low." His wingman had an eyeball on the missiles and both knew what to do. Fighting the increasing g's that were now about five plus, Bill flipped on his jammer and shoved the nose down toward the rapidly climbing missiles. In the seconds he had before he had to make a hairy, but usually successful maneuver, Bill looked around for the tell-tale dust plumes made by the SAM leaving the launcher. All he could see were two small puffs of smoke in a jungle valley below.

Big Mother 40

By now the missiles were almost inside of a mile of the two diving F-105s and the closing speed was above Mach 4 when the RAW's gear shifted tone from the deeper "You're locked up by a fire control radar" to the higher-pitched warbling that told the pilot that the missile's terminal seeker was on. When he was about a quarter mile from the missile, he pushed the rudder pedal and the stick hard to the left and rolled the Thud around an imaginary barrel about five hundred yards in diameter.

The missile wobbled as the seeker tried to guide the missile to the target, but its small fins and high speed made it impossible for it to change its heading fast enough to get within range of its proximity fuse. They flew past the F-105s before someone on the ground detonated both SAMs. Bill grunted and contracted his belly as he strained against the seven g's he was generating as the F-105, now well past Mach 1, pulled out of its dive.

The radio came alive. "Three Two is with you at your four. That was exciting. Let's compare notes when we get back."

Chapter 7

IN HACK

The air flowing through the open doors and windows of Big Mother 40 made the oppressive hundred-degree heat and eighty percent humidity just bearable. Two hours into the mission, a bored Jack D'Onofrio was flying the helicopter at two hundred feet in a lazy, random race track pattern above the glassy brownish-green water three to four miles off the coast. Nonetheless, a daylight mission was a pleasant change of pace from the usual middle-of-night sorties.

Josh Haman cursed the designer of the seat as he squirmed to find a comfortable position. His movement sprung the acrid, recognizable smell of his sweaty body odor from his armpits. Before his first tour in Vietnam, he thought the smell was manly. Now, it was just another smell that was processed and in this case, pungent as it was, ignored. He was bored but alert, scanning and studying the greenish-brown shore line that sent up a mixed smell of dung-filled rice paddies and spicy food being cooked.

The screeching of the beeper jolted everyone in the matte black helicopter from a relaxed state of alertness to one of tension and heightened awareness. A second, similar high-pitched warbling tone began to compete with the first, which added another layer of sweat from fear to the one from the heat.

"Big Mother 40, Eagle Eye Seven Zero Two. Steel Tiger Five Oh Five is down. Copy?"

Steel Tiger Five Oh Five was an A-6E Intruder that was the source of the two beepers. Eagle Eye was the all-weather attack aircraft Hawkeye with the side number 702 from Airborne Early Warning Squadron 116, based on the USS *Ranger*, and orbiting at 25,000 feet and seventy-five miles to the southeast of the helicopter. In its darkened, red-lit cabin, four Naval flight officers and one enlisted operations specialist were maintaining a radar picture of the Hanoi/Haiphong area, ready to change missions and vector fighters to incept MiGs that might venture near either rescue or other aircraft on the strike.

Josh, who, for the moment was the non-flying pilot, and whose primary duties were navigation and communication, keyed the microphone using the switch by his left foot. "Big Mother 40 copies."

"Big Mother 40, Eagle Eye Seven Zero Two. Meet me on new CSAR frequency of two nine five point two."

Josh pointed to his chest and Jack held up his hands to show he'd given up control of the helicopter before he spun the wheels on the UHF radio on the center console and keyed the mike. "Big Mother's up." He tried to keep his voice under control; this was his second combat rescue.

The first for the twenty-four-year old University of Pennsylvania graduate had been a routine pick up three days ago of a pilot who had landed a little over a half mile from the coast just north of Vinh. Jack noted in his personal log book that the first green ink entry was less than thirty days after arriving in the Philippines and less than five months from getting his wings in Pensacola.

They didn't draw fire off Vinh until Big Mother had slowed to a hover. The different sizes of the green 'golf balls' passing over them were clearly discernible as the North Vietnamese gunners adjusted their aim on their medium-bore anti-aircraft 23mm and 37mm guns. At first Jack thought it looked just like the movies, and then as the splashes and tracers got closer, his gut clenched and he tried not to puke.

Jack squirmed in his seat as he pulled his shoulder and lap belt tighter. They emitted the now familiar and distinctive smell ingrained into the cushion's fabric that was a mixture of jet fuel, grease, and body odor. He suspected he was about to learn another lesson in the dangerous business of combat search and rescue.

"Big Mother 40, Eagle Eye Seven Zero Two. Swordsmen Three Zero Seven and Three One One are orbiting the harbor at angels eleven and saw two chutes. They're standing by with twenty mike mike. Have two more A-7 Corsairs with ordnance inbound to support rescue. Call signs are flight leader Blue Diamond Four One Zero, and Four One Two. Say intentions, over?"

"Big Mother 40 is buster en route to the survivors." Jack D'Onofrio pushed the switch on the IFF transponder marked IDENT to flag their position on the radar operator's scope in the E-2 Hawkeye. The movement of flashing blip would catch his attention and he'd snag it so he could track Big Mother 40's altitude, course, and ground speed.

The operator knew from the blip that the helicopter had left its orbit which, at its closest point of approach, kept it over three miles from the southeast tip of Cat Hai Island and just outside the Haiphong Harbor estuary, and could estimate the helicopter's time of arrival at the survivors which, flying as fast as it could—buster—was about a hundred-ten knots/hour at its current weight and age.

"Okay guys, listen up." Josh pulled back on the upper half of the mike switch to use the intercom. "If you haven't heard, we've got a pilot and bombardier-navigator from an Intruder about to land in Haiphong Harbor and we're going to get them. On the way in, we'll keep the freighters about two to three hundred yards to our right and stay at about a hundred feet. Vance, you're only going into the water if one of them is injured and can't get in the horse collar or is tangled in his chute."

"We've rigged the horse collar to the hoist cable for rescue and all stations are manned and ready," Van der Jagt answered, standing behind the mini-gun mount's inch-thick steel armor plate; the electrical power to the gun was turned on so it was ready to fire at 2,000 rounds/minute. He had the option to select a slower rate of fire of 1,200 rounds/minute, or the faster one at 4,000, with the flip of a switch.

Josh heard the loud humming sound that changed pitch which told him that Van der Jagt was checking out all three rates of fire on the mini-gun. He rarely fired at the 4,000 round-per-minute rate because the barrel would heat up fast and need to be replaced. Changing the barrel meant he would not be able to provide suppressive fire during the minute or so that it took to unlock and remove the hot barrel, unlatch and get one of the two spares from the rack in the cabin and put it on the gun. Not having the mini-gun in action could jeopardize a rescue.

John Vance peeled off his flight suit and stuffed it into his helmet bag, then stashed the bag under the canvas troop seat opposite the cargo door. He cinched the small, black, inflatable diver's vest tight over his brown t-shirt and khaki swim trunks and made sure his mask and swim fins were within easy reach just inside the fuselage rib that framed the cargo door. He would keep his helmet on until just before he slid off the cabin floor and dropped into the water.

Nicholas Kostas slid the bolt back to chamber a round in the M-60 mounted on the side of the passenger door just behind the co-pilot. Kostas took control of the six-barreled weapon in a rescue when the mini-gun was needed and Vance was in the water or on the ground.

"All right, we're about to enter the estuary," Josh keyed the intercom. "Remember the ROE. There are lots of ships in the harbor who are supposed to be neutral, so we cannot shoot unless we are fired on."

Josh was hoping that the gun crews manning the huge anti-aircraft guns on the long, thin Cau Rao peninsula on their left would be afraid of hitting the ships filled with munitions from China and the Soviet Union and fuel from Indonesia.

Josh flexed the fingers of both hands to keep his grip loose so he could maintain just enough pressure to move the cyclic but not enough to lose his feel for the helicopter. Normally, he held the cyclic between his thumb and forefinger, which changed the pitch of the main rotor blades depending on where they were as they rotated around the main shaft to bank, climb or descend. Now, his hand was wrapped around the black, multi-button grip. He shivered despite the heat and sweat running down his face and back.

The pungent and distinctive smell of gun oil and solvent reached Josh in time for him to watch Jack break open the breach of the grenade launcher, slip in a M381 high-explosive 40mm grenade and snap it shut. Twenty-three grenades were left in the custom-fitted aluminum box in the console between the pilot and co-pilot seats.

The crew could see hilly Cat Hai Island to the north from a hundred feet above the calm and muddy waters. To the west, the Cau Rao peninsula, which was only a few feet above sea level, was a thin brown line on the horizon.

D'Onofrio reached into the nav bag hanging on his seat frame and pulled out an 8"x10" black-and-white photo taken the day before, which showed ships anchored in two groups; the bigger in the shallow water on the east side had twelve ships. The one on the west had only six.

"All these are freighters."

He pointed to a group of shapes near what looked like an island. "There's a group of four tankers all by themselves out in the middle of the estuary. There's another six freighters out in deeper water to the west off Cat Hai." D'Onofrio held the photo where Josh could see it.

"Got it. Get pictures of them as we go by."

Jack held up the Navy-issued Beseler Topcon camera as an acknowledgement. Before he could answer, a voice in his headset stopped him from talking.

"Big Mother 40, Eagle Eye Seven Zero Two. Swordsman Three Oh Seven reports both survivors are in the water about two miles southwest of Dinh Vu at the north end of the bay and about same west of that little island. They are about a half a mile apart. Swordsman Three Oh Seven is the SARCAP commander."

D'Onofrio pulled back the bottom of the two position mike rocker switches on the cyclic, careful not to apply any pressure that would counteract Josh's subtle movements. Rock the switch to the top and you talked on the intercom. Pull back on the bottom and you transmitted on whatever radio was selected. "Big Mother 40 copies." He took a black grease pencil out of his sleeve pocket and put a small "X" on the photo to mark the survivors' reported location and then drew a small arrow on the bottom to show Josh the direction from which they were approaching the bay. He estimated they were about ten minutes away and assumed that the radar operator on the Hawkeye had already figured that out or would have asked for an ETA.

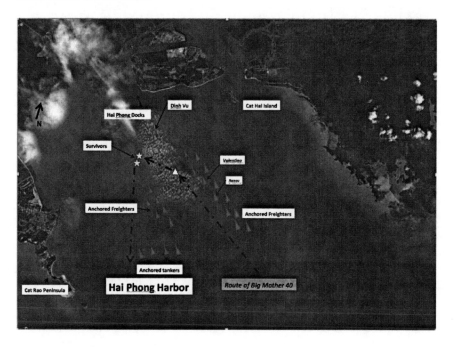

"Three large splashes at two o'clock, two hundred yards." Van der Jagt's announcement meant that the North Vietnamese spotters on the ridges were calling the shots for the 85mm anti-aircraft guns that dotted the island.

Josh started a series of erratic, sharp, forty-five-degree banks to throw off their aim. Each turn would head them toward the last plume of water as he chased the splashes in front of the helicopter. The theory was that the enemy gunners were constantly adjusting their aim and shells were not likely to land in the same place twice. A hit by one of the seventeen and half pound projectiles would send them into the bay in a spinning multi-piece fireball.

Josh pulled back on the cyclic sharply and lowered the collective in a coordinated, smooth maneuver that slowed the shuddering helicopter from about one hundred ten knots to less than seventy. "Time two minutes."

D'Onofrio pushed the button that started the stopwatch on the instrument panel as Josh kept the helicopter steady at a hundred feet above the water, muddy brown with patches of blue green, and rolled the slowing helicopter to a new heading thirty degrees from the old one. The distinctive smell from the estuary's blend of mud, swamp, sewage, and seawater flooded the helicopter.

"Thirty seconds." D'Onofrio watched the second hand notch its way around the dial. "Two minutes, go, go, GO!"

Josh pulled up on the collective pitch lever to increase power and pushed the nose over with the cyclic to gain speed. Less than thirty seconds later, the nineteen thousand pound helicopter was back at one hundred ten knots.

"Timing three minutes," D'Onofrio called out the next interval.

Josh was hoping they were creating tracking problems for the North Vietnamese radar operators directing the guns, because the computers in the Russian radar dumped tracks of targets flying below eighty knots. But they couldn't stay below eighty knots—they had to get two the survivors as fast as possible.

Intelligence reports stated that it took about two minutes for the revolving antenna to get enough hits on the aircraft to create a firing solution. By changing heading each time the helicopter slowed, they were hoping to create a series of tracks on the operator's scope that looked like chicken scratches which would disguise their true position. Josh, as well as everyone on board, assumed the NVA gunners and radar operators knew about where Big Mother was going, but the more difficult they made it, the greater their chances for survival. The erratic stop-start maneuvering made their progress toward the two survivors slower than they wanted, but it was a necessary compromise.

"Okay, on the next sprint we're going to head over to that line of ships and stay about three hundred yards to the starboard, and when we get close to the end of the line, we'll go like hell for the guys in the water."

"Yes, sir. We're locked and loaded," Van der Jagt replied.

Crew members on the closest freighter, which was flying the blue-and-red squares and stars of the Panamanian flag, waved as the matte black helicopter passed, happy they had ringside seats to watch a small battle without the risk of actual participation.

Josh rolled the helicopter onto a track almost parallel to the ragged line of freighters anchored a couple hundred yards apart along the edge of the shipping channel. When they were about two miles from the western shore of Cat Hai Island, Jack held up the photo again. "We'll need to head west toward the guys in the water when we pass the fifth freighter."

Josh clicked the mike twice and nodded.

"Next freighter is flying the Liberian flag and the third freighter is Russian. Name on the stern is *Razov*." D'Onofrio put his binoculars down on the window frame by his knee. The red band on the funnel with the gold hammer and sickle was clearly visible and the last splash from the 85mm shells was now a half mile behind them. "Looks like they have given up trying to drop an 85mm round on top of us for fear of hitting one of these ships, particularly the Russian ones, which are probably filled with things that go bang."

"What the fuck?" Jack's words were punctuated by the distinctive pinging sound of bullets going through the skin of the helicopter. Josh looked to the right and saw the remains of a series of vertical splashes coming toward the helicopter and yanked the collective up and yawed the helicopter with the rudder pedals.

"I'm on it." The distinctive humming sound from short mini-gun bursts that was a cross between a loud sewing machine and ripping paper told everyone that Van der Jagt was in action.

D'Onofrio keyed the intercom. "Take out the big-assed machine gun in a sandbagged position on the *Razov*'s superstructure." He watched two sets of tracers going in opposite directions. One was reaching out to the gyrating helicopter and the other was ripping sand bags apart, and he could see tracers ricocheting off the steel structure of the ship. He hated the sound, which was a lower pitch version of someone tapping a fork on a high quality crystal glass in rapid succession. He waited a few seconds before keying the mike again. "Anyone hurt?"

Vance stuck his head between the two pilot seats as he grabbed four 40mm grenades and the loaded M-79. "No sir. No leaks, either. But the big raft took at least one hit and is torn up pretty bad. The forward ammo tray for the mini-gun took at least two. Don't know what the damage is, but I'll inspect the belts as Van der Jagt shoots."

Josh pulled up on the collective a bit more, but the increased shuddering and vibrations told him that the helicopter was approaching blade stall, and at one hundred twelve knots Big Mother 40 was going as fast as it could. His brain processed the bongs made by the M-79 but he was too intent on jinking the big helicopter to keep it or its crew from being hit.

"Not bad. Looks like the first grenade went through one of the windows on the bridge and the second one hit the superstructure just to the right of the gun position." D'Onofrio split his time between scanning the gauges and taking pictures. "Good shooting, guys."

"Shit, more trouble." As splashes from another DshK went past the nose, Josh jinked the helicopter hard right and then toward the left. Van der Jagt fired a long burst that sprayed bullets all over the stern of the next ship in line, which was named the *Valentinov*. It had a Russian merchant marine flag on the stern but no markings on the funnel.

Josh could see the splashes walking toward the helicopter out of the corner of his eye; he heard three more pings before he could move. Shoving the rudder left for a few seconds and then back to the right as he rolled the helicopter back and forth added more variables to the Russian gunner's tracking solution. Josh was trying to find a balance of keeping the turn rate and angle of bank at a point where Van der Jagt could accurately return fire and still make it difficult for the enemy gunner.

"Got the bastards," Vance blurted out. "Don't think they are going to shoot at us for a while."

"I got a picture of the explosion. Vance got a direct hit on the ship's structure with one of the grenades. I think we got most of the gunners."

"Any major damage?"

"No, sir." Van der Jagt spoke up. "Just did a security check. We took ten hits that I can see. One about two feet aft of me and it just missed the control cables, two went into the raft, two into the ammo hopper and the other five are in the tail cone. You can see light on both sides where the bullets went right through."

Josh thought he'd only heard three or four hits. What else had he missed? He was flying mechanically and rolled the HH-3A to a heading of three four zero without realizing what he was doing.

"That looks good." Jack put his finger on the map and then eyeballed the distance. "I'm estimating it's less than five miles from where the A-7s think the survivors are."

"Big Mother 40, this is Swordsman Three Zero Seven. I've got radio contact with both Steel Tigers. We made one low pass and Steel Tiger Five Oh Five Bravo is having trouble getting out of his chute. He said both legs are numb and only one arm is working. Copy?"

"Swordsman Three Zero Seven, do you have a visual on Big Mother 40?" Josh had to know if the victims could see them.

It seemed like minutes, but in reality the radio was silent for about thirty seconds. "Big Mother 40, Swordsman Three Zero Seven has a tally. You should run over Steel Tiger Five Oh Five Bravo's dye marker on your current heading. Five Oh Five Alpha is about five hundred yards to the north and closer to shore with no marker. Copy?"

"Roger. Tell Five Oh Five Alpha to make white water after we drop the swimmer to help Five Oh Five Bravo so we can find him fast."

Two clicks told the helicopter crew that Swordsman Three Zero Seven would do as asked.

"Listen up everyone. We're going to drop Vance to help the bombardier/navigator who's having trouble getting out of his chute and then go pick up the pilot. Van der Jagt, hopefully Five Oh Five Alpha can get into the horse collar by himself. If not, we'll drop Kostas into the water, fly around until he gets the pilot ready and then hoist them up when they're ready. Vance, as soon as you have Five Oh Five Bravo clear of his chute and ready to get him into the horse collar, make enough white water with splashes so we see it a few hundred yards away. Thumbs down means we've got to lower the Stokes litter. For the record, I am going to remind everyone that the longer we sit in a hover, the greater the chance we collect a large caliber bullet which will ruin our day." Josh turned around to look into the cabin and saw the three smiling crew members giving him thumbs up.

Vance was a stocky, strong, and about five foot five on a good day. He had a large K-Bar style knife strapped to his left leg. He pulled on his black fins before sliding into position just inside the aft cargo door. When Josh flared the helicopter to get it below ten feet off the water, he'd move into the open door.

Vance had never spent much time swimming, growing up on a wheat farm in northern Minnesota. He fished and hunted around the tree-lined lakes, but rarely went into the cold water. While many of his classmates struggled with the survival phase of training, Vance was comfortable in the woods; the same tactics he used to stalk game helped him avoid pursuers in the evasion portion of survival school, and then again when he went through the Jungle Escape and Survival Training course in the Philippines. Then to the surprise of his instructors, he also proved to be a natural swimmer. In the warm water of the pool and then in the Gulf of Mexico, Vance was relaxed and swam with smooth, powerful strokes that let him glide through the water with minimal effort, whether he was swimming alone or towing another student in a drill.

Both Van der Jagt and Kostas were wearing oxygen masks stripped of all equipment except the microphone that eliminated wind noise when they stuck their heads out the HH-3A's doors but also muffled their voices. They searched the 180 degree arcs on the left and right sides while Jack had the front and monitored the instruments. At this point, there was no need to navigate, just find the survivors and get them aboard as fast as they could.

"Survivor ten o'clock at about five hundred yards," Kostas called out. The sodden nylon parachute would eventually drag the man down, even with his survival vest inflated. "Turn left about ten degrees."

"Got him." Josh keyed the mike as soon as he saw the glint from the reflective tape on the bombardier/navigator's helmet, then began to slow the helicopter and descend to forty feet.

Big Mother shuddered as the nose pitched up and the twenty-five-foot-long blades flexed and twisted. At forty knots, Josh eased the nose forward and lowered the collective.

"Thirty feet, twenty knots." Jack based his calls on what he saw outside as well as on the radar altimeter and airspeed indicator. "Ten knots, twenty feet." Seconds later: "Ten feet, less than ten knots. Jump, jump, JUMP."

On the third "jump," Josh didn't wait for the "Swimmer away" call because he assumed Vance was out of the helicopter, and pulled the collective up and shoved the nose down with the cyclic to get the big helicopter to accelerate.

"Thumbs up from Vance approaching Five Oh Five Bravo," Van der Jagt called out from his station in the cargo door of the helicopter where the mini-gun and the one inch thick steel gun shield was pulled back into the cabin. In response to the call, Josh rolled the helicopter to the right and accelerated in the general direction of where Steel Tiger Five Oh Five Alpha was supposed to be.

"Five Oh Five Alpha is about three hundred yards just off the nose at one o'clock." Van der Jagt's voice was slightly distorted by the mask and the wind.

"Put me on top of him." Josh had lost sight of the survivor and wanted Van der Jagt to direct him.

"Yes sir. Come right ten degrees. Survivor two hundred and fifty yards."

A second later, Josh keyed the mike. "I've got him in sight."

"Steady, two hundred yards."

Josh came to a hover a few yards from the survivor. Spray whipped up in front of the windshield, causing him to momentarily lose sight of the man in the water.

Van der Jagt had his head out the cabin door so he could give precise directions to Josh to get the hoist right above the survivor. "Horse collar is in the water. Slow forward. Ten yards."

Josh nudged the cyclic forward and felt the helicopter settle slightly, so he compensated by raising the cyclic a fraction of an inch. For a few seconds he admired the small rainbow that appeared in the billowing spray in front of the hovering HH-3A.

"Easy forward. Five yards. Easy … Stop! Steady hover. Steady …" Van der Jagt's commanded. "Survivor is getting into the collar…. Survivor is in the collar…. Survivor is clear of the water."

Hearing the last bit of information, Josh pulled up on the collective and nosed down to gain speed and altitude. The helicopter was passing seventy knots when four plumes of water erupted within a hundred feet of where the A-6 Intruder pilot had been floating.

"Eagle Eye, this is Big Mother 40, we have Steel Tiger Five Oh Five Alpha on board."

"Big Mother 40, Swordsman Three Zero Seven. We've got trouble. There are four fast-moving boats and a junk heading out to you. The boats are coming out of Dinh Vu and the junk is in the middle of the channel. We've got enough twenty mike mike for one, maybe two passes."

"Swordsman Three Zero Seven. How far away are they?" D'Onofrio tried unsuccessfully to keep the pitch in his voice from rising and the bile in his stomach from entering his throat.

"Two of the fast movers are about a mile away from you. The other two are maybe a mile and a half. The junk is about two miles, but it looks like it has some kind of small cannon on the bow that the crew is getting ready to fire. Copy?"

"Boss, Vance has his arms crossed above his head. Don't think he's ready for us."

Josh pointed at his face to indicate he'd talk. Before keying the mike, he reminded himself that this was not a secure circuit and didn't want to tell the bad guys any more than he had to. "Eagle Eye Seven Zero Two and Swordsman Three Zero Seven, I need the A-7s to take out the fast movers and the junk as well as figure out where the 85mm shells are coming from. They had us pretty well marked."

"Big Mother 40, Eagle Eye copies. Break, break. Swordsmen say state?"

"Swordsmen Three Zero Seven and Three One One have plenty of gas."

"Swordsmen Three Zero Seven and Three One One, Eagle Eye Seven Zero Two, you're cleared in hot on the closest fast movers. Break, break. Diamond Four One Zero and Four Zero Four, you have the junk headed for Big Mother 40. I have the cavalry coming for what you can't take out. Diamond Four One Two and Four Zero Eight stand-by, I'll have targeting for you shortly. Acknowledge."

"Three Zero Seven is in hot. Three One One will yo-yo with me for cover."

"Diamond Four One Two copies for all the Diamonds. Diamond Four One Two and Four Zero Four will roll in hot as soon as the Swordsmen finish their pass. Will call roll in."

Josh flew the helicopter in a series of ragged circles about five hundred yards to the seaward of Vance and his project. He climbed up to five hundred feet to get a better view on one orbit and as soon as they passed three hundred feet, three strings of six large green balls from a rapid fire 57mm gun passed just a few hundred feet from the helicopter.

Before Josh keyed the intercom, the thought flashed through his mind that the bastards knew where they were and this could get ugly in a hurry. "Van der Jagt, how long will it take to get the survivor into the Stokes litter?"

"Too long. Four or five minutes in a hover, if we're lucky." Hovering that long would bring a rain of 85mm shells down on the helicopter. "Boss, I have an idea we've played around with back at Cubi. It's not perfect, but Kostas and I believe it may work." He came forward to a position just behind the pilot and co-pilots' seats. "We had the riggers make several wide Velcro straps in case we needed to strap someone to a back board. If Vance can wrap these around the pilot and the backboard, then we should be able to get both up the hoist in seconds. All Vance will have to do is deflate his vest and the pilot's LPA and attach the D-rings on their harnesses to the hook, and then away we go. With a little luck, we won't make the guy's injuries any worse."

"I like it. Get ready to drop it."

"I've got the board sandwiched in a big piece of Styrofoam to make sure it floats. I'll show it to him on the run-in so he'll know what to do. All we have to do is give him some time to strap the pilot to the board."

"Swordsmen Three Zero Seven and Three One One are Winchester. Believe we sunk three of the four boats and the other is dead in the water."

"Roger, Swordsman Three Zero Seven. Stand by and maintain visual contact until Diamond flight arrives. Break, break. Diamond Four One Zero and Four Zero Four, this is Eagle Eye Seven Zero Two. Do you both have a visual on Big Mother 40?"

"Diamond Four One Two plus Diamond Four Oh Eight is on trail of Diamond Four Zero Four and we also have a visual on Big Mother."

"Eagle Eye, Diamond Four One Two. We got the junk, but took an awful lot of flak from the area around Dinh Vo. Believe that's where the heavy triple-A is coming from. We can also see several 57mm positions along the road toward Cau Rao on the west side of the bay. Do you want the rest of the Diamonds to hit them?"

"Diamond Four Oh Two, Eagle Eye Seven Zero Two. Affirmative."

While the crew of Big Mother 40 was waiting for Vance, every few seconds a string of four or five splashes in a row would erupt in the harbor. Some were closer than others. It would take only one of the 37 or 57mm shells to send them crashing into the water. To make the black helo harder to spot and track, Josh made erratic turns at forty to seventy-five feet, keeping the tips of the main rotor blades just a few feet above the harbor's dirty brown surface.

"Josh, we're going to have to make the pick-up in ten minutes or less or we may be swimming back to the boat." Jack tapped the fuel totalizer with his gloved finger, not so much for emphasis but to make sure that none of the fuel gauge needles were sticking. "We're down to less than twenty-two hundred pounds—at one hundred ten knots, we'll burn fourteen to fifteen hundred pounds per hour. To be on the safe side, we need two thousand pounds to get back to the *Oklahoma City*, which is the closest surface ship."

"Got it. Tell Eagle Eye to ask the ship to close the distance. My guess is that we'll be down to about eighteen hundred pounds or less when we leave here."

"That's my guess, too."

Josh concentrated on jinking the helicopter and Jack kept an eye on Vance. From the shell splashes it was clear the Vietnamese were unable to accurately target the men in the water or the helo.

"Sir, I've got lots of white water from Vance, so he should have the pilot strapped to the board. He's at about two o'clock and about five hundred yards."

Van der Jagt's words prompted Josh to tighten the turn. He planned to slow at the last possible moment to minimize the time the North Vietnamese gunners would have to zero-in on the hovering helicopter. He wanted to be in forward flight thirty seconds or at most a minute after they stopped. Any longer and they would be sitting ducks.

"Hundred feet."

He pulled the cyclic stick back at the same time he lowered the collective to maintain a hover. As soon as the shaking and shuddering helicopter began to settle, he added a bunch of power to keep it at forty feet above the water.

"Ten seconds. Twenty seconds," D'onofrio counted.

"Vance has the hook and is latching it to their harnesses." A few long, painful, slow seconds passed. "Got a thumbs up." The pitch in Van

Der Jagt's voice increased even though he was trying to maintain his cool, calm image. "Raising Vance and the survivor."

"Sixty seconds."

Two large splashes erupted about seventy-five yards at eleven o'clock, followed by two more in front of them, a hundred yards away.

"Survivor's clear of the water. Let's get the fuck out of here."

Josh smoothly shoved the nose over and raised the collective as he headed for the last series of large splashes. He looked at the fuel gauges and saw they had seventeen hundred pounds. Based on where the *Oklahoma City* was when they took off, they would have to ditch about thirty miles from the ship.

"Eagle Eye, Big Mother 40. Both survivors are on board and we're checking them out. Say pigeons to *Sooner*. We will be low state prior to arrival."

"*Sooner* is closing your area at twenty plus. As soon as able, climb to one thousand feet for radar vectors. She'll have a ready deck on arrival and medical team waiting."

THURSDAY, 3 DAYS LATER, MAY 11, 1972, 0812 LOCAL TIME, YANKEE STATION AIRCRAFT CARRIER, GULF OF TONKIN

Josh and Jack walked into the ready room that HC-7's Detachment 110 shared with the reconnaissance squadron that flew Vigilantes off the USS *Ranger*. The heavy attack recon squadron only had about fifteen officers and had lots of extra space.

"Lieutenant Haman and Lieutenant Junior Grade D'Onofrio!" The commanding voice came from one of the vinyl-covered ready room chairs.

Josh turned to see a commander coming toward them from the back of the ready room. "Yes, sir."

"The chief of staff wants to see you, and I am to escort both of you to his office *now*." The commander pointed to the door as if to emphasize the last word. It was then that Josh saw the Judge Advocate General's insignia on his collar. His name tag had the CTF 77 logo and 'Winthrop' in white letters.

Commander Winthrop ushered them into a large—by shipboard standards—office and then sat in a chair in the corner, leaving both lieutenants standing in front of the captain's desk. It had a large name plate with the logo Commander, Task Force 77 on the corner, along with the name 'Martin Ruppert' in gold letters. The man with eagles on his collars was flipping impatiently between pages in two folders flat on his desk.

"You are at attention." The captain spat out the words in a command voice and shifted his gaze from one folder to the other as both aviators stood in a rigid position of attention. "Do either of you know what rules of engagement are for?"

"Yes, sir." Both Jack and Josh answered almost simultaneously.

"Enlighten me. What are the ROE for ships from neutral nations?" Ruppert's head came up and his eyes bored holes in the two junior officers.

"They are not to be fired upon." Josh paused for a second before adding, "Unless they commit a hostile act that puts U.S. forces in danger. Then we are supposed to either evade and withdraw or return fire with enough force to stop the hostile action."

Josh wasn't sure whether it was annoyance or anger, but whatever it was, Ruppert was closer to a boil than a simmer. What the hell was this about? They'd both just been briefed on the ROE and both had passed the written test.

"Who was the commander on the HH-3A during the rescue on May eight?"

"Sir, I was," Josh said.

"And you're Lieutenant Haman." It was more of a statement than a question. The captain tossed one of the folders aside.

"Yes, sir. I was the mission commander."

"Why did you order your crewman to fire on neutral ships?"

"We fired on the *Valentinov* and the *Razov* only after they fired on us with DshKs which could have easily shot us down."

"Why didn't you evade or withdraw?"

Josh paused for a second. "Two reasons, sir. First, we had already taken hits. Second, if we had not fired back my crew and the helicopter would have been exposed to more gunfire that would probably have shot us down, because it would have been several minutes before we could get out of range. So we encouraged them to stop firing. As you know, we routinely fly near anchored ships in the harbor because we know that the North Vietnamese don't want to hit them. No one has told us not to do it."

"Don't be cute with words with me, Lieutenant. Both of you and your crew are in a lot of hot water. You've created a goddamn international incident." The captain's face flushed with anger as he tossed copies of *Izvestia* and *Pravda* to the front of the desk. Both had pictures of an HH-3A with tracers streaming from the mini-gun. "These were couriered to me from CINCPAC and let me tell you what the articles say."

"No need to, sir, I speak and read Russian. The headline on Pravda says 'U.S. helicopter attacks innocent Soviet merchant ship.' The—" Josh started to reach for the paper but it was pulled back. Josh wondered why the captain was getting so upset by Soviet propaganda. And what about the rescue?

"Lieutenant, you are at attention!" Ruppert slammed his hand down on the desk and then took a deep breath, but his cheeks flamed bright red. "Not only did this make the Russian papers, but the *New York* fucking *Times* carried the *Izvestia* story with the fucking Russian journalist's by-line." Captain Ruppert threw the front page of the U.S. paper across the desk. "You idiots killed at least ten Soviet merchant marine sailors and wounded two dozen more. The State Department wants your heads along with your crew's on a silver platter. They're trying to contain this war and you've just tried to expand it."

"Sir, if you read—"

"I'm talking, and you, Lieutenant Haman, you are listening."

"Yes, sir."

"Lieutenant, this is an order and don't fuck it up. You and your crew are in hack. All of you are to pack your gear and board the next COD to Subic Bay. There, you will report to the HC-7 Support Detachment O-in-C as well as to the JAG officer at the Cubi Point Naval Air Station. You are also grounded and will not leave the Cubi Point facility until the pending judicial action, which will probably be a general court-martial, is completed. You will be confined to the BOQ and only go to work and the officers club for meals. You will also be in your rooms after nineteen-thirty. If you violate these conditions, you will be confined in the brig." Captain Ruppert fumbled around for a manila folder. "These are your formal orders. Now, get out of my office and get off this ship."

"Yes, sir."

Neither said anything until they got back to their stateroom where Josh turned to Jack. "What did you do with the film from the Topcon?"

"It's still in my helmet bag; I forgot to turn it in." Jack paused for a second. "You don't want to talk about what is going to happen to us? It sounds like we're going to be poster boys for a public execution."

"Good, and not yet. First, when the smoke clears, cooler heads will prevail. If not, our careers are over unless we want to hire some expensive lawyers. So, what we have to do is be prepared to prove our innocence."

"And you're an expert on this?" Jack's voice dripped with sarcasm.

"Not exactly, but this is not the first time I've been in hack." Josh looked into his friend's face. Action, not worrying, was needed. "I've got the film from my Nikon. When we get to Subic, we'll go to the Hobby Shop photo lab, process the film and see what we can see."

"But he said we were not allowed to go anywhere except the BOQ, the club to eat, and the squadron. The Hobby Shop Photo Lab was not on the list."

"I know, but it is in the building next door to the BOQ. Are you going to tell anyone we made a slight detour for an hour or so?"

"Okay. Just so you know, I'm pretty sure the guys manning the guns were Spetznaz. I could see the blue-and-white striped jerseys they wear under their fatigues." Jack fished out two rolls of film and stuffed them in his pocket. "Are you sure we're not going to get hammered? I can live with getting tossed out of the Navy, but breaking big rocks into small rocks at Leavenworth for years, no way."

"My gut says we're going to be okay." He was just as scared as Jack, but right now he was focused on exoneration. "Right now, the armchair admirals are looking for someone to hang to show they are forcing the warriors to play by their politicians' ridiculous rules."

"So what chance do we have? There are probably admirals lining up to make examples out of us so they can tell their buddies how they are helping win the war."

"Here's what I think happened. Somebody in the State Department got his panties in a wad because he had to work late one night answering a bunch of questions from some high mucky-muck about how do we deal with this instead of what caused it. Fixing blame is more important than figuring out why." Josh popped open a can of Coke. "When the smoke clears and someone at CINCPAC comes to their senses they will realize that, first, we picked up two guys in the middle of Haiphong Harbor. Second, we took a fair amount of fire from two Russian ships. Third, if they string us up—figuratively speaking— no one will go into Haiphong to pick guys who land there. This is not a message they want to send to the air wings. And fourth, last time I checked, we were doing our job. The Russians shot at us, we shot back, and I think the Russians are pissed they didn't bag us. Now they have a couple of shot-up ships and casualties that they have to explain at home, so why not blame the Americans and try to create a diplomatic incident?"

Jack wasn't yet convinced, but worrying wasn't going to help. "We need to tell the guys, and they are gonna be pissed."

Big Mother 40

A growing, unrecognizable shriek stopped Thai in his tracks for a second while he listened. The intensity grew to a point that, even a hundred feet below the jungle canopy, he could feel the pressure wave of the jet, which he now recognized as an F-105, that passed overhead. The deafening noise hadn't receded when he heard the unmistakable crump of exploding bombs, each one louder than the next. He could feel the concussion from the weapons as he ran to the command center. The attack was over by the time he got there, less than ten minutes later.

"What happened?" Thai gasped out, his heart pumping overtime from adrenaline.

"We were bombed by what we think were four F-105s," Loi answered, holding one of the hand sets. "The air defense sector didn't alert us that they were coming. The first we knew was when one of our lookouts spotted them and called the command center. They were in and out of the valley so fast we did not have time to engage them."

"Casualties first, damage second."

Major Loi hung up the handset. "One string of bombs landed right in B Company's bivouac area. The phone line is out so they had to use the radio and the caller said that casualties were heavy. We dispatched our regimental doctor along with a truck. We won't have an estimate of the casualties until he gets there in about ten minutes."

"Anything else?" Thai stood in the middle of the room looking at the shell-shocked faces of the men around him. It was clear that this was the first time many of them had been on the receiving end of American airpower.

"Yes. The lookouts in that area are pretty sure that three of the four guns in the nearby Krait anti-aircraft battery were wiped out, along with their fire control radar. We don't have any communication with them, so the squad that is on the truck is going to hike up to their position and radio in a report."

"Send someone in a vehicle up there right now, along with some extra medics. Tell them to re-establish telephone communications as soon as possible and to stay off the radio unless they are under attack."

"Yes, sir," Loi replied. "I think we were pretty lucky. Two of the bombs landed on either side of one of the hidden missile launch pads, and from what we understand none of the ropes were cut, but they are being checked out. We'll have to replace some of the camouflage. One of the cranes used to load missiles on the launcher has a few extra holes, but we do not think the damage will prevent us from using it. We talked to

114

the Russians; they are just starting an inspection of the missile on the launcher and they have not called us back yet. The rest of the bombs landed in the jungle and did no damage." Major Loi walked over to the map. "I have ordered all the companies to deploy into the field and patrol their sectors to make sure that there aren't any American special forces hiding in the base. C Company is sending a platoon to help search B Company's area and I am going to take a small platoon from the headquarters to support them as well."

"Excellent idea, but Major Loi, I need you here to coordinate the movements and actions of the company commanders. Have someone get another truck to take them up there and I will go with them." Thai paused, collecting his thoughts. "Koniev, where is he?"

"Right behind you."

Thai swiveled around. "Any idea of what happened?"

"Yes, my guess is that the F-105s came from bases in Thailand below our radar coverage and entered the valley going as fast as they could and dropped their bombs. The F-105 was designed for that type of attack. Our radar never saw them, which is why we didn't get any warning."

"You had no idea the Americans would try something like this?"

"No, I did not."

"No intelligence, nothing from your embassy or the air defense center?"

"No, I just got off the phone with them and the raid was a surprise to them as well."

"Interesting." Thai started to the cave mouth. "Colonel Koniev, do you want to come with me?"

"Yes."

The trip would give Thai the chance to grill Koniev about what he really knew. Sometime, he would have to tell him *We know you are reading the American's messages,* but not now. The Vietnamese colonel waited while Koniev finished buckling the load-bearing harness with the six magazines and slung his AKM over his shoulder.

The trail to B Company's area took the two men along with a radio operator across the valley and then up onto the ridge on the east side of the valley. As they came around a bend near B Company's bivouac area, the company commander and his radio operator were sitting by a tree waiting for them to arrive.

"Sir, all wounded have already been brought down from the 57mm battery. We're going to bring the dead down later. The battery commander is one of the dead."

"Very good." Thai counted fifteen men with bloody bandages lying in a row. Some were still on stretchers and others were lying on the ground. "A platoon will be up here in a few minutes to help you. Have you seen how badly the battery was hit?"

"Yes, sir, I just came down with the last of the wounded."

"Good, lead the way up there." Thai turned to Koniev. "Do you need a breather?"

Koniev finished the swallow of water from his canteen. "No. Let's get moving." His workouts must have been helping because the thirty minute, mostly uphill walk didn't have him breathing hard.

As he followed the two Vietnamese officers along the path that wove back and forth, zig-zagging up the ridgeline, Koniev wondered how they managed to get the guns up to the site. The captain held up his hand and the group stopped.

"One of the bombs hit over there." The captain led the men through the trees to a hole that was about ten meters wide and at the center, about the same deep. "There are pieces of trees all over the place but no one was hurt by this bomb. We felt it explode down in our area."

Ten minutes later, they entered a clearing that had been, at one time, covered by camouflage netting. There were the same size holes in the ground where two of the hooches Koniev had seen all over the base used to be, and a third hooch that was half its normal size. The other side had collapsed in a splintered heap. The fourth, while still standing, was shredded by shrapnel.

Thai pointed at the holes. "My guess that these holes were made by either 350 kilogram or 450 kilogram bombs. I'll take you to see the guns."

Another ten minutes of climbing the steep path and they came to the second in a line of cleared patches. The bent barrel and frame of one gun was on its side a few feet from a bomb crater; there were only fragments of what used to be a S-60 57mm gun near the other hole. A bloody uniform, probably still containing body parts, was still dripping blood into a growing red-brown pool that was slowly being absorbed by the ground.

Koniev went over to inspect the damaged gun where Thai joined him.

"You know, a lot of work went into getting these guns up here. We had to disassemble them into pieces that could be carried by a team of men who carried them up to where they were placed. Then, once we had all the parts, we had re-assemble the guns in position where we wanted them."

"How long did that take?"

"Working day and night, about a week per gun." Thai waited for a few seconds. "Did you know this attack was coming?"

"No." Koniev suspected he knew where Thai was going with his questions.

"Colonel, are you aware that we know that you are getting messages that tell you when the Americans are coming?"

"Officially? No. Unofficially, I am not surprised."

"Then why didn't you share the information? We are in the same war, we share the same dangers, we are supposedly allies."

"Our commanders have different chains of command and have given us different orders."

"Alexei, you didn't answer the question."

"The honest answer is because I have specific orders not to tell you. Only a handful of my countrymen know that we have this information. I know it is a horrible excuse, but it is the truth."

"I am glad it was not your decision." Thai waited for a few seconds. "Now that you know that I know, can you give us more information on when American airstrikes are coming and where they will drop their bombs?"

"No. I can only give you what I use when we shoot missiles. Even that is violating my orders."

"What about this bombing? What do you know about it?"

"Nothing. And if you are decoding our messages then you know or will find out that this mission was a surprise to us."

"Yes, I will find out the truth. You didn't answer my question."

"I know. I will have to figure out a way to share more without my superior's knowing."

FRIDAY, 2 DAYS LATER, MAY 14, 1972, 1113 LOCAL TIME, TAKHLI AIR BASE, THAILAND

Two days later, Gus Thomes was being guided to a parking spot when he saw a Jeep approaching fast. He finished the F-105's short shutdown check list and climbed down.

"Sir, you have a visitor in your office." The officer was very nervous.

"Great. I'll see him after I post-flight the airplane and finish the debrief."

"Sir, General Jameson ordered me to pick you up and ordered me to tell you that the other pilots can debrief without you."

Thomes pulled his helmet off and tossed it, along with the navigation bag, onto the back seat of the Jeep. "Well, then, Lieutenant Smithson, let us not keep the General waiting."

"Gus, tell everyone to leave the outer office and then close the door." General Jameson was sitting in his chair and Gus took a seat in one of the desk chairs, not worried that his flight suit was soaked with sweat. He placed his bottle of water on the corner of the desk.

"What kind of mission did you complete two days ago?"

"Went on a low-level training hop." He knew where this conversation going. If he was relieved and retired as a result of this mission, it was worth it. While it was not a secret within the wing, the only place the flight was listed was on the daily flight plan, which was not shared outside the wing. All someone had to do was compare the number of sorties and bombs dropped to the totals on the ATO for the day and see that there were four extra flights and twenty-four more bombs expended.

"In Thailand, in the middle of a war?"

"We don't practice those very often and the 333rd wasn't tasked that day."

"The training hop wasn't on the air tasking order issued by either Seventh or Thirteen Air Force."

"Doesn't have to be. As the wing commander I can authorize it."

"With live ordnance?"

"I can authorize that, too. Why else would you fly a low-level training mission? It is what we are supposed to be able to do."

"Who planned the mission?"

"I did." Thomes kept his answers short and to the point; he didn't want anyone else implicated. He wasn't sure if the man on the other side of the desk was going to be able to control his temper.

"How'd you select the pilots?"

"They volunteered." He couldn't, but wanted to tell the general that when he asked for volunteers all the pilots in the room had raised their hands.

"Did you fly over Laos and Vietnam?"

"Yes, sir." Gus looked at the desk and saw his chart from the mission opened on the desk.

"Why?"

"Because northwest Vietnam is a good place to dump some extra bombs on a training mission in a valley where no one at Seventh or Thirteenth Air Force believes there is missile base. They think we saw a cloud. Well, if you visit our photo lab, we can show you pictures of an S-60 57mm radar-directed anti-aircraft gun flying through the air, courtesy of a Mark 83 thousand-pound bomb. Also, dash four in the flight will tell you that the tree tops in the floor of the valley rippled in a funny way that he's never seen before as he followed his flight leader over it at close to five hundred-plus knots. And, as your intelligence officers will tell you, radar-directed S-60s are the favorite defensive gun around SAM sites. Ask any Wild Weasel pilot."

"How'd you get there and back without tankers?"

"Simple. If you look at the kneeboard card that was with the chart on my desk, you'd see the flight plan." Gus waited until the general picked up the white 5"x7" card with the smudged pencil notes. "We took off and cruise-climbed to about fifteen thousand feet; as we approached the North Vietnamese radar horizon we descended down to five hundred feet, and as we approached the target area from the southeast we went into burner. After dropping the bombs and when we were clear of the target area, we climbed back to ten thousand, landed at Nakhom Phenom with about twenty minutes of fuel left, got gas, and flew home. Total flight time was about three and a half hours. And, oh, by the way, not a round was fired in our direction and everyone came home."

General Jameson studied the kneeboard card and glanced at the chart before putting it down deliberately as if it were contaminated. "You know I could relieve you for this."

"You could."

"I could also have you court-martialed, run out of the Air Force, and you'd be sent to Leavenworth and you'd lose your pension."

"Yes, sir, you could." *And you won't.*

The General rubbed his face. He was looking at one of the finest combat leaders and pilots in the Air Force. Relieving him was the by-the-book answer but it would also be stupid and could backfire. "I'll make a deal with you: Promise me you won't continue this vendetta. In other words, no more freelance missions. On my side, I'll push Seventh and Thirteenth Air Forces as well as Commac-V to find and eliminate this base. If needed, I'll be aggressive and insubordinate to the point it may get me relieved. And, if we get more proof there is a base in that area and if there is an air strike involved, you get to lead it."

"I'll agree on one condition."

"And that is?"

"You find out in the next thirty days. We can't keep losing planes and pilots at this rate. My gut tells me that valley is where the missile base is."

"Trouble is, Commac-V won't act unless he has facts." The General tapped the desk with his forefinger. "And right now, he is very short on facts."

"Then figure out how to get him the facts. An S-60 battery in the middle of nowhere should arouse their curiosity. That's a fact. Missiles appearing out of nowhere well outside the range of those at known sites around Hanoi and Haiphong are facts. What does it take?"

"I'll push the intelligence folks to take a deeper look. How about ninety days?"

"Thirty, as in four weeks from today."

"How about we talk about progress in thirty days?"

"Done, but if you are not sitting in this office with definitive progress that impresses me, deal is off."

"Agreed." The general held out his hand, which Gus shook.

"Beer is on the General because he makes more money than the Colonel."

TUESDAY, NEXT DAY, MAY 16, 1972, 0830 LOCAL TIME, SEAL COMPOUND, CAM RANH BAY, 180 MILES NORTH OF SAIGON, SOUTH VIETNAM

"Generals, what brings you up here to this posh beachside resort so early on a Sunday morning?"

Captain Mancuso's friendly sarcasm was appreciated by his audience, but the visit by two generals and four staff officers and its purpose was a surprise. Marine Major General Hector Cruz, Chief of Staff for Operations for Commac-V, and an Air Force three-star Mike Jameson, the Thirteenth Air Force's commander, plus four Air Force colonels whose name tags said Snyder, Griffin, Richards, and Paladoro were crammed into the SEALs' briefing room. Only Snyder and Paladoro wore wings on their sweat-stained khakis. Before they walked into the room, Mancuso's SEALs covered the charts hanging on the side walls with black drapes.

"We want to change the mission we talked about a few days ago," General Cruz stated.

"Okay, why?"

"Over the last few months," Jameson said, "we've been losing airplanes from each strike package every day, and typically, it's tail-end

Charlie. We know roughly where they went down on the western end of Route Packs Five and Six."

The colonel whose name tag said Deputy Chief of Staff, Intelligence, under the name Griffin, rolled out a Tactical Navigation Chart with a dozen Xs marked in a cluster in northwestern North Vietnam.

"In most cases no one saw them until it was too late," Jameson continued. "All we get, if we're lucky, is a missile call followed by a mayday and then maybe a beeper. Every one of the pilots who survived was captured within minutes of hitting the ground. It is beginning to affect morale and we're getting questions from the wing commanders for which we don't have any good answers. These extra losses are increasing the loss rate, which is already high, to the point where it is both unacceptable and unsustainable."

"We do have a couple of pilots who thought, emphasize, *thought* they saw the puffs of smoke from the missile launches, but the area doesn't have any visible missile sites and is a mountainous part of North Vietnam. We're not sure if they saw a cloud or smoke because they were evading two missiles. So, for the past three days we sent Wild Weasels into these areas here and here." Jameson pointed to an orbit southeast of Ha Giang and another about fifty miles farther southeast. "The Wild Weasel missions were added on a random basis, and when they were flying nothing happened. Then, the next package loses an F-105. Pilot ejected, talked for a minute or two on the ground before he had to evade. We are assuming he was captured because we have not heard from him since."

"So, what you're telling me is that you think there's some sort of missile base up here and you want my SEALs to find it."

"That's it."

"What about the other mission to take a look at the rail yard outside Ha Giang?"

General Cruz took over. "It is on hold until we find this place, if it exists. We will share whatever we have in the way of intelligence and then let you figure out the best way to find the base."

Mancuso looked at Jameson. "Who else knows about this?"

"Right now, just the people in this room," Cruz answered. "Pac-Af and CINCPAC haven't been sent our analysis yet. We have the mission reports and pilot debriefs from the strike packages where the Air Force lost F-105s from two wings. We also have the debrief from a strike into a valley where one of the wing commanders thought the missiles were being fired. Let me emphasize that his estimate has not been confirmed by any intelligence. None of these guys know this conversation is taking place."

"Let's keep it this way."

"We have to tell CINCPAC and Pac-Af," Colonel Griffin said.

"No, we don't," Mancuso said. "At least not yet. They don't have to know anything until we have a plan. All they need to do is provide us with the reconnaissance assets that we will task. Tell them that if they need to know more, either come here or we'll go to Hawaii. Nothing, I repeat, absolutely nothing goes in messages."

"We'll need their help," Griffin persisted.

"Are you telling me Seventh and Thirteenth Air Force doesn't have the stuff already here in Vietnam to (a) do some reconnaissance and (b) analyze the info we gather?"

"Captain," Cruz said in a way to prevent Mancuso from embarrassing Griffin in front of his boss, Jameson, "what do you need to find this base?"

"Three things. First, the ability to task photo and electronic reconnaissance aircraft as needed. Second, a couple of dedicated helicopters and crews experienced in long-range insertion and extraction operations. And third, we need total and absolute secrecy."

Mancuso looked at the Air Force officers; he knew Cruz already knew what was coming and had probably warned them in advance, so he was not expecting an argument. "Here are principles that we will use to govern this operation, and they will not be violated. If they are, we're out. All communications will be face-to-face. No messages, and no phone calls other than to schedule meetings. We will not discuss the subject matter of the meetings in calls either. I will personally approve any and all written messages. After being inserted, my teams will be on the ground for no more than five, maybe six days. If the shit hits the fan, I expect the Seventh and Thirteenth Air Forces and CTF 77 to stop what they're doing and provide whatever assets I need to get my men out. Whoever is assigned to me, works for me. Not for Seventh Air Force, not for Thirteenth Air Force, not for CTF 77, but for me, Commander, Navy Special Warfare Forces, Vietnam. That means I will have operational control of their mission tasking and they do what I want them to do, which includes if, how, and when they communicate with their former chain of commands."

"Agreed." The Marine General looked at his Air Force counterpart, who had a pained look on his face.

"How long do you think it will take to find the base?" Jameson asked when he found his voice.

"I have no idea, General. We could get lucky and find it on the first mission. Or it could take longer. Each time we insert a team into such a confined area crawling with NVA, we increase the risk. If we don't find it right away, we'll probably have to come up with plan B, or even C or D. So we want to do what we can to maximize the chances that we find it on the first mission."

"I have to check with my boss before we give you a blank check." Jameson didn't like losing assets to a sister service's command for an indefinite period of time, and inside the Air Force it could be considered political and career suicide. He needed "air cover" before he agreed to Mancuso's and Cruz's demand. But then again, it was the right thing to do; and if they retired him, he could live with that because he'd had a great career and been promoted well beyond his dreams.

General Cruz looked at his Air Force counterpart. "I'll take care of getting Pac-Af's support. CINCPAC's ops officer is a personal friend and classmate, and I know his boss as well. We were on the football team together at the academy and he never would have gained a yard if I hadn't blocked for him. I'm sure Pac-Af will go along if it will cut down his losses."

"Thank you, General, I appreciate your help. Just let me know what support you need from the Air Force." General Jameson turned to Captain Mancuso. "Do you have a place where I can make a secure phone call?"

"Yes, sir, you can use my office or our command center." Mancuso showed the way to his office past several officers who were waiting to enter the mission planning room.

Mancuso waited until the Jameson was on the phone to his command center at Tan San Nut before tapping his Marine general friend on the shoulder and nodding toward the corner. "I want a couple of crews from HC-7. I hear a guy by the name of Josh Haman is back in theater. My guys worked with him on his first tour and say he is top notch. If you can, let him pick his crew. Get him first and then we'll let him help us pick the second crew later."

"I'll make it happen. Great choice."

WEDNESDAY, NEXT DAY, MAY 17, 1972,

0845 LOCAL TIME, VENOM BASE

"Colonel Thai here," Thai said, seated at his desk.

"Excellent, Colonel. General Chung and I wanted to share information with you that is for your ears only."

Thai recognized the high-pitched voice of General Van Dong, the head of the Northwest Air Defense Sector to whom he reported. In a small room, the tenor could grate on one's nerves, but the hollow sounds on the secure circuit toned it down.

"First, I am sorry you lost so many men. I will have the replacements sent to you later in the week. Before I called, I listened to our Soviet advisors as well as our own experts who studied this attack, and both have come to the conclusion that it was a complete surprise. We are considering recommendations that may be able to prevent such attacks in the future, but we are not sure if the Americans will continue to use this tactic. Until they do, we won't change our defenses. Second, I want to congratulate you on the success you are having. The reports on the shoot downs and the base's operation are most impressive. We want you to continue to work with Koniev and increase the rate you are shooting down airplanes." The General spoke slowly to accommodate the encryption equipment.

"Thank you, sir."

"The information I am going to tell you is not to be shared with anyone. Normally, this intelligence would not be provided, but we think you can use it to your advantage."

"Yes, General, I understand." Thai made sure that he had an extra pen to take notes which he would study then burn.

"First, I want to let you know that the American Thirteenth Air Force has designated a hundred kilometer by two hundred kilometer area in the northwest part of our country that includes Venom as a special area of interest and is marked on the commander's charts and others in his headquarters."

"I understand. We will take precautions to protect the base from attack. My men are disbursed throughout the base on continuous patrol. This will make it harder for the Americans to kill us or penetrate the base." Thai realized that Von Dong hadn't mentioned minimizing risk to the base. Was that a change?

"Very good. We also want to let you know that we think the Russians know when the Americans are coming." General Van Dong stopped to let his words sink in. "We are able to decipher some of the messages sent to Koniev because we use the same equipment and the encryption keys for the message traffic we share. When we apply those keys to the special messages he is getting, we are able to partially decode them."

Thai wondered why he was being told this. The Russians had a room that no one but Koniev and his four GRU officers were allowed in. The room was guarded by the extra Spetnaz soldiers that Koniev could not assign to Thai's companies. Koniev was sure the extra men were not Spetnaz but special GRU security people, and there were specific limits on what he could order them to do. Did Van Dong want his men to spy on Koniev? If the Russian commander found out, it would ruin their relationship.

"We want you to monitor how he uses that intelligence which gives him information on the route and the target as well as the number of airplanes. You may want to ask him how he picks his targets. You're very clever, so I am confident you will figure something out."

Thai waited until he thought the general was finished. "You want me to do two things. One, find out how Koniev knows when the airplanes are coming. And two, make sure Koniev doesn't miss any opportunities to shoot down American airplanes." It was more of a statement than a question.

"Exactly."

"How do I know when Koniev is getting this kind of information? Are you going to provide me with that information?" Thai wondered how they were going to prevent any more surprise attacks. He was sure General Van Dong was not concerned about the attacks unless they destroyed the base, and if they did, he would be ordered set up another one. The men on the ground, Thai included, did not matter to him.

"We will call you so there is no record to let you know when he is being sent a message that has information."

While Colonel Thai was on the phone, Koniev was plotting the information from the translation of tomorrow's American air-tasking-order message when his secure line rang. He looked at his watch and was surprised it was late afternoon.

"Good afternoon." Koniev assumed it was Rokossovsky because he was the only one who ever called him on this line.

"Are you alone?" Different voice. Nikishev's.

"Yes, I am."

"First, the air strike was a complete surprise to our people as well as to our local comrades. I had the people in Moscow take another look at that day's list of air strikes and it was not there. We are not sure what happened on the American side because that is not like their Air Force, which is absolutely anal about putting every possible piece of information into their air-tasking orders. Some in Moscow think it was a rogue attack by some renegade officer."

"You do know that the F-105 was designed for low-level strike missions."

"I do know that." Nikishev paused for a second. "I am glad that none of our men were hurt in that attack."

"We didn't know they were coming until we heard the jets and the bombs started exploding." Koniev stopped for a second. "More than fifty of Thai's men were killed and almost the same number wounded."

"Yes, Colonel, we heard." Nikishev paused to take a long drag on his ever-present cigarette. "Colonel, Rokossovsky is with me and we want to pass information to you that may affect the way Moscow views your operation, as well as other activities we have here in North Vietnam."

Koniev thought the general's words sounded ominous so he reached for a pad to take notes. "What happened?"

"A few days ago, an American A-6 Intruder was shot down and the crew landed in Haiphong Harbor. As usual, the Americans sent in one of their rescue helicopters. This crew was very clever because they flew close to all the ships anchored in the estuary waiting to dock. Among those were several Soviet ships, two of which, the *Razov* and the *Valentinov*, were carrying the new versions of the S-75 Divina missile."

Koniev pressed the handset into his ear as chain-smoking Nikishev wheezed and took another puff off his cigarette. He was about to say something when the general started talking again.

"There was an exchange of gunfire between the American helicopter and the *Razov* and the *Valentinov*. Normally, the Americans just fly near the ships and wave. We don't know who started shooting first, but there were Spetznaz on both ships and you never know what those hot heads will try. Twelve of our countrymen were killed and over twenty wounded."

Koniev thought it safe to venture an opinion. "Knowing the Americans, they had no reason to shoot at the ships; a firefight makes getting in and out of the harbor more difficult."

"We agree; typically they just use the ships as a shield. However, we don't know what our local comrades-in-arms did or what Moscow will tell us they did. My guess is they are turning this into a propaganda event."

"That wouldn't surprise me."

"We would be interested if and what the Vietnamese say, if anything, about the incident."

"Yes, sir. I will call if Thai says anything. My guess is that he doesn't know about the incident." Koniev waited a second before asking the question he'd wanted to ask since he'd arrived in Vietnam. "How many other Soviet soldiers have died in this war?"

Koniev imagined the old general sitting in a room with a dense cloud of cigarette smoke working its way down from the ceiling and guessed he was taking a long drag while he decided whether or not to answer his question. "We are well over one thousand killed and about half that many wounded in the three years I have been here. The actual number is not known outside this embassy and certain offices in Moscow. Let us keep it that way."

"Thank you, General." The implied threat of the general's last statement was very clear.

"You are welcome. Keep up the good work, and be careful."

Chapter 8

REPRIEVE

"Sir, I couldn't find you, but this message came in about twenty minutes ago." The petty officer handed Josh a yellow government phone message form that had a name and a phone number.

"Wonder what this is about?" he said to no one in particular as he spun the dial on the black rotary government-issue phone that looked like it had been designed in the 1930s and barely survived World War II. When he hung up the phone less than a minute later, he turned to Jack, who was sitting on the desk. "Some Captain by the name of Mancuso wants to see both of us ASAP. They're sending a jeep over right away. Must be important."

"Maybe they've already decided what they want to do with us, and Mancuso is the messenger who tells us we're going to be put in front of a firing squad!"

"Oh ye of little faith!"

The two aviators waited in the shade of the hangar that housed HC-7s maintenance operations at the end of the ramp the squadron used to park its helicopters. It was at the end of the pier where the Navy could and often did, dock two carriers end-to-end. Damaged or aircraft needing more maintenance than the ship could provide were craned off and towed to the rework facility on the other side of the air station's nine thousand foot runway.

By the time the gray Jeep arrived, sweat stains were beginning to show under their arm pits of their khaki uniforms. The enlisted man was wearing a dungaree top and bottoms that had seen better days. "Lieutenant's Haman and D'Onofrio?" He said the last name as if he was a second grader sounding out a new word.

"Yup."

129

"Hop in."

Josh got into the front seat while Jack climbed into the flat bench that served as a back seat. No sooner were they in the vehicle then the driver dropped the clutch, burned a little rubber and took off down the ramp. Josh grabbed the handle on the side of the windscreen and turned around to see a wide-eyed Jack with a death grip on the two handles on either side of the rear seat as the young man at the wheel drove as if he were a grand prix driver. He screeched to a stop in front of a small cluster of buildings surrounded by two rows of chain-link fences six feet apart and topped with razor wire. Unlike other buildings on the base, there were no signs describing its use or occupants. A single narrow gravel pathway crunched as they walked toward the guard shack. The driver pulled his badge from a back pocket and then turned. "Lieutenants, please show your ID cards."

After the armed guard, who was wearing shorts and a t-shirt, checked their names against a list, he unlocked the gate. As they went into the building, Josh could see the tree-covered hills of Sand Island, about three miles away in the middle of the shark-infested Subic Bay.

They were escorted to a small conference room that had two large maps, one of the Philippines, and the other of Vietnam, tacked to the wall, metal folding chairs scattered around the room, and gray tables lined up together. Whatever was on the other walls was covered by black drapes.

"Sodas and bottled water are in the fridge at the end. Both are a quarter and there is a cup full of change." The petty officer closed the door as he left.

Josh put two quarters in the can. "What do you want: Coke, Pepsi, water?"

"My career back! You may be used to this, but to me, it's almost as bad as being shot at."

"Look at the bright side. They haven't sent you to JEST yet. So besides that, what do you want to drink?"

"Coffee. It is way too early in the morning for a soda. Is this what I think it is?" Jack walked along the wall, looking at the maps.

"Yeah, it's the SEAL compound. Maybe they're planning to offer us a suicide mission and just like in the movie *The Dirty Dozen*, if we survive, we get pardoned."

"It'll be a lot more interesting than that." A new voice entered the conversation. Both officers turned and came to attention.

"At ease, gentlemen, I'm Captain Tony Mancuso. Please sit down."

Marc Liebman

After shaking hands, he spun one of the chairs around and crossed his tanned, muscular arms across the back of the chair. "For the record, I am the commander of the SEAL teams assigned to Commander, U.S. Forces Vietnam, and I have two areas of operations. One, Lieutenant Haman, you know about, which is working the Mekong River Delta all the way up into Cambodia. You worked for me on a couple of operations on your last tour. I have another area that is, shall we say, new and different. Ops for these missions are planned out of our new base at Cam Ranh Bay. And my guess is that both of you are wondering why the fuck you're here."

"Yes, sir." Both Jack and Josh spoke at the same time.

"You and your crew come very highly recommended. Lieutenant Haman, I understand this is your second tour with HC-7; and Lieutenant D'Onofrio, this is your first trip to Southeast Asia. Is that correct?"

"Yes, sir." Josh spoke up. "After my first tour, I was a RAG instructor but it was boring, so after about six months they let me come back. Jack and I met in the RAG. He volunteered for HC-7 and was one of my students."

Mancuso nodded. Josh wore ribbons that showed he had been awarded two Silver Stars and three Distinguished Flying Crosses, which confirmed his warrior credentials. Jack had his Bronze Star ribbon with a Combat V next to his red-and-yellow "Alive in 65" medal. "My guys tell me that last summer, you were the HAC who inserted and extracted a couple of SEAL teams on ops around Vinh and along the trail in Laos and Cambodia. You got them in and out with very little drama and got very, very high marks from my SEALs."

"Thank you, sir." Josh nodded. "All my crew did was help them pick better LZs and work out signals and alternatives that we knew couldn't be compromised."

"Lieutenant Haman, you are understating the point, because the detailed planning and those alternative extraction plans are what enabled you to get them out safe and sound when a team was on the run."

"It was pretty simple, sir," Josh said, not sure how much Mancuso knew.

"Then there was the recent rescue of the Marine Recon team north of the DMZ. I've heard several stories about that one. Major General Hector Cruz, who is now Commac-V's head of operations, is a good friend of mine, and my boss. He's a Recon Marine and we go way back. What happened?"

Josh looked at Jack and it was Jack who spoke first. "You tell him and I'll speak up if you leave out anything important."

"Sir, here's the *Reader's Digest* version. We'd flown up to Phu Bai to use a hoist and work stands to change a tail rotor gearbox that had reached the end of it service life. While we in the sixty-minute test hover, the tower called and asked how many passengers could we carry? We said, 'It depends, why?' The tower controller said there was a seventeen-man Marine Recon team trapped by the NVA and in danger of being overrun and captured. We had full fuel, so I pulled out of the hover and Jack asked them where they were."

"We didn't have a chart that went that far north so the tower turned us over to a pair of Marine OV-10s who briefed us and vectored us toward the landing zone between calling in air strikes that were keeping the NVA at bay. We knew from talking to the Marines who helped us that all the H-46s at Phu Bai were grounded for a gearbox problem. The Marines didn't have enough Hueys, plus, as we found out when we got there, you couldn't fit the three UH-1s safely into the LZ at the same time to get the Marines out in one lift."

Josh took a sip of his Coke before he continued. "We chugged up over the hills, followed by two Huey's with rockets, and just as we got there, a flight of four Intruders laid canisters of napalm along the tree lines. The Marines had their recognition panel out and we told them they would be loading from the helicopter's right and left sides. I came up over the hill, flared, and plopped it down right on the recognition panel, which came up off the ground in the rotator wash. I was afraid it would get caught in the rotors, but it went sailing merrily away. The Marines were defending a wide ravine and we took fire from every direction."

Josh drained his can of Coke as details from the mission flooded his mind. "Two DshK machine gun rounds went into the overhead circuit-breaker panel and blew the emergency throttles right out of Jack's hand. Hits from AKs on the instrument panel sprayed both of us with glass. Just as the Marine lieutenant leading the platoon stuck his head between our seats to tell us to go, I got hit by a DshK round right in the back of the seat. I thought my blood and guts would be all over the cockpit, but it got slowed by the broom closet." Josh saw the puzzled look on Mancuso's face and realized he needed a bit more explanation. "The cyclic and collective controls in the cockpit are all connected to the hydraulic actuators for the rotor system, which are all grouped together in a section of the air frame we call the broom closet because, behind the access panel, the four actuators are all lined up in a neat row. And when Sikorsky modified the helicopters, they installed armor made of a boron epoxy laminate that's about three quarters of an inch thick on three sides, because if these get shot up, you can't fly the helicopter. Anyway, the armor in the broom closet dissipated much of the bullet's energy before it slammed into the same type of armor on my seat; otherwise, I wouldn't be sitting here."

Unconsciously, Josh leaned forward and rubbed the back of his rib cage where the large, long-since-healed black and blue mark had been. His memory led him right to the spot. "All it did was give me a big bruise."

Jack started talking. "As Josh was trying to get us out of there, I turned around and saw a Marine just sitting down, not doing anything. We'd told recon team's radio operator to pass the word that once they got on board to fire out through the windows. So I yelled at the platoon leader to tell that man to fire. Being a good Marine, he did as he was told. Just as we lifted off, we heard and felt this WHOOOOOSH, along with a flash of flame, and the cabin filled with smoke. Apparently, the only thing he had left to shoot was this one-shot bazooka-thing called a LAW and he fired it. Luckily, no one was hurt and the back blast didn't turn us into a fireball."

Mancuso chuckled; before you pulled the trigger on the Light Anti-Tank weapon, the last thing you did was make sure no one was behind you, because the flame could start a fire or burn someone really bad.

"By the time we took off, our caution panel was lit up like a Christmas tree, showing several problems with our electrical and hydraulic systems." Josh said. "I think, at least initially, they came on because the circuit breaker panel was messed up from the bullet that went through it. Anyway, as we were taking off, the lieutenant was standing between Jack and me, when two NVA soldiers popped up out of the elephant grass about fifty feet in front of us just as we were gaining speed. Craig Green was the lieutenant's name, and he fired a burst from his M-14 right through the windscreen and both NVA soldiers went down."

Josh swirled his can of Coke as a way to see how much was left in the can. "We managed to get to about a thousand feet over the terrain so the Hueys could slide under us to look us over. We were losing fuel and hydraulic fluid. Then, after about twenty minutes of flying, the secondary hydraulic system started to fail and we shut it down. Without hydraulics, you can't control the HH-3A, so once we started seeing fluctuations in the primary hydraulic system pressure and started getting random kicks in the controls we started looking for a place to put it down. We put it in a rice paddy near a grove of trees. Everyone got out and about twenty minutes later two H-53s arrived from Quang Tri with a large security team.

"The next day, we pulled the main rotor blades off the helicopter and stuffed them into the back of an H-53 before it lifted off and then slung the helo back to Phu Bai with cables hooked to rings on the fuselage. When we got it on the ramp, we counted one hundred sixty-six 7.62 and 12.7mm holes in the fuselage as well as a couple of 12.7mm hits in the belly that we didn't know about, and the tail rotor blades looked like sieves."

"I know that's not the end of the story," Captain Mancuso prodded.

"No, sir, it's not." Josh put his can down carefully, as if he was measuring his words. "The CO of HC-7 is a commander by the name of Nagano and is based in Japan. He tried to have us arrested and court-martialed for carrying out unauthorized maintenance at an unauthorized base and flying an unauthorized mission. General Cruz wouldn't let us go back to Da Nang for a few days to let things cool down. When we flew back to PI to get a new helicopter, Nagano grounded us, saying we were unsafe."

The memories of the conversations still burned in his mind. Nagano had threatened to find something on which to base a court-martial, and no Marine General was getting in his way.

Mancuso held up his mug. "Often makes you wonder which side some people are on, doesn't it?"

"Yes, sir, it does." Josh understood the reference to his current situation. "I don't know who General Cruz spoke to, but a few days later, Nagano changes his tune and we're told to take another HH-3A to Yankee Station on the next carrier leaving Cubi."

"General Cruz gave me some more details on who he talked to in Nagano's chain of command, but you are the type of pilot we are looking for. He also told me about the conversation he had with you after he pinned Silver Stars on your chests." Mancuso reached for his cup of coffee and took a long sip. "I have a deal for you guys. I need an HH-3A and crew to support my ops. They involve inserting and extracting SEAL teams in interesting places. If you say yes, we'll read you in and tell you more. And, I promise you, all the shit you are getting from that great rescue in Haiphong Harbor will go away, and Nagano won't be able to bother you either. One more thing, and I don't know if this will make a difference, but Marty Cabot says hello and his team will be the one you'll be putting on the ground."

"I'm pretty sure my whole crew will go along. When do we start?"

"As soon as I can get you an HH-3A, and any maintenance people and parts you need to our compound at Cam Ranh. I need a list of the skills, and if you want, the names of the people you need so my yeoman can cut the orders."

Jack grabbed Josh's shoulder as soon as they got out of the Jeep after another wild ride to the HC-7 ramp. "Who's Marty Cabot?"

"A SEAL I worked with a lot on my last tour. We took his team in and out of Cambodia, Laos, and North Vietnam and a couple of other places. UCLA ROTC grad, was on their swim team, likes to surf and even ski a bit. You'll like him."

"So he's the Josh Haman of the SEAL community?"

"I wouldn't say that."

"Keeping up with one of you is enough. Two may be more than I can handle."

"Well, if you can't keep up, take notes. Or you can quit … I won't be offended."

"No, I'm hooked on this adrenaline-junkie thing. This will be a show worth telling my kids and grandkids about."

"If you live that long."

"Yeah, well, you keep saying two things: one, you're gonna die sometime; and two, you only get to do it once. It applies to me to."

The next morning, while both aviators were slogging through the pile of new messages on the clipboard, a courier arrived at the HC-7 hangar with the written orders from Captain Mancuso. By then, Josh had already made seven copies of the message, one for each member of his crew, one for each of their personnel files, and one for the admin file of message orders.

He'd also used the message as authority to select an HH-3A undergoing maintenance and was standing on one of the armored fold-down platforms that, when closed, was also an engine cowling, when Derek Van der Jagt yelled across the un-air conditioned hangar. The petty officer looked awkward and uncoordinated as he moved toward the helicopter to make sure that his aircraft commander heard him.

Van der Jagt had come to the Navy via the New York City court system. He excelled in school, but had a penchant for getting into trouble, which a psychiatrist would tell you were screams for the attention he never got from his widowed mother who struggled at being both a mother and breadwinner. A local court judge who was told about Van der Jagt's excellent academic record told the seventeen year old, "You have four choices: jail, Army, Navy, or Marine Corps. Pick one." The Air Force wasn't interested in defendants who appeared before the judge, and the one recruiter in the courtroom was from the Navy.

"Lieutenant Haman, sir, you have a call."

"What?" Haman yelled back from the platform where he was pre-flighting the left engine and left side of the rotor head.

"Commander Nagano is on the phone. Wants to talk to you and won't accept that you're not available."

"Tell him I'll be right there. Jack, finish the pre-flight. Hopefully, this won't take long." Josh climbed down and then jogged across the hangar. Even thought it was mid-May and not raining, the humidity was close to a hundred percent and his flight suit was a lot sweatier than when he'd started the pre-flight.

Van der Jagt handed him the phone and motioned the other enlisted men to leave the shaded area. Josh suspected that, at the other end of the line, Nagano was ensconced in his office, fuming over something.

When the squadron had been formed, Nagano, who was proud of his Nisei heritage, had established the command and administrative element, as he liked to refer to them, in vacant spaces at the Atsugi Naval Air Station near Yokosuka, Japan. The move had come after he found out that he would not get combat pay or the combat zone tax deduction by working from an office in the Philippines on his two-year tour as the unit's commanding officer. Nagano contended that Japan provided better access to fleet administrative support, despite the fact that the jungles and waters of the Philippines made for an ideal training base. He created Detachment 1, based at the Naval Air Station's Cubi Point in the Philippines, to provide heavy maintenance support to the detachments operating off ships in the Gulf of Tonkin. Det 1 had a bare bones personnel section to support its own operations and the men flying helicopters off carriers and other ships. Once ensconced at Atsugi, Nagano had only visited Cubi Point twice: once to inspect the facilities, and a second time because he was required to attend a conference on the air station. He never went to sea with any of his detachments.

Josh had met the overweight officer twice on his first tour: on his way out to the Philippines and Vietnam, and then on his way back to the States, when he was asked to stay at Atsugi for a few days and ordered to give Nagano a NATOPS check.

During the check ride, Josh pulled one engine to idle to simulate an engine failure. Nagano missed key memory items on the check list, and then he botched the run-on landing so badly Josh had to shove the idling engine back to the "normal" range and assume command of the helicopter. That was after Nagano couldn't hold a steady forty foot hover over the bay. Any one of these failures was enough to give the commander a "down." Josh remembered the conversation, after the flight when they were alone, in which he had tried to suggest to Nagano that he needed to stop flying.

Later, Josh had heard that the squadron NATOPS officer was afraid he'd get a bad performance evaluation, known in the Navy as a "fitness report," if he grounded Nagano. So, the NATOPS officer was willing to let Nagano continue to fly until he rolled a helo in a ball and killed someone besides himself. Josh thought of Nagano as the typical rear-echelon type who got people killed. Nobody wanted to fly with him because he was unsafe.

"Lieutenant Haman."

"Haman, this is Commander Nagano."

"Yes, sir, what can I do for you?"

"It is not what you can do for me, but what you can do for your career."

Josh took a deep breath and forced himself to listen.

"I just wanted to let you know that I spoke to General Hector Cruz, as well as with an Admiral Hastings on the CINCPAC staff. General Cruz had …"

Nagano paused and Josh knew the next words were not going to come out easy.

"Well, a lot of nice things to say about you and your crew. You did save seventeen of his Marines from certain death or capture in the DMZ. And, Admiral Hastings says that CINCPAC has decided not to pursue the judicial actions against you that I recommended. I have been directed to send you and your crew to Cam Ranh Bay as soon as you can get there. You're to select one of the helicopters at Cubi, make sure it is ready to go, and depart on the next ship with a helo deck headed to the Gulf."

"Thank you, sir." Josh thought that was the best thing to say.

"I know you and I don't agree on a lot of things, but I want you to be careful. You have the potential to be an excellent officer, but if I may, let me give you some advice. Fly only what you are authorized to fly. Not every mission will come out as well as your pick-up of the Marines. You tend to act like a cowboy and if you continue doing that, people will die and it will have a negative affect on your career, if you don't get yourself killed."

Josh had to restrain himself. Asshole. Nagano was worried about careers when they had guys shot down and waiting pick up a few miles from the beach, or SEALS being chased by bad guys. If he thought they could dash in and get a downed crew with a reasonable chance of getting in and out in one piece, he was going in. Josh waited a few seconds before speaking. "Commander, thank you, I'll keep that in mind."

"If you do, you won't get your helicopter all shot up like you did and put others at risk."

Risk? As in risk to your career. Josh bit his tongue. "I understand, sir."

"And, to put a fine point on it, you won't always have a two-star general or admiral around to cover for you."

Now Nagano was getting to the real point. General Cruz must have put him in his place, and when Nagano discussed administrative action with Admiral Hastings, whoever he was, he was probably told that a general court-martial would not be supported by CINCPAC. And since shit flows downhill, Nagano was now passing some on to him. Josh thought it best just get off the phone. "Sir, if there is nothing else, we've got to finish a preflight and get a test flight done so we'll have the helo ready to go. Just so you know, it has the side number Four Zero."

"Yes, please get Big Mother 40 back up so we can show it on our readiness report. General Cruz told me that the official certificates and paperwork for your medals from that mission are working their way through channels. Where do you want me to send them?"

"Cam Ranh Bay. That's where we're going to be based for the foreseeable future and they can forward it if needed. I'll tell the crew they're coming. Thank you, sir." Josh didn't want to have to carry the certificates around in his baggage. When they arrived, he could send them to his dad from the Navy base in South Vietnam, along with his latest letter.

"Good luck. I don't know what they are planning for you, but I am sure you will find it interesting."

"Thank you, sir." Josh waited for a dial tone before he hung up the phone.

"What was that about?" After Van der Jagt had said who was on the phone, Jack could listen to only one side of the call.

"I believe Nagano has seen the light." Josh pointed toward his friend. "He has suddenly gained wisdom via short conversations with General Hector Cruz and an Admiral Hastings, who is on the CINCPAC staff, in which he—Nagano—was in the 'receive,' as opposed to the 'transmit' mode. Commander Nagano has officially informed me that we are back on flight status and heading out to the Gulf when the helo is ready to go on the next ship that can carry us. The good commander was civil and encouraged me to think about my career as opposed to telling me that I am on the route to being thrown out of the Navy in disgrace. I call that progress."

"Indeed. Anything else?"

"Yeah, I'll get to tell the guys that the paperwork, medals, and citations are on their way."

"Why did they get Bronze Stars and we got Silver Stars? We were all there in the same helicopter sharing the same enemy fire?"

"That's the way the system works. The enlisted guys get one level lower than the pilots. The policy is that the HAC gets the top medal, then the co-pilot gets one lower, and then the crew are given medals another level down, with the senior air crewman getting the top medal and everyone else one level below. In this case, General Cruz was very specific on what he wanted and overrode, at least for us, the awards instruction. We got Silver Stars and everyone in the back got Bronze Stars. Anyway, I agree it doesn't make sense, but I don't make the rules. Some shithead at CINCPAC did. This is one windmill I don't want to take on."

WEDNESDAY, 13 DAYS LATER, MAY 31ST, 1972, 1021 LOCAL TIME, 20 MILES WEST OF HANOI

Gus Thomes was coming off a mission to destroy a bridge that was on a road that went from Hanoi into the Peoples' Republic of China. His F-105D was climbing past twelve thousand feet when he keyed the mike to execute what both General Jameson and he agreed was "progress" defined by an approved mission on the Thirteen Air Force ATO that let him bomb the valley to send a message that the Air Force knew something was going on there AND to freedom to choose his tactics.

"This is Ramrod One Six; I'm off the target with hung ordnance. Ramrod Five Five, you've got the lead. Ramrod Six Two will stay with me." To the others in the flight, Thomes' voice had that muffled hollow sound of someone wearing an oxygen mask, but it was perfectly audible.

"Ramrod Five Five, roger, I have the lead."

Gus cruise-climbed to about seventeen thousand feet to save fuel and rolled out on a different heading from that flown by the other sixteen F-105s from the 334th Tactical Fighter Squadron. Off to his right, he could see Ramrod Six Two, which also had a full load of six Mark 83 thousand-pound bombs and jamming pods on the outboard ordnance station on each wing. On flights deep into North Vietnam, each F-105 carried two electronic counter measure pods set to broadcast on the frequencies used to guide SA-2 missiles.

At four hundred knots, it took only about ten minutes to reach the valley which Gus recognized from the earlier mission. He scanned the jungle below, looking for something to aim at. He picked a U-shaped notch in the ridgeline and decided to aim at the valley floor at the base of the ridge.

He waggled his wings and got a similar rocking acknowledgement from his wingman. Satisfied, Gus shoved the throttle up to full military power and rolled the F-105 into a sixty-degree dive.

With his nose down and the Thud accelerating fast, he put the piper on the gun sight on the floor of the valley at the base of the notch, and at ten thousand feet, released all his bombs and pulled the stick back and to the left to roll the big fighter bomber so he could see where his bombs hit. The concussion sent rings of humid air out from where the bombs exploded, but other than smoke from the explosions, he was convinced that all he and his wingman had done was turn trees into matchsticks. Still, he hoped the twelve bombs sent a message.

WEDNESDAY, SAME DAY, MAY 31ST, 1972, 1040 LOCAL TIME, VENOM BASE

The explosions followed by the ringing phone brought Thai from his bathroom to his office. He listened for a few seconds before hanging up, then buckled his pants and ran down to his command center where Koniev was waiting.

"What do we know?" Thai asked Loi.

"Not much. American fighter bombers, which we think were F-105s, just dive-bombed the valley."

"What did they hit?"

"Nothing. The bombs landed in the southeast end of the valley and may have damaged the access road, which should be easy to fix. We are checking on that now." Major Loi hung up the phone. "We didn't have any men in the area other than the men on the observation platform."

"Colonel Koniev, any idea of what happened and why?"

"No, Colonel Thai. I think it was just two F-105s because the rest of their formation passed to the north of us about five minutes ahead of them. We tracked them to Hanoi, and two airplanes hung back after making their dives on the target. Perhaps they couldn't keep up with the others and then dropped their bombs. We need to see if we have any radio intercepts so we can try to figure out why they dropped their bombs here. We know this is an area of interest, but this attack, like the one earlier, appeared to be random and not part of a campaign to destroy the base. Believe me, if the Americans wanted to bomb us to hell, they could do it no matter how many missiles we fired."

"I am not so sure. Again, do you think they know where we are?"

Koniev paused for a few seconds, contemplating what to tell his counterpart and then decided to tell him the truth. "No, I don't." He could not add that there had not been any missions in the Air-Tasking Orders that sent airplanes to bomb this area.

THURSDAY, NEXT DAY, JUNE 1, 1972, 0815 LOCAL TIME, CAM RANH BAY, 180 MILES NORTH OF SAIGON, SOUTH VIETNAM

"What are we doing here?" Jack looked at the table in front of him that had several different kinds of rifles and pistols in rows, with their barrels pointing to the Gulf of Tonkin. The only ones he recognized were the AK-47, the M-16, and the .45. Why were the Russian guns there? He barely qualified with the .38 caliber pistol back in San Diego as part of the RAG syllabus for pilots and air crewmen going to HC-7. That half day on the range was the first time in his life he'd ever fired a gun.

"Practice and train. If you want to operate with us, you have to shoot like we do." Marty Cabot picket up a .45-caliber Model 1911. "If the taxi has to be parked someplace at an unplanned location and we have to walk home or wait for another one, we need to be confident that you can help us stay alive. And, since I am sure that none of you have practiced our drills recently, we're going to practice every day we can. Once we are confident in your marksmanship, we'll teach you our basic tactics and then take you on some patrols so you can learn how to move through the jungle and not sound like a herd of elephants."

Jack nodded and looked at the targets set on frames in the sand.

"So," Marty continued, "we're going to start with the .45 and then shift to the rifles and then to the M-60, which you are already familiar with, and one of our special toys, the Stoner. We'll also get you familiar with the Soviet weapons the North Vietnamese carry for two reasons. One, so you know what they sound like, and two, in case you need to use one, you'll know how. Questions before the Master Chief goes over some safety rules."

Heads shook no. Marty could see Josh's smiling face, knowing his friend enjoyed shooting. "Okay, this is, as Lieutenant Haman and Petty Officer Van der Jagt know, not going to be just standing here and pumping rounds into the Gulf. Once we're comfortable that you are more dangerous to the enemy than to us, we'll move into shoot-and-move drills. And, oh yes, there will be some competition involved in which the low man buys the beer." He turned to look at his friend. "I have to win some money back because your HAC keeps beating not only me, but many members of our team."

Chapter 9
RESCUE

"What's eating you?" D'Onofrio put his hand on his friend's shoulder as they sat down in the bunker used as a mess hall for the base's officers. They'd just finished refueling and securing the helicopter's main rotor blades to the fuselage in a revetment after an uneventful flight south down the spine of North Vietnam. X-Ray, near where the Khe Sanh Firebase used to be, had been picked as a staging area as it was about ninety minutes flying time from Sierra Six's operating area. Earlier that morning, Marty Cabot and five other SEALs had jumped out on a ridgeline in the first sector to be searched.

"Here; read for yourself." Josh pulled a folded, well-read letter out of the breast pocket of his flight suit and shoved at his copilot. "I got it yesterday before we left Cam Ranh Bay."

Shit, Jack thought, *this looks like a dear John letter. If it is, I'll kill the bitch when I get back home.* He carefully unfolded the sheets, which had the pungent-sweet mix of sweat and expensive perfume, and recognized Carla's handwriting, which he'd seen in the few letters they had exchanged since he left San Diego. For a milli-second, he wondered why Carla was writing to Josh and prayed it was not bad news.

May 27th, 1972

Dear Josh,

I hope this letter gets to you quickly and you are well. By now you must be pulling your hair out because you probably haven't heard from Natalie for a few days. She asked me to write this letter because she is very, very ill. As you know, since the accident, she has had one blood infection after another as well as swelling and tenderness in her stump.

Yesterday, she was at our house and looked very feverish so I took her temperature. It was 102 so I took her to the UC San Diego Medical

Center Emergency Room where my dad works. They did a blood test and immediately admitted her to the hospital and began pumping her full of antibiotics. One of the ER doctors is a Navy Reservist who just came back from Vietnam and he had some X-rays taken and believed, after he talked to her for about thirty minutes, that he knew the cause of the infections. I don't know what all the medical terms are but he is sure there is a large abscess inside her stump and the bone is, to use the doctor's words, dying. He said it was like gangrene from the inside and if not treated, is fatal.

This morning they made a decision to remove what the remains of her leg at the hip. The docs are convinced that the abscess and the diseased bone are causing the infections. The doctors told her that she would keep getting weaker and weaker and they might lose her to the fever. They felt that, since her fever was slowly coming down, the risk of surgery was less than losing her to the infection, which would spread throughout her body and permanently damage her organs and ultimately, when they went septic, kill her. That's when she told me she said to take her leg off and signed the papers. She's over twenty-one or we would have had to wait for her parents.

I called Natalie's parents as soon as they admitted her to the hospital. They were on a vacation near Bodega Bay and Natalie had their itinerary in her purse. They got here just after she came out of surgery.

We're all outside the intensive care unit where Natalie is resting comfortably. The great news is that her fever seems to be staying down despite the operation and is now below 100, which is good!

The doctors are very optimistic that she will make a full recovery. Her one question to the surgeon when they told her what they wanted to do was "Will I recover in time to fly to Hawaii in September?" When they told her "yes," she said, "What are you waiting for, get started." That's my friend Natalie; all she was thinking of was seeing you again.

By the way, the answer she got was that it should take about three to four weeks for the amputation to heal, maybe longer, but she should be able to make the flight. How fast she builds up her strength and stamina will be up to her. Knowing her, she'll be a workout maniac!

She also told me that she would tape a letter to you as soon as she can. Take care.

Carla

Josh waited until his friend looked up. "I was wondering why I hadn't heard from her. Now I find out she was lying in intensive care when this letter was written and she's probably alive, but could be dead. I'm out here in the fucking boondocks and don't know. Look at the date."

"I take it as good news. They found the problem and Natalie made it through surgery okay. It's just a matter of time and she'll be back to normal." Jack folded the letter, paying careful attention to the creases, and then slid it back into the envelope, trying not to get the grime from his hands onto the paper.

"Thanks, I hope so... God only knows when we'll get mail again."

"I'm confident you'll have another letter when we get back to Cam Ranh."

"Lieutenants, the boss wants to see you." A Marine captain was standing in the doorway with his rifle in his hand and two bandoliers of magazines for his M-16 slung over his shoulders. "He wants to know how fast you can get airborne, and can you act as an airborne FAC?"

"Short answer is less than two minutes from the time we get to the helicopter and yes, if need be. Why?"

"You'll find out." The captain smiled. "Follow-me. The CP is just a few hundred feet away."

On the way to the command center, which was at the highest point on the base, he could see eight inch howitzers and 155mm artillery pieces were dug into the ground so their barrels looked like telephone poles stuck into the ground at odd angles. A recent rain had tamped down the dust and outside the door of the command center, the beds of two U.S. Military M274 Truck, Platform, Utility, 1/2 Ton, 4X4, a.k.a. "Mules" were piled high with ammo cans. He could tell from the size of the olive-drab boxes which ones were full of magazines for M-16s, two and fifty round belts of 7.62mm for the M-60s and hundred round belts of .50 caliber for the M-2 heavy machine gun the Marines dubbed "Ma Deuce."

"Welcome to Firebase X-Ray" The three officers shook hands. "I'm Colonel Nathan Becker. For the record, Firebase X-Ray's primary mission is to interdict traffic moving down the Ho Chi Minh Trail and from the DMZ, as well as to provide artillery support for Marine and South Vietnamese Army units operating in the area. Since Khe Sanh was shut down, we are the only large Marine outpost that is close to the northwest corner of South Vietnam. There are about eight hundred Marines based here on X-Ray."

"Sir, thank you for allowing us to use your base as a staging area while we wait to extract a team. It shortens our response and transit time by over an hour or more. We should be gone in three or four days."

"My pleasure to have you here. When General Hector Cruz calls and asks a favor, my answer, ninety-nine percent of the time, is yes, and if it's in the one percent range, then I ask for twenty-four hours to figure out how to say yes."

Both Jack and Josh smiled at the colonel's reference to Cruz, which indicated that the two had more than a casual relationship.

"There are two reasons why I asked you to come down here. One, I feel obligated to warn you that helicopters that spend the night here are mortar magnets. We expect to have more than an occasional round shot at your helo. Let's hope they don't get lucky. Good news is the revetment we put the helo in is out of range for anything they can shoot at it unless they use an 85mm gun. They've been reluctant to do that lately because we respond with a barrage of eight inch and 155mm shells that end the discussion.

"Second, if you are here, we could use you either tonight or tomorrow night to act as a spotter. We're getting info from our recon teams that the NVA may hit us sometime in the next forty-eight to seventy-two hours and, based on what you said, you may still be here. This won't be the first time, because they don't like us shelling the Ho Chi Minh Trail, so every few weeks they take a crack at us, which we think they are about to do again."

"No problem, sir. If you want, we can take one of your officers with us as a spotter. If we get airborne, we have about four to five hours of gas. Getting the chopper safely airborne fast will be the trick. If we take off in the midst of a firefight, there's the risk of us crashing someplace on the firebase."

"That's what General Cruz told me you'd say. I need you to spot the bad guys' movements. We'll fire a bunch of flare rounds to light up the kill zones, but it will be a big help if you can give me a picture of what's going on from overhead. The NVA typically throw two or three regiments at us—that's two to three thousand men. Any close air support you can provide with the mini-gun would be most appreciated."

"Sir, how much warning can you give us?"

"We don't know when the attack will start. If we're lucky, we get maybe an hour. Some nights we get just a few minutes. We never know. My recon teams are coming in tonight and I'll know more then."

"We'll be ready, sir. My crew was planning to stay at one of the bunkers near the helo pad. I'll have them take the blade tie-downs off so all we have to do is start the engines, engage the rotors, and go. Where do you want Jack and me?"

"Stay in the officers' bunker so we know where you are. My ops guys will brief you after we talk so you know the lay of the land. This way, when the shit hits the fan, we can tell you where we need help and you'll be familiar with the base."

"Yes, sir. In the meantime, we'll try to get some sleep. We've been up all night."

TUESDAY, NEXT DAY, JUNE 6, 1972,
2105 LOCAL TIME, VENOM BASE

"Koniev, Rokossovsky here."

"And what can I do for the good colonel at this late hour?"

"We just heard from Moscow. It is, as you know, late afternoon there and they probably don't have a lot to do on a nice summer afternoon." Rokossovsky knew Koniev would enjoy his sarcastic reference to their comrades in the center of the Soviet universe. "They are convinced from reading the Americans' messages going back and forth to Hawaii and Washington that they are going to make a maximum effort to find and destroy Venom."

"Are you telling me that they are going to try to attack us with hundreds of fighter bombers or B-52s, or launch a ground assault, or both?"

"Moscow doesn't know how they are going to do it, just that an attack will be coming after they find Venom. Right now they don't know where it is, so they cannot attack. I would not be surprised if they use commandos like they did back in nineteen-seventy when they tried to rescue their POWs held at the Son Tay camp. Expect something in the next few weeks."

"Interesting." Koniev's mind was racing. That vindicated Thai's obsession with realistic training and plans.

"That's an odd choice of words."

Koniev wasn't annoyed just surprised that Rokossovsky didn't see the irony of his comments. "You're telling me that Moscow is certain that we are going to be attacked but can't tell me when or how. All they can say is that one is coming. Then you tell me the enemy doesn't know where we are so they can't attack us. Doesn't that seem odd to you?"

"I am just passing on what the geniuses in Moscow think."

"We haven't seen any drones or reconnaissance aircraft in the past few days, so how do we know if they have located Venom?" He'd already told Rokossovsky about the latest nuisance bombing by the two F-105s. The intelligence report said that they were just releasing hung ordnance and the location was a coincidence. Koniev was, when he got the report, skeptical, thinking that it could be part of a deception operation but also realized that it could be accurate.

"We don't, but we hope we see it in their message traffic." Exasperated, Rokossovsky wanted to end the debate. "Look, I was asked to give you this information. I've done my job, now you do yours."

And what, you asshole, is that, besides keep shooting down the Americans, knowing that every time we launch a missile, we increase the possibility that it will bring a rain of bombs down on our heads? And then what was he supposed to do? And if the Americans knew where they were, they would've been bombed day and night after their anti-radar missiles took out our radar.

"Can I share this with Colonel Thai?"

"No!" The annoyed, shouted word came through the tinny sound of the secure phone and he was left listening to an aggravating dial tone.

Koniev wondered what Thai really knew. The Vietnamese surely had their sources. How could he broach the idea to Thai that the Soviets were pretty sure that the Americans would attack? *We just don't know how or when.* They couldn't stop operating, because the North Vietnamese would complain, nor could they increase the risk of being located or they'd be attacked, so they'd just have to pick their targets to minimize the chances that the Americans would locate the base.

WEDNESDAY, NEXT DAY, JUNE 7, 1972, 0016 LOCAL TIME, FIREBASE X-RAY, I CORPS AREA OF OPERATIONS, SOUTH VIETNAM

The crump of exploding mortar rounds and artillery shells jolted Josh awake. Jack had volunteered to take the 2400-0400 watch at the command center; Josh had gone to bed in a spare rack.

During the past two days, while waiting for a possible early extraction, they'd flown Becker and his intelligence officer around the area, looking for signs of NVA activity. Each three-hour flight covered a specific sector and gave the colonel an opportunity to take a detailed look that convinced him that, despite the Marine close air support that he had called in and the artillery strikes he'd ordered, the NVA was massing for an attack against X-Ray. Becker thought that the attack would begin about 0130 that night; if anything changed, he would send a runner to get him.

Before lying down on his back in his flight suit, he had hung his M-16 and bandoleer of ten thirty-round magazines on a hook welded to the bed frame and stuffed his .45 into the thigh pocket where it would be easy to reach. Three magazines, each with seven rounds, went into the leg pockets of his flight suit instead of the chest pockets. This way, if he turned over, the sharp steel corners of the magazines wouldn't poke him in his chest and wake him up.

As he emerged from the bunker, a Marine shoved him into a trench seconds before an 85mm shell smacked into the red earth a few feet from where they were standing. The dive and the blast sent his M-16 and bandoleer flying in one direction as Josh tumbled in another.

Josh could see tracers were flying everywhere in the dim light from the flares; he was certain that trying to make it to the command center was suicide. He turned to ask the Marine, who a few seconds before had been lying near him, what was the best route to the command center, but the man was gone.

Josh chambered a round in the .45 without thinking, and jogged, head down, along the trench toward the sound of machine guns and the occasional thump of a mortar. As he turned a corner, two NVA soldiers carrying satchel charges in one hand and their AK-47s in the other jumped in the trench. Josh fired two rounds at the closest man, who staggered backward from the impact of the 230-grain slugs. Josh beat the second man to the trigger and fired three more rounds, one of which hit the man in the face. The first man was still struggling to bring his AK to bear when Josh fired a round into his forehead.

Around the next corner of the trench that zig-zagged away from the bunkhouse, he heard a .50 caliber machine gun and then felt the concussion from its muzzle blast. Clearly, this wasn't the command post! "What can I do to help?" Josh asked the man directing fire from the mortar tube and three machine guns in a large pit surrounded by sandbags.

"The first thing you can do is put the .45 away. Do you know how to load a mortar?"

Josh nodded. His total experience was dropping a couple of rounds into a mortar tube during one of his ROTC summer "cruises" when he spent a week with the Marines. It would do for a start. Sand flew as shrapnel from two mortar rounds ripped jagged holes in the three-sandbag-thick wall. Gunners and their loaders were pumping out bursts from their M-60s through apertures that looked to be two-sandbags-wide and two tall.

"Good. Drop two rounds in and then stop." The gunnery sergeant looked at him again. "If I want you to change your point of aim, I'll call out left or right and tell you how many stakes to slide into the base plate. Each stake around the tube is ten degrees. Don't worry about the range, we're zeroed in on the wire. Just slide the base plate to change the point of aim."

Josh nodded and picked up two rounds. As he dropped the first into the mortar, he held the second ready to go until he heard the faint plunk of the round leaving the tube, then he dropped the second one in and heard it fire. The gunny grabbed him by the arm. "When I want you to shoot flare rounds, I'll let you know. They're in a separate pile over there."

Another nod from the aviator was followed by the distinctive sound of the mortar being fired, followed by a harsh white glow from a burning flare about two thousand feet above them. His next round was drowned out by the staccato barking of the M-2 .50-caliber machine gun at the front of the pit and the M-60s on either side.

"We need more ammo!" the gunnery sergeant yelled to no one in particular. "You two!" He pointed at Josh and one of the other Marines in the pit. "Get as much M-60 ammo as you can carry. Then go back and get some fifty caliber rounds."

Josh followed the Marine down the slit trench to a bunker, popping his head up long enough to see that he should have turned left to go to the command center instead of going right. He kept his head above the sandbags long enough to see his helicopter still in the revetment and tracer rounds spitting out from several positions on the revetment. He hoped it wasn't damaged beyond what they could repair quickly. Loud smacking sounds and a spray of sand brought him back to reality.

"Carry these." The Marine helped him sling a pack with twelve 40mm mortar rounds on his back, then stacked four olive-drab cans, each with a 250-round belt of 7.62mm ammo. Before picking up the cans, each of which weighed about fifteen pounds, he helped the Marine shoulder a similar pack with mortar rounds and grabbed the four cans before they both headed back down the trench to the firing pit. Josh dropped two cans by each of the M-60s.

"Now you know the way, go get some more!"

Josh looked at the gunny, took a deep breath and headed back down the trench. As he came out of the ammo bunker, this time with two cans of M-2 .50-cal, another pack of mortar rounds, and a belt of 7.62s around his shoulders, a burst from an AK-47 stitched a line into the sandbags just behind his head and walked down the dirt. To avoid the next burst, Josh flopped to the ground amid a pile of empty ammo cans and let go of what was tucked under his arms and in his hands before moving toward the source. As he turned the corner, two NVA soldiers dropped into the trench and Josh got off two rounds with his .45 at the first one who staggered, but did not go down. The other man tried to stab him with the bayonet on his AK but it caught in the sandbags lining the trench, which gave Josh a chance to fire two more rounds at point blank range into his chest. To make sure, he fired a third to the head before he turned around to make sure that the first soldier was dead.

He didn't want to trip over dead NVA soldiers, so he heaved their bloody bodies out of the trench, retrieved the ammo cans and returned to the mortar and machine-gun pit to find a mortar round had collapsed the back wall. The two Marines that took most of the blast were lying in the bottom of the pit holding bandages against the worst of their wounds. The gunnery sergeant was applying pressure bandage to a wound in his side, so Josh took over one of the M-60s and began firing. He switched from one M-60 to the other, helped by a Marine who shoved ammo boxes at him and pointed out targets while he tried to keep himself from bleeding to death by holding a bandage to his gut.

At 0336, the gunnery sergeant put a hand on his shoulder. "Cease firing, cease firing."

Josh had been spitting out short bursts at NVA soldiers retreating through gaps in the wire. Josh took a moment to look around and realized he was in the fighting position closest to the camp's gate. As he peered over the top sandbag, he could see bodies and moaning men in tan uniforms strewn around the camp's open areas, and larger clusters in the wire and by the gate.

The gunnery sergeant saluted him when he saw the wings on Haman's flight suit. "Lieutenant Haman, you can fight in my hole any time."

Still high on adrenaline, Josh flopped down on a pile of empty shell casings, not feeling the sharp edges on his butt and thighs, and helped a medic tend to the wounded Marines before helping carry them to the camp's infirmary.

"Where have you been?" Jack looked at his dirty, exhausted friend.

"Out there…" Josh waved an arm toward the perimeter. "Where were you?" came out muffled as Josh drank from the water bottle.

"In the command center like I was supposed to be. Someone told Colonel Becker that I am, shall we say, inexperienced with firearms and he said the safest place for me was in the command center because that way I wouldn't kill any innocent Marines."

"How many did we lose?"

"No one in the crew has a scratch. Colonel Becker said that they have about two dozen seriously wounded that will have to be Medevac'd and five dead."

"How's the helo?"

"They're looking at it now. I talked to Van der Jagt a few minutes ago; he said it has a few extra holes in the fuselage but nothing a little thousand-mile-an-hour tape couldn't fix. We'll need daylight to make sure." Jack looked at his friend. "You look like hell. I'll take care of getting the bird ready to fly."

Josh, slumped in a chair, had just finished guzzling a bottle of water when Colonel Becker walked up to the aviator. "Lieutenant Haman, I just talked to Master Gunny Longstreet down in the pit by the main gate. He had a lot of very nice things to say about you. If his position had been overrun, we'd have been in a world of hurt. He said, despite the fact you are a swabbie helo pilot, he could remake you into a fine Marine officer. He also said, if it wasn't for you, his whole team would be dead and this command post would now be crawling with NVA."

"Tell him thank you. But I really didn't know what I was doing."

"I don't believe that for a minute, Lieutenant. For the record, this is the third tour Master Gunny Longstreet has been with me here in 'Nam and he doesn't give out that kind of praise easy. He comes from a long line of fine military men. His lineage goes back to a Civil War general by the name of Longstreet. You may have heard of him?"

Josh nodded numbly. "Yes, sir, I have."

WEDNESDAY, SAME DAY, JUNE 7, 1972, 1530 LOCAL TIME, FIREBASE X-RAY, I CORPS AREA OF OPERATIONS, SOUTH VIETNAM

Colonel Becker had come to a skidding, dirt-spraying stop in front of the HH-3A at 1430 with news that Sierra Six was being chased by bad guys and needed to be extracted as soon as they could get there. By 1530, Josh and his crew had been airborne for almost an hour. Jack was head down plotting their route north, staying one leg ahead of the one they were flying.

"Jack, we're going to get one pass at the LZ. If they're on time, we should get in and out before the North Vietnamese show up and ruin our party. The fact that they asked for a pick-up in daylight tells me they are in a world of hurt."

"What about some support?" Jack was trying to mentally match the photo of the LZ to the contour lines on the map.

"Until we get a call from either Red Crown or Billiard Ball or someone else, we have to assume we're going in alone. If we get help, great. If not, we get Marty and his team out by ourselves. Simple as that."

"And you have a plan to do that without getting us shot down?"

"Not yet. Not until I know which LZ it is and I can see it."

"Based on how fast we're covering ground, I'm estimating that we're about thirty minutes out from the closest LZ and about thirty-five from the farthest."

WEDNESDAY, SAME DAY, JUNE 7, 972, 1615 LOCAL TIME, 90 NAUTICAL MILES NORTH-NORTHWEST OF FIREBASE X-RAY ALONG THE NORTH VIETNAMESE/LAOTIAN BORDER

Forty miles north of Big Mother 40, Marty Cabot and his five SEALs were spread out in an inverted-V of three two-man fire teams. Cabot was sitting with his back against a tree filling his lungs with the hot humid air.

"How far do you think we are from our primary LZ?" he whispered to Chief Jenkins, who was handling navigation.

"Best guess is that we're about ten minutes away. We'll need to make sure we'll be the only ones there."

Marty pointed at his radioman and made the gesture that he wanted to use the radio. The cracking sound of a dry branch froze all of them for a second before they eased their M-16s into firing position without making a sound. A few seconds passed before the first North Vietnamese soldiers appeared downhill from their position, headed toward the clearing that was their LZ.

After making sure all the NVA troops had passed, Sierra Six moved diagonally away from its position. Twenty minutes later, Marty picked up the handset and cupped his hands around the mouthpiece. "Big Mother 40, Sierra Six."

"Sierra Six, Big Mother 40. Go," Jack answered immediately.

"Extract Rossignol Two Zero Three, repeat Rossignol Two Zero Three. ETA plus thirty. Copy?"

"Rossignol Two Zero Three in plus thirty. We'll be there."

Josh waited until Jack released the mike. "Where's Rossignol Two Zero Three from here?"

"About ten miles. Head zero two five to start. That should get us close. What's the plan?"

"Are there any other clearings nearby?"

Jack looked at the chart and then pulled out several photos from the nav bag that contained charts, photos, and a NATOPS manual. The LZ on each photo was circled with black magic marker to make them easy to see. "Yeah, two. There are a couple of terraced rice paddies about two miles away and another smaller clearing in a large group of trees about a mile away. Why?"

"Here's what we're going to do: We'll pass over Rossi Two Zero Three at ninety knots headed toward the smaller one of the two. Then we'll slow up and orbit over the paddies near the smaller clearings as if we're waiting for them. If we take fire, we'll move away and then when Marty calls again, we'll dash toward Rossi Two Zero Three and pick them up."

Jack looked at his friend wide-eyed as if to ask, "Is that it?"

"Big Mother 40, this is Sandy Two Oh and Sandy Two Two. Understand you may need some help. Sandy Two One and Sandy Two Six are about five minutes behind us. We understand that some fast-movers are also on the way. ETA plus fifteen. Copy?"

"Sandy Two Oh and Two Two. Welcome to the party. Glad you are here. Brief in about five mikes. TACAN on Channel 95. Call when you've got a visual or within five miles. Over."

Josh gave Jack a thumbs up. "It's gonna be a walk in the park."

WEDNESDAY, SAME DAY, JUNE 7, 1972,
1654 LOCAL TIME, VENOM BASE

"What's going on?" Koniev had been watching the radar scopes in one of the missile control vans and had seen the converging blips on an area about thirty kilometers south of Venom.

Colonel Thai, who was standing behind one of his radar operators, spoke without turning around. "The Americans are trying to pick up a reconnaissance team that we've been chasing for three days. I trained the commander, but he has only three under-strength companies because all the men are being sent to the south and what he has is not enough. If he is lucky, his companies will have about half the men they are supposed to have. They thought they had them trapped twice, but each time they got away. From what we have heard on the radio, the Americans may escape."

"Do the Americans send these teams in often?"

"Yes. Sometimes one or two a month. They are very tough to catch, and when you do, expect to get a very bloody nose."

WEDNESDAY, SAME DAY, JUNE 7, 1972, 1715 LOCAL TIME,
LZ ROSSIGNOL 203

"Sierra Six. Say location in the LZ."

"Middle, east side. Tell me when you want me to pop a smoke."

"Sierra Six, stand by. Sandys Two Oh and Two Two, do you have a visual on 40?"

"Roger that, we're about three thousand feet above and behind you with one pair on either side. Sandy Two Oh has the lead and Sandys Two One and Two Six have joined the party."

"Sandy Two Oh, LZ is to north, about five miles from my present position. It is egg-shaped and about a quarter mile long. Sierra Six is going to pop a smoke on my command. When he does, plaster both the west and north sides of the LZ and then the south side after I land. Feel free to suppress any enemy you see shooting at us."

"Sandy Two Oh copies for the flight. Good luck."

"Two minutes to the LZ. It is just to the right of the nose." Jack pointed in the general direction.

"Got it. Tell Marty to pop the smoke."

Josh could feel the concussion from the string of five-hundred pound bombs dropped by Sandy Two Two that passed the HH-3A as it began to slow. He timed his entry into the LZ to allow about thirty seconds to pass so the shrapnel from the bombs could fall to the ground. Even as he flared, Josh felt the heat from the blast and the fires along the tree line through the open side window.

Orange smoke wafted up from the elephant grass, making the pick-up location easy to spot. The men of Sierra Six were clearly visible along the tree line and Van der Jagt didn't have to use the mini-gun and the NVA was nowhere to be seen. While the SEALS were clambering on board through the cargo door on the right side, the helicopter was jolted by a series of large explosions. Everyone on board who was looking out could see and feel the dirt and debris raining down through the rotors.

"You okay, Big Mother 40?"

"No sure yet, but we think so. What happened?"

"Big Mother 40, this is Sandy Two Oh. We got a very large secondary explosion on the south side of the LZ. It looks like we hit a pile of ordnance hidden in the trees or a tunnel, because it's still burning and exploding. Suggest you get out as soon as you can."

"Big Mother 40 has everyone aboard. Lifting."

They could feel the concussion of each explosion in the southern end of the LZ as it happened. Josh pulled the collective almost to the upper stop and dumped the nose to get the helicopter out of the area as quickly as he could. As he did, everyone on board heard and then felt another, larger explosion which stood the HH-3A on its nose when it was still less than twenty feet from the ground. Josh hauled back on the cyclic and pulled the cyclic up to the stop and watched as the tips of the rotor blades chewed through the top of the elephant grass before the helicopter began to climb. If the tips of the big helo's rotor blades had hit the ground, he'd have lost control and they would have been incinerated in an out-of-control fireball. It had been close—maybe a foot difference between fire and flight.

As they passed one thousand feet, Josh motioned to Jack to take over flying.

"Josh, that was the first time I've ever seen or heard of using the rotor blades of an H-3 as a lawnmower!"

Josh held up his middle finger on his right hand. With Jack flying and the immediate danger passed, now that they were following what they believed was a relatively safe route south into the Republic of South Vietnam, Josh looked back into the cabin to check on the team. The SEALS were sprawled out on the cabin floor sleeping despite the piercing, high-pitched engine whine and noise from the transmission amid piles of equipment. Marty said thanks over the intercom as soon as they were climbing to altitude but other than that, few words were spoken.

WEDNESDAY, SAME DAY, JUNE 7, 1972, 1730 LOCAL TIME, VENOM BASE

Colonel Thai had started toward the door of his hooch when the secure phone rang. For a second, he debated not answering and then put the handset to his ear.

"Colonel, General Van Dong is on the phone. May I put him through?"

Thai almost snapped and said, "Of course you can, you idiot," but caught himself. He was annoyed and impatient because the call was delaying a trip to visit B company after its commander made repeated mistakes during a training exercise with live ammunition, first in pursuing an enemy patrol and then stumbling into a simulated ambush. He took a deep breath before picking up the ringing phone. "Good evening, Comrade General," he said, forcing himself to be pleasant while he wondered what the general who tended to call at the end of the work day to give a task that had to be competed by the morning wanted.

"Good evening, Colonel Thai. I would like to pass along some information that you should find interesting."

The understatement in the reedy voice got Thai's attention. He sat down and pulled his pad and pen into a position to take notes.

Marc Liebman

"First, I don't know if you had heard, but today one of your former students failed to catch an American SEAL team with the call sign Sierra Six, which was rescued by a helicopter we are sure was based at Cam Ranh Bay. We must do a better job catching these teams when we give tour commanders what we believe is very accurate intelligence. The Americans outwitted the battalion commander. I may bring you back to Hanoi for a day to review this action."

And by implication, assuming that battalion commander was using the tactics I taught, him, he'll be reviewing me. How can I be blamed? I wasn't there. It sounded like a witch hunt, and some poor officer was going to have his career ruined, probably by something out of his control. Facts be dammed, the general staff wants someone to blame.

Thai wanted to interrupt the General, but thought better of it. He knew from experience that army headquarters had assigned a battalion which was, in all likelihood, a couple of under-strength and maybe under-trained companies. The battalion commander either didn't have enough men to set a trap or the area he was given was much too large for the number of men under his command. He thought maybe he'd ask later after the General finished, but it was probably best left unsaid. He made a mental note to see if he could find out through officers he knew.

"As our former colonial occupiers liked to say, what will be will be." The General paused and Thai knew that the silence meant the second part of the conversation was about to begin. "We have learned that the American SEAL base at Cam Ranh now has two of those black helicopters with the call sign of Big Mother; one is designated Big Mother 40 and the other Big Mother 16. We found that notable because it is usual to have one helicopter at the American naval base and it stays for only a few days. Our sources in the south believe that both will be staying for a while. Big Mother 40 was the one that made the pick-up of the SEAL team, Sierra Six. We know that for sure because we recorded all their transmissions."

That was nice to know, but Thai wondered how it affected him. He'd listened to the recordings before but it had not helped him catch the Americans.

"You might want to write this down." The voice sounded tiny, almost like the small man who owned it. "We now know the pilot of Big Mother 40 is Joshua Haman, and Sierra Six, which just escaped our grasp today, is led by a SEAL lieutenant by the name of Martin Cabot. Our intelligence is ninety percent sure that Cabot was the team leader that chewed up your unit in those two firefights in Cambodia."

Thai sat back in his chair as if he'd been shot. "Sir, I thought the Americans spent just one year in Vietnam?"

"Some Marines, Green Berets, and SEALs make several tours. This is both officers' second tours and, from what we have gathered from announcements in the American papers, Haman and Cabot have some of the Americans' highest decorations for bravery."

"General Dong, sir, why are you telling me this?"

"We believe, and this is an educated guess by our intelligence officers based on the reports they are getting from the south, that Cabot will lead a reconnaissance mission to find Venom. His pilot will be, according to our intelligence officers, Haman."

"Thank you for telling me, sir. We are ready for them."

"Do not share what I just told you with your fellow officers or the Russians. We don't want them getting cold feet and pulling out."

"Sir, I understand."

FRIDAY, 2 DAYS LATER, JUNE 9, 1972, 1545 LOCAL TIME, CAM RANH BAY, 180 MILES NORTH OF SAIGON, SOUTH VIETNAM

"Attention on deck." Master Chief Petty Officer Tannenbaum made sure the door to the debriefing room was wide open. Marty Cabot along with Josh and Jack jumped to attention causing several of the folding metal chairs to clatter to the concrete floor.

"As you were, gentleman," General Cruz said as he came in, followed by Captain Mancuso and a two-star admiral wearing wings. "Let me introduce you to Admiral Hastings, CINCPAC's Chief of Staff for Operations. Lieutenant Cabot, I want you to tell him what you just told Captain Mancuso earlier today which he passed on to me. Admiral Hastings is on his way back to CINCPAC and he needs to hear it right from the horse's mouth."

"Yes, sir." Marty re-rolled out the map they'd been studying. "We did all the planning by the book for what should have been a routine reconnaissance mission inside North Vietnam. The insertion went as planned but as soon as we were on ground, it was clear the NVA knew where we were operating, so I assumed the mission was compromised and began moving toward our extraction LZs."

"Why do you think that?"

"Couple of things. First, normally, it takes a least day or two for them to begin tracking us. Yeah, they hear and maybe even see the helo bringing us in, but we do fake insertions to disguise where we land. It confuses them a bit and lets us get away from the insertion LZ, and unless we stumble into one of their units we have a head start. We found signs that they had all the extraction LZs staked out and were waiting for us. All three landing zones were listed in the mission plan which was messaged to CINCPAC. My instinct said change the insertion point, so I had Lieutenant Haman drop us off in a back-up LZ that wasn't listed on any message traffic."

"Then what?"

"I decided to change the rules of the game. To evade, we started following them and watched the NVA set up ambushes for the helo with DshKs at the primary and secondary extraction LZs we listed in the message. We decided we needed to get out in a hurry."

Marty waited until Josh had finished putting empty M-16 magazines on the corners of the map. "Right along in here, we were pretty sure we were being pushed into an L-shaped ambush. I'd seen the tactic before so we struck back. Normally, there's a gap at the base of the L with only a small command element, so we went through there and hammered them pretty bad. I found the bodies of an NVA major and another officer as we were moving away and grabbed their map cases."

As if ordered, Josh rolled out the captured chart and held down the corners with empty coffee mugs. "My Vietnamese isn't very good, but the guys who speak it say that the writing on the chart shows each of our insertion and extraction LZs, along with the day we were supposed to be picked up. They're marked here and here, and if you compare them to our chart, they're pretty accurate."

"So how did you get out without getting caught in a big firefight?"

"Lieutenant Haman and I have alternative pick up plans. His favorite sport is snow-skiing, so we designate the alternative extraction LZs by a brand of ski and a size. I have codes that I can tell him about my favorite sport, which is surfing, which tells him our situation. Only he and his crew and my team know them. Because the back-up extraction LZs weren't in the message, there wasn't an NVA soldier in sight. When we got to Rossignol 207, the primary designated LZ, we spotted a platoon-sized patrol moving through the area; and it was apparent after watching them they were going someplace else. Just to be safe, we changed LZs to 203 because the sound of the helo would have brought them back to Rossignol 207, and I didn't want to risk a firefight when we didn't have to."

"So, Lieutenant, what you are telling me is that someone tipped off the NVA that you were in their backyard, and that they knew the location of all the insertion and extraction LZs along with the dates for insertion and pick-up?"

"Yes, sir, in a nutshell, that's what happened and, Admiral, I'd bet my life on it because that is what just happened. These charts are proof that they had everything: op area, LZs, radio frequencies, and recognition codes. They were just waiting for us. All that info was on papers in the map case."

The admiral looked at General Cruz and Captain Mancuso, who both had "I told you so" looks.

JUNE 10, 1972, SATURDAY, NEXT DAY, 1117 LOCAL TIME, HA GIANG, NORTH VIETNAM

Gus Thomes' wingman was holding station on his right at about ten feet of step down and twenty feet in trail. The other two F-105Ds maintained the same separation on the left as the four airplanes cruised at four hundred knots at eighteen thousand feet in a formation known as the "finger four." About half a mile away, on the right and left, there were two more flights of four F-105Ds, all carrying the same load of six low-drag Mark 83 thousand-pound bombs.

Last night, when he'd read the section of the air-tasking order that detailed the mission, he'd called General Jameson to complain. He'd thought that they had agreed that this strike would be in and out on the deck to minimize the warning time the North Vietnamese had, but the air tasking order had them coming in at their current altitude.

While the General agreed that the low-level run-in made more sense, they couldn't allocate enough tankers to support a twelve plane strike and didn't want the planes diverting to Nahkom Phenom. So, it was climb high, tank in total radio silence, then drop down to low level for the last fifty miles and then, after they got out of the target area, climb back to eighteen thousand feet and tank on the way home to Takhli.

During the conversation, he and Jameson had had a good laugh at the flight's call sign: Roscoe Zero One; because both knew that Roscoe was the name of the General's German shepherd. The General had listened to his arguments and then before he hung up, Jameson said, "Gus, the raid goes as per the ATO."

At that point, he had no choice but to say, despite his misgivings, "Yes, sir."

So, cruise in high, dive down to the deck to drop their bombs, and then climb back to altitude once they are out of the target area. Other than a few puffy clouds, there was nothing to mar the bright blue sky which, in his mind, made a perfect day for flying better because they were going to bomb the hell out of a marshaling yard that the intelligence folks believed supplied the missiles to the North Vietnamese that were bringing down his pilots.

Looking down, he saw they were nearing the point where the twelve F-105s would spread out into a combat formation as they descended. By the time they reached five hundred feet, they would be less than fifty miles from the target which, at about .95 Mach or six hundred-odd knots, they should cover in less than six minutes.

Gus rocked the wings of the F-105 and out of the corner of his eye saw the four planes move away from each other and as they did so, Gus eased the nose down into a thirty degree dive. Thomes told them in the briefing that once he was at five hundred feet he was going to keep his airplane as close as possible to Mach 1 and as soon as he released his bombs, he expected the airplane to jump to Mach 1.1. He'd prefer to come through the target area at a higher speed, but the drag from the bombs wouldn't let them go faster.

He had two reasons behind the supersonic pass. One was that the noise and shock waves might cause the NVA gunners to pause for a few precious seconds and the second was to minimize the time the fighter bombers would be in the Quang Trung/Ha Giang Valley. He wanted the whole formation to be in and out of the target area in ninety seconds or less, which meant the three flights of four would be dropping their bombs less than thirty seconds apart. Their speed, separation into separate tracks, and five hundred foot altitude should prevent any one of them from flying through the blast from the bombs of the planes in front of them.

He adjusted the stick and throttle with gloved hands to keep his dive speed right at .98 Mach, and the airspeed indicator confirmed that the Thud was descending like a lead sled. Any faster, and he would feel the vibration from the external tanks and jamming pods on the wings and bombs on the belly rack. As he began to level off and slow, as confirmed by the digital indicator and the movement of Mach needle on the airspeed indicator, Gus keyed the mike with the only radio command he planned to issue during the strike: "Selecting burner now, *now*, **now**."

On the third now, he moved the throttle, already close to military power, to the left and into the detent that sent a continuous spray of raw jet fuel into the J-57's exhaust. The result was a noticeable extra push and the fighter bomber, now down to about forty-five thousand pounds from its fifty-two thousand pound maximum take-off weight, settled down at about .94 Mach in the hot humid air, at a true airspeed of about five hundred ninety knots.

As soon as he came around the ridge to the north and west of Quang Trung, Thomes could see the railroad marshaling yard with the rail cars parked on the two most western tracks under the jungle canopy. He reached down with his left hand and flipped on the switch for the jamming pods on the outboard wing stations to the "on" position. In a quick glance down, he saw the green light that told him they were "on" and transmitting. The clock on the instrument panel said the F-105s were right on time and his eyeballs saw that they were where they were supposed to be.

Gus put the bomb sight's piper on the last two cars in the line and waited until the ring flashed before mashing the button on the stick with his left thumb. The F-105 leaped at least a hundred feet in altitude and accelerated to .99 Mach as soon as the bombs fell free. Out of the corner of his eye, he saw the Mach needle pass 1.0 when he heard a muted bang and felt both a thump and the F-105 slow and shudder.

Thinking that engine had come out of burner, he pulled the throttle back and then slammed it against the stop, but the fire warning and master caution lights told him he wasn't going to complete this mission.

He could see four S-60 anti-aircraft guns and a truck a on small plateau on the ridge to his right ahead of him. He selected "guns" on the stick, hoping the dying fighter still had electrical power, and nudged the rudder so that the nose of the F-105 was pointed at the battery.

As soon as the battery filled his gun sight, he pulled the trigger back as far as it could go, and let the tracers from the 20mm M-61 Vulcan cannon dance all over the S-60s as erratic control inputs from the dying hydraulic systems caused the nose to yaw to the left and right and pitch up and down.

"Roscoe lead, get out. Get out! Get out! You're on fire!"

He ignored the radio call and eased back on the stick to get what altitude he could. A quick glance in his rearview mirror told him that the back of the airplane was engulfed in fire as the F-105's inertia took it to over three thousand feet as it slowed below three hundred knots. He thought he still had a few seconds and wondered if he should ride it in, or punch out.

"Roscoe lead, eject, eject! This is Roscoe Six Six. The back half of your airplane is on fire. Eject, eject, EJECT NOW!"

Thomes unhooked his mask and shoved the target area charts into one of the pockets of his flight suit and the others into a well on the right side of the instrument panel before squeezing the handles on either side of the seat. He wasn't ready nor did he believe it was his time to die.

The roar of the ejection and blast of the wind was replaced by total silence as his chute opened and he floated down to the trees below. Turning in his harness, he looked back at the rail yard and saw two things. One, all the F-105 pilots had put their bombs right on target and it would be a while before the North Vietnamese used the rail yard again. And two, the railcars that were supposed to be filled with missiles were, in fact, empty.

Thomes had just enough time to cross his arms and legs and tuck his chin in before he crashed into the tree tops. It only took a few seconds, but after the noisy descent through the jungle, he was suddenly swaying in silence. Before he released his harness, he straightened his helmet so he could see and pulled off his oxygen mask. Looking down, he was only about three feet from the ground, so he released the fittings and dropped to the spongy surface with a soft thud and no searing pains.

He sat in the mud and took a quick inventory of his body; other than a few scratches under his torn flight suit, nothing seemed amiss, no broken bones, no puncture wounds. It was time to get moving and remember his survival and evasion training because he was deep in Indian country and getting him out from this hot area was going to be dangerous work for whoever came to pick him up.

He knew that the others had seen him eject and two planes in his flight had rocked their wings as they passed him in his chute. When they got home, the pilots would confirm that he had gotten out of the F-105 safely. Now the difficult task of finding him and then getting him out of North Vietnam would begin. His job was to evade capture for as long as he could.

After moving what he thought was several hundred yards through the jungle as quietly as he could, Thomes found a large tree under which there was a clear flat area where he could take inventory of what was in his survival vest. The break also gave him time to gulp down one of the sixteen ounce bottles of water he carried; he made sure the cap on the empty bottle was screwed on tight when he was finished to keep the dirt out and to make sure he would not lose it as he moved through the jungle.

The PRC-90 radio was in the front pocket. He pulled out the earpiece and plugged it into the radio, and after turning it on, pushed the transmit button. As soon as he heard a side tone, he spoke, "Any station, this is Roscoe Zero One, repeat this is Roscoe Zero One, over."

"Roscoe Zero One, this is Billiard Ball Two Two, say status."

"This is Roscoe Zero One. Unhurt. Evading toward safe area, copy."

"Roscoe Zero One. Keep the faith. Will advise plans at next scheduled reporting time. Keep moving. Copy?"

"Roscoe Zero One copies." Without saying it out loud, they'd just told him that no one was coming to get him in the next few hours or days. The evasion game was on and this time it was for real.

The next item he took out was his .45, which he cocked to put a round in the chamber before engaging the safety. Then he took out his three spare magazines and put one in each boot top pocket and the other in the pocket on his left bicep.

Inventory complete and nothing—based on his memory of what should be in the vest—was missing, Gus took out the chart and, based on their pre-flight briefing, determined from where he thought he landed was the best direction for evasion and pick-up: west along the ridgeline. He was surprised to see, when he looked at his watch, that it was 1355 and guessed that he'd been on the ground for about two hours. He took a few minutes to let the compass from his survival kit settle down on the chart and then, orienting himself as best he could, he figured that as long as uphill to the top of the ridgeline was on the right, he was generally heading west.

Now ready to move, Gus hesitated and listened, surprised how noisy the jungle had become. After he dropped through the tree tops it had been remarkably silent, as if the resident bugs and animals had been waiting for him to make the first move. Now, as he sat there, he tried to separate the chirping of different birds and the clicking and clacking of bugs from any sounds made by humans, particularly those with hammers and sickles on their uniforms. After about fifteen minutes, Gus was satisfied he was alone and he moved out. He was not ready to make a reservation in the Hanoi Hilton.

Chapter 10
MORE DUMB LOSSES

Captain Nyguen Binh eased his head out of the surf and then steadied his binoculars with his elbows notched in the soft sand. Before peering through the East German made lenses, he looked left and right and saw other heads emerging to take a breath before dropping down. Behind him, in a buoyant pack now held between his feet, was an AK-47 with ten thirty-round magazines, six grenades, and a flare gun with a single flare.

The buildings in front of him looked just like images in the photos he'd used to build a cardboard model for training. The only difference was now they were surreal in the harsh yellow-orange glow of the arc lights on the top of towers spaced evenly along the two rows of chain-link fence topped with razor wire. A meter separated the two fences, which was again consistent with the reconnaissance photos. Mentally, he congratulated his comrades on the accuracy of their work. Captain Binh could see the boat ramp fifty meters to his left through his binoculars that led to a wide gate that was padlocked in three places with steel posts on each side of the gate buried deep in the ground.

There was a watch tower on each corner of the complex, with what he'd been told was two centimeters thick armor on the sides. In each, he could see a solitary figure scanning the water and a mounted M-60 machine gun in the two on the beach side.

The swim in from the western edge of Cam Binh Island had been a lot easier than he'd expected. They'd been gathering there for two days, waiting for a moonless night to make the two-mile swim. Lying in the warm surf gave him time to catch his breath. He looked at his watch. His two four-man blocking teams, each with an RPG and four rockets, should be in their positions along the road on the far side that linked the complex with the air base on the north end and the naval base and port facility of the west side of the Cam Ranh peninsula.

Big Mother 40

Before pushing back into the surf, he tapped the man next to him on the head, who nodded and slid back into the water, and by the time Captain Binh had reached the shelter of the boat ramp, both sniper teams had the bipods of their Dragunov semi-automatic sniper rifles resting on the sand just below the water's edge. When he got about halfway up the ramp, four men slid past him and went about five meters in the shadows before stopping. Captain Binh looked at his diving watch and pulled a small flashlight out of his pants' pocket. Checking first that the green lens was still in place, he tested it before flashing it three times toward the four men in the water with the Dragunovs.

When the snipers fired, the four men in front of Binh rushed forward and placed two half kilogram bricks of Semtex on the posts and pulled the ten-second fuses. Binh saw that one of the guards in the tower had slumped down. He heard a loud ping as another 7.62x54mm bullet shattered on the armor plate of the second tower. Before the startled surviving sentry could rake the beach with his M-60, a second 150-grain round from one of the Dragunov rifles flung him back and out of sight.

He wasn't sure which came first, the blast from the Semtex or someone sounding an alarm. The noise from the klaxon was deafening as the twenty-four men, divided into four six-man squads, charged through the opening. Each headed for a specific building with a mission to kill as many Americans as possible, then blow up the operations center and the two barracks before Binh blew his whistle three times and fired the flare that would tell them to retreat to the water. Once away, they'd swim out to a fishing boat that should be waiting a couple hundred meters from shore.

Mancuso rolled from his bunk inside the command center, grabbing his .45 and the shoulder holster with two spare magazines before heading to the main door. Hearing a pounding and shouts at the side door, he unbolted it to let Chiefs Jenkins and Tannenbaum in. The two senior enlisted men unlocked the armory and handed out M-16s along with ammo cans filled with loaded thirty-round magazines to those who were on watch inside the command center.

Elsewhere, SEALs tumbled out of their bunks with their side arms and M-16s and headed for pre-planned defensive positions. At first, some thought it was another one of Mancuso's drills, but the staccato from AK-47s, green tracers crisscrossing the compound and grenade blasts told them otherwise.

Marty and the two pilots were trapped in the officers' quarters. They didn't want to risk trying to sprint the fifty yards or so to the main building with firing all around them. They had their pistols with limited ammo: only two magazines apiece. They turned off the lights and built a barricade from overturned desks and mattresses and awaited an attack they thought was inevitable.

The first two SEALs emerging from the enlisted bunkhouse were cut down in a hail of gunfire. A grenade tossed by an NVA commando bounced off the door jam and then outside before shredding the area around the door with fragments. Four men, two from each side of the door, returned fire, cutting down six attackers. With two providing covering fire, Van der Jagt, Vance, and Kostas, alerted by a phone call from the barracks, ran down a path bordered by a single chain-link fence to the main building and pounded on the door, which opened to let them in.

Inside, Chief Tannebaum handed them weapons and ammo and directed them to positions behind file cabinets and safes now arranged in rough arcs around either door.

Captain Binh watched while one of his swimmers put small Semtex bricks on either side of what he thought was the back door of the main building and his primary target. Ten seconds later, there was a large hole in the reinforced concrete structure. Two grenades were rolled in and Binh heard a warning shout just before both went off.

The first two men through the door staggered from double taps from a .45 from very close range. The next two made it in but collapsed in a hail of bullets. Binh, now next to the door, pulled the pins from two grenades, tossed one, and rolled the other inside. The first came flying back out the door and he dove for the ground as it hissed to a non-explosion. The second went off and he dove thought the door followed by four of his men.

There was an eerie silence for a few seconds as his eyes burned from the thick smoke. Binh could see large dark objects a few feet away and a rapid series of flashes winking at him, followed by searing pain and then nothing.

Marty and Josh climbed the lookout tower on the southeast corner as the sun came up. By the time they got there, the body of the SEAL had been lowered, but there were still fragments of brain and bone along the back wall of the platform, even though it had been washed with a hose. Neither said much as they surveyed the grisly scene from fifty feet above what used to be a battlefield.

"Morning, gents."

Both turned around to see Captain Mancuso, who had just climbed up the tower without, it appeared, spilling his coffee. "Good morning, sir," they said at the same time.

"We killed twenty-six and captured six more who are awaiting transport to the hospital." Mancuso surveyed the scene below.

"It was pretty ugly, sir. It looks like we got caught with our pants down." Marty shared what Josh was thinking.

"Yeah." Mancuso's grim face reflected his mood. "Our intelligence didn't give them a credible capability in this area, so how'd they get here? And are they going to try again?"

"Sir, how many did we lose?" Marty asked.

"Six dead, three wounded, including Chief Tannenbaum, who has a bunch of shrapnel wounds and will have to go to the hospital for a while. Chief Tannenbaum should be back in a day or two, but everyone, including me and the helo crew, who were in the command center, have shrapnel wounds from the grenades and shit that was flying around. None are serious, but we'll all have to go to the hospital later to be checked out."

"The maintenance guys are checking the helicopter to see if they left us any presents. It looks like they ignored it in their rush to get to the quarters and the ops building."

"Once it's cleared, get the helo ready so we can use it if we need to. We're going to stand down for a few days to clean up the mess." Mancuso spread out a rolled up piece of paper he was holding. "I thought you guys would like to see this. I pulled it out of a pouch on a captain who made it into the command center. It looks like they had the layout of this place pretty well scoped out. Plus, they had two blocking positions along the road, here and here. Marty, I want you to take a team out as soon as you can and check them out. My guess is that they are gone, but maybe you can find some clues on how many came ashore. I'd assume that there were several two- or four-man teams."

"Yes, sir. We'll leave right away."

"One more thing. Be careful." Mancuso pulled a handful of shell casings out a pocket. "Tide is going out and we found this, along with what the guys think were bi-pod marks in the sand. Apparently, they had two sniper teams right on the water's edge. That makes thirty-six. If you assume two or four men at each of the blocking positions, that's a total of forty to forty-four men."

Neither junior officer said anything.

"Josh, how soon can you get your whirlybird airborne?"

"As soon as we finish checking it out, and if there's nothing wrong with it, we can be airborne in five minutes, sir."

"My hunch is that they came from Cam Binh Island, and I was pretty sure I saw a fishing boat a couple of hundred yards off the beach when we came out after the firefight. Can't give you much of a description other than it looked like thousands of other junks in the South China Sea. Only my guess is that this one is high-tailing it north. I'd like you to look for any fishing boats that look suspicious. It may be a wild goose chase, but it will, if nothing else, make me feel better. They've got about a four hour head start, but at ten knots, that's only forty miles. Meanwhile, I'll send a team over to Cam Bin Island by boat to have a look around. Probably won't find much, but it is worth checking out."

MONDAY, 2 DAYS LATER, JUNE 12, 1972, 0723 LOCAL TIME, MOUNTAINS WEST-SOUTHWEST OF THE QUANG TRUNG/HA GIANG VALLEY

Gus Thomes looked at his watch and was surprised he had slept so long.

"Shit, I've slept for eight hours and I'm still exhausted."

The throbbing in his groin strongly suggested that he relieve himself.

This was day two of his practical exam in survival and evasion. He'd spent the first day moving cautiously and listening for other human sounds. Each time he checked in with Billiard Ball, he was encouraged to keep moving west and promised that a rescue would happen. Even though he was well west of the target, Gus assumed from his strike briefing that the anti-aircraft sites in the vicinity of Ha Giang would make it much too risky to send in the Jolly Greens.

He lay motionless for about two minutes under the large, leafy branches that he'd cut just before dark, after he'd moved what he estimated was about two miles west of where he'd spent his first night in the jungle. The Billiard Ball controller had asked him two of his authentication questions on his call before he bedded down for the first night. Satisfied, the controller had said that they were working on a plan to extract him, and to keep moving toward the pick-up area.

Light was beginning to filter through the trees, which he estimated to be between fifty and seventy-five feet high. He shook off the dirt from his flight suit and unzipped it so he could inspect his body for ticks and other creatures that may have decided to use him as a source of nutrition. The leaves that were once his bed were used to smooth over his tracks and then were tossed on the ground in what he thought was a random pattern.

The noise from animals beginning their daily hunt for food was, if not deafening, loud. Satisfied there were no humans around him, he took stock of what were now his only possessions in his survival vest and torn and muddy flight suit. The inventory showed that he had his two bottles of water, which he'd refilled in a stream, safe to drink now that the halazone tables had dissolved, but no food, which meant he needed to find something to eat if he were to survive very long. Both food and water, according to his training, should be plentiful in the jungle. He couldn't wait to set a trap and didn't want to shoot anything because the sound of his .45, which was not the most accurate hunting weapon anyway, would alert the NVA to where he was.

Gus didn't see any fish in the stream, so he had to find something to eat. If needed, he would start eating bugs because, as the survival instructors pointed out, they were full of protein. Gus wasn't that hungry yet, but close. The bigger question was would the NVA give him the time to forage for food?

He'd taken the time, when he'd stopped for water late yesterday, to clean the cuts and apply the first aid ointment to hopefully minimize infection. As he did so, he saw several areas on his forearms and thighs that were yellowing and turning black and blue. He wasn't sure if it were the hiking or the descent through the trees or both that caused his aching joints and muscles.

Thomes turned on the PRC-90 at his briefing time of fifty-three past the hour, and listened before transmitting. Billiard Ball Seven Two was on duty and didn't have any news for him other than to keep moving west. The communication helped assuage the loneliness he felt as he moved through the jungle. Getting rescued was his only goal.

MONDAY, SAME DAY, JUNE 12, 1972,
0919 LOCAL TIME, VENOM BASE

Thai entered the command cave and saw the lieutenant officer of the watch holding up the phone.

"Colonel Thai, I have an urgent call for you."

As he handed the field handset to his commander, the young lieutenant made sure a fresh pad of paper and a pen were conveniently located on the table for his colonel to use. Thai nodded and the lieutenant withdrew to a discreet distance away.

"Colonel Thai." After speaking his name, he nestled the handset between his neck and shoulder, grabbed the pen and scribbled some numbers and other information on the pad before looking at his watch. "I know the area and we'll be there in six hours."

The lieutenant stepped forward when he saw his commander hang up.

"Lieutenant, where is Major Loi?"

"He is on his way to C Company to observe an ambush exercise on the live firing range."

"Call the range and tell them that the exercise is cancelled and that Major Loi and all four platoons from C Company are to be trucked to the command center immediately. The machine gun squads in both platoons will stay here. Then, contact the commissary and have them prepare three days' worth of rations for them. We have a mission and need to leave within an hour. Tell the Company C commander that we are going hunting. I'll brief the officers when we get to where we are going."

MONDAY, SAME DAY, JUNE 12, 1972, 1127 LOCAL TIME, RIDGELINE WEST-SOUTHWEST OF HA GIANG

The rock outcropping at the top of the ridgeline forced a clearing in the vegetation and was a perfect place to hide that still gave him a clear, unobstructed view of the sky. He had found the place about two hours after he woke up and felt it was as fine a spot as any to tell the world that Gus Thomes was still alive and well. Considering that he'd spent the day before carefully picking his way through the rocks and vines trying not to leave a trail, Thomes decided he needed to rest a bit; he didn't think he was being followed.

He was tired and hungry and every joint in his body ached, and he wondered how he would have felt had he *not* worked out five to six days a week. He stank and wondered if his smell would make him easy to track; it was such a different smell from the fragrances of the tropical flowers, which themselves provided a stark contrast to the smell of decaying vegetation. In a moment of reflection, Gus thought if the consequences of getting caught weren't so bad, this could be, in another time and place, almost fun.

A look at his watch and it was time. Looking up, Thomes could see contrails and thought *Perfect* as he keyed the mike on the AN/PRC-90 survival radio. "Billiard Ball Seven Two, this is Roscoe Zero One. Are you up?"

He started timing down a minute before he'd transmit again, but after about thirty seconds, the radio cackled through his ear piece. "Roscoe Zero One, this is Billiard Ball Zero Nine, stand by. Seven Two returned to base."

Gus clicked the mike switch twice. The controller on the EC-121 that flew command and control missions for a variety of "customers" operating up and down the border between Laos and Vietnam was in an orbit that was about thirty or forty miles long. He thought it had to be boring flying and figured the controller was contacting the 355th's command center and asking them to pass on more authentication questions and answers via a secure radio link.

"Roscoe One, this is Billiard Ball Zero Nine. Ready for authentication. Make sure you are on SAR frequency. Over."

It was more of a statement than a question. Thomes rotated the selector switch to the UHF Guard position and then back past off to the UHF search and rescue position to make sure the radio was tuned to 282.5 megacycles. "Roscoe Zero One is up on SAR frequency. Standing by with answers."

"Roscoe Zero One, what type of dog does your boss have?"

Thomes chuckled. "German shepherd." That was an unusual question and it was not on the secure list of personal questions that pilots left behind with their squadrons so rescuers could determine whether the call was a hoax. This particular question told him that Jameson was in the Wing's command center.

"Roger, copy, second question. Roscoe Zero One, what is your favorite sport?"

"Tennis." He'd keep his answers short to conserve battery juice.

"Roger, copy. Third question. Roscoe Zero One, what kind of truck do you own?"

"Negative truck, have sports cars. One 'sixty-nine 911S and one 'sixty-three Lotus Elite 100."

"Roger. Roscoe Zero One, say your condition."

"No major injuries. Am mobile, but bruised, sore, hungry, tired and very ready to be picked up."

"Copy that. Roscoe Zero One, can you stay put and contact us in two hours?"

"Yes, and will do."

Gus knew the controller was going to relay the conversation to Thirteenth Air Force along with a decision on whether or not they wanted to attempt a rescue. His answers should have told the controller that he was the genuine article and there were enough of them to, hopefully, get a rough fix on his position. Had he been captured and forced to use the radio, he would have used the word "battered" when replying the truck or car question, to tell the listener that he'd been coerced or tortured, or "used" to imply that he was being used by the NVA as bait.

He hadn't seen or heard another soul so far, but that didn't mean they weren't out there, just that he hadn't run across them. Thomes believed the NVA had begun a meticulous search for him and hadn't yet picked up his trail. He lay back and closed his eyes; he needed a nap.

MONDAY, SAME DAY, JUNE 12, 1972, 1437 LOCAL TIME, HIGHWAY 2C, NORTHWEST OF HA GIANG

C Company's captain stood on the top of the truck's cab to survey the tree-covered ridgeline in front of him, trying to get a visual picture of the terrain before he submerged into the jungle. Satisfied his notes on his map matched what he saw, he clambered down the hood and then to the ground. Once there, his four lieutenants and sergeants gathered around as he spread the map out on the ground.

"Before we enter the jungle, let me once again remind you to make sure you tell your men that no matter what happens, we are not to harm the American pilot in any way, even if it means taking casualties. Colonel Thai was clear that we are to treat him with respect. Our mission is to capture him and bring him back to our base before he is transferred to Hanoi. Anyone who violates the Colonel's instructions will be punished." The captain, whose father was a member of the Central Committee, was as emphatic as his commander who, along with Major Loi, had taken him aside just before they'd boarded the trucks. He was also looking forward to practicing the English his father insisted he learn.

Two of his four platoons were going to enter at this location. Two more were going several kilometers up the road and would enter there. The hope was that the American pilot was hiding someplace in between them.

"Good luck." He shook the senior lieutenant's hand, the man who was going to lead the First and Second platoons. Their first goal was to find the pilot's parachute and determine if in fact he'd survived. If he had, they'd look for signs for which direction the pilot went and would adjust their search plan. A four-man communications team would move into the village and use the telephone line to communicate with Venom Base and the platoon leaders by radio.

MONDAY, SAME DAY, JUNE 12, 1972, 1653 LOCAL TIME, RIDGELINE WEST-SOUTHWEST OF HA GIANG

"Roscoe Zero One, Billiard Ball One Six. Are you up?"

"Roscoe Zero One is with you." New call sign and a different mission number, but probably one of the same EC-121s that flew the

Billiard Ball missions. At least he was now part of their mission brief and he didn't have to initiate the conversation.

"Roscoe Zero One, need you to move from your present position west by at least one kilometer. Are you able?"

"Roger. Can do tomorrow." Both participants knew that moving at night in the jungle for someone not trained to do so was difficult and dangerous. Both also knew that the best way to keep the NVA's radio direction-finding teams from pinpointing Thomes was to keep his transmissions short.

"Contact Billiard Ball if your situation changes or when at new location and we'll brief you on what happens next. Copy?"

Thomes pushed the transmit button twice in rapid succession. At first he was disappointed and then angry that after three days of being on the run, the Jolly Greens still weren't on their way. What the fuck was going on? But he was deep in Indian country and a rescue in this area was going to be a challenge. *Well*, he thought, *at least I'm still free.*

Monday, same day, June 12, 1972,
1745 local time, Cam Ranh Bay

The twenty-two year old enlisted photo interpreter with thick, black-framed glasses pulled out the mosaic of photos, carefully glued together, compiled from a Buffalo Hunter drone mission completed the day before, and pushed them to the front of the table. "Sirs, I've put small blue circles on the photos where we know where a plane went down, along with the aircraft type, call sign, and date of the shoot down. This is not all the planes that went down in the area, only the ones in which I had enough data to plot a position with some accuracy."

Josh studied the photos for a few seconds. "French, how do we know their positions?"

The jet-powered, six-hundred-mph AQM-34L drones flew pre-planned, low-altitude routes known by their code name, Buffalo Hunter, over North Vietnam after launching from airborne Air Force DC-130s. He'd learned from a briefing document provided by the Air Force that after the drone climbed to twenty thousand feet or more, the engine shut down and a parachute deployed. Specially modified Air Force H-3s snagged the parachute and carried the drone to a base where the pictures were developed. Josh studied the high-resolution pictures and marveled at both the camera and technology that was much more sophisticated than the radio control airplanes he and his father had built and flown when he was in his teens. It was something he planned to do with his children, if and when he and Natalie had them.

"Sir, it is based on the last known position from either SIGINT data or debriefs from the other crews in the flight. The five-mile diameter circle represents the area in which the plane probably went down. The one for Big Mother 22 is based on a couple of sources: one was the route that we know it was taking, and another was that there were intermittent IFF hits from an Air Force EC-121 with the call sign Billiard Ball. It's the biggest blue circle because of the uncertainty."

"What are these markings for, Petty Officer French?" Marty asked, unfamiliar with the symbols that showed radar sites.

"Sir, I dug up a report from VQ-1 that was sent about a month ago to NICPAC that showed emitters in our area of interest. It came from a Mustang by the name of Greg Winston who is a legend in the ELINT community. He wouldn't have sent out the report unless he was sure it was accurate. So I plotted all the ELINT hits that he noted that are consistent with the Fan Song A and B fire control radar used with SA-2 Guideline missiles. The bad news was that the whale, sorry sir, the EA-3, he was flying in was too far from the emitters to get a good solid bearing line so I plotted the spread based on the plane's track."

"Got it."

"One more thing. You'll notice that the twenty airplanes went down in three clusters. I drew the range rings from each of the locations to show you where the missiles could be. Those are the bigger circles in red. This intersection of all the range circles suggests the base is in this area." French unfolded a chart. "I did this on this map and am about to plot it on the mosaic."

Master Chief Tannenbaum stuck his head in the room and used a voice just loud enough to make sure he was heard. "Lieutenants, boss wants to see you in his office on the double."

"Close the door, Master Chief, and all of you sit down because you're not going to fucking believe this." Mancuso opened a folder with a yellow Top Secret cover. "I just got this. Apparently, Thirteenth Air Force got a wild hair up its collective ass and launched a recon mission with their Air Commandos. From what I understand, Thirteenth Air Force still doesn't believe that the North Vietnamese have a secret base right under Route Pack Five. That was right after they had a bunch of F-105s bomb the shit out of rail yard and lost one. Pilot got out but his status is unknown. The post strike photos are, to use the word General Cruz said the Air Force used, were 'inconclusive.' To me that means, assuming that the bombs hit the target, what the Air Force thought was hidden in the rail yard wasn't."

Big Mother 40

Mancuso took long swig from his coffee mug. "The astonishing answer is that the Air Force still thinks the missiles are being fired from sites just south of the Chicom border at a town call Ha Giang. They support that conclusion with the belief, based on the amount of flak the F-105s ran into, that the NVA are defending missile shipments coming into North Vietnam by rail from the PRC. I find that hard to believe because the North Vietnamese don't trust the Chinese any farther than they can throw them, and all the known missile sites are near Hanoi and Haiphong and Vinh. Add in that moving the missiles from Ha Giang to Hanoi by truck or train would make them vulnerable to air strikes, while what's on the docks in Haiphong, for reasons only known to our glorious president and his wonderful whiz kids, are off limits to being bombed. Plus, we have photos of missiles being unloaded from ships and none from trains. To this old frogman, it makes no sense, but it is what we are dealing with."

Mancuso laughed when he saw the puzzled looks on the two officers' faces. "I'm not making this up! Those supposed missile sites on the Chicom border have never fired at one of our airplanes before, so for all we know they could be dummies, not operational, or more likely, non-existent. Also, if I were a betting man, the Vietnamese sites on the border were built in case they and the Chinese start fighting again. But, I digress..."

The captain was dressed in his usual uniform of brown t-shirt and utilities cut off just below the pouch pockets, with white socks and canvas-and-leather jungle boots. "Anyway, the helos with the Air Commandos went in about four hours before dawn on the eleventh with three Jolly Greens and six A-1s to insert a recon team of their own south of Ha Giang and got the shit shot out of them. According to the message, one of the Jolly Greens with a crew of six and half of the twenty-man team was shot down in flames and they're pretty sure there were no survivors. An A-1 was shot up so bad the pilot parachuted out and was picked up by the Jolly Green that had the other half of the assault team, but in the process, they got shot up and barely made it back to base. Two guys in the Jolly Green were killed and several others wounded. All three of the other A-1s and the spare H-3 received substantial battle damage from small arms fire and 12.7mm and 23mm guns."

Josh winced. "Sounds like the NVA were waiting for them."

"It gets worse. General Cruz told me that the Thirteenth Air Force commander, General Jameson, exchanged a series of messages with Pac-Af describing what he was about to do and wasn't told no! He authorized this raid on his own with his own assets and didn't bother to tell any of the other folks in theater what he was doing. What blows my mind is that

Jameson didn't bother to brief Commac-V, much less try to coordinate the operation with anybody other than Pac-Af. General Cruz, along with his boss, Commac-V are, shall we say, pissed off big time. Seventh Air Force's face is all red because he didn't know about the mission and CINCPAC isn't a happy camper, either."

Mancuso held up his hand while he drank from his coffee mug. "There's more. These dumb-ass Air Force generals. Excuse me, my bad. We—that's defined as Thirteen and Seventh Air Force, a.k.a. the before-mentioned dumb-assed individuals, CTF-77 and me, are supposed to be working under the direction of Commac-V to come up with a plan for a covert reconnaissance in this general area to find this hidden fucking missile base. One would think that stirring up a hornet's nest in the area of interest is not the smartest thing to do."

Mancuso took a deep breath. "I ain't done yet. Apparently, when Jameson authorized the planning of this raid, he didn't, or more than likely, the planners didn't take into account that Thirteenth Air Force didn't have enough assets to execute the raid and meet its combat search-and-rescue commitments. They only had eight helos available in Thailand, and apparently two were down for major maintenance. Now suddenly, they lose one, get another two shot up, they only have four left to support strikes along the trail in Laos and into North Vietnam. As a result, when they took off, anybody who got bagged was shit out of luck. With the losses they took on the raid, they couldn't go after the F-105 driver who was shot down on the June tenth strike on the marshaling yard outside Ha Giang. So, this guy has been on the ground for the better part of three days and they've been stringing him along until they can dash in and get him without a major effort."

The SEAL captain suddenly stopped talking before he added, "Sorry guys, this rant is off the record, but the fact that I am pissed off is not. General Cruz said Admiral Hastings was, his words, apoplectic when he found out and CINCPAC wanted heads on a silver platter."

"Is there any good news in this?" Marty asked, not trying to be cute.

"There is. First, we're going to get another helo and crew from HC-7. Josh, you get to pick them. Second, Commac-V is about to hand-deliver to each of his commanders involved in our little search for the hidden base a Top Secret directive that says the Commander, Naval Special Warfare Forces, Vietnam—that's me—is to run *all* recon missions and that no one is to do anything without my express permission. Third, we're to get top priority on Buffalo Hunter assets. And fourth, Thirteenth Air Force—that's Jameson—gets a personal emissary from CINCPAC to explain the facts of life and my gut says there is a strong possibility that Jameson gets relieved over this. So, until the smoke clears in Saigon and someone tells us different, other than for tasking reconnaissance flights, we're in a holding pattern. No one, and that includes us, goes into that area until CINCPAC okays it, except for a rescue."

French was looking at another pile of photos when Marty and Josh returned to the room with the photo-mosaic now taped to a 4'x8' sheet of plywood. The small-boned, 5'4" petty officer was smiling from ear to ear when he stood up as the two officers entered the room.

"French, you look like the cat that swallowed the canary. What do you have?"

"First, Lieutenant Haman, Petty Officer Van Der Jagt brought me this letter and cassette and asked me to give it to you along with this tape recorder and said if I didn't, he would personally castrate me."

Marty watched as his friend put the two items on a chair behind him before nodding to the photo interpreter to continue.

"Sirs, I plotted the bearings from the Fan Song radar I got from NICPAC and the range rings on the mosaic from the last known location of all the airplanes that were shot down and on the chart. What that tells me is that the launchers have to be in one of these four valleys, all of which are right under the Air Force's Route Pack Five's typical ingress and egress routes marked with blue tape."

The petty officer let the officers peer over the chart.

"Here's the interesting part: if you look at this photo carefully, you can see the end of a gravel road from Highway Two and a submerged bridge that leads to nowhere. So I asked myself: Why would the NVA put a bridge there?, and if you look at this"—the petty officer unfolded another chart—"you'll notice that it leads to an area, based on the distance between contour lines, where one could build a road into this valley which is almost in the center of where all the range rings intersect."

"So you believe the base is in this valley?"

"I can't confirm it yet because I found eight other ends of gravel roads off highways in the area, but none of them led into a valley big enough to support SA-2 launches."

"What you're telling us, French, is that you're pretty sure that you've narrowed the location down to a single valley." Marty's eyes shifted between the chart and the mosaic.

"Yes, sir. I would rank this one as Number One. There are three more that are all possible candidates, but this one would be at the top of my list." French got pensive for a minute. "Lieutenant Haman, could the North Vietnamese use a SA-2 to shoot down an H-3?"

"Could they? Yes. Are they likely to shoot one at a helo? No, because we don't fly high or fast enough."

"That's what I thought. Thank you, sir."

"Whoa, French. Where did that question come from?"

"I plotted the full route for Big Mother 22 with this yellow tape. Here's the last recorded radar hit and here's the planned route which goes right through the intersection of all the range rings. I guess what I'm asking is, what kind of gun could shoot down a helo with one or two hits so that it couldn't get off a mayday?"

"They'd have to kill the crew instantly or blow one of the blades off. A 12.7mm or 23mm gun could do it, but they'd have to be very accurate and close, particularly at night, and get multiple hits. A hit by a 37mm or 57mm gun could be fatal, if it took off a rotor blade. Again, French, why?"

"That partially explains these photos which I got from NICPAC. On several nights in April and May, RA-5s and drones photographed 57mm guns being towed up from Hanoi, and I can't find where they've been placed. Based on the photos, I'd guess between eight and twelve or even sixteen guns moved down the road. The S-60s are very common around SA-2 sites, so they've either gone down the Ho Chi Minh Trail or they're someplace in this area. Then there is this Air Force RF-101 photo of my Number One valley, and it shows several up-ended S-60s after some F-105s ran through and laid several strings of bombs. I just can't be sure, but again, a lot of signs point to this valley as the missile base."

"Great work. Keep digging. Josh, D'Onofrio and I will go see if Mancuso can get us the go-ahead for the next mission." Marty pushed Josh in the direction of a row of doors. "You go find someplace private to read your letter and listen to the tape. You'll be useless until you do and then only marginal for a few hours after."

Josh laughed and moved off to a corner of the ops room where he slit open the letter with the blade on his pocket knife and slumped into a chair.

June 2nd, 1973

My dear Josh,

I am dictating this letter to Carla because both my arms have IVs in them and are taped to a board, so it's difficult to write or hold a mike for a recorder. I hope this letter gets to you soon and that you are safe.

Big Mother 40

The great news is that I am going to make it to Hawaii in September. I had Carla bring me a calendar and started marking off the days until the flight leaves. It will be motivation for me to build up my strength and stamina as fast as I can. They will have to kill me to prevent me from going. We'll be able to spend a precious week together.

Carla played all the tapes you sent me and they gave me added strength and encouragement to make it through this. I was determined not to die. If for nothing else, it would piss both of us off.

Just so you know, the last infection along with the cause is gone, hopefully never to return, and I am definitely on the mend. I'm pretty weak, but I already feel better than I have in a long time. No temperature and no infection anywhere in my body and my blood work is now normal.

Carla said she told you about the operation, so you know that there's nothing below my left hip. The medical term is a left hip disarticulation or LHD. The residual limb that you liked to caress is gone and muscle from my thigh and butt was stitched together in front of where the top of the thigh bone used to fit into the hip socket. Right now, it's sore mound of flesh where the doctors tell me there will be a long scar. You'll have to help me find out how sensitive it is. They tell me that at first, I will have trouble sitting, but will learn to adjust to not having a left thigh and my left butt will be smaller than my right because of the way the stitched the muscles together. I guess that makes me half-assed!

Anyway, I'll give you all the gory details in a tape in a few days. Carla took some pictures of me here in the hospital but I don't want her to send photos because I look horrible.

Supposedly, they are going to take out all the IVs tonight and remove the big pressure bandage that is around my waist and left hip. Carla and my mom and dad have pushed me around the hospital in a wheelchair but they won't let me use my crutches for at least 24 hours after the IVs come out. Once I get up on them, I'll find out how far I have to go to regain my strength.

The doctors think I'll be able to leave the hospital in about a week. After everyone's leaves tonight and the IVs are gone, I'll try to tape a longer letter to you, but please be patient with me; I don't have much stamina, but that will come.

See you soon.
All my love,
Natalie

Marc Liebman

Exhausted, Gus Thomes had lost count of his paces but he believed he'd moved about nine hundred plus yards as he zigzagged along the rocky ridgeline. He was trying to maintain a straight line, but it was difficult, because trees and rock outcroppings forced him into one detour after another. There was no way he could check his position, so he hoped that his count was correct. To make sure, he was going to add another five hundred strides before he called it a day.

The heat and humidity, along with the difficult terrain, was sapping his strength. His stomach had long since stopped grumbling from lack of food and it was now, as they said in survival school, a matter of will. The ground was uneven, sometimes muddy, and sometimes rocks, slippery from the humidity, caused him to fall many times, banging and scraping his kneecaps. Each time, he had to restrain himself from cursing out loud as his body accumulated more cuts and black-and-blue marks.

The only saving grace was that he'd again filled his two water bottles from a pool in a small stream and dropped in the halazone tablets to hopefully kill any gremlins that would give him the shits. Near the stream, he'd found a tree with a grapefruit-sized, apple-looking fruit. After slitting one open and tasting it, he was sure it was a pomelo and quickly carved it into chunks and ate it. Then he'd picked three that looked and smelled like they were ripe and stuffed them into his survival vest, alongside his first aid kit with its diminishing supplies, the two water bottles, a spare battery for the radio, a fishing kit, some coiled up shroud line he'd taken from the parachute, as well as an orange section he'd cut from one of the panels right after he landed. The signaling mirror as well as a pencil flare gun with six flares were kept handy in outside pouches.

He rubbed his nose as he sat on a rock and was greeted by a raunchy, acidic, penetrating stench from his dirty, sweaty, body. After looking at a strange, grimy face with several days of stubble in his survival mirror, he decided that he wouldn't scare himself again. And after smelling himself, decided he'd pay a lot for a bath or a shower.

As Gus Thomes was sitting in a nest of boulders with sharp edges, the captain commanding C Company was on the radio listening to the leader of First Platoon describe the site around the American pilot's parachute. After a couple of squads searched the area, they'd found boot tracks a couple hundred meters to the west and were going to follow them until dark and then camp out. After studying his map, he switched frequencies and re-positioned his third and fourth platoons, then picked up the phone.

Thomes looked at his watch now that he was set-up for the night. So far, the three pomelos hadn't caused an eruption in his bowels, and while he wasn't full by any measure, his stomach had stopped its growling protests. As soon as the second hand on his government-issued watch hit twelve, he keyed the mike to check in with Billiard Ball before he went to sleep. "Roscoe Zero One is up."

"Roscoe Zero One, Billiard Ball Six Two copies. Give me a short count."

"Say again?" Gus didn't scream "Are you *trying* to get me captured?" He played dumb to keep from saying anything.

"Need a quick short count."

"One, two, three, four, five. Five, four, three, two, one." The NVA knew the SAR frequency of 282.5. He wondered why Billiard Ball Six Two wanted to risk giving his position away.

"Roscoe Zero One. Got it. Need you to continue same direction in the morning for another click and then we'll send in the cavalry. Let us know when you think you are there. Copy?"

He used two clicks of the mike to acknowledge the call and then sat back against a large rock. So they knew where he was and tomorrow they would get him out.

Thomes didn't know whether he could move another kilometer without getting captured or falling down a ravine and killing himself, or worse, hurting himself so bad he became an attractive meal for some unknown predator. So far, all he'd seen were birds and monkeys and nothing else. He'd heard a lot more, but not seen them. *And, thank God, no snakes.*

How far can your mind push your body? The farther you can, the better your chances of survival. He had no choice but to keep on going, even if it meant talking and swearing at himself while he pushed himself beyond what he thought was possible. What amazed him was how clearly he could now recall some of the lectures, which proved that he had been paying attention. The thought made him chuckle. If and when he got back, he was sure he would be plunked in front of a video camera and told to tell his story. The tape would become one of many that future Air Force pilots would, like he did, have to sit through. Smiling, he wondered if the NVA would find his odor before his tracks—one of the good things about the gravelly surface at the top of the ridge was that he was leaving very few, if any, footprints.

Thomes found a small clearing that let him see the sky on day four of his jungle hiking adventure. He lowered himself to sitting position against a large tree and pulled out his pistol and flipped the radio to the on position. Through the hole, the Jolly Green could lower the jungle penetrator and he would clip the "D" ring on his harness to the fitting and hang on for dear life as they lifted him out of the trees for a ride back to Thailand. It was perfect.

"Roscoe Zero One is up."

"Roscoe Zero One, Billiard Ball Two Five, say status."

"Same as before, just more tired, more hungry, more scratches and cuts and more smelly."

"Copy Roscoe Zero One. Almost over. Jolly Greens are less than thirty minutes out. Authentication question: Name of your wife?"

"Diane."

Gus was about to key the mike when he saw the four NVA soldiers emerge from the far side of the clearing with their AK-47s leveled at him.

His heart sank. He keyed the mike before he raised his hands. "Roscoe Zero One is about to be captured, repeat, Roscoe One is about to be captured." He then raised his hands.

He heard the "Roger" before one of the NVA soldiers removed the earpiece while another picked up his .45. One held out his hand and pulled him to his feet while another removed his survival vest and patted him down. Convinced that he was now unarmed, they motioned in the direction of the valley floor. Thomes followed the first two soldiers and realized there were about fifteen more around him which, to his tired mind, meant that there was no way he was going to escape.

Always the cynic, he wondered if the conversations with the Billiard Ball controllers had given him away, but then realized the NVA knew where he landed, so it had always been a race between getting rescued or caught. He'd lost this race.

Big Mother 40

Colonel Thai and Koniev were waiting at the back of the truck when Gus Thomes was helped down. "Colonel Thomes, I am Colonel Thai and this is Colonel Koniev. Welcome to our base."

Gus Thomes stood upright, at attention, somewhat surprised to see both a Vietnamese and a Russian officer standing in front of him speaking English. Without thinking, he saluted the two officers. "Colonel Gustav Thomes, United States Air Force."

Koniev wrinkled his nose a bit at the smell coming from the man in the tattered flight suit standing in front of him. "You can take a shower in our officers' quarters. After which we will have our doctor take a look at you, and then you can have dinner with the officers in this command who speak English. I need to remind you that any attempt at escape is fruitless and Colonel Thai's men will shoot you if you try. Tomorrow, we will put you on a truck to Hanoi. Do you understand?"

"I do."

"Excellent. Colonel Thai's men will show you to where you can clean up. We will give you some clean clothes from my men that will fit."

"Thank you." Thomes was surprised at his treatment; it wasn't what he'd expected. But then, he wasn't at the Hanoi Hilton yet. Still, these bastards were the ones he was trying to kill and who were in turn trying to kill him. Should be an interesting dinner discussion.

Thai waited until after he and Koniev had walked back to his cave after saying goodbye to Colonel Thomes. Before his hands were tied, the three men shook hands, and Thomes saluted after he thanked them for both dinner and the shower. Then he was driven off in a small, four-wheel-drive truck.

The two colonels often used his cave because it was private, as Koniev was the sole occupant and they could talk about any topic without worrying about someone listening. Plus, Koniev had all the charts needed to have a discussion about tactics and the defense of the base.

Thai sat down on one of the crude wooden chairs near the large table with the map marked with all the missile engagements.

"I never thought about it, but this is Colonel Thomes' third war; and at fifty, he was much older than I expected. War is for young men, because we believe that we will live forever." Thai paused for a second to allow for a change in subject; he didn't want the discussion to get philosophical. "Thomes didn't say much other than the Americans were coming after us, and when they do, their Air Force will destroy this base. You know much more about the Americans' tactics than I do; what do you think they will do next?"

"Reconnaissance and more reconnaissance. They won't do anything until they have found us. The more difficult we make it for them, the longer it will take. Thomes didn't say anything, even when I asked him directly, that led me to believe that they know where Venom is located. Therefore, they can't bomb us."

"But they have lots of reconnaissance planes. Won't they fill the sky with them?"

"Yes and no. Even the Americans don't have unlimited numbers of planes. We should see more drones and more reconnaissance planes, particularly during the day. Your army's expertise with camouflage will be very important. The more we make Venom look like just another jungle valley, the harder it will be for them to find us."

"I think we should shoot down the drones whenever we can. The Americans won't know when or where they have been shot down."

"They can figure that out. I believe that the drones have a radio link back to the plane that launched them. Plus they know the route, so, even if the drone is blown off course by the wind, they will know about when and where the drone was shot down when the radio link fails."

"Are you sure about that?"

"Yes."

"We need to keep fighting. My government will not allow us to hide and wait until we are attacked."

"Drones are hard to hit because they are so small. Plus they are cheap and you don't kill or capture a pilot. I think we should be very selective in which manned aircraft we choose as targets because there are so many. That should minimize the risk of detection."

"I will think about it."

Big Mother 40

"You'll be interested in this." Captain Mancuso tossed a printed message on the conference table that was covered with maps and photos. "On Thursday, the Air Force tried to execute low-level reconnaissance missions over northwest Vietnam. An Air Force RF-101 is missing and presumed lost or captured, and a Vigilante off the *Ranger* was shot up. They made it out to the water before punching out and both guys were rescued."

"Let me guess, the mission was in the Thirteenth Air Force ATO message." Marty was making coffee in the corner of the conference room.

"Yup. And in the Air Plan from the *Ranger* that was sent to both Commac-V and CINCPAC. But here's the best part. Not a SAM was fired in the northwestern part of the North Vietnam. The Voodoo and the Viggie were bounced by MiGs, and the escorting Navy fighters got four MiGs and the Air Force got two."

Mancuso held up his hand to stop any questions. "I just got off the phone with General Cruz. Written authorization for additional missions is being delivered by a courier today. You are going out to the *Ranger* and meet with CTF 77, who will then authorize further Navy reconnaissance missions over North Vietnam. You'll help plan them and bring the photos and negatives back here. However, the orders are clear that these sorties are not to be mentioned in any messages and are to be part of 'routine' strike operations. Stay on the *Ranger* until you think you've got the photos you need. I'll have Big Mother 16 bring mail and other stuff that I need to send to you by courier. FYI, DET 110 is on the *Constellation* and we think that it best that you stay separated unless you need their help for maintenance. That'll avoid any unnecessary questions that you'll have to answer with silence. Oh, yes, and one more thing, the orders give you authorization to communicate directly via message to me or General Cruz, so if you two want to talk in codes that are not in the books, think that through and brief both Master Chief Tannenbaum and me before you leave. Questions?"

"None yet." Josh chuckled as he spoke.

Mancuso laughed. "Let me know when you plan to take off. Oh, and one more thing. This just came in and I thought you rotor-heads would find it interesting." Mancuso slid another message across the table.

"Nagano is retiring and his change of command is the 28th of September." Josh handed the message to his friend.

Jack read the whole message and then looked up. "Are you surprised? I thought he extended for another year?"

"Short answer is no."

"Why?"

"Because he flunked his NATOPS check just before I left to go to the RAG. Nagano was unsafe and air crewman had to be given direct orders to fly with him."

"Is that a rumor, or fact?"

"Fact. I gave him the NATOPS check on my way home to the states last fall. My fitness report was already done and the Ops Oh asked me to give him the check ride since I was essentially bullet proof. When it was evident halfway through the check ride that he wasn't going to pass, we went on a short across country and when we landed, the senior air crewman got everyone out of the airplane and Nagano and I had a short conversation. I told him that I could flunk him and have it on his fitness report, which meant he would never make captain, or he could retire at the end of the fiscal year."

"He was that bad?" Jack was surprised at Josh's candor.

"Yeah ... Scary unsafe, and worse, both he and I knew it. If I wrote up all the mistakes there was no way that anyone who read the report would allow him to fly again. He needed to go back to the RAG for a full refresher course. Nagano was flying the bare minimum of a couple hours a month; and then on each flight, he bored around the sky for about an hour or so before flying three GCAs at the end to keep his instrument qualification, followed by three landings. The guy was just hanging on, thinking that once he left HC-7 he'd never have to crawl into a cockpit again. Captain, as a Naval Aviator, if you blow a check ride, the CO has to note it in the remarks section of your fitness report unless there were extenuating circumstances. We all screw one up occasionally and then pass on the recheck. It goes in your training record, but not in your fitness report. In Nagano's case, the one before was marginal as well. My predecessor had given him a passing grade by a point as a courtesy and that was wrong."

"Ouch."

"What I just told you is not common knowledge. The only people who know are the squadron's former Ops Oh and the current XO."

Chapter 11

LUCK

Colonel Thai put down his chopsticks and watched his Soviet counterpart dunk a chunk of fish into the sauce before putting it in his mouth. "I saw the picture of your wife and daughter on your table. They are beautiful, but you don't talk about them at all. Why?"

"Because they are both dead." Koniev tried to say it without any emotion, yet just the words hurt.

"May I ask what happened?"

Koniev looked around; there wasn't anyone near the table where they were eating. "After my three-year tour in East Germany, I was sent to command a missile regiment guarding our Northern Fleet headquartered outside a town called Archangel. They only have two seasons there: lots of winter and less winter. It is very nice in the summer, but the winters are dark, very long, and very cold. And there is not much to do because you can't go outside for very long."

He plucked another piece of fish from the bowl and put it in his mouth. After enjoying the spicy flavor, he continued. "Four years ago this past January, my wife and daughter both caught the flu, which turned into pneumonia. The doctors at first didn't treat them because, as I found out later, there was a shortage of antibiotics, just like there is of almost everything in the Soviet Union. So, they cut back on doses. Some genius said that soldiers should get priority and sick civilians would only be treated in extreme cases. So what happened was that the few drugs they got were not strong enough, which just prolonged their suffering."

Thai took a deep breath and didn't say anything. They had the same problem here. The regimental clinic was, if it weren't so serious during a war, a joke. His experience in Paris as a student had taught him that Western countries' doctors had plenty of medicine.

"The pneumonia spread to both lungs and they died, one week apart." Tears flowed down Koniev's cheeks.

189

"I am so sorry."

"Oh, that's just one part of the sad story. Most of the doctors in the clinics and hospitals were drunk on either medicinal alcohol or vodka, and often, when they administered medicines, they used the wrong ones or gave the patient improper doses. My wife and daughter were among several hundred, maybe thousands who died that winter. No one knows how many because it's a state secret."

"Was anyone punished?"

"No. The head of the local hospital's brother was a member of the Central Committee, and those of us who lost loved ones were told to mind our own business or we would be reported to the KGB for counter-revolutionary activities."

Thai didn't say anything but thought that was one of the "joys" in living in a Communist paradise: political connections were more important than competency.

"I was grief-stricken and angry and I started drinking. I finished my tour and said a few things to some senior officers that I shouldn't have and was about to be retired when the head of the Air Defense Artillery School rescued me from myself. He brought me to the school and kept me from doing something really stupid, like kill the fucking doctor, and got me to stop drinking. That was over two years ago and I haven't had more than a drink a day since then. And now the experts on the General Staff in Moscow, who never shot a missile in their life, think I am Communism's and God's gift to surface-to-air missile tactics. So, I guess I have been rehabilitated, and that's why I am here."

Koniev looked at Thai, who was finishing his bowl of rice. "You don't talk about your family either."

"Because I don't have one."

"No wife or girlfriend?"

"No. I have been at war for as long as I can remember so I never had time to find a wife."

"There's more to that story than what you are telling me, I suspect."

"There is. I spent two years at the Sorbonne which, if you don't know, is in Paris. There, I met a young woman who was the daughter of a French legionnaire and a Vietnamese woman. We wanted to get married, but they forbade her to come back to Vietnam with me. My parents, who had both studied in France, put pressure on me to come home to serve my country. When I got back, I found out that the regime had been reading my letters and knew I was considering staying in France."

Koniev was silent for a moment. "What about your parents? Isn't it unusual for someone to go to the Sorbonne?"

Thai pushed his bowl to the side and put his chop sticks across the top. "Yes, it is, but you have to know whole story. My father was a good friend of Ho Chi Minh's. They met in France and together they fought the French, and then the Japanese, and then the French again. He was a member of the government's inner circle for many years, even though he wasn't a member of the Politburo. He was able to use his influence and power to get official permission to send me abroad for up to three years to finish my education. I did that, but by the end of the second year I was in love and my girlfriend's father offered me a position in his export/import business. The mistake I made was that I wrote home and asked my father for advice."

Koniev shook his head, because he and his wife had always suspected that the KGB, or at least the political officers, read their mail when he was stationed in East Germany. He and his wife had agreed upon code words or phrases that used in a certain context would tell a different story from what was being said in the letter.

"By the time I arrived in Haiphong, both my parents were in re-education camps and I was immediately drafted into the army as I got off the ship. It was almost a year before I saw them again, and by then it was clear the camp had broken their spirit. They were teaching in a school in a fishing village near Vinh, but in reality, they were waiting to die. I was in South Vietnam in nineteen sixty-six when they passed away. I was never officially told they had died. The way I found out was that, when they knew they did not have much time to live, they arranged for a trusted friend's son, who was assigned to a regiment in the division in which I was serving, to carry a letter to me. He carried it in a special pouch so that it wouldn't get wet as he made his way south. The journey, if you have not heard, is made on foot. It takes several months and is very dangerous. You can be bombed day and night, you can get sick, and then there are the poisonous snakes."

"Yes, several officers have told me that. Many of your subordinates are happy they do not have to take that walk. How did you become an officer?"

"Fate, I think." Thai was pensive for a minute. "I was sent to the South to a front line infantry regiment because those who sent me assumed my chances of survival were slim. And, when I was killed, my family's lineage, so to speak, would end, which would make those in the secret police and my father's former friends happy. But I was not ready to die, nor did I accept it as my fate."

Thai sipped his tea, then put the cup on the table as the memories flooded back. "In my first skirmish, the platoon leader panicked and ran away from the enemy and the sergeant was killed; so I started directing the men, and ultimately we captured the gun position we were attacking. So, the regimental commander made me a sergeant on the spot. About a month later, we were attacking a fortified enemy village and the company commander was killed, as was my lieutenant; I led my platoon and what was left of the company and kept them from being annihilated by the Americans. We went into that battle with almost two hundred men and came out with less than one hundred, at which point, my regimental commander told me that I was a very good leader and soldier and made me a captain and gave me a company to lead."

"You never went to any officers' school?"

"I'll get to that in a minute." Thai smiled. "The regimental commander told me that I was one of his best officers and was going to send me to officer candidate school even though I was already a captain. The political officer, who did not know my history, wrote a glowing report on me and, along with the division commander's and the regimental commander's recommendations, I got ordered to the school. It took me about two months to get there.

"When I arrived, the school did a detailed check on my background and political reliability ... and I was confined to quarters while they figured out what to do with me. That took over a month, but the need for competent combat leaders overrode political expediency and I was allowed to finish the course which, by now, I could teach. In fact, I had the highest scores and many of the instructors were asking me questions rather than teaching me."

Thai refreshed his tea cup. "Then I was sent back to the same division. It took over a month to walk and ride to where they were based in Laos. I was given a company, and one of my first assignments was to chase American reconnaissance teams that were searching for our bases in that country and then calling in air strikes. It was frustrating work, but I did eliminate several before my company was ordered to get ready for a major assault. Then this happened."

Thai pointed to his face. "We were getting ready to attack an American unit when we were napalmed. Almost my whole company was killed and I was lucky to survive because I was up front, watching the Americans. It was six months before my wounds healed. The trip north was very painful because my burned skin kept cracking and getting infected. I didn't want morphine, which was all the doctors had to relieve the pain. The medics kept washing the wounds with sterile water that they would boil over a campfire and then let cool. I had a bottle of antibiotics that a medic from my company stole from the hospital. Between those and the pills they gave me I survived, but by the time I got back north, I was weak and had lost a lot of weight. And, again after I regained my strength, I was sent back south, now as a major to lead a battalion that would specialize in hunting American reconnaissance teams. I didn't want to go back, but I had no choice; the country is at war and they needed experienced commanders."

Thai took a long sip from his tea cup because it gave him time to remember. This was also the only time he'd shared his feelings about what happened. "It was difficult, but we had enough success so that I was given a second battalion to train and promoted to lieutenant colonel. I had many battles with the American special forces, and in most cases, I hate to admit, they got away. There was a SEAL team I chased several times in Cambodia and they were like ghosts. One time we thought we had them cornered, but what they were doing was setting up an ambush on us. We lost over a hundred men in about fifteen minutes in that firefight and I was wounded again. After I was healthy enough to ride, I was sent back north to recover and was teaching in the school for new infantry officers when I got a call to go to a meeting with my old regimental commander, who is now a three-star general. And, as you said, here I am."

WEDNESDAY, NEXT DAY, JUNE 21, 1972, 1625 LOCAL TIME, USS *RANGER* (CV-61)

Josh unlaced his steel-toed leather boots and pulled off his sweaty flight suit before climbing into the upper rack in the four-man stateroom whose forward bulkhead was the back of the water brake for the number three catapult.

"Nothing for you," he said to Jack, referring to the earlier mail call announcement which had sent him visiting each of the *Ranger*'s seven ready rooms to see where their mail was delivered.

En route to the spaces they shared with the reconnaissance squadron that flew Vigilantes, Josh had been stopped by the admiral's aide, who gave him a dirty, off-white sack containing the crew's mail. Mancuso had given it to the C-2's loadmaster just before it left Cam Ranh Bay with instructions to give it to the admiral's aide, who would know where his officers and enlisted men were bunked onboard the carrier. It also had a note that Big Mother 11 was down with a hydraulic actuator problem.

Jack looked up from his book. "You're going to be unavailable for the next hour while you devour Natalie's tape?"

"Not a tape, but a long letter."

"So that means you might consider dinner around eighteen hundred?"

"Sure."

Josh flipped the switch that turned on the small fluorescent light above the two pillows. Less than three feet above his head was asbestos cladding that provided some insulation from the heat generated by the sled sliding down the catapult track propelled by superheated steam. A conical-shaped piece of steel welded to the catapult sled slammed into a tank with a loud metallic bang every time the catapult was fired, a mere five feet from the end of his bunk. The force vaporized much of the fresh water in the tank as it absorbed the energy needed to sling forty-one thousand pounds of fully loaded F-4 into the sky. He'd gotten so used to the sliding sound followed by the loud clang that he could tell by the tone what kind of airplane had just launched and even sleep through the noise. He'd recorded the sounds onto a previous tape to Natalie so she could hear what he had to sleep through.

This line period the *Ranger*'s air wing had the day shift, which meant that the first launch would be around 0600 and the last at 1800. Flight quarters were announced about four, and right after that the catapult crews began their testing by firing what were known as "no loads." Around 2200, they'd venture down to the air wing's Integrated Operations and Intelligence Center known around the ship as IOIC or, as one wag dubbed it, "One hundred and One Clowns", to look at the last of the pictures taken by the RA-5Cs that day. They'd cull the ones they wanted from them, which they stored in a locker until they were ready to leave the ship.

He closed his eyes for a moment, visualizing the last time they were at the top of Point Loma sitting on the stone wall. He was laughing at Natalie's frustration because she was unable to keep the wind from blowing her shoulder length hair across of her face as he tried to take a picture. Then he opened her letter and began to read.

My dear Josh,

I'm at the UCSD library using their typewriters because they got a whole bunch of the new IBM Selectrics and I can type faster than I can write. They're really cool, easy to use, and have interchangeable balls so you can pick different type faces. This one is Arial Narrow Italic in case you are interested. I typed one of my papers last week on one of these Selectrics and the correcting feature made it easier and much faster.

My real reason is writing, er, typing, is that I ran out of tapes, so rather than wait another day, I thought I'd send you an old-fashioned

Marc Liebman

letter. I'll get another box of tapes today on the way home. As you know, I am saving all of your tapes and not recording over them. We can decide what to do with them when you get back.

Lots of good news. Assuming I pass the summer school exams for the courses I had to drop while I was sick this spring, I should graduate in January. It is a semester and a summer later than I had hoped, but considering all that happened, I'm happy to finish. Sometime after I get back from Hawaii, I plan to start looking for a job. That will be a hoot. Who the hell will want to hire me, a one-legged dietician with no experience?

Yesterday, I went back to see Dr. Haney for my 30-day checkup and he is very happy with my progress. My blood work is normal and there is no sign of infection. The best news of all is that I feel great and have fully recovered from the surgery. He wants to see me in December and then, if everything is normal, that's it. No more doctors and blood tests.

My right leg is also getting stronger and doesn't hurt from being tired all the time. I think that it felt tired all the time because it never fully healed from the accident and because I was sick so often. The bones in it have healed and because my body is not fighting infections all the time, I can work on getting it stronger. As you know, I was very afraid of breaking it again. The docs and the therapist have given me some exercises to strengthen my calf and thigh and I've started riding an exercise bike in the school's gym every day. Both will make my leg stronger and give me more stamina so you'd better be ready.

One of these days, I will get around to going back to the prosthetist. They showed me a leg they were making for someone else and it looks uncomfortable. My butt will have to go into a big plastic bucket that wraps around my waist. The socket, as it is called, is held together with several buckles. It just looks yucky and is very heavy because it has to have three joints, i.e. one for my hip, knee, and ankle. There's no rush to get fitted, and we can talk about whether or not I should get one when we see each other in Hawaii or when you get back.

I've tried several types of crutches over the past few weeks and like the forearm ones the best. The new lightweight fiberglass forearm crutches are a dream to use and I've also got a set of aluminum ones that adjust in height so that if I want to wear a high-heeled shoe, I can adjust the height of the crutches so the handles are at the right height. I'm sure that is more than you want to know.

The insurance company knows what happened as does the hospital where the original amputation was done. The insurance company has agreed in the settlement to provide me with a new leg every three years and pay any maintenance costs in between new limbs. To initiate the

195

policy, I have to get one. Whether or not I wear it is another story. So, at least it'll be free. We're working on a different settlement with the hospital due to the incompetence of the original doctor. When they found out that the Navy surgeon and his team would testify in court, they caved in because they don't want the publicity of a trial.

As you know, I've been wearing your class ring and the 22-carat gold wings you gave me on a chain around my neck and Dr. Haney recognized the ring. I told him that it was my boyfriend's and he said he knew several Army officers who went to Norwich. I can get the names if you want to know.

To celebrate my clean bill of health, Carla and I went out shopping —what else does a girl do?—for bathing suits of all things as well as for some clothes for the trip to Hawaii. I keep telling her that all I need are clothes for the flight over and back, a few T-shirts and shorts plus a couple of bathing suits. Not that I am planning to wear much of anything for the first few days! Anyway, I bought a several two-piece bathing suits that I think you'll like and a couple of other outfits that were on sale.

This will be the first time I go out in public in a bathing suit since my original amputation. All the times we were out on your boat, when I wore a bathing suit, it was just you and me. I guess I am still self-conscious even though I go out all the time and everybody knows I'm missing a leg. But this is different and I was thinking about having some cloth sewn over the left hip so people won't be able to see the scar. As I said to you before, there's just enough muscle to make a mound that sticks out a bit. Maybe it's just me and I am over-reacting, but I think it's ugly. You tell me what you think when we're together in Hawaii. And, I can tell from looking in the mirror that my left half of my butt is smaller and has a different shape than my right side. Oh, well.

Carla says I have the figure to wear a bikini and wanted me to get a couple of very skimpy ones, but I couldn't bring myself to buy one, even after trying it on. Anyway, I may go back because they have a great selection and everything is on sale until the Fourth of July.

Tomorrow, I am having lunch with the Warhawks' Wives Club. Sharon Butterworth, the CO's wife, along with a couple of the other wives, visited me several times in the hospital and insisted that I come to their lunches and meetings. She has also been very helpful in making sure I got a seat on the charter to Hawaii.

At first, I was a bit uncomfortable joining them. I am not a Navy wife nor are you part of HS-10 anymore, but when I told Sharon that, she said, (a) she didn't care, and (b) the wives wanted me to be a member and since they make the rules, they can break them. They treat me as an equal and they don't try to make allowances for my handicap. They know *that if I can't do it, I'll speak up. I love that because I hate when people cater to me just because they think I need help because I only have one leg.*

Anyway, I like them and they are a fun bunch, but you know we're just dating! If you believe that one, my love, I've got another story for you.

The group is eating at Fiona's downtown and it should be fun. There are several other wives whose husbands are going to HC-7 soon. All of them have asked me about you because they have heard so much about you from their husbands. They're all eager to fly with you. I don't know how the assignments work other than what you told me so I didn't say anything other than they'll get assigned to crews when they get to the Philippines. It's kind of weird hearing about some of the things that you've done for others. Anyway, the respect others have for you is very, very impressive but DON'T get a swelled head over it.

One more thing. Carla says to tell Jack that if he wants to meet good-looking, eligible girls when he finishes his tour and comes back to San Diego, she'll introduce him to a bunch of good-looking women who would like to meet him. She thinks he's got a lot to offer and just needs to find a good woman. I'll help as well.

I can't wait until we see each other in Hawaii. I have a calendar on my wall and cross off each day. My parents are excited about me going and want to see you again.

Please come back to me safe and sound. I miss you and love you with all my heart.

All my love and see you soon.

Natalie

THE SAME DAY, 1972, 1943 LOCAL TIME, USS *RANGER* (CV-61)

"Sir, Lieutenants Haman and D'Onofrio reporting as ordered."

The small space that was the wing commander's office was barely large enough for the steel desk that was bolted to the floor. It had its own entrance that could be closed off to give the captain some privacy, and two chairs with worn green seat cushions wedged against the bulkhead.

"At ease, gentlemen. Thanks for coming. I'm Captain Rick Framingham." They all shook hands. "I've got a brief in a few minutes, but I wanted to ask you if your crew would be willing to be a stand-by SAR asset. I know why you are out here and the admiral said it was up to you. Would you stand by on a thirty-minute alert? It'll take us that long to get the HH-3A out of the pack and the rotors spread."

"Sir, we'll be happy to do it."

"Great. Go down to strike planning and get yourselves up to speed on what we're doing tonight. We got some extra missions laid on and we're extending the air plan by three cycles. We should be done by midnight."

"We'll be ready if called."

When they got back to the stateroom, Jack said, "You could have said no."

"I could have. What would have been your answer?"

"Same as yours."

"I figured as much." Josh tapped his friend on his shoulder. "Let's go round up the guys and get organized. I guess we're going to watch movies in the Heavy Seven ready room tonight."

THURSDAY, JUNE 22, 1972, NEXT DAY, 0703 LOCAL TIME, VENOM BASE

"Enter." Thai was expecting the courier who rode in with the convoy that had delivered twelve new missiles.

The young lieutenant unlocked the handcuff and chain with a key and gave Colonel Thai a sealed envelope from the worn leather briefcase before stepping back into a rigid position of attention.

"Lieutenant, please make sure you get some breakfast and sleep so you can return to Hanoi tonight." Thai scribbled his name on the custody form that documented that he had received the briefcase.

"Thank you, Colonel. Sir, my orders are to remain here until after you have had a chance to study the contents of the briefcase and then carry back any response."

"I will look through the material right now and will send for you when I am finished."

"Thank you, sir." The young man saluted again, did an about-face, and left Colonel Thai wondering what was in the briefcase. The thick envelop was double sealed. He slit it open with the Fairborn fighting knife he'd taken off a dead U.S. Army Special Operations Group soldier in Cambodia.

Sliding the contents out on his desk left him with two rubber band wrapped piles of photos topped with a typewritten note:

Marc Liebman

Colonel,

We thought you might find these photographs and biographies interesting. What you have in your hands are photographs of U.S. Navy Lieutenants Martin Cabot and Joshua Haman. Cabot is a Navy SEAL and Haman is a helicopter pilot who has extensive experience getting in and out of our country undetected and was an instructor pilot training others in his tactics before he returned to this war.

The photographs were taken when they entered the Seventh Air Force Command Center at Tan San Nhut Air Base. With the help of some friends in the U.S., we were able to put together brief biographies of both officers who, like you, are very highly decorated and very competent warriors. What we learned about them is in the envelope along with the photographs.

We believe these officers have been tasked with finding Venom. Haman and Cabot have worked together in the past and are very experienced in getting in and out of our country.

Cabot is an expert at covert reconnaissance and an expert at setting ambushes and then escaping. We have good reason to believe that Cabot and you have met in Cambodia as well as in Vietnam.

Neither our sources nor our intelligence experts know how, when or if they will try to find you. What we do know is that they are operating as a special group outside their normal chain of command. Our sources in the south have been able to find out very little other than two of the black Sea King helicopters that have violated our airspace time and time again are at Cam Ranh Bay. Haman and Cabot are there as well.

We thought you would be interested in this information so that you know who your enemy is. This is more confirmation of what I told you earlier. How you use this intelligence is up to you.

General Chung

"So you're the bastard who killed my men." Thai held up the photo of Marty Cabot wearing fatigues and a .45 in a shoulder holster facing another similarly dressed man with the insignia of a U.S. Navy captain. He couldn't read the name tag, but he thought the first letter was "M." After trying to glean as much as he could from each photo, Thai began writing.

Big Mother 40

The admiral's aide, a.k.a. "the rope," was waiting outside the IOIC. "The admiral would like to see you at sixteen hundred sharp."

"About what, sir?"

"Don't know, Lieutenant. The admiral just asked me to make sure you were in his office at sixteen hundred. That's all I know." The newly minted lieutenant commander hurried off down the passageway toward the blue-tiled section of the 03 deck that denoted flag country.

After he left, Josh turned to his friend. "I guess that means we'll have to find clean flight suits."

The aide was waiting for them when they showed up at 1555. As soon as they approached the door, the aide knocked and they heard a faint, "Come in."

The aide opened the door, stuck his head in and announced, "Lieutenants Haman and D'Onofrio." A nod of his head told them to step in.

Josh almost came to a sudden, startled halt when he saw Captain Marvin Ruppert, the chief of staff for CTF-77 and the one who'd put Josh and Jack into hack, sitting at one end of the worn brown leather couch next to the admiral's desk. Admiral Allen Hastings sat the other end of the couch.

"I believe you two gentlemen have met Captain Ruppert and Admiral Hastings."

The admiral, who was the commander of Task Force 77, smiled when he spoke. "At ease and take a seat." The admiral motioned to the conference table on the other side of his office.

"Admiral Hastings came aboard when you went over to the *Kitty Hawk* to pick up some pictures and is going to leave on the COD that goes out at the end of the eighteen-hundred launch. Before he goes, he has something to share with you." CTF-77 nodded in the direction of the other flag officer. "Admiral."

"First, what I am about to tell you is Top Secret, specially compartmented information under the code words 'Phantom Arnold.' No one who is not in this room, including the staff's intelligence officer on this ship, is cleared for this information. Captain Mancuso, his head of intelligence, and Lieutenant Cabot are the only other individuals in this theater cleared for this information. Let's keep it that way."

"Yes, sir," both lieutenants said in sequence.

"Before I forget, the staff's N2 will have you sign the necessary paperwork that grants you access to the specially compartmented information with the code words Phantom Arnold after this meeting is over."

"We understand, sir," Josh said for both of them.

"About two weeks ago, we concluded an exercise in the North Pacific that proved, beyond a shadow of a doubt, that the Russians are reading our messages, or someone is providing them copies in near real time. Problem is, we don't know who or how they got them. What happened confirmed our hypothesis of a leak when the Russians acted just as we thought they would to the *Kitty Hawk's* and then the *Oriskany's* deployments."

Hastings let his words sink in; he suspected that this was the first time that Haman had heard any senior officer confirm his suspicions that there was a leak in the Navy's classified message traffic.

"As you know, the Soviets try to keep a trawler within a few miles of any carrier; but the trawlers, on a good day, can only make fifteen knots. The plan was for the *Kitty Hawk* to leave Hawaii on schedule and then steam at twenty-five knots for a couple of days heading northwest directly toward Petropavlosk, which is near the southern end of the Kamchatka peninsula. The *Oriskany* was in Japan for a break, and instead of heading south back to Vietnam, she headed north to rendezvous with the *Kitty Hawk* about four hundred miles east of Petro. What we know is that once the *Kitty Hawk* and *Oriskany* moved, the Russians scrambled every long-range reconnaissance aircraft they had to search for the carriers, starting with the route *that was in the message traffic*. After both carriers announced their presence by letting an E-2 emit at about one hundred and fifty miles from Petro, the Russians scrambled dozens of fighters and kept cycling them for a couple of days until they were sure they weren't being attacked. Then they lost a Bear when the pilot made a low pass over the *Kitty Hawk* and dug a wingtip when it turned in front of the carrier."

Admiral Hastings showed Josh and Jack photos of it cart-wheeling as it hit the water.

"The exercise got the *Kitty Hawk* and the *Oriskany* an extra week of liberty in Yokosuka. The *Kitty Hawk's* air wing flew their asses off from just off Petro until they were inside Japan's twelve-mile limit. The Russians had subs running from all over the Pacific to sit in trail once they found the *Kitty Hawk* and her escorts."

On the way back to their state room, Josh signed for a sealed, weighted bag that had both the negatives and the prints from the photos taken by the *Ranger*'s and *Constellation*'s RA-5Cs during the past seventy-two hours. Another, with tonight's missions, would be ready by the time they planned to take off just before the last recovery began at around 0530.

Josh could see Jack had something on his mind. As soon as they got into the room, Josh closed the door and motioned him to the bulkhead at the forward end of the stateroom. "Out with it."

"Why did Admiral Hastings share this?"

"My guess is because Marty found the info on those maps he captured that led to the exercise which confirmed what we suspected." Josh paused to let his brain finish the thought that was running through it. "Our job is to help Marty find the base, and what I think the admiral just told us was that if we can find it, CINCPAC will consider all options. And he wants us to look for more evidence of a traitor. From his point of view, it is very logical."

"Logical, hell." Jack tossed his arms in the air in frustration. "I joined the Navy to fly, not to go spy-hunting and I know what you are thinking."

"And that is?"

"You're betting that CINCPAC with Hastings and Mancuso's support has given or is about to give Marty a hunting license to go find that goddamn missile base. And then go back to put the place out of business."

"You're getting way too smart for a co-pilot."

SUNDAY, 3 DAYS LATER, JUNE 25, 1972, 2135 LOCAL TIME, HANOI

"What do you think of our boy, Koniev?" The question from the general came out of the blue. The half-empty bottle of vodka and two glasses next to an ashtray full of cigarette butts dressed the rough-hewn wooden table.

Rokossovsky looked at his boss, wondering where that question came from. They'd become confidants in the past year, but their diverse backgrounds would never allow them to become close friends. One reason: Nikishev knew from reading Rokossovsky's dossier that there was a notation that said "Of Jewish Origin," which could be a career-limiting fact in the Soviet Union. To anyone in the army or the KGB, the "of Jewish origin" entry gave the government a convenient excuse to charge Rokossovssky at any time of being a member of the global Zionist movement conspiring to overthrow the socialist republic, and to execute or send him to the Gulag. The old General was sure that Rokossovky had reached the rank of colonel only due to his ability to help his senior officers solve difficult, often career-threatening problems. It also gave those who knew of the note leverage over Rokossovsky to use when they needed a favor.

For many, the notation saying his parents were Jewish was a professional kiss of death, but for Rokossovsky, underneath it was another, much more serious notation that said "grandson of Zinoviev." The fact that Rokossovsky never knew his grandfather, because the man had been executed after one of Stalin's more famous show trials during the purges of 1933, which was before he was born, didn't matter. His family and his children would always be tainted by the KGB note.

Rokossovsky took a couple minutes to top off their glasses, conveniently giving himself time to think of what he should say about Koniev. "He's the right man for the job."

"That's a bullshit answer."

Rokossovsky thought that Nikishev's beady eyes were trying to bore a hole in his forehead to get at what was on his mind.

"Try again." Nikishev tipped his glass toward his deputy before taking a long swig.

Rokossovsky took a deep breath. "I think he's gone native."

"Better. Explain."

"First, he divided up the Spetznaz detachment among the four Vietnamese infantry companies to get what he believes is better training. And, I think he's right. Our men don't know shit about fighting in the jungle. Spetznaz always trains our allies rather than be trained by them, so Koniev's change didn't go over well in Moscow. But nobody told him to rescind the order. By the way, I think the Spetznaz like being out in the jungle with the Vietnamese. They are learning skills they can't get anywhere else. Second, he insists that his officers eat with their Vietnamese counterparts to get to know them. Third, I suspect that given the choice, he'll act in the Vietnamese's best interest rather than ours."

"Why do you suspect this?"

"Sir, I have my sources. I talk to several of the officers out at Venom when I call out there and before they put me through to Koniev. The political officer we sent with the Spetznaz hates him. Koniev doesn't let the political officer get involved in any operational decisions."

"Interesting." The general closed his eyes as he savored the fire from the clear, room-temperature liquid. He lit another cigarette, knowing not to ask the obvious question; the burly Colonel Rokossovsky was probably getting his information from one or two plants among the Russians. Maybe the political officer was his source. "What do you plan to do about it?"

"Nothing to do. He's doing what he was sent there to do in Moscow and our ally's eyes. So, as long as it doesn't affect our business, why worry? He's just a soldier doing his job, and as long as he obeys his orders, we have nothing to do anything about."

"When are you going to Vientiane?"

"First flight tomorrow." Rokossovsky emptied the bottle into both their glasses, careful to ensure there were equal amounts in both. "I will spend the morning with our military attaché, who will regale me with stories about our how our gallant Pathet Lao allies are killing our American-supplied enemies and tell me that he needs more guns and bullets. Then, after a lunch with our Laotian comrades-in-arms, who will confirm what I heard from our attaché, I will have a drink with our other employers who will hand me a large envelop stuffed with Swiss Francs after they tell me about the next series of shipments. When we finish, I will go to the local Credit Suisse office where I will make a deposit that is the equivalent of ten thousand U.S. dollars in each of our bank accounts."

"And then?"

"After I admire the balance in my account, I will go back to my hotel room where two beautiful half-French, half-Laotian women will be waiting to fuck my brains out. I will do it long enough to miss the afternoon flight back to Hanoi so I can continue to enjoy myself for another twenty-four hours before I return."

"You do know you can get laid here in Hanoi."

"I can and do. But I am much more careful here, because who knows who's watching?"

"And you don't have the same problem in Vientiane?"

"I do, but I don't think the local government cares. They're trying to stay in power and already know that our Vietnamese friends, with our support, supply the Pathet Lao." He stopped speaking, but he was thinking, *If I defected, what could I tell the Americans that they already didn't know*? "If the headline in the local newspaper read: RUSSIAN ARMY COLONEL HAS ORGY WITH LAOTIAN WHORES, who would care? The CIA maybe, and who gives a shit if they have pictures. What are they going to do with them? Show them to you? My superiors in Moscow? The KGB?" He almost added, "Me?"

Rokossovsky knew he would be very valuable value to the Americans if he defected, because he knew the Russians could read their messages. Shit, just that alone would be worth something. But what else? How many missiles they were bringing into Vietnam? They probably had a more accurate count than he did. He knew that if he walked into either the French embassy or the Swiss consulate, the Soviet embassy would know in minutes, and the only way he would leave Vientianne would be in a box.

The real reason he stayed in Hanoi was because it put off his retirement. What did he have to look forward to? A loveless marriage? He was almost convinced that he was better off not going back.

The discussion was getting uncomfortable and Rokossovsky wanted to end it. He was never going back to the socialist paradise whose capital was a drab Moscow, not if he could help it. The question of how it would end kept rattling around in his brain.

Someday, the KGB, if they didn't already know, would learn that every Russian airplane leaving Hanoi carried at least five hundred kilos of heroin. He made sure the suppliers' local representatives placed the drugs on the airplane and that it cleared customs. Or, if the drugs were already there, he make sure the plane wasn't searched thoroughly.

His trial, if he got one, would only delay the inevitable bullet in the back of the head in the basement of the Lubyanka. Maybe he should just disappear one day from Vientiane. They had flights to Thailand where he could seek asylum in the U.S. embassy. He'd need another passport; his Russian one wouldn't get him very far. If he went into the U.S.'s chargé d'affaires in Laos, the KGB would know within hours, and he suspected that he wouldn't leave the country alive. *But, then again, if the Americans could keep me alive, it would be a way out: paid to live in the U.S.!* Maybe that was the best way to go.

He drained his glass and stood up. "I'm going to bed because I have a long, profitable day ahead tomorrow."

Nikishev laughed as he did the same.

MONDAY, NEXT DAY, JUNE 26, 1972, 1410 LOCAL TIME, CAM RANH BAY, 180 MILES NORTH OF SAIGON, SOUTH VIETNAM

"So what do we know?" Marty asked, walking back and forth between three plywood sheets covered with black-and-white photographs pieced together to provide a detailed map of the search area, as well as potential helicopter ingress and egress routes. Typed notations and arrows pointing to their subject referred to other photos that provided more detail.

Petty Officer French, who was leading the photo analysis, said, "First, we have a good view of the terrain. We can see several hot spots in the jungle on the infrared map. They're either small huts, cooking fires, or could be missile control vans which give off a lot of heat. We don't know which is which, *yet.*" After a pause for emphasis, he said,

"We narrowed down which of the six roads probably ends at the missile base." He took the time to point them out. "Each could lead to a road under the jungle canopy or they could just end. Again, we don't know. I think you will find this interesting." He lifted a few photos that were piled on a map on the table. "We photographed this little convoy of six missiles just to the east of the area covered by the mosaic, which could be reloads for an SA-2 battery. Two facts make this convoy interesting. First, it is headed *away* from Hanoi and every other known SA-2 battery. Second, it has three of the little four-wheel-drive GAZ trucks, along with the normal complement of six KAMAZ trucks pulling missile trailers. Typically, there is one GAZ for the convoy commander, but this one has three. Why?"

"Humor me," Marty said, not following where French was going with this angle.

"Don't know for sure. Could be extra personnel, could be almost anything, but it's worth noting. Based on what we know about how the Russians and North Vietnamese deploy SA-2s, they can be set up in these three valleys. The SA-2 doesn't go straight up when it's fired, so it needs some room to maneuver, which means it needs room to accommodate the launch trajectory. Also each launcher needs a road to get its reloads."

French moved to a different position around the map board. "The good news is, we're down to our leading candidate, plus two other valleys. We're taking a detailed look at all three and should be able to rank them in order starting with the most likely and tell you why. We have another mosaic on the opposite wall of all the suitable LZs we can use for insertion and extraction to each of these three valleys. There aren't many, but enough for two, maybe three missions."

"Anything else?" Josh asked, studying the potential landing zones.

"Yes, sir. We have another pile of images from around the primary area of interest that we haven't gotten to yet because we focused on putting the mosaic together. We should find the information from them that we need to pick the most likely search area."

"The trick is picking the right valley first." Marty looked around the room and saw six tired men. "Why don't you guys go get some rest? Be back in the morning. Then you can start fresh."

After the photo interpreters left, Josh plopped a couple of the LZ photos on the table. "Did you talk to Admiral Hastings about Phantom Arnold while we were out on the *Ranger*?"

Marty laughed. "Mancuso told me. What did they tell you?"

"Hastings gave Jack and me a short brief on the exercise. Yeah, it was pretty amazing." Josh put both hands on the table. "Our suspicions were vindicated. Can you imagine the Russians' reaction when they learned a battle group got to within one hundred-fifty miles off Petropavlosk without their knowing it was coming?"

"Somebody had fun planning that op." Marty pulled two Cokes from the refrigerator in the back of the room.

Josh took a long swallow from the can before changing the subject. "So what's the plan?"

"Simple. We do a sneak and peek in the valley that's our top candidate. Your job, should you choose to accept is it, is, as usual, to get us in and out."

"No problem."

"You two guys are fucking nuts." Jack, who was looking at the big mosaics, turned and faced his friends with his hands on his hips.

"It's an all-volunteer outfit. You can drop out at anytime." Marty poked his finger in the direction of Josh's co-pilot with a smile on his face.

"No way. I don't know what's more fun, watching you guys stick sharp sticks in the eyes of the bad buys or seeing you deal with the REMFs on our side. Anyway, if nothing else, I get a ringside seat if we all go up in a ball of fire."

"That isn't going to happen," Marty shot back.

"Oh ye confident ones!" Jack shot back in one his mock tirades, which was Jack's way of venting before he focused on the difficult task of helping plan the mission.

Master Chief Tannenbaum opened the door and said the two magic words: "Mail call!" He tossed a small pile of letters on the table, plus a tape cassette. "Well, I guess you two love birds are about to disappear and leave me alone to figure everything out," Jack said, trying not to whine.

Marty handed Josh the tape before sorting through the envelopes. "Hey, Jack, you got a letter."

Jack looked at the return address. "Yeah, from my mother."

"Mothers are important."

"True. We wouldn't be here without them."

"If, and only if, you'd been able to keep a steady girlfriend instead of chasing every skirt you could find," Josh said as he slit open the wrapping around the cassette, "you too might have a nice, sweet-smelling letter of interest or two every day. If I remember back to when you were in the RAG in San Diego, you were introduced to several lovely ladies, beginning with Carla, who liked you, but you were more interested in getting them into bed than building a long-term relationship."

"Guilty as charged. But, as I feel compelled to remind you, all relationships start in the bedroom, which is where I prefer to keep them. I realize I am now paying for my shortsightedness, which as I would like to point out, enables me the freedom to chase any woman I choose."

"And, around here, what can you chase?"

"Good point... Not much." Jack slit the top of the letter with an X-Acto knife that was lying on the table. "There is always hope. From what I have seen, there are lots of available women at Cubi."

"Yeah …. Get in line behind the thousands of other horny men who are chasing them." Josh spoke as he was trying to decide whether to read the letter first or listen to the tape.

"You don't have to be so discouraging."

"Just trying to keep you grounded." Josh waved the letter to make sure he hadn't cut the sheets when he opened it.

"Here." Jack flipped the X-Acto knife end over end and was rewarded with soft thunk as the blade stuck into the plywood. "Go read. You'll be useless until you do."

> *My Josh,*
>
> *I'm sitting in the courtroom and while they're taking a break, I thought I'd drop you a quick note. The prosecutor asked me if I'd be here and take the stand if needed during the pre-trial hearing of the idiot who hit me.*
>
> *They keep going back and forth, and why they don't want to try him is still, despite all their explanations, a mystery to me. He was drunk as a skunk at four o'clock in the afternoon and he told police that he was going shopping. Yeah, right. They have witnesses who said he'd just stopped off at a liquor store to buy more booze and showed the receipts as evidence.*
>
> *Anyway, I've been here almost all day. It is hurry up and wait and very boring. They thought I might be called to testify this morning but the defense attorney asked the prosecutor if they could make a deal. So, the judge gave them a couple hours to come up with something or the DA has to decide whether or not to go to trial or walk away.*
>
> *Meanwhile, the rest of us are sitting around waiting. The guy's wife and kids are on the opposite side of the courtroom and*

the wife won't look me in the eye. On one hand, I feel sorry for her, but on the other, she has to know her husband is an alcoholic.

If I had my way, I would like to see him do some serious jail time, but I don't think that will happen. This is not the first accident the guy has had while shit-faced. He works nights at a local food-processing plant and then comes home, gets drunk and sleeps it off while the wife is at her job and the kids at school.

Since he has not spent any time in jail for prior DWI arrests, he has been able to go to work, so he hasn't lost his job. Too bad because his employer has to know what kind of drunk he is.

What I didn't know until a couple of days ago when I read the depositions and all the pre-trial stuff to prepare for my testimony was that this was his fifth accident in which he was drunk. It was the first in which someone, i.e., me, was badly hurt. As you know, his insurance company has settled with me so that part of the ugly episode is over.

The DA just came over and told me that there will be no trial. The bastard has agreed to give up his license, go to AA, and when they certify that he has been sober for at least two years, he can be retested for a license. His fine is $5,000 which he has to pay over two years. If at any time during the next five years he's arrested for driving drunk, or any other crime or misdemeanor in which he is drunk, then he will receive an automatic five-year sentence in the clink with no probation or time off for good behavior.

In other words, by going to AA and getting sober, he gets off scot free, while I lose a leg, have the other broken in two places, undergo two major operations and spend six month sick as a dog and damn near die in the process. Something tells me that this isn't fair.

Am going to end this letter and drop it in the mail on the way home. Will tape more tonight.

Love you and come home to me safe and sound. All my love.

Natalie

Big Mother 40

"Why didn't we shoot at the first and second flights of aircraft?" Thai asked Koniev, who was at his makeshift desk in his cave. On the pad in front of him, were his notes on the details of the latest shoot down.

"Because they would have seen the missile launches and the Americans would probably have located the base." This was not the first time they've had this discussion and Koniev wanted to keep to the two principals he believed were the keys to Venom's success:

> 1. Be efficient in using the minimum number of missiles to get the maximum number of kills; and,
>
> 2. Minimize the ability of the Americans to find the base.

"But we must shoot down more airplanes. That is our mission." Thai was insistent.

"We bagged two more out of the last formation and we'll get more every day," Koniev said, doing his best to be conciliatory. "Nguyen, our mission is to test new theories and shoot down as many American airplanes as we can without giving away our position."

"The Americans are not bombing your country. They are killing my countrymen. The families of my soldiers are in danger." Thai's tense rigid body was coiled as if to strike.

"I know that, but this base and my job are not solely responsible for the defense of your country. We are here testing new theories that you can employ to help you be more effective defending Vietnam."

"No, Colonel Koniev," Thai said, showing his anger with the proper title, "we are testing theories that the *Soviet's* can use. If they help us, so be it, but you are here for the benefit of the Soviet Union. If they help the Democratic Republic of Vietnam, so much the better. Is that not so?"

Koniev wasn't going to be baited into an argument that served no purpose other than to create more friction. He suspected Thai was complaining up his chain of command, but until Nikishev told him that he could compromise the base's location, he would only fire on selected targets. Nikishev's reluctance to ask Moscow to change his orders to enable him to fire more missiles was two-fold: one, getting the missiles to Venom was difficult and dangerous because the Americans were getting more efficient at finding and attacking the convoys. The NVA was shooting SA-2s in barrages of hundreds of missiles at every major American raid, so the overall missile expenditures were much higher than planned, which meant there was competition for missiles.

And two, Rokossovky had told him several times that Nikishev was trying to minimize Soviet casualties. As the Americans get more effective at attacking the missile sites, it put more and more Soviet officers and men in danger. Already, Soviet pilots had been grounded and most sent home because of the alarming number that had been shot down by the American Navy and Air Force fighters.

"That is not true." Koniev chose his words with care. "We are here to help you defend your country, and our soldiers and pilots are dying as well."

"Then we must do more. We *must* shoot down more Americans even if it increases the risk to Venom."

Koniev could see, hear, and feel the emotion in Thai's words. His response was the same as it always has been: "Have our orders changed by someone in Moscow, and then we will do our part."

"I need your help. You must convince your generals to let us change the rules of engagement." Thai's insistence was not new, but he was getting more aggressive each day. Koniev kept asking what was eating at him and never got a straight answer.

"You know I have made that request repeatedly." Koniev couldn't say, "And still no change, nor will there be," because that would infuriate Thai even more. Koniev stood there as his counterpart grabbed his AK-47 and left the cave, still angry.

Once he was sure the Vietnamese colonel was out of earshot, he picked up the secure phone.

"How can I help you, Colonel Koniev?" Rokossovsky was in a jovial mood.

"I just had another run-in with Colonel Thai. He wants us to shoot more. I told him that I can't until my orders change, but did not give him the real reason."

"Good. Nikishev is being steadfast as well. Moscow tells us that the NVA is shooting missiles faster than we can build and ship them. And forget it about the new models you're using. The last seventy-two are on a ship in Haiphong waiting to be unloaded. After they're gone, there will be no more for several months. So Nikishev is thinking about closing your operation when we run out, rather than letting you use conventional tactics which will result in an immediate American attack. If he does that, he may make you the senior advisor to the commander of their air defense forces."

Koniev thought that was an interesting wrinkle. "We have about thirty missiles left, and from what I was told, there are another fifty in a warehouse on a pier, and now you tell me there are seventy-two more available. Thai said the fifty are being shipped as soon as they can, but we are losing about fifteen percent during transit; about one out of every six re-supply convoys is attacked, and each suffers some losses. Is that accurate?" Koniev did a quick calculation in his head. At the present rate of consumption, they'd be out of business in a month or two. If they got two-thirds of the ones on the ship, they'd have another month's supply. *Then I guess it is off to the bunker outside Hanoi.*

"That is about right." Rokossovsky fished for a report from the many scattered around his desk. "The Vietnamese are asking why not send the new missiles and controllers to the batteries around Hanoi and Haiphong and not risk losing them. We keep showing them how the Americans are diverting reconnaissance and electronic warfare aircraft to first find and then destroy you, but I am afraid, my comrade in arms, it may be falling on deaf ears. The real answer is that you have the only set. When they are gone, there are no more in the supply pipeline."

"So are Thai's generals putting pressure on him to get me to change the rules of engagement?"

"We believe that is the case. They have no other choice because Nikishev has not gotten clearance from Moscow to change them. And, he won't take that risk if it means that more of our people die. Just yesterday, an American missile hit a control van and killed six officers and wounded several others. That pushed the number of our dead to above three thousand in the past five years."

"Just so you know, this is getting to be a daily argument with Thai." Koniev went back to the topic of the call and didn't care if the Vietnamese had tapped their phones, although Rokossovky had assured him on several occasions that scenario was not possible. According to him, they didn't have the technology or capability. Koniev wasn't so sure.

"That is why you are so well paid," Rokossovsky laughed as he hung up.

Chapter 12

WEST OF VINH

"Lieutenant Haman, please come to the command center. Captain Mancuso says it is urgent."

"Tell the captain I'll be there as soon as I can." Josh put the phone in the officers' bunkroom down. "Jack, go out to the helo and make sure the guys have finished the daily pre-flight. Something's up and I want to be ready to take off immediately. If not, we'll go fly anyway because we haven't flown it in almost a week."

"Thanks for coming." Mancuso handed Josh a piece of paper with a number written on it. "General Cruz called to ask you to call this number. Ask for a Navy lieutenant by the name of Rayborn. General Cruz said an A-7 Corsair off the *Constellation* went in west of Vinh and they had two HC-7 helos shot up last night trying to get the guy. The remaining Det 110 bird on the *Constellation* is down and needs a new main transmission and they won't be able to get one out to the ship for another twenty-four to forty-eight hours. The Air Force tried at first light today and couldn't get him out. Big Mother 16 and 40 are the only two helos available and General Cruz asked me to ask you if you can make the rescue."

"Sir, your answer was?"

"It's your call, Lieutenant."

"Are we still talking to the pilot?"

"Yes. Call sign is Argonaut Four Zero Six. Red Crown says he has authenticated correctly. From what we understand, he's got a broken leg and can't move around, but other than that, he's okay."

"Captain, please call General Cruz and tell him my crew will be airborne in less than fifteen minutes. Have someone ready to brief me over a secure phone when we land at Phu Bai to get gas. No messages, no Vietnamese involvement. Vinh is a nasty place to go down, but if he's west of Vinh, we've got a chance to get him."

"Good luck. I'll make the call. Let me know when you're on your way back."

"Round Top Seven One, Big Mother 40 is up," Jack said, looking at his notes. While they gassed up, he looked at a chart to plot the downed pilot's reported position and a route up there, noting that the A-7 pilot was less than twenty miles as the crow flies from the coastline in a mountainous area west of the North Vietnamese port. The two pilots agreed that the best way to get there was to cross the coast about ten miles north of the DMZ, fly west until they got to the mountains, then follow the ridges north to where they thought the pilot was.

"Big Mother 40, Round Top Seven Zero One, we have four A-7s orbiting plus two A-6s en route. More to follow. Copy?"

"Round Top, Big Mother 40 copies. What about additional authentication?"

"Round Top Seven Zero One, Big Mother 40. Squadron mate gave us some personal information we can use for authentication which is that he is a University of Massachusetts graduate and a former ski racer."

"Big Mother 40, Round Top Seven Zero One. Roger that. Meet me on Three Zero One point Five. Argonaut Four Oh Six is monitoring Two-Eight-Two point Five. Radar vectors available if you need them."

"Big Mother 40, roger. We'll request vectors if needed." Josh wondered what year Argonaut Four Oh Six graduated and if he'd raced against the guy. "Jack, leave the transponder on. I want Round Top to know where we are. Here's the deal: this shitty weather is good for us. You fly and let me navigate until we get close. Go as fast we can over the rice paddies, and then keep it between seventy knots at fifty to a hundred feet over the treetops about halfway up the ridgeline and under the clouds. When we get just west of where we think Argonaut Four Oh Six is located, we're going to cross the ridge to our right and head east. If we get lucky, we'll be able to see his chute, which, according to Lieutenant Rayborn, is on the west side of the ridge. If you get tired or need a break, let me know."

"No problem. Why don't I turn it over to you when we head east?"

"Fine. That'll be about in another thirty minutes."

"We're ready in the back."

"Good, you guys know as much as we do."

"Skipper, I've got my pack ready if I need to help the pilot out." Petty Officer Vance would be the one lowered to the ground if needed;

his pack was stuffed full of rations, a spare radio and batteries, medical supplies, and two quarts of water. In the jungle, he'd have a Heckler and Koch MP-5 with a collapsible stock and eight thirty-round magazines strapped to his harness, along with a Model 1911 in a thigh holster with four spare clips, each with seven rounds of .45 ammo.

"Vance, the last thing I want is two people to pick up."

"Sir, you may not have a choice." Even over the intercom, Josh could hear the determination in the young man's voice.

"Understand."

The wipers struggled to keep the windshield clear as they clunked back and forth. Despite being almost noon, the thick overcast and heavy rain made it dark outside the HH-3A and dark and damp inside. The moisture was so heavy you could taste it before it invaded your nostrils. The dampness and the distinctive jungle mix of rotting and fresh vegetation permeated the cabin and mixed with the pungent smell of evaporated jet fuel and the acidic smell of hot molybdenum disulfide grease. Underlying all of this was the rankness of body odor stored by the cockpit cushions and canvass crew seats. Any dramatic changes in this odd but normal mix was cause for someone to pay attention or even, in some cases, raise an alarm.

"Turn point in about two minutes. A saddle in the ridgeline should be coming up on your right. As soon as we see it, I'll take control."

"Got it."

"Guys, as soon as we turn east and get into the valley, start looking at the far ridgeline for the chute."

"Boss, how bad do you think it'll be?" Van der Jagt asked what everyone in the helo was thinking.

"In terms of triple-A?"

"Yes, sir."

"I don't know. I'm not worried about the North Vietnamese soldiers out searching for the guy. They'll have to shoot through the jungle canopy with their AKs and won't see us in time to have time to get a good shot at us. It's the heavier 23mm and 37mm stuff that scares me because we're going to be near Highway 89, the major road into Laos. We're going to be west of Vinh and next to Haiphong and Hanoi, where there's lots of triple-A. Our problem is we don't know what's in this valley or where it's located, and if we stumble on one of those guns at point-blank range, they could bag us."

Big Mother 40

Josh's crew could accept a blunt, frank answer rather than a bullshit one. They were all nervous and fear came with the combat SAR mission. The trick was not letting it prevent you from doing your job.

"Big Mother 40, Round Top Seven Oh One. Swordsmen Three Oh Four and Five are making their runs on AAA sites north of you. Also we have Sandys Two Three and Two Nine joining in about two minutes. Two more Sandys are about ten minutes out. Sandys Two Three and Two Nine should be just west of you and are familiar with the area and will call when they enter the valley."

"Roger Round Top Seven Oh One, heading in now." As soon as he cleared the ridge, he raised the collective and eased the nose over to increase their airspeed to a hundred knots.

They were still descending toward the valley floor when Van der Jagt called out. "Parachute, two o'clock, near the top of the ridge."

Josh rolled the HH-3A into a thirty degree bank to put the nose of the helicopter on the white-and-orange cloth stuck on a treetop. "Got it. Jack, ask Argonaut where the Trapp family has its lodge."

"Argonaut Four Oh Six, Big Mother 40. Authenticate. Where does the Trapp family have its lodge?"

"Stowe." The reply was almost instant.

"Be there in five."

"I'm ready. Fifty meters at four o'clock from the chute. I can't move."

"Roger."

"Sandys Two Three and Two Nine have a visual on Big Mother."

"Penetrator ready and we're rigged for rescue." Van der Jagt's muffled voice told Josh that he had the mask on and his head was outside the helicopter with his eyes focused on the parachute.

"Slowing." Josh keyed the intercom even though the crew would feel the helicopter pitch up and hear the change in engine sounds.

"Steady hover." Van der Jagt had his head out the door as Josh flared into a hover. "I can't see him."

"Argonaut, guide us over you."

"Twenty-five yards to the right ... ten yards ... five yards. On top."

"Can't see him. There's a gap in the trees to the right. Am going to move us right and send Vance down since Argonaut can't move," Van der Jagt said. The longer they hovered, the more vulnerable they were. He made the call without checking with Josh. "Vance is on the ground ... Got a thumbs up ... Penetrator clear."

"Round Top, found Argonaut Four Oh Six. Paramedic on the ground. Stand by for status." Josh dumped the nose and pulled almost full collective to get the HH-3A on the move.

"Big Mother 40, this is Nursemaid. Argonaut has lost a lot of blood and has a badly broken leg. Need to stop the bleeding and splint his leg before we can move him. Hopefully, we can get out without having to give him some plasma. Will notify you when we're ready."

Josh started a steep turn when the UHF radio crackled. "Big Mother 40, Sandy Two Three, break hard *right now*; you are taking ground fire from your six. Looks like a quad 23mm mount. Rolling in on the guns now."

With the helicopter in a steep bank, Josh craned his head to see behind him when a stream of green tracers passed under the nose. "Jesus H. Christ!" As he maneuvered, the HH-3A vibrated and shuddered in response as he rolled from one sixty-degree bank to another one steeper at forty-five, all the while changing altitude. He keyed the mike. "Big Mother 40 is taking fire from all quadrants. Sandy Two Three and Two Nine, you down here with me?"

"Yup. We're getting hosed by 23mm and 37mm, too. Exit the valley and give us some time to work our magic."

"Nursemaid, Big Mother 40, call when you are ready." Josh thought that if anyone could patch up the A-7 pilot fast, it was Vance. He'd just signed a strongly worded recommendation for him to attend the school for Navy Corpsmen. Vance spent his spare time taking college pre-med correspondence courses and wanted to be a doctor.

"Nursemaid, roger." Vance knew the drill and Josh would do everything he could to make sure that neither man became guests at the Hanoi Hilton.

Vance was child number four of six and used to being on his own. The young petty officer knew growing up that as soon as his older brothers said they wanted to run the family farm he'd have to find something else to do. Nothing interested him locally, so when he asked a Navy recruiter, who had a pair of shiny gold wings with the letters AC on a circle in the center, what they were, the petty officer said, "I was a helicopter air crewman," and described what he did. After listening, Vance said, "That's what I want. How do I get to a helicopter squadron where the action is?"

"Sandy Two Nine is hit. Losing gas out of my left wing tank. Sorry guys, gotta go home. Make them pay for damaging my bird."

Josh looked up and saw the plume of gas coming from a large jagged hole about halfway out of the wing as the A-1 flew by about four hundred yards away.

"Sandy Two Three is Winchester other than twenty mike mike. Got some of the triple-A suppressed at the southern end of the valley. Will stay until Sandy One Zero and One Three arrive."

"Nursemaid is ready. Will release a smoke if needed."

"Nursemaid, no, repeat, no smoke."

Josh turned the HH-3A one way and then wracked the shuddering helicopter into a near vertical bank and pulled back on the cyclic, putting two g's on the helicopter. The HH-3A groaned in protest and the vibrations from the flexing rotor blades increased.

"Watch the g's and the rotor RPM." Jack thought it pertinent to remind his HAC that if he pulled too many g's, they'd over-speed and over-stress the rotor head and possibly cause one of the hinges to fail. Loss of any blade meant instant death to everyone aboard.

"A hundred yards." Josh had the groaning helicopter's nose up in a flare. Pulling the nose up too fast could also cause the main rotors to flex down and cut off the tail pylon. That, too, would cause an uncontrolled crash that would kill them all.

"Penetrator's going down." The call from Van der Jagt came as the helo came to stop over the clearing and a stream of 23mm tracers went by the cockpit. The gunner had clearly not anticipated the quick stop. "Get the penetrator up. We're targeted." Josh hauled the helicopter up vertically by keeping the cyclic centered and pulling up on the collective.

"Ninety-six percent RPM and dropping"

Josh's two clicks acknowledged that as he dumped the nose as the rotor RPM passed ninety-five percent on its way to ninety-four percent. He was rewarded with another stream of 23mm bullets passing under the helicopter as the gunner over-corrected. The 23mm rounds were joined by a string of eight larger, more lethal 37mm golf balls from the eight-round clip that seemed to hang lazily in space as they passed by the nose.

"Sandy One Zero and playmate One Three are rolling in on the 23mm and 37mm sites. There are three that have you bracketed."

"Sandys are at your eleven o'clock and crossing." Jack could see the tops of the A-1s in their dirty brown and green camouflage, turning at sixty-plus-degree angles of bank. One was higher than the other; it pulled up and went straight and then reversed just as he passed overhead.

"Round Top Seven Oh One and Big Mother 40, Sandy Two Three, we could be in this valley for a week and not run out of targets. Go for it."

"Nursemaid, Big Mother, you ready?"

"Roger."

As they turned toward the location, they could see the A-7 pilot's orange and white parachute disappearing down into the jungle. "Jack and Van, mark this spot on a chart and in your brain in case we have to come back."

"How could I not remember? I've been getting a tour of the valley from a variety of vantage points and unusual attitudes."

Josh looked at his co-pilot and smiled at his gallows humor. This time, instead of heading straight across the valley, Josh flew down the ridgeline, a couple hundred feet below its tree-covered crest. Several streams of tracers snaked out toward the helicopter in a vain attempt to hit a target that was changing altitude and airspeed erratically. The hum of the helicopter's mini-gun added another distinctive note to the sound of a helicopter being pushed to the limit to avoid being hit.

Approaching the area where Vance and the pilot were hiding, Josh pulled the nose up about sixty degrees and then leveled just over the spot. No sooner were they level than the mini-gun hummed again while Kostas lowered the orange jungle penetrator.

The ping, ping, ping sound of bullets going through the thin aluminum skin added fear to Van der Jagt's voice. "Can't see Vance and the pilot. Taking hits. Penetrator is coming up! Let's get out of here."

Josh didn't wait. Nose down with forward cyclic and a healthy pull on the collective pulled the penetrator free and the helicopter began moving. "Nursemaid, Big Mother, we'll be back when we can quiet things down. Execute Plan Delta, repeat Delta."

"Nursemaid copies. Plan Delta."

It took a few minutes of dodging before the HH-3A exited the valley and headed south. "Round Top Seven Oh One, Big Mother 40."

"Big Mother 40, say intentions."

Jack keyed the intercom before Josh answered. "I'll bet they don't understand Plan Delta."

"Yup, and I am not going to tell them on the air." Josh rocked the mike switch from intercom to the UHF. "Round Top Seven Oh One. Need pigeons from entry point to Indian country to your home plate, over?"

"Big Mother 40, we're being relieved by Round Top Seven Oh ThreeSeven Oh Three and will pass your request on to them. Should have pigeons for you as soon as you turn east."

"Cool. That's a smart radar operator. He will note when we head east after we get south of the DMZ and then they will give us a heading and vectors back to the *Constellation.*" Again, he moved his finger from the top of the switch to the UHF. "Round Top Seven Oh One, Big Mother 40, roger that."

"I'll figure out how much gas we'll have when we arrive. My guess is not much," Jack said.

"Pessimist." Josh trimmed the helicopter to fly hands off and pressed the intercom mike switch on the floor. "Van der Jagt, how bad were we hit?"

"Unless there is some damage to the rotors or in the belly, I think all we did was take some 12.7mm rounds through the cabin and tail pylon and a couple in the armor plate in front of the mini-gun. We can look when we get on deck. They didn't like me firing back."

"Guys, we will go back and get Vance. I am not going to leave him on the ground any longer than we have to. He knows that Plan Delta means move to a place you can hide and we'll come back if we can later in the day or at dusk or as soon as it gets dark. That's about six to eight hours from now. If that doesn't work, we'll go back in the middle of the night and then again around dawn. We're going out to the *Constellation*, get some gas, ammo, talk to Argonaut Four Oh Six's squadron mates and tell the air wing what we need, and then come back."

Josh let the HH-3A cruise at one hundred knots at about three thousand feet. No one said much other than to respond to vectors from the E-2 and then normal calls based around checklists as they approached the *Constellation* for landing.

Josh found Jack slumped on the floor outside a head near the entrance to the *Constellation*'s flight deck. Dribbles of vomit were still on his chin.

"Josh, I don't know how you do it. There was so much shit shooting at us from all over that valley I could have caught a couple of the 23 and 37mm rounds in my hand. We damned near got bagged. Not once, but several times."

"The operative words are 'damned near.'" Josh handed him some paper towels. "We didn't because we were unpredictable and hard to track and we had good close air support." He watched his co-pilot wipe his chin. "I'll get you something to settle your stomach." When he came back a few minutes later, Jack hadn't moved. He handed him a can of Coke.

Jack opened the can with shaking hands and took a long swallow. "Will this work?"

"Yes. Either drink the Coke or I get you some coffee grinds to chew on. When you finish this one, I've got another one for you."

Jack nodded, feeling the ice-cold liquid go down into his queasy stomach. "I don't know how much longer I can do this."

Josh slid down the wall to be next to him. "Look, everyone in the helicopter, including me, is scared shitless. You're reaction tells me you are normal. After a lot of these missions, my knees shake so bad I'm afraid to walk."

"So you admit you're scared."

"Hell, yeah. Here's the thing: I'm too busy flying so I don't have time to worry or think about what could happen other than dodging the triple-A and making the pick-up. As the co-pilot, you have the hard part, which is watching everything that's going on around us and keeping me informed. And, what's worse, you just have to sit there and not do anything, so you're not in control. For us aviators who like to be in control of the world around us, that's hard to do. But you can do this; and don't let this go to your head, but you're good at it." He almost said "almost as good as me."

Instead he added, "And, you are acting as my alter ego to keep me from doing something really stupid by making me think and re-think some of the things that I do. A lot of times I act instinctively, and most of the time it is the right thing to do, but you help me by making sure that it is right."

"Yeah, right." Jack shook his head side to side.

"As I've told you before, the fear gnaws at me, too, but I find a way to let it out. Some guys go off and get drunk, others bang away at punching bags. You have to find your own way to deal with your fear. If you don't, it'll drive you to the funny farm. Talking about it is okay. If you weren't scared, I wouldn't let you fly with me."

Josh handed his co-pilot a second Coke. "We're going flying in about ten minutes. Go take a piss and I'll do the pre-flight. If you want some food, Van Der Jagt raided the enlisted mess and got stuff you can munch on while we're airborne."

"If I can keep it down."

The helicopter was ready for take off on the angle of the *Constellation* less than forty-five minutes after they'd landed. "Big Mother 40, this is War Chief tower. Wind is down the throat at fifteen. Cleared for take-off. Contact Round Top Seven Zero Three on Three Oh One point Five when able. Bring Argonaut Four Oh Six back to us. Good luck."

After making sure the detailed map of the valley with all the gun emplacements plotted was handy, Jack keyed the mike. "Take off checklist complete. I've got the throttles." Then he rocked the mike switch to the radio position. "Big Mother 40 lifting."

Big Mother 40

At two hundred feet, the heavy rain pelted the helicopter as it beat its way through the pitch-black night. A generous meteorologist would have said the visibility was half a mile. Josh guessed it at half that and hoped it would stay that way when they popped into the valley.

"Big Mother 40, Round Top Seven Oh Three Radar contact. Have four A-6s, call signs Steel Tiger Five Double Zero, Five Oh Three, Five Oh Six, and Five One Zero, ready and briefed. Two more are on five-minute alert, and War Chief and its playmate, Gray Eagle will provide additional aircraft as well. Let us know when you need help."

"Big Mother 40, roger." Josh rotated the UHF mike switch to the intercom. "With a little luck, we'll sneak in and get Vance and the pilot and get out without too much drama."

"Dreamer. They know we're coming, not when, but where. They're hunting Vance and he can't move fast because he has to take care of the pilot. Since Vance knows that, I hope he's taken the time to build a hide. And hopefully, the rain will make it harder on the bad guys, too."

The HH-3A entered the valley several miles south of where they believed Vance was hiding to try to confuse the NVA and make sure they knew which direction to turn. As soon as the helicopter nosed down and started to turn, Jack keyed the mike, hoping that Vance heard the helicopter and turned on his radio. "Nursemaid, Big Mother."

"We're up."

"Authenticate. Ask Argonaut what is the slogan of Mad River Glen?"

It took about thirty seconds. "Ski it if you can. Am two hundred meters NNE from last position. Will mark on top."

Josh clicked the mike twice as he adjusted Big Mother's heading and slowed to seventy knots. Jack looked back in the cabin and saw Van der Jagt leaning out the cargo door.

"Now, now, *now*." They could hear the noise of the helicopter being picked up by the microphone on Vance's radio.

"Got a light. Vance flashed a white light as we passed over him. Turn hard left; I think I can guide you in." Van der Jagt turned the hoist over to Kostas and Petty Officer Jeffrey Jackson, an air crewman from the *Constellation*'s plane guard helicopter detachment who'd volunteered to fly with them, taking over the M-60 in the passenger door on the left side. Kostas and Jackson had gone through boot camp and aircrew training together.

Josh slowed the helicopter to minimize the diameter of his turn. "Keep your eyes peeled. It is *way* too quiet."

Just as the helicopter was slowing past forty knots, four streams of tracers of different sizes lashed out, and when he saw them, Josh waved off, accelerated and started jinking. The low clouds forced him to stay two to three hundred feet above the trees. "How close were we?"

"Skipper, I don't know because I lost the precise spot when I saw the tracers." A pause. "Sorry, boss."

"Don't worry, we'll find him." Josh waited a second. "Nursemaid, you ready?"

"We were born ready."

"We're going to try again."

"We'll give you a colored light when you get close."

Josh clicked the mike twice.

"Big Mother 40, Round Top Seven Oh Three, do you need support?"

"Yes." Josh paused for a second, then keyed the UHF. "Round Top Seven Oh Three, ask the first two A-6s to lay a string of cluster bombs on both sides of the road that goes along the river down the center of the valley, one every five hundred yards as briefed. Have them call when they are in hot and dropping. Then call in the next group as planned."

After the controller on the E-2 acknowledged, Josh keyed the intercom. "And while they're creating fireworks of their own, we're going to attempt the pick-up."

"That's the plan?" Jack asked, not trying to be sarcastic.

"Steel Tiger Five Double Zero is in hot."

"Show's on." Josh grinned at Jack as he spoke. "Let's wait for the first couple of CBUs to start going off. The A-6s should get some secondaries, which will keep the bad guys' heads down."

Josh arched his back and stretched his arms to relieve the tension and aches caused by flying the helicopter for what his mind told him was now pushing twelve hours with just a short break. "Van de Jagt, am coming around to the left, to where D'Onofrio and I think Vance is. Correct us if we're wrong."

"You're good, boss. I think we're only a few hundred yards away."

They heard the bang before they felt the concussion. For a few seconds, the hillside was bathed in a yellow light which made the trees look an eerie shade of gray-green under the dark gray clouds.

Jack craned his head around, struggling to see behind them. "Looks like the A-6 got something. There are a bunch of explosions like ammo or fuel barrels exploding about a mile behind us."

"That's not good news. It'll light up the valley and we'll stick out like a sore thumb," Josh said, failing at trying not to sound worried.

"Easy forward, Boss. Got a mirror flash from Vance. We're about twenty yards out."

Josh heard loud bangs and felt the helo shudder. He added power and fed in right rudder and headed the helicopter downhill to pick up speed. "What the hell was that?"

No answer.

"No warning lights. All gauges are normal." Jack's voice was calm. "You keep flying and don't hit anything hard. I'll look in the cabin."

"Van der Jagt, what the hell is going on?"

Silence.

"Do you want me to un-strap and go back?" Jack was reaching for his lap belt to free the shoulder harness.

"Not yet … Loosen your belts so you can turn around and see what you can see."

"No need to." Van der Jagt's voice came on the intercom in a pitch several octaves higher. "We took two 23mm rounds. One hit the penetrator and it's all fucked up. The second hit the aft end of the armor plate under the mini-gun and exploded. No one's hurt but the shrapnel punched lots of holes in the floor and the fuselage by the door. It also cut my intercom cord so I had to dig out my spare."

"Any leaks?" Josh was more worried about hydraulic leaks than ones from the fuel cells in the belly of the helicopter. Without hydraulics the helicopter was uncontrollable and they were either dead or about to die.

"No. We're double-checking right now, but I don't think so, and I don't smell any oil, JP-5, or hydraulic fluid. I've got to figure out what to do with this penetrator and the hoist. Give me a few minutes."

"Round Top Seven Oh Three, Big Mother 40."

"Big Mother, go."

"We took some 23mm hits but are okay. Can you get us more A-6s? The first pass was successful, but I need at least two more for a total of four before we can make the rescue."

"Big Mother 40, Round Top Seven Oh Three, War Chief is launching two more. Be there in less than twenty minutes. Two more are getting ready."

Josh flew Big Mother out of the valley and began a random orbit about twenty miles to the west, being careful to stay east of the Ho Chi Minh Trail and its well-directed anti-aircraft guns. Fifteen minutes later, the radio came alive.

"Big Mother 40, Steel Tiger Five Oh Three with three playmates with you. What's on your mind?" The secure radio made it sound like the bombardier navigator in Steel Tiger 503 was speaking in a long, hollow tunnel.

Josh eased the nose down to get close to the trees. Ahead, he could see the reflected glow of the dying fires through the rain. The ceiling had come down to less than a thousand feet and the misty fog made it impossible to see across the valley.

The airspeed indicator oscillated between ninety and one hundred knots, which Josh knew was pushing it in this terrain and weather conditions, but speed was life.

Jack keyed the mike. "Steel Tigers, Big Mother is crossing the road and the river."

The A-6s had been orbiting in two pairs, one north and west just outside of missile range from the batteries based around Vinh, the Ho Chi Minh Trail, and just north of the DMZ. Both sections were between the cloud decks at about ten thousand and timing their circles so that they would enter the valley from the north three minutes after Jack made the radio call.

"Here's where the fun begins." Josh keyed the intercom. "Nursemaid, Big Mother. We're on our way again."

Two distinctive clicks let the crew know that Vance was alive and well. By now, the helicopter was only fifty feet above the rice paddies in the bottom of the valley.

"Steel Tiger Five Oh Six and Five One Oh are in hot."

"I see the A-6s," called Van der Jagt. "Lots of little explosions, some bigger ones."

"Okay everybody, this is when it gets hairy." The helicopter started to climb up the ridge line when Josh keyed the mike. "Nursemaid, authenticate, steepest run at Mad River."

The first A-6 Intruder passed five hundred feet overhead and the jet wash jarred the helicopter after the engines were past. Off to the south, twelve cluster bombs, each with six hundred and seventy bomblets, began to pepper the jungle and rice paddies with flashes of light.

"The Cliff."

"Nursemaid, do you hear Big Mother?"

"Roger, keep it coming, am twenty degrees right and about two hundred yards."

"Nursemaid, Van der Jagt says disconnect the penetrator and use the horse collar or D-ring to pull both of you up in one pass."

"Copy."

"Twenty yards. Got another mirror flash."

"Got him." Van der Jagt pushed the down button on the hoist as far as it would go.

Fifteen seconds later, Josh was relieved when he heard, "Big Mother, Nursemaid, we're on."

"Survivor coming up."

Josh didn't wait for the call that said Vance and the survivor were clear of the trees. He keyed the intercom as he pulled the collective up almost as far as it would go to climb straight up. "Hang on, here we go."

Van der Jagt used the two hundred foot per minute rate on the hoist to get them to just below the climbing helicopter that Josh kept below twenty knots. The HH-3A had burned about half of its fuel so it climbed easily.

"They're well clear of the trees." Van der Jagt's voice was very matter of fact as if he did this every day. "Boss, we have a problem. Hoist jammed."

"I'll keep it below twenty knots. Don't try to fix it, haul them in."

"Try to keep us out of the trees. I'll go help." Jack unstrapped and headed for the cabin. When he stuck his head out of the cabin, Vance and the A-7 pilot were about fifty feet below the helicopter. Van der Jagt had several loops of the hoist cable wrapped around the heavy glove used to steer the cable as it went up and down.

"Sir, get a gunner's belt on so you don't fall out, and then I think the four of us can haul them in."

Jack was surprised that the hoist cable wasn't smooth, and broken strands from the braided cable ripped the leather palms of his Nomex gloves apart before they started cutting his hands. When they got some slack in the cable, he looped it around the mini-gun mount to get a little more leverage.

It seemed like it took forever before they got the two men to the side of the helicopter just below the door. While Jack and the volunteer air-crewman struggled to keep the oiled cable from slipping through their hands, Van der Jagt lay down on his stomach and grasped Vance's hand and pulled. As they got closer to the floor of the H-3's cargo door, Kostas grabbed Vance's torso harness and got them a few inches closer so Van der Jagt could get his hands on the pilot's harness. Together, the four men heaved and got the pilot on board. Vance wrapped his arms around the mini-gun mount while his legs flailed, trying to find the rear weapon station so he could wedge himself against the fuselage. Van der Jagt and Kostas pulled Vance into the cabin and Argonaut Four Oh Six levered himself with his hands to get deeper into the cabin and out of the way.

"Boss, everyone is on board safe and sound."

"Good work." Josh added power and accelerated from the twenty knots he was maintaining to a hundred. "Round Top Seven Oh Three,

Big Mother 40, Argonaut Four Oh Six is on board and okay. Headed back to the barn. Need a litter on arrival."

FRIDAY, TWO DAYS LATER, JUNE 30, 1972, 0815 LOCAL TIME, CAM RANH BAY, 180 MILES NORTH OF SAIGON, SOUTH VIETNAM

"From what I read in the message, that was quite a rescue. Mancuso was impressed. He likes guys who don't quit. Well done," Marty said, standing across the desk that the three shared in the open area that served as an office.

"Yeah, well, somebody had to go get the guy." Josh took a long swig of his water. He was already sweaty and it was still early in the morning. "The A-6s must've hit several gun positions and a couple of ammo dumps and a fuel storage facility because the valley was lit up with several fires when we left."

"You were in the air for what, sixteen out of nineteen hours?"

"Something like that."

"Where's Jack?"

"At the helicopter, last I checked. They're patching bullet holes with tape, I think, and making sure that nothing vital was hit."

"Want to talk about it? Something tells me it was hairier than what's in the report."

"It had more than its share of scary moments. A walk in the park it was not. But the good guys got the job done." Josh smiled. "How about next time we have a beer after work?"

"I'm buying and we'll go to the club to have a real meal tonight."

"You're on." Josh pointed the top of the empty water bottle at his friend.

"While you were out playing hero, our photo interpreters came up with this. They found it in the treasure trove of stuff we got from the Air Force Buffalo Hunter missions." Marty plopped a picture on the desk.

"What am I looking at?" Josh looked at his friend before the picture.

"You tell me."

Josh studied the picture for a few seconds. "That looks like the remains of an H-3."

"Very good. It's the Air Force HH-3E that was shot down on that botched raid."

Josh looked at the picture again. "Who are all the people around it?"

"Good question." Marty handed him a blow-up of two officers standing by a GAZ-69 truck and looking up at the sky.

"One's European. My guess from his fatigues is that he's Russian. The other is Vietnamese. Both, from their insignia, are colonels."

"Look at this one." Marty plopped another photo on the desk. "The Russian's collar tabs say rocket artillery, but my guess is that his background is surface-to-air missiles."

"That would be logical."

"And, we think his name is Koniev."

"How on earth did you figure that out?" Josh was surprised they came up with a name.

"The photo guys used a marker to fill in the gaps in the lines on the enlargement. One of the guys reads Russian and he thinks that's the most likely name. Could be something else, but Koniev is good enough for me."

"So we find Koniev, we find the base."

"No, the other way around, dummy. Find the base, you find Koniev. But since great minds think alike, we sent NICPAC a note via a courier to see what's in the files about him and to respond the same way. It's a long shot, but you never know. The answer should be here sometime tomorrow."

"Wow. So you think Koniev and this Vietnamese colonel work together?"

"That'd be my guess. There are no other Russians in the photos, so my guess is that the Russian is an advisor to the Vietnamese colonel. Why else would he be there?"

Chapter 13
OPERATIONAL PLAN

Boris Rokossovsky was savoring the blessings of a second sanctioned trip to Vientiane in less than a month by sipping from the glass of fresh orange juice that room service had delivered with his breakfast when the phone rang. "Yes?"

"My name is Valentin Grushkin. I hope you had an enjoyable night." The voice on the other end let a few seconds pass as if it were sending a message. "We both work for the same people and I would like to spend a few minutes with you this afternoon after your lunch with our comrades from the Pathet Lao."

Who the fuck is this guy, and how does he know about my meeting and lunch? Rokossovsky told himself to be careful. "What would you like to talk about?"

"Your future. I have been asked to determine your interest and maybe make you an offer."

That was interesting. Rokossovsky would be at a disadvantage, though, because he had no way to call a friend in Moscow to check Grushkin out. "Where and when?"

"Your hotel will be fine. We can meet on the terrace and have a beer and talk. Say two-thirty. It will give you plenty of time to make your flight at seven."

"How will I find you?"

"Be on the terrace early and I will find you. See you then."

The man had piqued Rokossovsky's curiosity. However, being the cautious person that he was, after he hung up he field stripped his Makarov TT-33. Before he reassembled the semi-automatic pistol, he test inserted each round from the four 8-round magazines into the chamber to ensure they would load smoothly. He slid a round into the chamber before sliding the magazine into the pistol so he had nine rounds available if he drew the weapon. The holster in the small of his back was an ideal place to carry the Walther PPK/S size pistol when wearing civilian clothes in Southeast Asia's hot and steamy climate.

"My dear colonel, you look nervous," Valentin said to Boris in English as he arrived at precisely t2:30p.m.

"I was surprised by your call, to say the least." Rokossovsky spoke in his native tongue. He left the Makarov on the chair when he stood up to shake hands; when he sat down again it was between his legs and pointed at Grushkin.

"Let's speak in English. The reason will become very clear in a minute or two."

"Okay." Rokossovsky was looking at a well-dressed man, by Russian standards, of medium height and with a full head of blond hair. He looked more Aryan than Russian.

"We work for the same organization. I'm just in, shall we say, a different directorate."

Rokossovsky understood that the use of the word "directorate" wasn't a reference to the Army, KGB or the GRU.

"First, I want to let you know our common employer is very pleased with your assistance. Not a shipment has been intercepted and your documentation has been perfect. Others have learned from your work."

Boris nodded to acknowledge the compliment. He hoped his churning stomach wouldn't give him away.

"I understand that when your assignment is over in December, you return home and retire." It wasn't a question.

Another affirmative nod from Rokossovsky, who was figuring the less said the better.

"Your wife moved to Minsk when you came here. Is that where you want to retire?"

So, how much more does Grushkin know about me? "I am hoping to get one more assignment before I retire. We were both born and raised in Minsk and she still has family there. We thought it would be a good place for her to be while I am here. So, yes, for us, that is a logical place to retire." *But it is fucking cold there and I will have to live with the old cow in a loveless, childless marriage.*

"If you are interested, we can talk about another option."

"Such as?"

"We need a proven person we can trust. Because you speak English quite well, we want to offer you a position in America."

Of course I'm interested. Who wouldn't be? "What's the job?"

"We want you to... watch over things for us. We have legitimate interests and we need people who can manage our operations. We think you can do that."

I have no training in business. "What kind of businesses?"

"Hotels, clubs, and restaurants. We want you to oversee the managers and collect their financial statements and report back to our owners on what they are really doing. And, make recommendations on people."

The way he used the word "and" was interesting. "You know I have no training in business."

"Yes, we know that. Most of our people don't have that kind of knowledge because they grew up in our socialist paradise. But, you, Colonel Rokossovsky, have something we find very interesting. You are inquisitive, you are used to analyzing intelligence, you read people well and you get things done right the first time. They are important skills we need."

"Where in America?"

"Miami. It has much nicer weather than Minsk. We will, of course, pay you very well even by American standards. Your monthly income will be more than what we pay both you and Nikishev. We can provide a driver and a bodyguard, if you so desire. Or, you can drive yourself. That will be your decision."

"What about my wife?" *He must know that we don't have any children.* Rokossovsky wondered if they'd made this offer to Nikishev and he'd turned them down. Or, maybe they hadn't talked to him at all. *I do all the dirty work, getting the fake paperwork completed for the "technicians" who load the planes and make sure they have access to all the flights. He must know that Nikishev does nothing.*

"Ahhh, good question. We have several options for you to consider." He laughed. "It is like America, the land of choices: what cars to own, what home to buy, what to eat, where to shop." A pause. "What job to take?" Another deliberate pause. "We have two options for that. The Army could inform your wife that you died gloriously in the service of your country as a Hero of the Soviet Union and she will receive your full pension for the rest of her life. Or, we could arrange a divorce. It is up to you how much of your pension you would want to give her in that case. My recommendation would be that you give her a hundred percent, because of the money you have in your Credit Suisse account and what we would pay you would dwarf your paltry Soviet pension. My guess is that she doesn't know about the Swiss bank account. I can handle all the necessary paperwork for either option."

"How do you arrange for me to get out of Russia or Vietnam?"

"That will be answered once you decide whether or not to join us. You have to trust me to arrange everything."

"When do I have to give you an answer?"

"I am afraid you do not have much time. I am flying out tonight and have to know before I leave. All I need is a yes or no. If it is yes, then we will have further discussions. If it is no, then when you retire, you go back to the Soviet Union and you will never hear from us again."

Rokossovsky didn't believe that for a minute. If he went back to Russia, he'd be a loose end and he knew how the Mafya handled them. "How do I contact you?"

"Just leave me a note in an envelope with my name on it at the front desk. One word will be enough." Grushkin looked at his watch. "I'm sorry, I have to go and you need time to think." He stood up and offered his hand. He focused his blue eyes on Rokossovsky's face. "I do hope you will join us. It will be better for all of us. Have a good day."

SATURDAY, SAME DAY, 1445 LOCAL TIME, VENOM BASE

A little later than the time Rokossovky and Grushkin shook hands at the end of their brief meeting, Thai's orderly asked Koniev to follow him to his commander's building. When he entered, Thai was smiling.

"Sit down, you have to listen to this."

Koniev did as he was asked while Colonel Thai set a Japanese Akai tape recorder on the table and clumsily loaded a tape. "This is a recording of the radio transmissions from a few days ago when the Americans rescued one of their pilots in an area just west of Vinh. We have the radio transmissions between the helicopter, the pilot on the ground, as well as their bombers and radar control aircraft. Listen."

Thai played sections of the rescue and stopped at each break and excitedly provided more background information on what was happening on the ground at the same time the Americans were trying to make the rescue. "We never could find the pilot. We knew about where he was, but our soldiers never got close. One of the reasons was that there weren't enough of them there. Most of them were guarding the fuel and ammunition or assigned to the anti-aircraft batteries."

"Why are you playing these for me?" The tapes didn't have anything to do with Venom Base.

"I knew you'd ask that. These tell me how the Americans communicate and operate during a rescue so that we will be prepared. I want to set a trap for the Americans the next time we shoot down a pilot near Venom. We can either get him to make the radio transmissions or we can get one of our intelligence officers to play the part of the American on the ground."

Koniev could see the excitement in his counterpart's face and heard it in his voice. "But these were American Navy planes. They don't operate like their Air Force. They tend to be much more unpredictable. And the American rescue helicopters come from Thailand while the Navy's take off from ships in the Gulf and usually don't come this far inland for rescues."

"But there were American Air Force and Navy aircraft working together, no?"

"True, but they were under American Navy control. And the rescue was just a few miles inland." Koniev stopped for a few seconds. "From the reports I heard, the Air Force tried and couldn't get the downed pilot out and then the Navy went in because Vinh is on the coast and is a lot closer to their ships. That is the difference." Koniev wasn't sure of the command relationships, but his experience in Vietnam and his training told him there was a difference. He wanted to see if the Vietnamese colonel had thought this through completely before telling him it wouldn't work, so he asked the next question. "Even if you could get a Navy helicopter or plane to come this far, how are you going to come up with the answers to the authentication questions?"

"Ahhh." Thai sat back a bit and thought for a few seconds and then took a sip from his tea cup. "We get them from the American pilot. If we have to torture him to get the questions and answers that is what we will do."

"And if he gives you inaccurate information, or they ask different questions, then what?"

"That is a risk we have to take. If they figure out it is a trap, then they don't come and we still have shot down another American."

Koniev had learned that there were almost always two levels to conversations with Thai, so he wondered what this was really about. "The helicopter on the tape is Big Mother 40. Isn't that the one you call 'the ghost'?"

Thai's eyes sparkled as he smiled from ear to ear. "Yes, it is the one that works with Sierra Six. I want to draw them into a trap and kill them."

Big Mother 40

"Good morning, gents. I hope you enjoyed your vacation because it's time to go back to work."

The door was closed to Captain Mancuso's office. Chief Tannenbaum was standing outside to make sure that they were not disturbed or overheard.

"First, since you are TAD to me, I forwarded the rescue report along with some other paperwork to HC-7 and to CINCPAC via Commac-V. All of whom will be most impressed. I thought Petty Officer Vance's hand grenade booby trap of the penetrator he left on the ground was brilliant since he had all of what, ten seconds to set it up. Anyone who moves the penetrator is going to get a nasty surprise."

Josh nodded. "Thank you, sir. I'll tell him."

"We may recruit him as a SEAL. He was on the ground for about fourteen hours with an injured pilot that he carried about quarter a mile through the jungle to where you picked him up."

"Sir, I think that would require having you figure out a way to keep him from going to medical school. He's already taking college correspondence courses on biology and is passing with straight As. He is very focused on his plan to use his GI bill to get his degree and then, if he can get into medical school, take advantage of the Navy's program that pays for it along with his internship. He plans to do his residency at a Navy hospital and then spends a few years on active duty in return."

"I didn't know that." Mancuso also thought that there would be very few doctors in the Navy wearing the decorations that young man would have by the end of his first enlistment.

"Sir, Vance grew up in Minnesota and they hunted a lot because they couldn't afford meat. He said to me once before that carrying a live human is much more enjoyable than a dead deer. They weigh about the same, but at least you can talk to the human."

Mancuso chuckled. "Back to business. I just got off the phone with Admiral Hastings. He has authorized detailed planning. No messages, no phone calls with details of the mission as we required. When you know when you'll have the plan done, let me know and Admiral Hastings and his senior SEAL will fly here—sorry, no trip to Hawaii—for an in-person briefing and approval. Code name for the reconnaissance operation is Sunlight Sam and everything is TS/SCI. Admiral Hastings has talked to General Cruz and CTF-77 and anything you need to plan and execute will be provided. Questions?"

"Sir, who else will be involved in planning and the actual op?"

"Other than the people in this room, your team, and Haman's crew, no one, unless you want them involved. Everything is to be done here by us to keep it compartmentalized. If we need to bring in someone else, he comes here TAD and doesn't leave until the op is over."

"Thank you, sir."

This was Marty's world and Josh kept quiet. The crew wouldn't like it, but they'd understand why there would be no liberty until they came back.

"When do you think you'll have an initial concept of operations?" Mancuso asked Marty.

"Sir, we should be ready to tell Admiral Hastings when to come here by Friday our time." Marty looked at Josh, who nodded in agreement. They had done a lot of the planning already.

"I'll let him know. Keep me informed, particularly if anything changes."

Master Chief Tannenbaum had rounded up both Josh's crew and Marty's twelve-man team, along with the photo interpreters and intelligence analysts assigned to the project, by the time Josh, Jack, and Marty, walked into the room.

"Okay guys, gather 'round. We now have the go-ahead to plan the mission to find the missile base. What we've done so far is research and prep work, but now we have to put together the analysis that will support a series of missions."

Marty was in charge of mission planning, even though technically, by date of rank, Josh was senior.

"We need to know how soon we can have a full ops concept for the first recon mission ready. Then we get to brief it to a two-star when it is ready. Usual rules—no messages, no phone calls, no contact with the outside world from this point on without either Lieutenant Haman's or my specific authorization. We've got the communication inside the Navy under control and I want to make sure we have it under control inside the team. So, make sure you do not reference any of this in your letters and tapes to loved ones at home. This operation is TS/SCI, code word 'Sunlight Sam.' Chief Tannenbaum will have all the paperwork for you to sign in a few minutes."

Marty waited for the giggles to subside. "If we have to ask for outside help, we need to ask for it without telling them anything about the mission. If we get resistance, Captain Mancuso will arrange for an attitude adjustment conversation with a senior officer in the other person's chain of command."

Marty looked around the room. "Okay, first thing, Lieutenant Haman is in charge of figuring out to get us there and back. Petty Officer French, you're tasked with helping Lieutenant Haman because you have done most of the photo analysis of the region but you will be asked to help the others as needed."

"Yes, sir." French picked up a pile of photos.

Marty stabbed the table with his finger. "Just to be clear, our research shows there are three areas to search. I know we have one where we think the base is, but we need to put them all in order of priority based on the likelihood the base is not in the first search area. Each has to get the same level of evaluation so we can make our selection based on as many facts as we can, rather than just a gut feeling. That may be the ultimate deciding factor, but we have to have a strong base of sound intelligence."

Marty stopped and swallowed, not sure if he should share his next thought, but then realized they might as well know what might happen because they would all be involved and some at risk. "My gut feeling is that all the valleys are too close to China to allow B-52s to carpet bomb. And, unless we can figure out a way defoliate the target area so they can see their targets, fighter bombers aren't the answer, either. That leaves one option: a raid."

Again, the SEAL paused for a few seconds to let his words sink in. "If you include a raid as an option, worst case is that we have to recon three valleys and come back for the raid on the fourth. That suggests four trips. That translates to four reconnaissance plans, four different routes in and out, and four sets of insertion and extraction LZs."

Marty could see the concern on each face as he continued with the assignments. "Lieutenant D'Onofrio will be in charge of intelligence and logistics, which means he'll gather everything we can find about the base, plus the two SEALs tasked with getting us equipped will report to him. He doesn't know anything but we can count on him to ask dumb and penetrating questions." A few chuckles rambled through the room.

"Everyone else will work with me to figure out which area of interest to search first and build the reconnaissance plan for each. I'll have a couple of SEALs assigned to look at each valley in detail as part of our planning process. Then, after each op, we'll update the plans and adjust as necessary. Lieutenant D'Onofrio will split the rest of the Intel guys into two groups, one to help evaluate insertion and extraction routes and LZs to support Lieutenant Haman, and one to develop a detailed profile of each reconnaissance area to support our ranking of each of the valleys and the order in which we will search them. The rest of you will be getting our gear ready and helping to research answers to questions."

Marty looked around the room. "Lieutenant Haman will work out of that side of the room and I'll work out of the opposite end. I want the composite photo mosaic and map of the area on a large table in the middle. All, and I mean *all*, intelligence will be noted on it so we can all use it as a single point of reference. Everything stays in this room. If needed we'll work around the clock, but I think our normal sixteen to seventeen hour days will get the job done. Questions?"

A few chuckled at his reference to the normal work day at COMMACVNAVSPECWAR. There were none.

"Good. Once we get the valleys ranked, then we'll use that to make our recommendation to Admiral Hastings as to where we go first. I want to be able to show the admiral the different valleys, why they were picked, and our rationale for ranking them."

TUESDAY, NEXT DAY, JULY 4TH, 1972, 2246 LOCAL TIME, CAM RANH BAY, 180 MILES NORTH OF SAIGON, SOUTH VIETNAM

Josh gave up trying to sleep. The notion had been bugging him for weeks and finally, his brain organized it in such a way that he could actually write something he thought might be coherent. During his first tour in Vietnam, he wrote letters to both his parents that were to be mailed or given to them if he was killed or missing in action. That was BN, or "Before Natalie." Early in this tour, it was easy to redo the ones to his mother and father, but writing one to Natalie eluded him.

Now, with her about to be a bigger part of his life, he wanted to write one for her but could never make the words flow. Each time he tried, he tore up several sheets in frustration and stuffed them into the burn bags for classified material. That was until the past couple of days when he admitted to himself, deep, deep down in his subconscious that his bachelor days were over. Done. Gone. Never to return. He was going to spend the rest of his life with her.

When he got to the command center, there was no one there other than the duty officer and the three enlisted who manned the telephones and radios. They spent most of their watches sorting and logging messages. No one from his crew was there; Marty, his fellow workaholic, was sleeping in the bunkroom that the three of them shared. A stack of paper was next to the IBM Selectric, and after taking a few seconds to get the paper lined up, he began to type away, letting words, and tears, flow.

Big Mother 40

July 4ᵗʰ, 1972

My dear Natalie,

If you are reading this letter, it means that I have been killed or declared missing in action. I hope you never have to read this, but since the worst will have happened, I thought I would try to tell you in my own words now how much I love you and how I wanted to spend the rest of my life with you.

I have written similar letters for my mom and dad and have told them all about you. They too will get mailed if something bad happens to me. I have also given them your name, address and phone number so the three of you can contact each other if you choose to do so. I wrote their address and phone numbers on a separate piece of paper and put it in this envelop.

Our few months in San Diego were wonderful beyond my wildest dreams and I cannot put into words no matter how hard I try to say how much they meant to me. Here on the other side of the world, I cannot stop thinking about you. You are the love of my life.

As you know, I am doing something that I love. No, I don't like the killing, but I have come to realize that I am a warrior. It is who I am but I am not a war-lover nor do I have any romantic notions about the glory of dying for one's country. In fact, that's exactly what I am trying to avoid. I do what I do because I volunteered, because I like the flying, the excitement, and the challenges of what we do.

This is my fifth or sixth version of this letter. I seal them up, give them to the personnel people to put in their safe and then, a few days or weeks go by and I ask for it back and re-write it. It seems each one just doesn't say it the way I want to. So, I will say it as simply as I can. I love you with all my heart and soul and hope you never have to read this letter.

Josh

Relieved, he addressed a new envelop and put it on the desk with a note instructing the enlisted man who maintained the personnel records to mail it if he were killed.

Marc Liebman

This was the first day in a week where one saw blue sky through the clouds and could see across the valley. Thai was surprised at how easily General Nikishev, the aged, past retirement World War II veteran had climbed the ladder to the observation post nearest the cave complex, following Thai's suggestion that he scan the treetops looking for imperfections in their camouflage.

The embedded stench of stale tobacco in Nikishev's uniform mixed with his sweat warned you he was coming if you were downwind. Even a few feet away and upwind, one knew he was around.

Koniev wrinkled his nose at Nikishev's odor pollution which stood out in the damp, freshly washed air. Rokossovsky seemed preoccupied as he stood off to one side. Something was amiss; it appeared to Koniev that the intelligence officer's mind was on something else, although he was paying attention to what was happening. Koniev thought he'd been able to get past the colonel's caustic guard through their phone calls, and underneath Koniev had found, to his surprise, a very dedicated, capable officer. So the question was, what was up with Rokossovsky?

The Russian officers had come with a re-supply convoy before dawn and planned to leave after dark. It would be a slow trip back and their driver was given a place to take a nap so that at least one person in the GAZ-69 would be awake.

Nikishev was enjoying meeting his fellow Soviet soldiers as he walked among the men arrayed at attention at the missile control van. He smiled and chatted with them as he pinned medals on each man.

The old Soviet veteran was totally surprised at the launcher when the trees had been pulled back, revealing an acre of clear blue sky. His smile told everyone that he loved seeing how they'd kept the launch sites hidden when the leaf-filled netting sprang back into place.

"What's next?" Nikishev asked, eager to keep going.

"Lunch and a briefing by Colonel Thai's officers on the base's defenses."

Koniev sat next to Nikishev during the briefing by Thai's company commanders to make sure the general stayed awake, but that precaution proved unnecessary. The old man's penetrating questions turned the meeting into a two-hour session before the general stood, said "Thank you," and looked for someone to lead him to his next event.

Koniev excused the junior Soviet officers, who smiled when they realized that they would not have to entertain the visitors, and pointed in the direction of the cave complex which was about half a kilometer away.

It was a walk along the gravel road that the three senior Soviet officers took in silence, only acknowledging the greetings and salutes of the soldiers who passed by.

Now, alone with the two colonels, Nikishev looked around the excavated stone room, which he was seeing for the first time. He was clearly tired and looked as if he needed a nap. "Can anyone hear us outside the cave?"

"No, not unless your voice can penetrate rock." Koniev pulled out a bottle of vodka that had managed to make its way to his cave courtesy of Rokossovsky. By the time he'd opened the bottle, Rokossovsky had placed three glasses on the table for Koniev to fill.

"To Mother Russia." All three officers clinked and drained their glasses. Dutifully, Koniev refilled them as they sat at the rough-hewn wooden table stained by coffee, tea, and gun oil that had gotten deep into the wood's grain.

"Moscow thinks the Americans are dedicating reconnaissance planes to find Venom, which is like a very annoying itch you can't make go away." Nikishev paused to puff on his cigarette. "Our experts think that once the Americans find Venom, they will blast it to hell. Others think that they are more interested in just learning your tactics. Personally, I think they will bomb the shit out of this valley. That's what I would do."

If this was accurate, Koniev thought, then what Nikishev was telling him must be coming from a spy inside the U.S. military. Where else would they learn this? He was also telling him that he was about to die.

Nikishev swallowed one half of the glass's liquid in one gulp. "Rokossovsky here thinks Venom is too close to China to use B-52s, which leaves us with his very interesting theory. You want to tell him?"

"Sure." Rokossovsky finished about a third of the glass while Nikishev drained his and held it out for a refill. He let Koniev finish filling all the glasses before continuing. "My guess is that the Americans will try to pull off some kind of raid like they did at Song Tay. To do that, they need a lot of detailed intelligence which they don't have at the moment, but give them time. Because of Venom's location, the only way they get that is from someone on the inside, or by reconnaissance on foot."

"So you think there might be a traitor here?"

Rokossovsky laughed. "Fuck, no. And if there was how would he get the information out? The Americans are very sneaky bastards. They have photographic satellite, drones, and all sorts of planes that can take very, very good pictures. They may be able to find your jungle paradise with it if they get lucky. And for them to get lucky, someone here has to be careless." Rokossovsky paused to push the ashtray that Nikishev was rapidly filling closer to the General. "Or, they may send their special forces in to snoop around. They tried that once and we bagged them. But since then, we have not seen any information in their messages that suggests that type of mission. That in itself is suspicious, because we see other messages that are either reports or tasking for a raid or a reconnaissance. One can take the lack of traffic as that they are not planning, or that they are planning it with a higher level of secrecy. Being the suspicious sort, I would choose to believe the latter is happening. Please let me be clear, I have no proof."

Koniev realized that Rokossovsky had just confirmed that if the Americans found and attacked this place due to a perceived breach of security, he was the sacrificial lamb. They'd need someone to hang, literally, and that was him. "What if the Americans sent some of their Spetznaz in here to find us? Then they could send in the fighter bombers."

"Finding you should be very difficult." Rokossovsky stated it as if it were a fact. "You are in a remote corner of Vietnam, hidden in this lovely valley. That's why we helped the Vietnamese pick this place. Plus, from what I see, everything is so dispersed you would need a lot of F-105s to destroy this place. Everything is hidden under the trees so it would be very hard to find something to aim at."

Koniev didn't believe anyone from the Soviet Union had anything to do with picking this valley. *So you either were told what the Vietnamese are thinking, or dismissed it, or don't know. I'd bet on the latter.* "We've already been bombed twice. That leads me to think the Americans have a general idea of where we are."

"Koniev, as I told you on the phone, when you listen to the tapes of the American radio transmissions, in one case they were unloading bombs that they couldn't drop. In the other, we think it was a training mission to see if their low-level tactics will work here. This valley happened to be a convenient place to drop their bombs, no more, no less."

"I'm not so sure I agree with you." Koniev believed that it was just a matter of time before the Americans unleashed their fighter bombers against Venom.

Rokossovsky drained his glass. "What I think is that the Americans will put a recon team on the ground to find Venom. Just be careful. I wouldn't want any harm to come to you." The stocky Russian tilted his half-empty glass toward Koniev and then drained it.

Big Mother 40

Twenty people lined up outside the HH-3A, on the boat ramp that doubled as a helipad, with packs stuffed with the load that the SEALs thought they'd need for a raid. They'd been at it since 0730 in the morning and each man was drenched in sweat as they clambered into the helicopter, wearing backpacks which weighed an average of fifty pounds, and were guided to a specific position in the cabin in an exercise to see how many they could pack into the cabin.

"Josh, we need to think in twos, plus the five in your crew," Marty said, standing in the cargo door, holding a clipboard that showed the last configuration they'd tried.

"I know. Right now, the most we can cram into the helo is fourteen SEALs and the five of us, which gives us a total of nineteen on board. We could probably get two more guys in if we took the mini-gun out and the ammo tray, but I don't want to give up the fire power."

"Me, neither. How long do you think the flight will be?"

Josh had the kneeboard card with the waypoints and fuel-burn calculations in his hand. "Depending on the LZ, it will take us somewhere between an hour and a half flight to an hour and forty-five minutes each way. Fuel is not the problem. We're going to be very heavy so we'll just do a rolling takeoff. We've tried it about a half a dozen ways and fourteen of your guys is the max we can fit in the cabin."

"I'd like to have four four-man teams if we could, which means sixteen is the right number. We're three short." Marty stood with his hands on his hips looking back and forth between the row of packs and the helicopter's cabin.

"If we get to do a raid, I'd like to keep this a one-helo mission because it reduces the size of the LZ we'll need and makes the transit in and out much less complicated." Josh looked at his friend and smiled. "If they tell us to go, then we'll figure out a way to solve the head count problem. I'll noodle on it and come up with some ideas."

Chapter 14

RECON

"What if we just stopped shooting missiles for a few days, maybe a week?" Koniev turned to Thai as he put down the East German made Zeiss 10x50 binoculars he'd brought with him to Vietnam.

The two officers were on the platform near the caves for what they called the "daily show" of a morning reconnaissance flight. Sometimes it was an RF-101, which was easily identified by its small swept wings, other mornings it was the long nose of an RA-5C with its distinctive wings and Coke-bottle-shaped fuselage. On other days, it was a small, shark-nosed drone.

The planes the American Air Force called RF-101 Voodoos generally came from the west and flew about three hundred meters above the valley floor. Both officers were amazed at how predictable the Voodoos were; they were alerted by a call from the Northwest Air Defense Sector Command Center each day that one was coming, usually at about the same time. Koniev kept a log of the time, direction of flight, and his estimate of the altitude and speed for each flight that flew over or near Venom.

The Navy RA-5C Vigilantes flew over at around three thousand meters and were much harder to see. The Soviet operators who manned the fire control scopes at Venom followed their flights by relying on the radar repeaters from the Northwest Air Defense sector. Koniev had given his men explicit instructions to turn Venom's radar off and not to engage the high flying U.S. Navy reconnaissance planes with either missiles or guns.

The drones were entirely different. It was not just their speed and small size, which made them look fragile, but the engine noise was an eardrum-piercing shriek rather than a roar, and Venom's radar operators never had any advance warning of when they were coming. Sightings were plotted by hand in the Northwest Air Defense Sector command center, which sent out vague and often unreliable alerts. Thai had seen

243

several drones that had crashed, and from examining the remains he knew that some took pictures and some recorded electronic signals.

The glass windows hiding the camera lenses and the pilot's helmet in today's RF-101 flight were clearly visible from Koniev's perch through the high-quality lenses.

Koniev handed the binoculars to Thai, who studied the light-gray airplane for the few seconds it was silhouetted by the dark-gray clouds. "How fast do you think he's going?"

"Better than nine hundred kilometers per hour. He's relying on speed to make him hard to shoot down. You have to be very lucky with any kind of gun to hit an airplane that low, going that fast."

"Do you think he's hiding from our radar?"

Koniev knew the difficulty of seeing low-flying aircraft with their radar. "Maybe he is trying to take our picture! You didn't answer my question. What if we stopped shooting missiles for a few days?" Koniev persisted, though he already knew the answer.

"Because the answer has not changed. You are here to shoot down as many American airplanes as you can. Each one you shoot down or scare off is one less they can use to bomb my countrymen. My job is to protect the base from a ground attack. If we get bombed, that is a risk we all take, so the orders are the same. We don't take days off. When the weather clears and the Americans come, we shoot them down."

Koniev believed the Vietnamese colonel had long ago accepted as fate that it was a question of *when* they would be found and attacked, not if. Thai knew he had two options. One, if he kept them in the caves, they would be relatively safe from air attack, but could not find and engage in battle any commandos who attacked the base. Or two, he could keep them in the field, dispersed around the base knowing that they were vulnerable to air attack. But it would take a massive B-52 strike to wipe them all out, and if they were in the field, they were in a much better position to defend the base against an attack by ground forces.

Thai adamantly believed that it was better to be in the field, where you can maneuver and hide and engage the enemy at a time and place of your choosing. That philosophy was why his four companies were deployed around the base and only one platoon of each of the four companies was in their bivouac area at any time.

Koniev guessed that it wouldn't be long before he and Thai were told to start keeping the tracking radar on longer to shoot down more planes. When that happened, Koniev expected the Americans would find Venom in a few hours and attack, and Soviet casualties would increase disproportionately. The missiles and launchers would be the primary targets, all of which were manned by his people whose only protection was the jungle canopy. He knew it was not enough.

"Mount up. Launch in fifteen minutes," Josh said into the telephone.

Their matte-black HH-3A had been parked on the alert ramp along with four green-and-brown Air Force HH-3Es for several days. Not only was its paint different, but the boat hull of the Navy version didn't look at all like the square fuselage of the HH-3E, which ended in a ramp and a long, skinny tail boom.

Josh had used Udorn for prior forays into Laos and North Vietnam so it was not unusual for the black Navy HH-3A to be parked on the concrete apron with the other camouflaged helicopters. Usually they were there only parked for a few hours, but this time Big Mother 40 had been there since Friday night.

By the time Josh arrived in the van from the rescue command center, Jack had the number one engine turning and was ready to start number two. "What have we got as a cover for our insertion route?"

Josh slipped the metal loops of the shoulder straps into the three-inch-wide lap belt latch before he spoke. "An Air Force RF-4 was bagged in northwestern Vietnam and they got two beepers plus confirmation that both pilots are alive and well. Call sign is Rampart Seven Eight. Here's the estimate of their position. It's perfect for us. We join the Jolly Greens as part of the flight and stay at treetop level. When they get to their holding area, we head toward our LZ. Let's get the number two engine started and then we'll engage the rotors. We don't want to be the last one ready to go. We're Jolly Green Nine Six until we're out of Indian country and back here, and we talk on the radio only if there is an emergency. We only use Big Mother 40 if we have to talk to Marty on the ground."

In the cabin, Marty and the five other men in his team were sitting on the floor. Since there were only nine men in the cabin, three of the five 3-position troop seats were folded down so everyone in the cabin could strap in. As planned, three SEALs were on each side, and their backpacks and weapons were in a neat row lashed down against the cabin wall.

Big Mother 40 was going to insert the SEALs into the valley they thought was the most likely one to contain the missile base for a planned a five-day reconnaissance mission. If needed, Marty was willing to extend it a day, but only under extenuating circumstances; everyone involved knew that the longer they were in North Vietnam the greater the chances of getting caught in a firefight, or worse, being captured or killed.

Day one would be spent working their way from the insertion point into the valley. They'd spend days two and three reconnoitering the valley floor and then, if all went according to plan, they'd use day four to hike to the extraction LZ for pick up on day five. If Marty needed to change the extraction LZ or wanted to stay another day, he had pre-determined times to communicate with Billiard Ball. In an emergency, he could call at any time.

"Ready to engage." Josh released the rotor brake and the helicopter rocked on its main mounts as the rotor blades increased speed.

Jack waited until the rotor rpm was up to one hundred four percent, allowing for the inevitable drop in rpm that followed when they pulled power for the lift, then gave the signal to the plane captain to pull out the chocks. "Who picked Nine Six for the call number?"

"CO of the rescue unit," Josh smiled at the reference to the number. "He has a sense of humor and is a road-racing fan. It's the number his favorite driver Dan Gurney uses a lot on his Arcerio Brothers Lotus 19."

"What about the weather?"

"For us it is not ideal, but it is also not bad, either." Josh wanted to make sure he gave Jack the latest information. "We'll pass through some rain showers on the way in, but it is supposed to be clear around the LZs. Not much of a moon, so it will be hard to make out the landmarks. The CO said he's only authorized four A-1s, but to let Red Crown or the SARCAP know if we need more. Two more are standing by for the rescue, but also for us. He isn't in the loop—we're going in without communicating with anybody and if we need help, we'll call. But if we do, that's a bad thing. I did, though, thank him for the offer."

On the way into North Vietnam, they planned to listen to the same frequency that the Jolly Greens were going to use for two reasons: one, if they got into trouble, they were already on a commonly used rescue frequency and could call for help without changing frequencies; two, it was part of the deception.

The navigation lights on the blacked out Jolly Greens were green, white and red dots above the HH-3A as they maintained position as the number three helicopter in right echelon, about fifty feet below, fifty behind and about one hundred feet to the right of the number two Jolly Green in the formation. Josh wondered what the tension was like on the Air Force helicopters who would soon be asked to dash in and pick up the downed pilots once the Sandy's found them.

"Jack, we're about 10 minutes from where we depart the formation."

"Got it." Jack was flying because the number two Jolly Green was on the left, or Jack's side, which made station keeping in the formation much easier. "It is a lot smoother than I thought it would be out here. Forecast said there was supposed to be…"

"Jollys Five Five and Five Six, this is Sandy Three Three. I've got both Rampart Seven Eight Alpha and Bravo located. Head Oh Eight Five from bullseye. TACAN channel 15. Let me know when you have a lock and I'll guide you in. Survivors are about a half mile apart.

"That's our cue! I've got the helo. Plan says we fly Oh Nine Eight for fifteen minutes. Start the clock and I'll take us down into the weeds."

"Clock has started," Jack said, looking at the chart through a red lens. "Radar altimeter is set for eighty feet. We need to keep a steady ninety knots, and if we get a break in the rain showers we should see the notch that we'll cross over into the first valley. If not, we'll have to slow to sixty and feel our way in and adjust the leg flight times."

Josh clicked the mike twice and concentrated on keeping the helicopter out of the rice paddies that glistened below. Josh felt very exposed at this altitude, with no mountains to hide their noise. After about five minutes, the rice paddies were replaced by trees and what little ambient light there was enabled him to see that the ground was beginning to climb so he raised the nose and added power.

"Remind me, how high is this ridge?"

"Top is at about eighteen hundred feet where we want to cross. We'd need to climb to over twenty-two hundred if we're off by a half a mile in either direction."

"We're passing fifteen hundred." Josh kept his head in the cockpit and flew the helicopter on instruments. As the helo flew, jagged rifts of cloud looked like daggers trying to stab them into the ground.

"I think we have about another five hundred feet before we get into the clouds, and we're crossing the ridge right where we should be." Jack kept his finger on the chart where the next turn point was noted. "Come left to One One Five for two minutes, which should take us across the valley. As soon as you're steady on the new heading, I'll start the clock."

"Good. Steady on One One Five." Josh had struggled with planning the insertion route because there weren't a lot of good choices that used terrain-masking to hide the helicopter from the North Vietnamese radar's prying electronics and the eyes and ears of the civilian population. This route kept them over flat areas that did not mask the high-pitched whine of the engines or the beat of the helicopter's five main rotor blades. If they were off by as much as a minute in either direction, Big Mother 40 risked flying over small villages where they were sure the local government officials would report the time and the helicopter's direction of flight.

Their other choices for routes had even smaller margins for error. This expedition, like many others, forced them to make choices as they balanced the risk of detection and the time of flight versus how easily they could navigate visually at night. In the end, this particular one, like every other insertion and extraction route plan, was a series of compromises. Now they'd find out if they'd made the right choices.

It took the better part of an hour to fly the remaining five legs of varying lengths. The clouds gave way to a clear black sky with a quarter moon and bright stars. "Under ten minutes to go. LZ should be on nose. I'll wake up the boys in the back!" Jack put the map between the corner of the instrument panel and the Plexiglas side window.

"We're ready in the back. Disconnecting." Marty said, telling the two pilots and the rest of the crew that he was taking off the head set he'd been wearing for flight. He came forward and both Josh and Jack shook his hand and wished him good luck.

"Deploy the rope." The SEALs had decided during the development of the mission plan the fastest way to get into a small LZ like the one they'd targeted was to fast rope out of the H-3. During several night-time practice sessions in and around Cam Ranh Bay they also realized that perfecting the technique also gave them more LZ choices. By the time they took off, all six team members of Sierra Six knew they all could be on the ground from a fifty foot hover in less than twenty seconds.

"Rope going out." Van der Jagt tossed the one-and-a-half-inch diameter hemp rope out the cargo door.

"Jesus, this place looks a lot larger in the photos than it does in real life." Josh keyed the intercom as he slowed and descended into a hover with the belly of the helicopter fifty feet above the ground and the rotor blades just above the trees.

"SEALs out the door."

Twelve seconds later. "SEALS on the ground. Got a thumbs up."

Josh pulled the collective up and he eased the nose over as the HH-3A climbed. By the time the helicopter was passing forty knots and one hundred and fifty feet, Van der Jagt reported that the rope was back on board.

"Fly Two Five Five for four minutes. That will take us diagonally across this valley and then we'll fly Two Zero Five for fifteen minutes before heading west to Nakhom Phenom. You should be able to maintain ninety knots a hundred feet over the trees now that we can see them."

"Got it."

Marc Liebman

Thirty minutes after they dropped off the SEAL Team, Josh turned the helicopter on a heading of Two Seven Five, which would take them straight to the Air Force base outside Nakhom Phenom. "So far, so good. You fly for a while and I'll navigate."

Josh waited until he saw Jack's hands take the controls and then he held his hands in the air to indicate that he was no longer flying the helicopter.

"I got it."

"Jolly Green Nine Six, Billiard Ball Four Four."

Josh pulled the mike switch to the intercom position. "What the hell? We're not supposed to call him and he's not supposed to call us."

"Maybe they think we're late. Or they got us mixed up with another helo with the same call sign. Or worse, they need help."

"Yeah. Well, let's find out." Josh took a deep breath. "Billiard Ball Four Four, this is Jolly Green Nine Six over."

"Jolly Green Nine Six, Billiard Ball Four Four, say your playtime."

Josh keyed the intercom while he looked at the gauges for the forward and aft tanks. "They want to know how much fuel we have because they may want us to do something." After a little mental math, figuring they needed about twelve hundred pounds of fuel to get to Nakhom Phenom, he keyed the mike. "Billiard Ball Four Four, Jolly Green Nine Six has about Six Zero minutes of playtime from our present position. Copy?"

"Jolly Green Nine Six, copy Six Zero minutes of playtime. Proceed to original orbit One Five miles at Zero Seven Zero from bull's-eye, squawk Three One Six Two, ident and stand by this frequency. Copy?"

Josh held up his hand to tell Jack not to speak. "I know what you're thinking, but before we say something, let's listen in and see if we can figure out what's going on and what they want. My guess is that the rescue of Rampart Seven Eight is not going according to plan. Meanwhile, head Three Four Zero while I figure out a more precise heading and en route time."

"We can't jeopardize getting Marty and his guys out."

"Let's wait and see what's going on." Josh wasn't ready to commit to any new course of action but he didn't want to eliminate any either. "They might want us to follow a damaged helo home."

"Jolly Green Nine Six copies."

"Jolly Green Nine Six, Billiard Ball Four Four, report reaching assigned orbit. Do you have another call sign you prefer?"

"Jolly Green Nine Six. Negative another call sign and estimate reaching assigned orbit in approximately ten mikes." Josh rocked the mike to the intercom position. "I wonder what the fuck that is about?"

"My bet is that he has both call signs on his briefing sheet for Jolly Green Nine Six. If we came up as Big Mother 40, he'd have instructions to divert the world to help us. So he's asking us to clarify which mission by which call sign we want to use."

"Not bad thinking for a lowly co-pilot."

"We need to go into an orbit with one minute legs and standard rate turns. Just like basic instrument training. Keep it at one thousand feet above the terrain, which out here should be safe," Josh said into the intercom before keying the mike for the radio. "Billiard Ball Four Four, Jolly Green Nine Six on-station in assigned orbit, with Four Zero minutes of playtime before we have to return to base. Copy?" He switched back to the intercom. "Jack, that gives us about ten minutes of hover time and thirty minutes to bore holes in the sky out here and about an hour of fuel to get home."

"Jolly Green Nine Six, Billiard Ball copies. Standby, maintain orbit, we're still trying to fix the location of Rampart Seven Eight Bravo. We have two Sandys working the area, trying to re-establish contact. They are taking intermittent heavy fire, mostly 23mm and 37mm. Copy?"

Josh clicked the mike twice and looked at the map to try to figure out where Rampart Seven Eight went down. After looking at it for a while, he keyed the intercom. "If the pilot is where I think he went down, it's a nasty area. Good news is that it's well north of where Marty and his guys are. We're about fifteen minutes from where Rampart Seven Eight Bravo is, so figure forty from our present position there and back plus about another ten minutes of fuel for the pick-up. Add in an hour back to Nakhom Phenom means we should land with about twenty minutes of fuel. I can live with that even though the low fuel warning lights will be on."

"Anybody, this is Rampart Seven Eight Bravo, need pick up now! Enemy nearby."

Josh turned to his co-pilot. "That's not an American voice nor a word most pilots would use."

"What do you mean?"

"Diction is off. Wording is not what a pilot would use. I'll bet the person using the radio is not a native American speaker. He could be an immigrant or it could be a trap. My gut says trap."

"Jolly Green Five Six is going to make a run at getting Rampart Seven Eight Bravo out."

Josh pointed to his chest and keyed the mike. "Billiard Ball Four Four, Jolly Green Nine Six will close your area in case Jolly Five Six needs help. When did you last authenticate Rampart Seven Eight Bravo?" In the gap, Josh keyed the intercom. "I hope he gets the hint. If they don't, we may have to go get the guys from the Jolly Green."

"Billiard Ball Four Four, Jolly Green Five Six is taking hits but no major damage and waving off this pass. There is heavy 12.7mm and 23mm fire in the area. Am going to try to approach Rampart Seven Eight Bravo's position from another direction."

"Billiard Ball Four Four copies. Break, break. Rampart Seven Eight Bravo, where did you take your honeymoon?"

"San Francisco and we had bad weather." The diction was slightly different and strained.

"Jolly Green Five Six, this is Billiard Ball Four Four. Abort, repeat *abort* at once. Repeat, ABORT AT ONCE!"

"Billiard Ball Four Four, this is Jolly Green Five Six. Roger that. Abort mission. Heading home."

Josh keyed the mike once more. "Jolly Green Nine Six will orbit and then join Five Six for the trip back."

There was an interval of grim silence.

'What the fuck was that?" Jack finally asked.

"That was a trap that we almost got sucked into. 'Bad weather' was a signal that he was captured. When the NVA finds out what he did, they're going to beat the shit out of him."

Josh reached into his helmet bag and pulled out a bottle of water and took a long drink.

"The good news is they got one of the guys out. My guess is that Rampart Seven Eight Bravo was caught and there was an English-speaking Vietnamese nearby who made that call to draw one of us in and almost succeeded. The teaching point is that you keep authenticating every time you make a run in. Now you know why I keep asking the questions until the very last minute."

"Yeah. If nothing else, it's self-preservation."

"You got that right. Oh, and one more thing." Josh gulped the bottle down. "Billiard Ball, in its desire to rescue Rampart Seven Eight Bravo at all costs, almost put us in position of having to make an ugly choice— going to get a downed pilot and put Marty's mission—which is also our mission—at risk or tell them to piss off and risk leaving a fellow aviator on the ground to be captured. They had both call signs and asking us which one we prefer was just stupid. It tipped off the bad guys that we had another call sign and maybe another mission. And, oh by the way,

Marty would be really pissed if we weren't there to pick him up next week."

"If they had asked you to go get Rampart Seven Eight Bravo in a situation where there was lots of ground fire, what would you have done?"

"I don't know and I'm glad I didn't have to make that decision."

THURSDAY, SAME DAY, JULY 13, 1972,
2219 LOCAL TIME, VENOM BASE

"Colonel Thai, sorry to wake you, but we've had three calls saying they heard a helicopter."

"Do you know where?"

"Yes, sir, we have their locations plotted on our map. They are all outside the base but they don't make sense."

"I'll be right there."

Thai went right to the large map of the base on a table that dominated the cave. The walk gave him time to think. One helicopter meant it was a reconnaissance team that might be trying to walk into Venom, which gave him time to find them. That was the first move in the game of cat-and-mouse to find Venom that he was confident he'd win.

"How many reports to do we have?"

"We had three when we called. Now we have four." The officer pointed out the locations which, when he traced them by time, did not show a straight line to anyplace near. Thai thought this had all the signs of that pilot Haman. Where was he going? And was he on the way in or the way out? As noisy as that big black helicopter was, Haman was very skilled at finding ways to mask the noise. Thai would like to know how he did it.

"Any radio intercepts?"

"No, sir."

"Any other enemy activity?"

"No, sir. None of our patrols reported anything. No air raids other than the usual low-level flights by the American A-6s. However, northwest of Ha Giang an American F-4 was shot down. We got a full report on how they captured one of the pilots, but the Americans rescued the other pilot. Our intelligence says the Americans sent two helicopters and four of the airplanes with the call sign Sandy on each rescue mission. This time, we know there were three helicopters. That is the first thing that is unusual. Our intelligence people are still listening to the recordings of the radio transmissions and we have asked for a full

transcript, which should be delivered sometime late today or tomorrow."
The young lieutenant hesitated, and then added, "We also have a report
about the helicopter from a local policeman this morning."

"And that is?"

"Colonel, sir. The policeman in the village reported the helicopter
noise and says he saw it passing by about forty miles west of here."

"Interesting. Can we get him on the phone?"

"Yes, Comrade Colonel."

"Please do. And also, I want all companies to search their sectors
along perimeter of the base beginning at first light. They are to look for
any signs that an American reconnaissance team either is or was here."
This was just like SEAL Lieutenant Cabot. *He, too, is a ghost.* Now he
knew why he'd had trouble sleeping the night before: The Americans
were here!

TUESDAY, 4 DAYS LATER, JULY 18, 1972, 2213 LOCAL TIME, UDORN AIR BASE

Josh was taping a note to Natalie when the phone in the BOQ room
rang.

"Haman."

"Sir, you have an urgent Top Secret message here in the command
center."

"Who is it from?"

"Your friend. He'd like to change his return ticket. Our van should be
outside the BOQ by the time you get to the front door. Another one is
getting your crew."

Van der Jagt and the rest of the crew were pulling off the boots that
tied down the rotor blades and removing the engine intake and exhaust
covers as the two Naval Aviators entered the Air Force command center.
On the way over, Josh had to listen to a tale of woe about how much Air
Force money Jack was leaving on the table—a reference to Jack's
prowess at the pool table he'd developed in the pool halls back home in
Falmouth, Massachusetts. Josh had watched him hustle other aviators at
officers' clubs around San Diego. Last night he'd watched his co-pilot
take lots of money from Air Force pilots who swore revenge. Josh knew
their pride was soon to cost them what was in their wallets.

After showing his ID card and signing a form, he took a piece of
yellow teletype paper from the Air Force watch officer.

Big Mother 40

TO: BIG MOTHER 40

FROM: SIERRA SIX

NEED EXTRACTION ON 18 OR 19 FROM STRATO. NO DANGER YET. AUTHENTICATE ON SCHEDULE WHEN NEAR.

"When did this come in?"

"We got the hard copy about ten minutes ago. It was received by the Billiard Ball EC-121 that was on station. Their message to us said to call you as soon as it was decoded."

"Thank you, Captain. We'll be departing as soon as we can."

"Sir, do you need any assistance? There are four A-1s on five-minute alert."

"No. I don't want to make this a bigger deal than we have to. Sierra Six is telling us that he doesn't think he is being tracked or in danger, and that is good news. But that may change, and if we need some close air support, we'll call Billiard Ball."

TUESDAY, SAME DAY, JULY 18, 1972,
0313 LOCAL TIME, UDORN AIR BASE

"We found the fucking base!" Marty shouted happily, standing between the pilot and co-pilot's seat with a head set connected to the intercom. He had waited until they were well clear of the LZ and Jack had reported that Big Mother 40 was out of Indian country.

"That's great news. How?"

"We were sitting on top of a ridge line when we saw them launch two missiles. The bad news is that they bagged another F-105. But it was weird, the trees just opened, the missiles fired, and then the trees closed back up."

"How they'd do that?"

"That's what we wanted to know. When we explored the valley, we found a pretty sophisticated rope and pulley system that pulls the camouflage nets back and then lets them pop back into place as soon as the missile clears the trees, so there's no cloud of smoke even after just a few seconds. They use real branches and leaves in the nettings, which I'm sure they change all the time. The jungle canopy is thick all over the area, so it's easy to hide the base."

Despite the dirt and grime from being in the jungle for almost five days, Marty's sweaty face shone in the dim red light of the cabin. "They've got gravel roads all over the valley under the trees. They go from an extensive cave complex in the side of the mountain out to the launchers and three bivouac areas that we could find. There are also foot paths all around the base. We located four missile launchers and the control van plus the missile storage area. We didn't want to stay around much longer because the place is crawling with NVA. They must have a battalion-sized unit based there that is always patrolling the area, so they either have a commander who's on top of his game or they use it for training. And they patrol in force, generally two eight-man squads who leapfrog in a well-drilled manner. I saw that tactic in Cambodia."

Josh nodded, but kept his focus on the map on his lap because Big Mother 40 was approaching the waypoint where they would turn on the last leg that would take them out of Laos and directly to Udorn. He held up his hand as a signal to Marty to stop talking for a minute and keyed the intercom. "Jack, turn to one nine zero in one minute; ten minutes on that heading should take us right to Udorn. Stay at five thousand until we're in Thai airspace. I'll turn on the transponder and see if Udorn can pick us up on radar."

Jack clicked the mike twice, which was also a signal for Marty to continue talking.

"We saw a bunch of Russians there, too. Here's what's really nifty: there's a parallel foot path alongside the roads and just inside the tree line that are wide enough for two men to walk side by side. It's obvious that they've spent a lot of time building this base."

"Anything else?"

"Yeah, bad news. I think we stumbled onto the wreckage of Big Mother 22. We found a ten-foot chunk of a rotor blade that looks like it's from an H-3. We didn't take the time to look for the airframe but it's probably close by. I marked it on the map and you might want to see if you can figure out if this could be where they went in, or it could be a Russian helicopter that crashed."

"Thanks. If this war ever ends, we can see if we can come back and look for the remains." Josh paused for a couple of seconds while he thought about the guys who went down. He'd known both pilots well. "Where's the nearest good LZ?"

"Good question. We checked out a couple we knew about in the next valley that were on the reconnaissance plan. We should have several choices. My guys are pulling together their notes and we'll lay it all out on a map when we get back."

"Anybody see you?"

"We don't think so. We came close a couple of times, but no contact. They have bivouac huts all over the valley and each group can support at least a couple platoons."

"What about triple-A?"

"More bad news. We stumbled onto several 57mm gun emplacements. The crew of one was sleeping in a little hut off to the side of the gun. We also saw another one that had been destroyed by bombs. Based on what we know, there are typically a couple of four-gun batteries around each missile site. So I'd guess is that where's there's one, there are more."

"We'll be back at Udorn by about oh four hundred. We can all take a short nap, clean up, and then fly back to Cam Ranh Bay tomorrow and debrief. We'll call the duty officer when we land and he'll wake Mancuso if he's not already up," Josh said.

"Good idea. It'll take me a while to get to sleep. A hot shower and a stiff drink will help!" The moisture on Marty's muddy face and hands were a dull flat red from the dim lights in the cabin and it was clear that he needed a long shower.

"I can certainly agree that you need a shower. Your friendly co-pilot is officially tasked to provide adult beverages for every one board. There is a strong, well-founded rumor that he has a bottle stashed with his clothing. Before we rush off to bed, the Air Force is going to want some information," Josh said, reminding Marty that their friends in light blue would be curious.

"Just tell them that we accomplished the mission. More they don't need to know."

"Well, remember, they know about where you went. Inquiring minds will want to know." The commander of Air Force rescue command center suspected they were there to search for the secret missile base.

"'About' is not very precise and I'd like to keep it that way. They're not cleared for this and I'm not about to tell them. They can guess all they want, but nobody on this helicopter is going to confirm anything."

"Like I said, mission accomplished. The Air Force helped get us in and now we're back. Thank you very much. When we need more of your help we'll ask," Josh was laughing when he finished the statement.

Marty took off the headset and slumped down against the broom closet.

Marc Liebman

Koniev picked up the ringing phone and listened for a few seconds. "Colonel, it is for you."

"Colonel Thai." After listening for several minutes, the Vietnamese officer made a scribbling motion with his free hand and Koniev slid a pad of paper and a pen over to him. After writing a few numbers down on the paper, he read them back and then hung up after they were confirmed.

"One of our patrols believes they found a campsite that proves that the Americans were here, up near where the battery that was bombed, and they think they found a campsite where they spent the night near the destroyed 57mm battery. It has flattened leaves and branches that were cut with a knife or some kind of saw they either used for camouflage or bedding. They also found where they took a piss and a crap, and the Americans didn't do a very good job at burying it."

"How'd they find it?"

"By accident. One of the men went off the path to relieve himself and found a cut branch and then began searching around. They were careful to cover their tracks. Other than the smell of a recent shit, they found an occasional boot print, but they couldn't find anything that told them which direction they went. I told them to keep looking but I am not optimistic."

"So, you're making the assumption that the Americans have located Venom?" Koniev wanted to see if Thai's decision-making was going to be based on duty, revenge, or the pressure from his chain of command— or some combination.

"Yes, but it is not an assumption, it is a fact." Thai tapped the table for emphasis. "I am assuming that a reconnaissance team is still on this base or nearby. We will have every man out looking for the next day or so until we are convinced they have left."

"And then what?"

"First, we're going to go on alert and increase our patrols in case the Americans come back. And second, Colonel Koniev, we are going to be more aggressive in using this base to its maximum effectiveness until we either run out of missiles or it is destroyed. There is no longer a need to be covert."

"Don't you think you are jumping to conclusions? We should wait until we see what the Americans do."

"And wait for the B-52s to bomb us out of existence? Or send in some commandos while we do nothing? No, Colonel Koniev, we shoot at them and try to kill as many as we can before they kill us."

"Colonel Thai, let us not rush into anything. The smart thing to do is to keep ambushing their airplanes, which makes it difficult to find this place. We know the Americans are going to be very deliberate. First, they will make sure that know precisely where the base is so they can select what they call 'aim points.' These are needed by their fighter bombers or their B-52s. Then, second, they will make a plan. It will take days, if not weeks for them to figure that out because they have to get everything coordinated. So let's not make it easy for them. I'm confident that we will get some intelligence that suggests when the strikes are coming and then we can plan accordingly."

"And if you are wrong, we are put out of action and have not extracted a heavy enough price. We already had one surprise low-level attack that killed a lot of my men. They can do it again. You didn't know about that attack, and despite having spies around all the American air bases in Thailand and Vietnam, neither did we." Thai thought for a second. "No, Colonel, we get aggressive starting tomorrow, and by that, I mean shooting at every passing American flight of fighter bombers."

"Colonel Thai, I'm sorry, but my orders won't allow that and I can't authorize my men to shoot unless they follow the rules of engagement that brought us here. Those rules and tactics are working, and until we have some indication the Americans are planning a raid on Venom, we should continue with the plan agreed to by both our governments."

"Then I will have my men shoot your men one at a time until they do obey my orders."

Koniev took a deep breath before speaking. "You will have to start with me."

THURSDAY, NEXT DAY, JULY 20, 1972, 2130 LOCAL TIME, VENOM BASE

The official report documenting that they'd found a suspected hiding place of American commandos the day before stared back at Colonel Thai. Other than four vague reports of helicopter noise, some branches obviously cut by a very sharp knife, and the two piles of human waste, they had nothing. The page described in detail the intense search he'd ordered along the northern ridge and then down to the valley floor that had turned up nothing else. It also covered the patrol plan that would keep the regiment in the field looking for intruders. He reminded himself that he had to trust the men he trained and that Cabot and his men were very good at covering their tracks.

Thai signed the report, knowing that the truth was already in the regiment's log book. Thai wondered what he should tell Koniev to put in his official message. By now, he was sure that Koniev had talked to General Nikishev in Hanoi and the old general had sent something on to Moscow.

In his official log, Thai couched the words in the report very carefully so that the reader would conclude that they were not "certain" the Americans were actually inside Venom. If he weren't careful and the generals in Hanoi believed the Americans were on the base, they would want to know why his regiment hadn't found them. If he told them nothing, then if, no, *when* they returned, how could he explain the fact that he knew the Americans were here, and hadn't asked for help? So then, on what could he base his request for reinforcements?

Thai had used the recent bombing to support his request for replacements to bring B Company up to strength. His request had been denied, but the American reconnaissance team was a reason to send another request for more men.

So the real question in Thai's mind was, when and how were the Americans going to attack? By air? If so, what kind of bombers? Waves of fighter bombers would overwhelm their air defenses, and if Venom's four missile launchers were destroyed they would be defenseless unless the bombers came in at low level where the S-60s were effective. B-52s? They would get about ten minutes notice that the bombers were on the way. It was not enough to protect his men unless they were close to the caves. They wouldn't know they were under attack until the earth started to shake from explosions. By land? Or both? What could he do to prepare?

MONDAY, 4 DAYS LATER, JULY 24, 1972, 0846 LOCAL TIME, CAM RANH BAY, 180 MILES NORTH OF SAIGON, SOUTH VIETNAM

"Well, the shit must have really hit the fan because they're working in Hawaii. Someone must have found time between rounds of golf to read your report that we couriered over." Captain Mancuso looked at the three officers standing in front of him. The reference was that Monday in Vietnam was Sunday in Hawaii, which meant it usually was a quiet day, because those stationed in the headquarters' units in Hawaii weren't at their desks generating messages and asking inane questions.

"Cabot and Haman, you hit the jackpot. D'Onofrio, you lose because I'm going to hold you ransom because no one else around here will fly with Haman."

"Sir?" Jack blurted out the word.

Big Mother 40

Mancuso held up his hand. "It seems as though there is a political war going on at CINCPAC. According to Hastings, Pac-Af's proposal is to carpet bomb the valley and turn trees into matchsticks in their attempt to destroy the base, but with no guarantees that they can hit it. The Air Force solution is to send in waves of B-52s and follow it up by flights of F-105s and F-4s to destroy what the B-52s miss. They also say that the Navy doesn't have enough assets on the carriers in the Gulf to get the necessary results. Plus, since the base in one of their route packs, the Air Force wants to do the bombing."

Mancuso held up his ever-present cup of coffee. "Your fellow Naval Aviators say 'show us the targets and we'll put them out of business.' Their problem, along with the Air Force's, is we don't have any photos other than your notations on a chart to show them the actual targets, so they can't plot good aim points that they can see from twenty thousand feet. Without knowing precisely where the launchers and the storage areas are, bombing the valley is just guesswork. As I understand it, to get a high enough probability that the target will be destroyed by the first or second wave is impossible because you can't drop enough bombs to do the job. So, the strike planning wizards are all scratching their heads and arguing over formulas that tell you how many planes and bombs of what type are needed to destroy a target like this. And, each time, they come up with an answer they don't like."

Mancuso put his mug down. "That's why the raid idea has become the tie breaker. It is ballsy, doable and may catch the North Vietnamese with their pants down as we did with the Song Tay raid, which is why Hastings wants you to brief CINCPAC himself. Sooooo, later today, the regularly scheduled C-141 to Hickam Field in Hawaii will arrive and Lieutenants Haman and Cabot, with General Cruz going along as moral support, will get on it with TAD orders to stay in Hawaii until someone with three or four stars on his collar makes a decision. You'll be going as couriers carrying all the material you need to prepare. Once you're done, take a few extra days and enjoy civilization while the heavies contemplate their navels. It may take a day or so, or maybe a week or two. You are authorized to stay there on the government's nickel until they send you back to me. Lieutenant D'Onofrio will remain behind in this tropical paradise as my hostage to continue building the data base and make sure we are logistically prepared. That's the bad news."

"And the good news is?" Josh was confused.

"Besides the fact that you are getting out of this lovely beach resort?" Mancuso wasn't asking a question and the men standing in front of him smiled at his sarcasm as he slid a sheet of paper across the desk.

"Here is the authorization for Marty and Josh to make a personal AUTOVON call back to the states."

FRIDAY, 4 DAYS LATER, JULY 28, 1972,
1853 LOCAL TIME, HONOLULU

"Well, this has been interesting." Marty twirled his moisture-covered beer glass while enlarging a wet spot on the bar at the Halekoa Hotel in Waikiki. "I don't think they could have asked us any more questions."

"Trust me, they'll come up with more." Josh looked to make sure that no one was around.

"The Air Force is pretty pissed because they're taking the losses and no one likes their ideas. They think they can carpet bomb the valley and destroy everything but can't give anyone probability of destruction that is believable. I think that when we told them how we can take out the base, set it up for follow-on attack, and grab some intel in the process, it, became at least at a gut level an attractive option. I also think they're wrestling with the risk and the political implications of a raid."

"Yeah, and when CINCPAC asked Pac-Af if he would 'guarantee that a B-52 won't (a) get within twelve miles of Chinese airspace or (b), won't get lost and penetrate Chinese airspace or (c), if damaged, won't crash in China,' Pac-Af just shut up because he had no answer. I was amazed he did that in front of two very, very junior officers."

Josh tipped his half-empty bottle of Heineken to his friend as he looked around to make sure they were still alone. "I thought Pac-Af was going to fall out of his chair when we told him that you and I have been in and out of North Vietnam at least a dozen times on similar recon missions. He almost raised the bullshit flag, and I was just waiting for him to because I was going to offer copies of the mission reports but then say, 'Oh, sorry, sir, I can't send them to you because you aren't cleared.'"

"That would have been a hoot. Well, we're done for the time being. The duty officers and CINCPAC's aide and Admiral Hastings all have our hotel room numbers. So let's have some dinner, and a nice bottle of wine before the women get here."

"You know what was really strange about the questions? It just hit me."

"What just hit you?"

"All the questions were about the debate about bombing the base and the various ways to get it done versus a raid."

"And your point is?"

"No one asked us how we'd pull a raid off. We told them that we can do it and that we've got a plan, but no one has asked us can we *see* the plan."

"Yeah, that's right. Maybe they're assuming that we can pull it off." Marty put his empty bottle down on the bar.

"Boy, have we got them fooled." Josh emptied his.

The two of them chuckled and ordered another round before Marty broke the silence. "Different subject, when does Natalie arrive?"

"Tomorrow morning at ten on an American flight from LA, or about fifteen hours from now, not that I'm counting." Josh answered, knowing he *was* counting the hours and minutes. He couldn't wait.

"You haven't said much about it. Just wondering."

"I wanted to focus on what we are doing. We were the only lieutenants in the room and admirals and captains were asking our opinion." Josh stopped for a second, then decided to open up. "Every time I think of Natalie, I get this wonderful funny feeling. I didn't want anyone in the room to think I was here for just R & R."

"Josh, it is sooooo obvious that you are in love with her." Marty shook his head. "The heavies have never seen you devour one of Natalie's letters. You disappear for hours when you get a tape. I'm sorry I left San Diego before I met her; I never have seen the two of you together but D'Onofrio says you two are the perfect description of lovebirds. Now I get my chance to meet the woman who brought the great Josh Haman the Bachelor down."

"I'm not trying to hide my affection for her."

Marty laughed. "That's because you can't. My, how the mighty have fallen. When we first met, you would chase anything with a skirt. In fact, and I'll never forget this, one time when we were in a bar in Hong Kong, you said that one of the reasons you wanted to come to Asia was to sample all kinds of women. Now you're the devoted boyfriend. My, how times have changed. By the way, I think Ma'i is on the same flight. She was having trouble getting a seat, but last I heard she was pretty confident she would be on the same one."

"That means we both can go the airport together." Josh finished his beer.

"After we get their luggage, do you want to get together while we're here?"

"Let's play it by ear. I think the women will make that decision. They're going to want to be alone with us for a while." Josh wasn't sure he wanted to share his time with Natalie, even with his good friend.

Marc Liebman

"Keep in mind, starting Monday we're on call so they may wind up having to spend some time alone, and I thought they'd want someone to hang out with."

"Good idea, but doesn't Ma'i have family on the big island?"

"Yeah, they live on the big island. She said she would go there after I left to go back to Vietnam because she doesn't want to lose any time with me. Anyway, I don't want to fly to Hilo because I might not be able to get back in time for a meeting." Marty's shoulders slumped as he relaxed. "What are you going to do?"

"Besides enjoy her company to the fullest?"

"You know what I mean."

"As in propose?"

"Something like that."

"I wanted to propose before I left for Vietnam but she made it clear that she didn't want to be a 'war fiancée widow.' Those were her words, not mine. I don't think that has changed, but we have gotten a lot closer via the tapes."

"You're afraid she'll say no."

"Yeah."

SUNDAY, 2 DAYS LATER, JULY 30, 1972, 0923 LOCAL TIME, HALEKOA HOTEL, HONOLULU

"What are you looking at?" Natalie asked, standing in front of the mirror brushing her shoulder-length, jet black hair. In the mirror, she could see Josh propped up on a pillow with a portion of the sheet covering his nakedness.

"The most beautiful woman in the world." He thought about the sight of her standing on the balcony when he woke up. All she'd had on was the negligee she'd worn to bed. The gentle breeze made it caress her body while the rising sun silhouetted her body. He marveled at how gracefully she'd stepped back and then turned around on her crutches to come back into the room.

"Right. You must be thinking of one of the many other girls you used to sleep with."

"Nope, I'm looking at her." Josh put a pillow behind his head and lay back against the headboard. "I saw you hopping to the vanity. You seemed to have gotten pretty good at it since I left."

"My balance is much better since I've been practicing. My leg was so weak after the accident, and I couldn't stand on it without support for very long. But, now without my body having to battle infections, and

263

Big Mother 40

since I'm now a workout demon, I've gotten a lot stronger. The therapists gave me exercises to strengthen my thigh and calf muscles, but I have to be careful not to overdo it and hurt my knee. Anyway, I'm still not as good or confident at hopping as I'd like to be."

"Could have fooled me. I like to watch you move, it turns me on." Josh walked over and put his arms around her waist and pulled her close. "And, the most beautiful woman in the world also has the most wonderful smell in the world."

"What's next?" Natalie leaned back against her lover.

"Besides more sex?" Josh dropped his hand to stroke her.

"Stop it."

"Stop what?"

"What you are doing." Natalie pulled his hand away from her groin. "How do you expect me to finish getting dressed?"

"I like what the docs did ... I can cup my hand on your vagina and stroke it like this and you can't close your legs to keep my hand out."

"Mmmmm, I'm glad you like it and if you keep doing that and we may never do anything else."

Josh kept stroking her clitoris. "Ahhh, you've discovered my secret plan to keep you locked up in this room naked until you go home."

"Seriously ...."

"I was thinking about a stroll down the beach, find someplace to have something to eat, go swimming, and then figure out what to do next. I'm okay just sitting on the beach with you. We don't have to be 'doing something' every minute during the day." Josh moved so he could face her while he had his back to the vanity.

"You don't have to work?"

"Nope. I just have to check in every four hours or so to make sure."

"And you're sure that you'll be back here in late September?"

"Yup. Call this a Navy Good Deal." Josh French-kissed her for a long time. "The Navy's picking up my expenses and I'm not getting charged for leave. Why do you keep asking me this?"

"Because others who are in Vietnam don't get extra trips to Hawaii unless they were wounded or sick."

"Trust me, I found out I was coming here about ten minutes before I called you."

"You can call me with that kind of news any time." Natalie leaned her crutches on the sink counter as she sat down to pull on her panties and a short, mid-thigh skirt. "Why don't you get dressed?"

"Good idea. I will be dressed in a flash." Josh yanked out a golf shirt and a pair of shorts.

Later that afternoon, Josh carried the towels and a small duffle bag as Natalie gingerly negotiated her crutches onto the sand. "I haven't been out on a beach in a while."

"Since the accident?"

"Yeah." Natalie stopped and tested the sand to see how far the crutch tips would sink in. "Before this moment, you were the only person to see me in a bathing suit and that was on your boat, away from everyone."

"That's why trying on bikinis was such a big deal?"

"Yeah, and then only Carla and the sales clerk saw me, so I have never really been out in public."

"Great. You looked wonderful in a two piece bathing suit last spring."

"How about a bikini?"

"Even better."

After spreading out the towels out on the sand, Natalie looked at Josh. "Let's get wet."

"Okay, let's go over to the water's edge where you can drop your crutches and I'll carry you in."

"Okay, sounds like a plan. Let's go." She pulled off the oversized t-shirt so she could model a skimpy bathing suit for him for the first time.

"Oh, wow. I love the suit and what's in it." Josh took her in his arms and kissed her.

The phone rang in Josh Haman's room. He listened for a few seconds before saying, "I'll tell him."

Natalie waited until he left a message with the front desk. "What's going on?"

"Marty and I have to be at CINCPAC at oh-eight-thirty tomorrow morning."

"How long are you going to be there?"

"I don't know. It could be anything from 'Thank you very much for the work you've done, go get on the next plane back to Vietnam because we'll take it from here,' to 'We want you to do this, go figure out how to do what you suggested and then come back to us with a plan.'"

"You're worried." Natalie let a crutch dangle by the cuff as she touched his arm.

"About meeting a bunch of admirals? No. It is what they may ask us to do that worries me because we will then have to figure out how the hell we can pull it off without getting a bunch of people killed in the process. That's the real problem."

"You mean you could wind up dead?" Natalie looked directly into her lover's eyes, searching for an answer.

"Yes, everyone could. Marty ... my crew ... his team ... me. My goal on every mission is to bring everyone home alive and without extra holes in their bodies. So far, I've been very lucky. But I know they can, if they want, order us on a one-way mission. That's why I often wonder if I'll get killed, and then how and when."

Natalie furrowed her brow. "I think to a large extent you make your own luck by being smart about what you do."

"Thank you for being a fan. There are others who think I'm reckless, even a loose cannon." Josh pulled her close to him.

"Do you know where Marty and Ma'i are?" Natalie leaned back to keep her face in front of his.

"No, other than they said they were going to go out shopping and would be back around dinner time."

"Do you want to meet them for dinner?"

"Sure. Why not?

SUNDAY, A WEEK LATER, AUGUST 6, 1972, 1420 LOCAL TIME, CAM RANH BAY, 180 MILES NORTH OF SAIGON, SOUTH VIETNAM

Jack fidgeted while he waited in the front passenger's seat of the air-conditioned van that was behind and below the cockpit of an Air Force four-engine cargo plane that had just parked on the ramp. "Welcome back to paradise," Jack said as soon Marty and Josh slid into the first row of seats. "I see both of you are freshly fucked."

"Up yours, RHIP." Josh slung the heavy briefcase handcuffed to his wrist onto his lap. "We worked our asses off."

"Of that I am sure. The question is what ass were you working on or off? Anyway, Mancuso wants me to bring you to his office for a quick chat. The guys will get your bags when they get unloaded."

Jack didn't wait for an answer. "Josh, both helos in Mancuso's taxi service are up and ready to go with no major gripes. We've flown each one for about two hours every day. We have our own fuel truck now. The maintenance guys drive it back and forth every day or so to keep it topped off, so we don't have to wait for them to drive down to fuel us."

After that exchange, they rode in silence. Josh spent the ride enjoying the memories of the last week and trying to still enjoy Natalie's musk, which was getting fainter and fainter by the minute.

"I understand you enjoyed yourselves and managed to stay out of trouble." Mancuso waved them to the chairs in his office. "Now that you're back, I hope you're still capable of working with a lowly captain like me and his dedicated minions after hobnobbing with admirals and generals for the better part of two weeks."

"Yes, sir, we appreciated the break," Marty spoke for both of them. "And we didn't forget our roots."

"Good, I just got off the phone with Admiral Hastings. He was, as was everyone at CINCPAC, very impressed with you two, but don't let it go to your head because I have to work with you on a daily basis. As you know, your concept of operations has been blessed, and while CINCPAC takes care of getting the operation approved by the high mucky-mucks in the five-sided puzzle palace in DC, Hastings wants to know how long it'll take to finish the detailed planning."

"We'll have it done by Friday." Marty looked at Josh, who nodded. "If we can crash for a few hours, we can start tonight. We brought a bunch of new stuff back with us: electronic intelligence, photos, as well as our notes and more charts. The guys can sort it out while we sack out for a couple of hours and then come back after dinner."

"Where are the briefcases?"

"We gave them to Master Chief Tannenbaum to log in all the TS/SCI stuff. We have a bunch of secret material in sealed envelopes in our bags. When we go back to our quarters, we'll dig them out and Jack can bring them back here."

"Good. Get out of here. Both of you look like shit."

"It is amazing what a shower and a shave will do for one's attitude," Josh said four hours later as he entered the building that functioned as an operations command nerve center. It still showed the scars, both inside and out, from the June attack. Mancuso had limited the repairs to only those items that either increased protection or got it back up and running. He wanted the chips gouged out of the concrete to stay as reminders of what could have been a disaster

"Yeah. Out with it! Curiosity is killing the cat," Jack demanded, sitting at the map table.

"Out with what?"

"Well, are you engaged?"

"Sort of."

"How can you be sort of engaged?"

"Well, I asked her one day on the beach if she would consider spending a lot of time with me."

Jack said, "I can't believe I am being the straight man for this...And Natalie asked, 'As in wife, not as in camp follower?'"

"To which I said yes."

"And she then asked, 'Are you proposing?'"

"And I said, yes. At which point I handed her an IOU card."

"An IOU? For what?"

"A ring. I gave her a picture of a diamond ring cut out from a magazine and taped to a piece of paper on which I wrote: 'IOU a formal proposal and a diamond ring.'"

"Did she hit you?"

"No, she laughed and said 'I accept.' Then we went back to the room and made love to seal the deal."

"You're serious."

"I am. Natalie told Ma'i about it at dinner one night. The formal engagement will be announced as soon as I can get back and buy a ring and put it on her finger."

"Can we go back to work now?" Neither had seen Marty come into the room. "Only a fucked up Naval Aviator would use an IOU to propose."

Chapter 15

FEET DRY

Even after two years, Rokossovsky never got used to the annoying, tinny ring of the phone in his office. "Rokossovsky."

"Sir, you have a call from Russia. He identified himself as an Army Colonel and gave his name as Valentin Grushkin."

"Put it through." In their conversations, Grushkin never mentioned his rank or service. The fact that he could call from Russia said a lot about the influence, power, and status of the man, or the people he worked for.

"Good morning, Colonel, what can I do for you?" He resisted the temptation to make a sarcastic comment about Moscow or some other Soviet city. One never knew who was listening and Rokossovsky suspected the embassy operator taped all calls just to cover her fat ass. They would be reviewed, and if nothing seemed amiss, stored. If something suspicious was said, a transcript would be made and turned over to the KGB, who would then listen to the tape and decide whether to put a note in your file, arrest you, or let it go.

"I am calling to discuss your next assignment."

"Excellent. I'm glad you called. I was wondering when it would be."

"Where would you like to go?"

"Are there any openings at the Marshal Budyonny Military Academy of Communications near Leningrad or Frunze? I'd like to finish out my career as an instructor." Rokossovsky was thinking that Moscow had flights to the west and from Leningrad, it was a short ferry trip to Helsinki.

"I am assuming you still want to leave Hanoi in December?"

"Yes, Colonel Grushkin, that would be perfect."

"I will check for you and call you back. In the meantime, I have some paperwork for you to complete so that I can prepare your orders. I will put an envelope for you on the Aeroflot flight that goes from

269

Tashkent to Peking and then to Hanoi before returning to Tashkent. If you could pick it up from the crew and then give it back to them before they leave the next morning, I will have someone get it from them in Tashkent. Is that possible?"

The bastard had just told him that he was going to put a load on the direct flight from Hanoi to Tashkent. Why was he telling him that? It was not the normal communication channel. *Am I am being set up for an arrest?* "Yes, that should not be a problem if the paperwork won't take a lot of time to complete."

"It won't. The envelope contains only ten sheets of paper."

Shit, Rokossovsky thought, the shipment was going to be 1,000 kilos, which was going to be hard to hide. It will have to be in two sealed pallets, each with about two hundred and fifty two kilo bricks. "I will make sure I give the crew the documents before they take off."

"Excellent. I will call as soon as your new orders are ready, which should be sometime in October, as soon as we know who your relief will be. Thank you and have a good day."

Rokossovsky wondered if Grushkin was really a colonel. Was he in the Army, the KGB, or GRU? Was he an officer at all? He wondered where Grushkin had called from. Whoever he was, Grushkin had enough power to get a phone line to call a Soviet embassy in another country.

MONDAY, SAME DAY, AUGUST 7, 1972, 0956 LOCAL TIME, CAM RANH BAY

Josh sat on the passenger door that, when folded down, was also the stairway to the HH-3A's cabin. It was a convenient place to sit to review the yellow sheets that covered all the maintenance squawks and actions that corrected them. His fight suit was peeled down to the waist, held up by the arms tied around his hips. And, like everyone else, his t-shirt was already wet with sweat, although it wasn't even ten in the morning.

"So, Jack, what did you do to further the cause of democracy while I was gone?"

"The guys on the *Shitty Kitty* had a main transmission chip light, and the helo is acting like a parts bin until it gets a new transmission. When they checked the chip detector, it had chunks of metal against the magnet; and then when they drained the oil, they got more pieces of gear teeth. When this happened, the detachment was down to just one flyable helicopter because the other was still in pieces on the hangar deck for scheduled maintenance. The supply guys on the *Kitty Hawk* told them that it would be a week or more before they could get a new transmission flown out from San Diego. So, after they called us to see what we had,

Van de Jagt and I rummaged around Cam Ranh and lo and behold, found one. The paperwork said it was overhauled in nineteen seventy. We opened the container and it looked like it had just come out of the rework facility. We used Big Mother 40 to sling it from the storage area to here."

"Why didn't you put it on a truck or have the COD take it out to the *Kitty?*"

"The C-2s are still grounded due to the crash where the tail came off. And it won't fit in a C-1. Soooo, we said we'd be happy to fly it out there. My first thought was that we'd just slide the can into the cabin through the cargo door on a forklift, but the gun mount and the ammo tray would have to have been removed to make room. We even thought about taking it out of the can and putting it in the cabin on a mattress, but there still wasn't enough room. Then there was the minor problem of actually getting the transmission into the cabin. That's when we re-sealed the can and hooked it up to a sling the guys made using two sets of cables to make sure we wouldn't lose it and hauled it out to the *Kitty Hawk.*"

"You did what?"

"We slung it out to the *Kitty.* It only weighed about four hundred pounds, or that's what the marking on the container said. You do remember we practice vertical replenishment in the RAG because it is a secondary mission?"

"You slung it a hundred miles or so? You're not a HAC. Who went with you?"

"Actually, it was about a hundred sixty miles and it took us a little over two hours to get there at seventy knots." Jack chose to ignore the question about who was the HAC. "When we got there, we put it down on some mattresses and then we slid off while they got a forklift to move it so we could land and fill up will fuel and fly home with a load of mail and two guys going on emergency leave. Piece of cake."

Josh didn't know whether to chew his co-pilot out or say good work. He was sure everyone in the Det had helped him and was sure the irrepressible Van der Jaqt was one of the ringleaders. Only D'Onofrio would think of going on a scavenger hunt at a Navy logistics center. He just smiled, thinking, *the guy is learning fast.* "Well done."

FRIDAY, FOUR DAYS LATER, AUGUST 11TH, 1972,
2002 LOCAL TIME, CAM RANH BAY

"How'd you and Braxton get along while I was gone?" Josh picked at his bag of potato chips at the O Club bar.

"Fine. I knew his co-pilot, Carlos Villareal, from the RAG and the training command. We went out to dinner a lot at the O Club here at the base since there wasn't much going on. Mancuso let CTF-77 task us for a lot of logistics missions out to the ships in the Gulf, and when we weren't flying mail and parts runs we flew each helo, alternating days so they are up and ready to go. Everything, and I mean everything, works in both of them."

"Good work. When did Braxton actually show up?"

"About two days after you and Marty left on your Hawaiian boondoggle. They came out on the back of an oiler coming from Subic Bay."

Jack looked over his shoulder to make sure that no one was around. Braxton and Villereal had left to go watch a movie. "I've got a bone to pick with you."

"Why?"

"We're supposed to be a team and share and share alike."

"We are. So?" Josh had no idea of where this was going.

"Well, first, you never told me that Bill Braxton was your 2P when you dropped Cabot and his Sierra Six team inside the PRC. In fact, you never told me anything about those missions." Jack stuffed a large French fry oozing oil in his mouth for emphasis. "Second, you and Cabot worked together a lot, not just on a few missions into Cambodia. My guess is that as soon as he knew you were back in-theater, he went looking for you. In fact, I'll bet you two talked about working together again before he came back for his second tour." Another French fry was devoured. "Need I continue?"

Josh looked around to make sure they were alone. "The recon missions into the PRC were a very highly classified program called Slinky Scout. Braxton shouldn't have said anything. Very few people know about them and it should stay that way. We got Marty in and out of the PRC four times without taking any fire. They got the intelligence on the trains going from the PRC into Vietnam they needed, so they were a success. Thankfully, the CIA didn't ask us to push our luck. End of the story."

Jack was boring in like a lion chasing a wounded deer. "Braxton said you were fifty miles or more inside the PRC more than once."

"On the first two, we left from Nakhon Phenom in Thailand, flew north over Laos and into the PRC. The LZs were near the railroad that went from Kunming to Lao Cai in North Vietnam. We could see the lights of Kunming, which means we were probably closer to seventy-five miles inside, rather than fifty. On the second two, Braxton and I entered the PRC north of Hainan Island in the northern end of the Gulf of Tonkin and put Marty's team in to take pictures of the railroad traffic going into Dong Dang in North Vietnam. That's why Marty and I know and CINCPAC knows there are, or were, no SAMs coming into Vietnam from the PRC. The Air Force refuses to accept the facts. Anyway, in the midst of planning a third set of the Slinky Scout missions, we were told to stop. No reason was given. We found out later that Nixon was getting ready to visit the PRC and didn't want anyone to upset the apple cart with another Gary Powers incident." Josh took a sip of his coke. "Does that answer that question?"

"It's a start."

Josh ignored the sarcasm, which he took as normal. "It's all you're going to get from me on those missions. Marty and I worked together off and on. In those days, crews were assigned to SEAL missions on an ad hoc basis. HC-7 would get tasked to provide a crew and one would be sent. Marty felt very strongly that the helo crew and the SEAL team should be paired and then train and operate together. I agreed, so I asked my crew before I volunteered to be the guinea pig and to work with the SEALs to create standard operating procedures on how we plan and execute these types of missions. It also includes a lot of the lessons learned. Marty's view was that we were more than a taxi service and insisted that we learned their tactics, how to shoot, react in a firefight, move quietly through the jungle and so on. That's why we train with them on the ground, and why we are going to start doing it before guys get to Vietnam. The concept worked. Marty rotated back before I did and then came back to South Vietnam about a month or so before I came back."

"OK," Jack said as a way to encourage his friend to continue.

"What you don't know is that I spent a lot of time in Coronado with the SEALs talking about helicopter insertion and extraction tactics, the type of equipment needed and more. There aren't many aviators out there who understand the SEAL mission or, more importantly, who SEALs trust. I don't know if that's a good thing or a bad thing, but in my view, the more we train with them, the better we can support them. Anyway, the RAG CO and XO knew and blessed what I was doing and were, when I left, trying to get some of this stuff included in the syllabus for the guys going to HC-7." Josh stopped to remember the other question. "And yes, Marty and I are friends, and he and his wife Ma'i and I have gone out on double dates. We've also spent more than one afternoon drinking beer at his house or mine. Outside of the Navy, Marty and I talked and hung around together because we are good friends. Then after he left, I met Natalie."

"And your whole world changed."

"You could say that. Anyway, Mancuso arrived after Marty left and, as you know, he was given more SEAL platoons and tasked with carrying out missions all over Southeast Asia, not just in the Mekong Delta. We're at Cam Ranh because we're closer to North Vietnam and it helps to compartmentalize the operations to help maintain security. Before he headed back to Southeast Asia, Marty never told me that while he was in Coronado, he was preparing to lead recon missions that were going to go deep into North Vietnam. He couldn't because I wasn't cleared for that information. When I finally got my orders, I sent him a letter telling him I was coming back. That's how he knew and told Mancuso that when they needed a helo driver and crew, to come looking for me."

"You do know that Mancuso and Master Chief Tannenbaum go way back. Both were UDT and are Korean War vets."

"No, I didn't know that." Josh dropped the end of his hamburger into the paper plate. "I assumed by the way they work together that they knew each other well."

"Here's another tidbit. Major General Hector Cruz is more or less the father of Marine Recon. He was a company commander during Korea and then, after that war, led the way to create what we now know as Marine Recon, and Mancuso helped him do that. Apparently, Tannenbaum and Mancuso met in Korea and worked on and off again throughout their careers."

"Didn't know that, either."

"Figured as much."

"Is that why you're still flying with me? You are now my personal intelligence and gossip officer. I gather you bought a lot of beers for Bill as you pumped him for information." Josh wasn't sure whether or not to be mad at Braxton for the breach of security. He decided to trust his former co-pilot's judgment and give him a pass.

"It didn't take much. He said you taught him a lot and that I should, hard as it may be, to listen and learn. By the way, Braxton said you can be a real hard ass sometimes."

"Bill's a good guy for a ring-knocker, and it took a while for me to drum the automatic 'Yes sir' out of his brain, because it can get you killed in a hurry. Sometimes it was a battle to get him to think on his own and not wait for someone to tell him what to do."

"Is that why he is with us?"

"When Mancuso asked HC-7 for another crew and helo along with some maintenance people, I was told Braxton and his crew volunteered, along with everyone else."

"Not quite true. It was a cat fight among many of the 2Ps you trained who are now HACs to be in the crew Nagano picked. Braxton and his 2P, Villareal, who was in my same flight at Ellison and then at HS-10, both volunteered to extend for six months just to join us. Amazingly, Nagano agreed without a fight, which is even more out of character for him because anytime the name Josh Haman comes up, Nagano starts twitching."

"Dumb bastards."

MONDAY, 21 DAYS LATER, AUGUST 28, 1972,
1102 LOCAL TIME, CAM RANH BAY

"Sir, Captain Mancuso just called." Roy Vance appeared from the shack that was one part workshop, one part protection from the sun, and one part maintenance office. "He'd like to talk to both of you. Kostas is getting the Jeep and will run you over."

"Thanks." Josh didn't need to put on a clean flight suit for Mancuso.

"Good morning, you three; glad you could all make it. Take a seat, gentlemen." Mancuso held up his coffee cup and Master Chief Tannenbaum took the empty one and replaced it with one full of steaming hot coffee. Josh couldn't believe the captain could drink the hot stuff when it was a hundred degrees outside, but he did, cup after cup.

"I just got off the phone with Admiral Hastings. We seem to be talking daily. Officially, we're a go when we're ready. We just need to tell them the date. He told me that CINCPAC got JCS's blessing and it went all the way to the president. Nixon knows what we're about to do."

"I hope no one sent a message," Marty said.

"No. Hastings told me that he and CINCPAC personally briefed the Joint Chiefs, the President, and the Sec/Def. They were the only people in the room. Apparently CINCPAC got their attention when he told them that if anyone sent a message about Sunlight Sam, which has now been changed to Sunset Sam, he would authorize SEALs to hunt them down and use dull serrated knives on their private parts before they fed them to the sharks. Seriously, they got the point and agreed to the need for very tight security. None of their staffs know about the operation. And they know and are very concerned about the leak. In the middle of all this, Hastings said Pac-Af went to the Air Force Chief of Staff with an alternative Air Force only plan. Needless to say, CINCPAC was pissed that Pac-Af went around him and his plan was dismissed. I'm sure we'll soon see a message saying that Pac-Af is either retiring or getting re-assigned. It's about that time that flag officers start playing musical chairs, because the end of the fiscal year is coming, so it wouldn't be a big deal. But I digress."

"So we're good to go?" Marty asked.

"Yup. All we need is cooperation from Mother Nature." He took a sip of the coffee, which was no longer sending up a wisp of heat. "Hastings said CINCPAC wants you to go before the monsoon is in full swing so we'll have a better chance of success for any follow-up bombing missions."

"We'll start working on a date."

THURSDAY, 3 DAYS LATER, AUGUST 31, 1972, 1102 LOCAL TIME, VENOM BASE

"Good morning, Comrade Colonel." Koniev recognized Rokossovsky's cheerful voice on the other end of the phone despite the distortion caused by the encryption.

"Good morning. It is nice of you to call."

"As you know, I am always the bearer of good news." Rokossovsky chuckled at his attempt at humor. Koniev had learned that the man, at least on the surface, didn't take himself too seriously. Underneath the sarcasm, Koniev knew Rokossovsky was a passionate, very capable intelligence and infantry officer.

"And what gifts do you have this morning?" Koniev loved to play along, if for no other reason, it was a break from the serious, often tense conversations he was now having with Thai.

Koniev was sure that Thai had been pressured into asking him to take more risks to increase their score. Koniev acquiesced, but on several occasions, he flatly said no because he was convinced that the more risks they took, the sooner the Americans would attack. His refusal got him another tirade from Thai about Americans bombing his countrymen and he and his fellow Russians not doing enough to help defend his country.

"As I am talking to you, your cryptographers should be decoding two very interesting messages. I will leave it up to you to decide how much you share with our Vietnamese comrades in arms, but suffice it to say, the messages confirm how interested the Americans are in Venom. They also confirm that you must be hurting them badly, so congratulations."

"Thank you."

"Don't let it go to your handsome head. Enjoy reading."

The line went dead at the same time the captain who was cryptographer on duty entered his cave. After handing him a folder with several sheets of paper, the young officer remained at attention.

"You may return to your duties, Captain; I was expecting these messages." As soon as the words came out of his mouth, Koniev realized that the captain knew what was in the message. "You will say nothing about what you read."

"Yes, sir, Comrade Colonel."

The translation into Russian of the first confirmed that the U.S. was going to dedicate reconnaissance efforts to find the hidden missile base in northwestern North Vietnam so that it could be destroyed before the monsoon season. That wasn't anything new. It was just another confirmation that the Americans were trying to locate the missile launchers with enough accuracy so they could attack. The second explained the captain's reluctance to leave his cave because it was in English and discussed the plans the Americans were considering.

Someone in Moscow's GRU headquarters had decided to send the actual message rather than a translation into Russian, knowing that Koniev spoke English, along with Russian, German, and Vietnamese. The Russian text stated the contents were extracted from a CINCPAC message. Koniev wondered what the GRU was trying to tell him besides what he was about to read.

FROM: CINCPAC

TO: COMMACV, THIRTEENTH AIR FORCE, SEVENTH AIR FORCE, CTF77

INFO: CINPACFLT, CINCPACAF, COMMARFORPAC

SUBJ: OPTIONS FOR DESTRUCTION OF SECRET MISSILE BASE IN NORTHWEST VIETNAM

1 (TS/NOFORN): ASSESSMENT: CONTINUED HEAVY LOSS OF AIR FORCE AIRCRAFT TRANSITING AREA FROM HIDDEN BASE IN NORTHWEST NORTH VIETNAM UNDER ROUTE PACKS FIVE AND SIX IS CONSIDERED UNACCEPTABLE. FORCES IN THEATER ARE DIRECTED TO USE ALL AVAILABLE ASSETS TO LOCATE THE MISSILE BASE FOR SUBSEQUENT DESTRUCTION PRIOR TO THE MONSOON SEASON. COMMACV IS TASKED WITH COORDINATING THE RECONNAISSANCE EFFORT AND ANY STRIKE.

2 (UNCLAS): RISKS:

    (A)   (TS/NOFORN) OTHER THAN LOSSES DUE TO ENEMY FIRE, MAJOR RISK IS POLITICAL VIA AN ACCIDENTAL OVERFLIGHT OF THE PRC DUE TO THE BASE'S PROBABLE PROXIMITY TO THE PRC/NORTH VIETNAMESE BORDER. UNDER NO

CIRCUMSTANCES SHOULD ATTACKING OR RECONNAISSANCE AIRCRAFT FLY WITHIN 25 NAUTICAL MILES OF THE BORDER.

(B)   (TS/NOFORN) CINCPAC'S ASSUMPTION, SUPPORTED BY HIS N2 AND NICPAC, IS THE THREAT IS A CURRENT GENERATION SA-2 GUIDELINE MISSILE AND NOT A NEW VERSION OR TOTALLY NEW MODEL FOR WHICH COUNTERMEASURES HAVE NOT BEEN DEVELOPED. ASSESSMENT CONCLUDES THAT NEW TACTICS RATHER THAN A NEW VERSION ARE BEING USED TO INCREASE THE SA-2'S LETHALITY. DEPLOYMENT OF THE NEW SA-3 GOA IS A POSSIBILITY BUT NO SUPPORTING DATA EXISTS TO SUPPORT THE CONCLUSION THAT THE SA-3 IS IN THEATER. BASED ON THE DATA GAINED FROM CREWS TRANSITING THE AREA WHERE AIRCRAFT HAVE BEEN SHOT DOWN IN THE WESTERN END OF ROUTE PACKS FIVE AND SIX, THE SHORT ENGAGEMENT TIME (RADAR DETECTION TO MISSILE IMPACT) STRONGLY SUGGESTS NEW SA-2 TACTICS.

(3) (UNCLAS) FOUR POSSIBLE STRIKE OPTIONS ARE CURRENTLY BEING EVALUATED AT CINCPAC:

(A) (TS/NOFORN) OPTION 1—AIR STRIKES FROM THAILAND USING F-111S, F-105S AND F-4S SUPPORTED HEAVILY BY ELECTRONIC WARFARE ASSETS. AIRCRAFT ARE AVAILABLE BUT NEED PRECISE TARGETING WHICH IS CURRENTLY UNAVAILABLE. RADAR GUIDANCE FROM LIMA SITE 85 CAN BE USED TO DIRECT HIGH LEVEL STRIKES BUT ACCURACY MAY SUFFER. THIS OPTION CAN BE COMBINED WITH (B) TO PROVIDE ENOUGH AIRCRAFT TO SATURATE TARGET AREA AND ENSURE ENTIRE COMPLEX IS DESTROYED ONCE LOCATED.

(B) (TS/NOFORN) OPTION 2—NAVAL AIR STRIKES FROM GULF OF TONKIN: TWO CARRIERS IN GULF CAN BE AUGMENTED WITH A THIRD DURING TURNOVER. A-6S PLUS AIR FORCE F-105S AND F-111S IDEAL FOR LOW LEVEL, BAD WEATHER STRIKES AND CAN BE AUGMENTED

BY MARINE A-6S BASED IN VN. LOW LEVEL CAPABILITIES OF AIRCRAFT NOTED ABOVE MAY PROVIDE TACTICAL OPTIONS THAT COULD MINIMIZE LOSSES. F-4S ARE ALSO AVAILABLE FROM BOTH LOCATIONS IF DESIRED. OPTION WOULD ALSO NEED EXTENSIVE ELECTRONIC WARFARE AND TANKER SUPPORT.

(C)(TS/NORFON) OPTION 3—B-52 STRIKES USING AIRCRAFT BASED IN THAILAND AND/OR GUAM. ANY STRIKE ROUTE WOULD HAVE TO COME FROM EAST AND WEST. APPROACH FROM THE WEST REQUIRES EGRESS OVER HEAVILY DEFENDED HANOI/HAIPHONG AREA. EASTERN APPROACH INCREASES WARNING TIME AS WELL AS REQUIRES TRANSIT OVER HEAVILY DEFENDED CAPITAL REGION BEFORE REACHING THE TARGET AREA. SOUTHERN APPROACH OR DEPARTURE OPTION WOULD INCREASE THE RISK OF UNACCEPTABLE OVERFLIGHT OF THE PRC AND AIRCRAFT WOULD NOT HAVE SUFFICIENT TIME TO SET UP FOR AN ACCURATE BOMBING RUN. CINCPAC BELIEVES B-52 INGRESS/EGRESS ROUTE OPTIONS LIMITED DUE TO PROXIMITY TO THE PRC BORDER. RAIDS WOULD NEED EXTENSIVE ELECTRONIC WARFARE SUPPORT AND FIGHTER ESCORT.

(D)(TS/NOFORN) OPTION 4—SPECIAL FORCES RAID USING VN BASED ASSETS: OPTION COULD BE EXECUTED ONCE BASE HAS BEEN LOCATED AND MORE INFORMATION KNOWN ABOUT ITS DEFENSES. RAID COULD BE LAUNCHED FROM SHIPS IN THE GULF, BASES IN VIETNAM, AND/ OR THAILAND. FORCES IN THEATER HAVE ENOUGH ASSETS IN THEATER TO PLAN AND EXECUTE SUCH A HIGH RISK MISSION.

(E)(TS/NOFORN) CINCPAC INTENT—PLANNING FOR COMBINATION OF (A) AND (B) AUTHORIZED. CONCEPT OF OPERATIONS BEING PREPARED BY CINCPAC TO MORE ACCURATELY IDENTIFY ASSETS NEEDED. OPTION (C) A POSSIBILITY AFTER RECONNAISSANCE PROVIDES PRECISE LOCATION. OPTION (D) SHOULD BE HELD IN

Big Mother 40

Koniev's first thought was the message was part of an elaborate disinformation campaign. After studying the contents and putting himself in the American commander's position, the more logical and plausible the contents became. Until the American's found Venom, they couldn't attack, which meant he had to keep the base hidden for as long as possible. He agreed that carpet bombing by B-52s was impractical because of the potential losses and political risks. Attacks from the east or west would force the big bombers to fly over the Hanoi/Haiphong area, which would lead, he believed, to unacceptable losses. This message, assuming it was genuine and based on the intelligence that Rokossovsky had been sending him, confirmed what he had been telling Thai, i.e.: the Americans were trying to find Venom so that they could attack it in a very logical, methodical way. And the attack was not imminent, so the longer they stayed undetected, the longer it would take the Americans to attack.

What should I tell Colonel Thai? Thai was already paranoid with pictures of a U.S. Navy lieutenant SEAL tacked to his wall that the good colonel believed had been tasked to kill him. If he showed Thai the American commander's message, Option 4 would only increase his paranoia because he would rationalize the other options as an elaborate deception. Koniev was convinced that Thai believed he would die defending Venom and it was just a question of when and how many Americans he would take with him.

The distinctive clattering of a 57mm gun interrupted Koniev's thoughts, even muted as it was by about a thousand feet of rock. The phone rang, which stopped him from leaving the cave. After listening for a few seconds, Koniev said, "I'll be right there." He put on the harness that held six magazines and, now, two grenades, and slung his AKM over his shoulder as he headed to the command center to meet Thai.

It took about an hour to hike through the jungle from one of the 57mm gun batteries to reach the drone crash site. There wasn't much left of the aircraft and the cameras were smashed, exposing the film to sunlight and fogging any images that might be on the film. Thai handed Koniev a bent piece of metal from the drone, one of many that had been dotting their radarscopes for the past few days.

"Souvenir." It was the data plate riveted to the thin aluminum skin that said it was an AQM-34J manufactured by Teledyne Ryan Aircraft along with the serial number. "I gave orders to shoot at these things from the rear quarter, so that if it survives the cameras won't be able to see the gun positions. They only take pictures to the side and down and are very hard to hit, but today we got lucky."

"You do know that the Americans can track their flight and know about when and where a drone goes down."

"Yes, Colonel Koniev, we have had this discussion before."

Thai only addressed Koniev by his rank when he was in front of others or when he was pissed at him.

"Our intelligence says they fly a predetermined path and there is no way to track them as they fly. They can't tell you where they crashed, and until they download the data or develop the pictures, they can't tell you if the drone was on its correct flight path. Our intelligence also suggests the drones don't always fly their planned routes. Anyway, shooting them down is a risk we have to take to keep from being discovered. The Americans don't know if the drone crashed due to a malfunction or our guns."

"You are sure that the Americans have no way of tracking these drones in flight?"

"Yes, Colonel. I have been assured by our intelligence people, who have spoken with our technicians, who have thoroughly examined these drones. The only transmitter is the one that goes off near the end of the flight so they can home-in on the drone to catch it after a parachute opens. We even have pictures of specially equipped aircraft catching the parachutes."

Koniev nodded rather than answer, so as not to get into another argument. He went to inspect the wreckage more closely and pulled a circuit board from a dented black box. It further confirmed everything he'd seen about the quality of American avionics.

Later that night, Koniev sat staring at the map showing all the kills made by his missiles. He had a set of cards in his lap on which he noted the date of the intercept, the serial number of the missile, and all the parameters recorded by the control van, such as the heading, airspeed, and altitude of the target and the time the missile exploded. Also on the cards was information pulled from the American ATOs and correlated as best he could with the information he had collected from the intercept, along with any data on whether or not the pilot survived. These were all numbered triangles on his map.

The pilot's survival gave him data on where the missile exploded in relationship to the airplane. Typically, if it blew up in front, shrapnel from the explosion either incapacitated the pilot or killed him outright. If it blew up behind the wing, the pilot was, in most cases, able to eject.

The map on the table showed clusters of shoot-downs. He'd thought it would enable him to spot patterns so he could change tactics if needed. The Americans were, in a way, cooperating because they were very consistent in their routes, even times of day.

Everything seemed to be working as planned except his relationship with Thai. As his days at Venom wore on, he was thinking more and more about how he could make it better, but he'd come to the conclusion that there was nothing he could do to improve it. It was, all at the same time, cordial, professional, tense, and friendly. Koniev was determined not to let it, literally, kill him.

As his relationship with Thai grew more difficult, he thought about recommending to Nikishev and the air defense artillery academy that his theories and tactics had been proven, and that he should return to the academy to supervise a detailed analysis of the shoot downs from the past few months. This way he could document the lessons learned so they could become part of Soviet air defense doctrine.

While that might make sense to someone in Moscow who was looking at Venom as a test, it would not go over well with the North Vietnamese, who were being bombed daily. And it might even be seen by some as an admission of cowardice. In the end, each time he thought about suggesting an end to the Soviet role at Venom, he dismissed it as being dangerous to his career and politically unpalatable.

The thought of dying made him look at the picture of his wife and daughter. It reminded him that he and Thai should be working together much in the way a marriage worked. He and Valentina had been very happy together and shared everything. They always managed to compromise when they didn't agree. Thai would bend somewhat, but he always came back with his mantra that Venom should shoot down more airplanes.

Koniev could do that, but with only two launchers available for use, they were limited to firing two missiles at a time. Reloading took about ten to fifteen minutes per launcher, which meant that by the time they reloaded, the targeted airplanes were well out of range.

Nikishev's clear instructions and orders were that he was to test his theories, shoot down what he could, while at the same time minimize the risk of discovery of Soviet personnel. He was to write a paper documenting what they'd learned at the end of his tour, which was why he was also keeping a diary of his experience, including notes on his discussions with Thai.

He didn't have the heart to tell Thai that they were running out of the specially modified missiles. When they were gone, then what were they supposed to do? It was a logical time to end this experiment.

It was clear that while the marriage analogy was pretty accurate, it was just as clear that they were headed for divorce. Thai tolerated him, but more and more, his frustration with Koniev's reluctance to attempt to fire missiles at any airplane that was within range was growing and becoming obvious to those around him. Koniev had a growing sense of unease that this was going to end badly, but what he could not decide was, for whom? There were way too many scenarios.

Would he be recalled to the Soviet Union in disgrace?

Or, would he go back and teach at the rocket artillery school?

Or, would he be promoted as promised?

Or, would both of them die here?

Or, would one of them survive? If so, which one?

He decided not to lose sleep over it. He poured a small glass of vodka and sipped it, thinking of possible scenarios until it was gone. Then he looked at the picture of his wife and daughter, turned out the light and laid down on his cot.

Chapter 16
LABOR DAY

Jack settled into the co-pilot's seat and interrupted buckling his shoulder straps to key the intercom. "Do you know what today is?"

"No."

"It's Labor Day and an official U.S. government holiday. As government employees, we're not supposed to be working."

Josh just shook his head, smiled. "Normal start check list, please."

It was totally silent in the darkened cabin as they taxied out to the runway. Terse and correct checklist challenges and replies replaced the usual intercom banter as they readied for takeoff. Behind them, fourteen SEALS and their equipment were crammed in the darkened cabin.

The rain, which had been off and on for the past few hours, left the ramp full of shallow puddles when they started the H-3's two T-58 engines. The unseen base of the clouds was almost five thousand feet: no rain, no low visibility to use to hide from sight. Just an overcast sky.

"We've got a green light."

"Acknowledged." Jack turned the helicopter's position lights on and off twice to make sure the tower saw their signal before leaving the switches in the OFF position. After rolling for about two hundred feet, the heavily laden helicopter lifted off.

The incessant rain was like nothing Koniev had ever seen before. The phrase *sheets of rain* wasn't an adequate description. Thick walls would be better. Back home, thunderstorms would dump rain for a few hours at most, but it was not like a monsoon. He observed that the rain continued for most of the day, and then it would stop for a few hours

285

before starting again. During the monsoon, he was told that they could expect to get fifteen to twenty centimeters a day, or more. Even at one thousand meters above sea level, would he, by the end of the monsoon, need an ark?

In his cave, drawing lines on charts required care because too much pressure on the paper caused it to rip. He rolled the maps up into tubes and put them in a bucket to store them. To protect them from the water dripping from the ceiling, he draped a spare poncho over the top. Outside in the streaming rain, his rubber poncho was a help, but all that really meant was that when he went outside, he got less wet.

The walls of the command cave were now dripping and buckets were placed under low points in the cave's ceilings that seemed to drip more. Equipment was moved to keep it dry, but it was musical chairs: one night, the water streamed down from one place and the next, it was two meters over. It made going into the command center an adventure because one never knew where anything was.

"It looks like last night we had several flights of American A-6s and F-111s, no?" Koniev said, looking at the map board on which the Vietnamese were plotting aircraft. Since his last visit, the Vietnamese had built a wood frame with a cover over the plotting board that collected water and let it flow to where it dripped into a bucket. Every once in a while, the officer in charge of the board would walk over to the radar scope that was linked to the Northwest Sector's command center and issue a command.

"Yes, it does. The Americans are up to something despite the bad weather. I just don't know what it is yet." Thai looked across the board at the Russian, wondering what he was really thinking.

After studying the layout for a few seconds, Koniev turned to the Vietnamese officer whose drier uniform suggested he'd been in the cave longer. "By the way, those blips are moving and the way we lose radar contact every so often, they are probably all A-6s on armed reconnaissance missions looking for convoys and any other military targets."

"Yes, sir, that is what we think," the Vietnamese captain continued. "There are three pairs, two from the carriers and one from South Vietnam. Two new pairs arrive almost every hour. Every so often, two high speed targets that we have identified as F-111s come from Thailand and attack one of our airfields. We only see them when they climb high enough to be picked up by our radar."

"Are we seeing any formations gathering over the Gulf?" Koniev wondered if the American Navy and Air Force activity indicated they were going with a combination of options A and B described in that recent message. If they were, that would mean they knew where Venom was, but there had been no indication in the intercepted and decoded communications that they knew.

"No, sir. We were told that the weather is very bad in the Gulf and we think they launched just a few A-6s. They have a couple of tankers flying, a radar airplane, and four fighters airborne, but none of those have approached the coast."

"What are those plots for?" Koniev pointed to two dotted lines, one just west of Vinh and the other just south of Haiphong.

"That is what I am most curious about." Thai had approached the map and was gazing intently at the lines. "We have had reports of American helicopters around Vinh and north of Haiphong. We think they are dropping off reconnaissance teams, but we are not sure for what purpose. The missile sites in that part of the country are out in the open."

"Are your men hunting them?"

"Oh yes." Colonel Thai looked at his Russian counterpart. "We have at least a battalion looking for each one of them, but so far, nothing. They are too far away to be a threat to us."

"Are you sure they put men on the ground?"

"Quite sure."

"How do you know that?" Koniev wanted the answer before he suggested they could be decoys. After he spoke, he realized that the first steps in Option A and B may be starting and Option D might come later, in which case the message wasn't a fake. However, he was going to let events play out a little more before he said anything. Right now, he was just a very interested spectator.

"In the past, the Americans left us calling cards in the form of booby traps, mines, and blown bridges that make it difficult to resupply launch sites in those areas with missiles. We expect they will do the same this time."

"Do you think they are just routine raids?" Despite what he saw on the charts, Koniev was convinced the Americans were executing option D. That would be the only reason there was no mention of it in the message traffic. Not even a hint. If he were running that kind of raid, he'd have the teams isolated until the attack took place. Thai didn't see it that way, so the question was whether those teams south of Venom were decoys to disguise the main effort, or part of the real effort that attacked targets all over the country. Or was he completely wrong?

And did the Americans know where Venom was? The more he watched what was happening, the more he thought they did. After Thai had told him he was sure that the Americans were on the base, their actions tonight made sense if you believed they were going to conduct a raid, followed by intensive bombing, or vice versa. "What do you think the Americans are going to do, conduct a raid first and then bomb the hell out of us? Or, chew us up with their bombs and send in a raid to finish us off?

"I'm not so sure." Thai sounded, to the Russian, more apprehensive than usual. "If you believe that to bomb us, they need to see the targets, then it is a raid first. If, on the other hand, if you believe they have located us well enough to send in the B-52s and fighter bombers, then the commandos can come in later to pick over our bones." Thai took a deep breath sucking air noisily through his teeth. "I believe the Americans don't have enough information to send in the fighter bombers. So that leaves me with a commando raid and the question of when, not how."

Koniev thought Thai suspected an attack was coming and his death was near. "Why?

"Because about half of these armed reconnaissance flights, as you called them, are up here by us. Why? What are they trying to do? What are they a cover for?" Thai pointed out the tracks of the airplanes on the manual plot kept with black grease pencils on a plastic sheet laid over a map.

"Are they finding targets up in this area?" Koniev suspected Thai was obsessed with annihilating Sierra Six and was letting emotion cloud his judgment.

"Oh, yes. They destroyed two convoys just south and west of us on Route 2 last night and took out six missiles in one attack and several supply trucks in another. We think, based on their speed, two F-111s hit the rail yard just south of Ha Giang and destroyed a train that was unloading ammunition. So, yes, they are active in this area."

"That makes sense. The Americans will keep coming as long as they can find targets they can bomb. We can't get them with our missiles at the altitude they are flying," Koniev said, to make sure Thai understood the tactics the Americans could employ with these airplanes.

"You seem so sure that these are just routine raids," Thai pushed back.

"They are following their doctrine." Koniev stated what was obvious to him. "They can't use F-105s and F-4s so they are using the A-6 Intruder and the F-111 just for this type of bad weather and mission. It is what they were designed for."

"I am suspicious. These helicopters came from the Gulf and from the south but not the west. In the past, they used routes from the west, south, and east to bring in reconnaissance teams by helicopter, but nothing came from the west last night or tonight. Again, why?"

"It could be they don't have enough reconnaissance teams, or helicopters, or both, or they think those are the safest routes into Vietnam. Or they don't want to deploy them all at once. It could be they are searching south of us first and this part of the country is next. It could be that the Air Force is not part of this operation. I could give you ten reasons why or why not." Koniev paused. "Or it could be a deception."

"Ah, Colonel Koniev, for once we are in agreement. I think it is some type of deception, which is why I have all my companies in the field looking for intruders. We will be ready if the Americans come." Thai paused for a few seconds. "It is not their Air Force I am worried about, it is their Navy. They can be very unpredictable and I am sure they know where Venom is. They cannot see us from the air so they will attack on the ground. I am sure of it, but not when they will come. That is what I do not know, but my men are prepared and waiting. And if that SEAL Cabot is with them, it will be my duty and pleasure to kill him."

The sound of 57mm guns caused both of them to look up. Just then, the phone in the command center rang. Thai picked it up.

Attack on Venom Base

Josh was slowing as they approached the LZ when the radio buzzed. "Eagle Eye Seven Oh Two, Steel Tiger Five One Zero, my playmate, Five Oh Six is hit, losing fuel. We just bombed a triple-A site south of Ha Giang. Steel Tiger Five One Zero is in trail of Five Oh Six. Will advise."

"The A-6s are forcing the North Vietnamese to pay attention to them, which is good for us." Josh was speaking to the crew as well as to Marty who was the only SEAL plugged into the intercom. The rest were poised to get out of the cargo door in the rear or the passenger door in the front behind the co-pilot's seat.

"Tail is clear of trees." Van der Jagt had his head out of the cargo door. "This area looks good, you can land here."

"Be right back. Saw something." With that, Vance, who was leaning out the cargo door to look for large boulders that would damage the main landing gear, jumped out and disappeared into the trees fifty feet away.

"Shut it down." Josh took a deep breath as they all felt the helicopter settle on its wheels, signaling they had arrived at LZ Dynastar. *Phase one of the mission is complete.* His brain began racing. *Now all we have to do is, one, find the base; two, destroy the missile launchers; three, hike back*

*to the helicopter; and four, assuming I am not dead or wounded, fly
everyone home. And, we have to do all this without the North Vietnamese
or a mythical man called Murphy stopping us.*

Jack pulled the throttles to both engines back to idle cut-off; Josh
disengaged the rotors and applied the rotor brake as soon as the engines
began to wind down. Behind him, the fourteen SEALs fanned out around
the helicopter to secure the LZ, while the crackling noises of hot jet
engines cooling down joined the night noises of the jungle as it came
back to life now that that the helicopter was no longer scaring its
denizens into silence. If the helicopter stayed there for very long, it
would become a place for the jungle wildlife to explore for food, and
some would make it their home.

Jack stayed in the cockpit for a few seconds to reposition all the
switches so all they had to do was flip on the battery and start the
engines. Once that was completed, he helped Kostas and Van der Jagt
toss the camouflage netting over the HH-3A as they had practiced a
dozen times in a darkened, closed up hangar at Cam Ranh.

"Skipper …" Vance had returned silently; his voice was a whisper.

"Where'd you go?"

"I thought I saw a fire being stomped out. There was a red glow and
then some sparks. I followed the tree line until I surprised two NVA
soldiers watching the LZ. I didn't find any communications gear like a
field phone or a walkie talkie, but we can look again in daylight.
Anyway, they are no longer a threat." He tossed two AK-47s on the
ground along with the harnesses and ammo pouches and four grenades.
"I used this." Vance held up a suppressed modified Smith & Wesson
Model 39. "I also found this in one of the shirt pockets. It looks like their
orders."

Marty had joined the little group with two more SEALS who
confirmed that they didn't believe there were more than the two men.
One of the SEALS looked at the flimsy paper through the red lens of a
flashlight. "Skipper, they're supposed to stay here until relieved at oh
eight hundred tomorrow. Their orders were, if they see something,
identify it, and then return to their company's position and report it. They
were not to engage unless attacked."

"Okay, I don't think we're compromised, but we need to hurry
because they may have roving patrols to check on them. If nothing else,
we have to be out of here by 0730. My guess is that they've staked out
most of the potential LZs around the perimeter of the base to let them
know if someone shows up. This means we attack tonight as planned,
which may force us into a daylight takeoff tomorrow," Marty said.

"Yeah." It was all Josh could say. Daylight trips through Indian country were bad enough. This time, it would mean that the Indians would be more pissed than usual.

"Vance, how many rounds did you use?" Marty asked.

"Three, sir. One to kill the first and two to take out the second, because I wasn't sure where I hit him. Just wanted to make sure, but it was a wasted shot."

"Let's move out. First rest stop, we review the plan," Marty said, wanting the time to think through any changes he may want to make to the operational plan.

"See you in about twelve hours or so." Josh shook Jack's hand.

If things went to hell, Jack's orders were to get airborne and call for help. The rest would execute what they called their walk-out plan. It had been Josh's idea to reduce the helo's security team to three—one SEAL, Jack, and Van der Jagt. Vance, Kostas and he would join the SEALs in the attacking force.

"Guys, we'll monitor the radios as per the timeline or if we hear a lot of shooting. Call us when you get about twenty to thirty minutes out and we'll be ready to rock and roll."

Josh hefted his web gear, remembering the fifty-pound-pack rule from when they figured out how many people they could stuff into the back of an HH-3A that was ready to go to war. In his load, along with a spare 150-round box magazine for his team's Stoner light machine gun, he was carrying three hundred rounds of 9mm ammunition in ten thirty-round magazines for his Heckler & Koch MP5A3, two 3.5 pound Mk 14 A1 Claymore mines, two fragmentation grenades, two two-pound bricks of C4 with detonators, two quarts of water, a Model 1911 .45 pistol with four spare magazines and four four-ounce D ration bars. All told, with the 6.8 pound MP5, Josh figured he was carrying every one of the fifty pounds, maybe a few more.

Under the dense canopy of the jungle not much grew; so despite all the rain, the ground on their mapped-out route was spongy but not muddy. It didn't smell any different from the jungle near Cam Ranh Bay where they'd trained, and the animals, sensing the helicopter was no longer a threat, were coming back to life, making the jungle its usual, noisy place.

As they neared the crest on the ridge that bordered the missile base, the point man held up his hand. All the rest kneeled and scanned their assigned sector. It was a drill that Marty insisted Big Mother 40's crew learn as they trained for the mission, along with becoming very disciplined and accurate, if not expert, shots.

Vance and his SEAL fire teammate crept through the woods, moving a few yards at a time and then pausing for a few seconds to look and listen, until they were just below the crest. After waiting for a few minutes, they motioned the rest of the team to come forward. Off to their left, they could see two 57mm mounts that had been up-ended by bombs. No soldiers were in sight, but they heard several talking and then counted the members of a NVA twenty-four-man patrol hurrying along one of the paths cut through the jungle.

Confident there weren't more enemy soldiers coming, they passed by the Fan Song B radar and stopping momentarily so one of the SEALS could inspect it for damage. After making a note where chunks of shrapnel had blown holes in the antenna and started a fire in the electronics compartment, they moved on.

From the 57mm site on a ledge cut into the ridge, they headed down to the edge of a clearing where a missile launcher stood ready. The flattening terrain told them that they had reached the bottom of the valley.

"Okay, it's twenty-two fifty-seven. We're about an hour behind schedule." They'd been on the ground for a little under three hours. Marty's voice was hushed but loud enough for all to hear. Each team was grouped around their leader. "From here, everyone should be in position by double-oh-thirty. Remember, be careful. There are lots of patrols moving around. Avoid a firefight if you can, but if you need engage, do so to get fire supremacy as fast as possible and then use it to disengage. Use the Claymores to protect your withdrawal if you have to, but I would like to save at least one per man in case we have to fight our way out. Rendezvous at the rally point no later than oh three hundred. I want to be on the other side of the ridge by oh four-thirty and back at the chopper by about oh six-thirty or sooner. Teams 1 and 2 are with me and we have the launcher complex. Chief Jenkins and Team 3 have the missile storage area and the generators, and Lieutenant Haman and Team 4 are the blocking force and have the caves. When you split up into two-man fire teams, keep the radio chatter to a minimum, but check in so we don't stumble into each other and get into a firefight with ourselves. Questions?"

No one said a word. "Josh, are you still comfortable taking on the cave complex and the hooches? There could be a lot of bad guys to deal with."

"Yes. We're going to cause a distraction if we hear gunfire, kill as many as we can, leave some presents to cover our withdrawal and pull out fast."

Big Mother 40

"Good. Team 2 will be covering the withdrawal of Teams 1 and 2. Don't do anything I wouldn't do." There were a bunch of suppressed chuckles. "Let's get to work. Good luck."

TUESDAY, 35 MINUTES LATER, SEPTEMBER 4, 1972, 0022 LOCAL TIME, VENOM BASE

Even though the wooden framed building was twenty feet from where he lay, Josh was sure that no one could see his dirt smeared face through the vegetation separating him from the path and the building. Josh pushed the extraneous thought out of his mind of how different this was from the hikes in the woods in Central Germany he'd taken as a Boy Scout. The jungle's damp, dank, musty smell was a lot different from the pleasing smells of pine and hardwood forests.

A hand guided his head toward a solitary figure in the structure to his right. The SEAL mouthed "NVA officer" and showed the suppressed Smith and Wesson, which one person on each four-man team carried.

Josh held up his hand; he'd recognized Koniev as he passed twenty feet away. He watched the Russian enter a tunnel ten yards up the gravel path. The SEAL nodded and then Josh pointed at an NVA officer in the hooch next to where they were hiding and drew his hand across his throat. He whispered, "Pass the word, you and I will go get the Russian, and the others will provide cover."

Three thumbs-up preceded the SEALs' slow movement and placement of two Claymore mines well in front of their firing position that would send hundreds of steel balls down the gravel road in front of the caves. When Josh looked at his watch, it was after double-oh-thirty-three; he knew that they could act now that his fire team was in place to slow down, if not stop, any reinforcements trying reach the other three teams.

When he finished crawling to the edge of the jungle near the hooch he nodded, and heard a soft PFFFFT. The North Vietnamese officer's head jerked and Josh saw a trickle of blood flow down his forehead as it flopped to the side.

Josh dashed up the wooden steps while his fire teammate crouched nearby in the shadow of a large tree. He made sure it was empty before he went back to the working area. There, the black and white photos of Marty, Mancuso and himself, pinned on a separate board next to the chart, brought him up short for a few seconds and he wondered—*where the fuck did they get these?*

The shoulder boards showed that the dead officer was a major and a political officer, not a colonel. He pulled the large map of the base and the photos off the wall, folding the map so that it would protect the photos, and stuffed them and the notebook the major had been reading into his pack.

TUESDAY, 19 MINUTES LATER, SEPTEMBER 5, 1972, 0041 LOCAL TIME, VENOM BASE

A quarter mile away, Marty Cabot nodded to the SEAL on the other side of the control van's doorway. Already, the C4 was in place on the bottom of the van, ready for the fuse to be set; but Marty wanted to get whatever intelligence there was inside. As he started up the stairs, the door opened and the surprised Russian captain was mowed down by a burst from Marty's suppressed MP5. Rather than dive into the unknown space, he tossed a grenade inside.

Another Russian emerged before the grenade went off with a muffled thump and was cut down by a well-aimed burst from a suppressed MP-5. Inside, Marty stepped over the bodies of three more Russians and grabbed three thick manuals off a rack. As he leapt out, his fire teammate set the fuse for ten minutes.

At the first launcher they found, Marty shoved his last one pound brick C4 onto the launcher, setting it even with the missile's rocket motor, before inserting the detonator set for ten minutes. At the next launcher, Marty and Petty Officer Benton repeated the process and used their last two bricks on two trailers with spare missiles.

Finished, the two-man fire teams were halfway across the launch zone when several NVA soldiers spotted them and ran in their direction, firing bursts that spattered in the gravel and then whined past and overhead. The NVA soldiers were between Marty and his fire team's route to the jungle and the rendezvous point.

Hearing the gunfire, the other SEALs setting the fuses on the missile storage area and the generators and their fuel tanks set them for five minutes. The plan was that once the fighting broke out, they would communicate and withdraw in different directions to confuse the NVA, even though they would all be moving toward the rally point. It gave the teams the option of attacking the NVA soldiers from different directions to distract them before fading into the jungle and escaping toward the rally point. The range of their small radios varied from a few hundred feet to at best two hundred yards, but did give them an advantage of knowing where the enemy was vis à vis their location. Marty was relying on their training and experience in these types of actions and wanted each team leader free to act to carry out their assigned tasks and then modify how they supported the withdrawal as the battle unfolded. Each team member was confident and knew their role as well as the others in the overall plan. They would communicate and adapt and overcome as they always did.

Staying dispersed was a risk that Marty felt was justified, given their small numbers. He was counting on their ability to destroy the launchers, start a large enough fire that could be used as an aiming point for the fighter bombers, and escape before they were engaged by a much larger force of the NVA.

Marty and his teammate were holed up in a blast ditch around the launcher, firing sporadically at a dozen NVA soldiers, knowing that just a few yards away, the fuse on a pound of C4 was ticking down. Each time they popped up to fire a burst, it seemed as if there were more NVA. The other two members of Team 1, even though they were lying flat, were exposed on the open ground between the launcher and the jungle.

"Three, this is One Actual, we're pinned down in open by the eastern most launcher. Need some covering fire." Anyone listening on the net knew that One Actual was Marty's call sign.

"Three is about to engage. Move when we start firing."

Team 3 coming from the missile storage area was first on the scene and caught a squad of NVA trying to get behind Marty. Several short bursts ended the threat and enabled Marty's Team 1 to get to the side of the clearing where the others waited. One of the SEALs from Team 3 stuck a brick of C4 into the retraction mechanism of the forest camouflage and set the fuse for one minute. The blast dropped the net to the ground and covered their movement into the jungle.

For the moment, the eight SEALs of Teams 1 and 3 were out of harm's way. Then they heard shouting and several long exchanges of gunfire: the SEALs of Team 2 were under fire, and from the distinctive ripping sound of AK-47s, it was clear that the NVA were gaining fire supremacy. Marty tried to contact Josh, talking into the radio's throat mike. After he got what he thought were two clicks, Marty pointed in the direction of the gunfire and the seven other SEALs nodded and moved out.

TUESDAY, 15 MINUTES LATER, SEPTEMBER 5TH, 1972, 0056 LOCAL TIME, VENOM BASE

At the other end of the complex, two three-round bursts from Josh's suppressed MP-5 dropped the two soldiers running by Koniev's cave into lifeless heaps. About half a dozen NVA soldiers came out of the cave as he started across the gravel road. He emptied a magazine in ten three-round bursts, dropping many men as he dove into the nearest cave. He could hear the SEAL with the Stoner light machine gun across the road firing short bursts, gaining enough time for Josh's fire teammate to cross the road.

Josh eased his way into the doorway of the first cave and saw that the wall continued at right angles to the entrance for several yards; he could see the glow of light shining off the damp rocks at the end.

Taking a deep breath, Josh stepped around the corner and knelt down, staying in the shadows as he crept around the L-shaped entranceway into a large room. Fear that any moment he would get a chest full of bullets gnawed at him. He hoped he would die fast if that happened.

He dove to the ground as the flashing of an automatic weapon at close range and AK-47 rounds ricocheted off the rocks above him, showering him with small chunks of stone. His teammate held up a grenade, pulled the pin, and rolled it into the room. After the blast, both raced in, looking for targets. Another burst from an AK was high and wide. Josh fired his MP-5 in the direction of the shooter while the SEAL dove to another spot on the floor behind what looked like a large typewriter. Again, another burst aimed at where Josh was a few seconds before sent sharp shards of rock flying that he could feel digging into his exposed neck.

"Clear." The English voice in his headset suggested he stand up, and he saw his teammate standing over the body of a Russian captain. A quick check showed three more bloody corpses in the cave. He picked up two books next to what he recognized as teletype machines that printed out decoded messages and flipped them open. Code books! This was not the cave he wanted to go into, but it was a bonanza and the books went into his pack, more than replacing the weight of the expended ammo.

The two men stuck their heads out of the entrance and pulled back in when they were greeted by a hail of bullets from a position a couple of hundred feet down the road. When they heard the shout "Go!" they emerged from the cave under the cover of short bursts from the Stoner. They raced back up the road and ducked into another cave mouth.

Josh turned to his teammate and held out his hand with the thumb up; he mouthed the word, "Ready?"

Acknowledging the nod he got in return, Josh moved down the entrance to where it opened into the cave, which had the same type of entrance as the other one. This time, he slid on his belly into the room.

He blinked in the bright light and saw from his position on the dirt floor what looked like a messy living room office more than a command center. Off to one side, there was a bank of radios, two radar monitors, a massive computer terminal, and several green file cabinet safes that looked like the ones used by the U.S. Navy. He could see two sets of boots by the file cabinets and pointed them out to his teammate. On the count of three, they rose and fired their MP-5s at point-blank range at the two surprised Spetznaz soldiers. They collapsed on the floor with three red splotches in tight groups in their upper chests as the brass cartridges tinkling on the floor broke the silence.

Josh looked at the bodies. Neither was the Russian colonel. Where was he?

Josh turned to get a better view of the room, which had a small kitchen area behind him and two doors along the plywood back wall that portioned the space. The SEAL pushed open the first door, which revealed a cot in what was an empty bedroom and held up his fist, signaling Josh to freeze. He made sure, as he flattened himself against the wall, that he was in the shadows on the side of the door.

The first thing to emerge from the door was the barrel of an AK-47. His SEAL teammate raised his MP-5 to get ready to stitch the door with a burst but something made Josh shake his head. His SEAL fire teammate nodded and sought cover behind one of the file cabinets and got out of the direct line of fire of the person holding the AK.

"Don't move or I'll blow your head off," Josh said in Russian as he stuck the barrel of his MP-5 into the base of neck of the stocky Caucasian man as he emerged from the door.

The man dropped his weapon and raised his hands in surrender. "I understand. Please, not kill me. I Colonel Alexei Koniev of Soviet Army." He annunciated his words in Russian accented and stilted but clear English. "I expect you and want defect."

"How did you know we were coming?"

"My country reads your coded messages. I know you found base and would bomb it. I also thought you would conduct some kind of Spetznaz raid. You know Spetznaz?"

My country reads your messages? Josh shook his head to think about that later. "Why do you want to defect?"

"I don't like live in Communism. All lies that cover bad government." Koniev paused for a few seconds, knowing that both Americans were surprised and probably wondering where he learned English. "I have proof that you have traitor giving us your communication codes so we can read your messages. They are in large envelopes in safe."

"Is the safe booby-trapped?"

"It is unlocked. After I take out files, I set off thermite grenades, will burn everything and set fire in cave to burn for many days. Make hard for my comrades to identify bodies."

"Get the envelopes, but if you try anything, you'll have more holes in you than you can count before you die." Josh prodded Koniev with the barrel of his MP-5 in the direction of the safes.

"I understand." Koniev hurried to open the top drawer. As he stuffed a half a dozen large envelopes into a pack, he turned to Josh. "I got call from embassy in Hanoi, telling me you might be coming. They did not believe it possible. I did, and prepared envelopes. Have messages, maps, logs and notes, everything. And, now, you are here. That is good, no?"

Koniev grabbed a photo off his desk, dismantled the frame, and slid the photo into the pack.

"Who's that?"

"My wife and daughter. It is all I have left. They are dead."

Josh heard several bursts from the Stoner as they rounded the entrance's blast barrier. His SEAL teammate grunted as he ran across the gravel path. When he got to the other side of the road, he held up a grenade and threw it in the direction of the NVA soldiers to cause them to take cover. Koniev was next out the door after it exploded in front of another cave entrance twenty yards down the road, sending shrapnel pinging off the rock outside where Josh was hiding. Using the cover of the explosion Josh emptied a clip in a spray of bullets in the general direction of where he thought the NVA soldiers were hiding as he dashed across the road.

Another series of bursts from several AK-47s chewed up the dirt and pinned Josh against a tree. He knelt down and fired back from one side and then the other of the three-foot-diameter trunk. Each time he stuck his head around to fire, he could see teams of NVA soldiers leapfrogging toward his position.

The distinctive bang from an exploding Claymore stopped the NVA soldiers' rush and gave the five of them the opportunity to move. Fifty yards into the jungle, the men stopped and listened. Josh looked at his fire teammate and could see a stain spreading down his left shoulder.

"How bad?"

"Just below my collar bone. It hurts, but I'll live."

"Let's get the bleeding stopped."

"I've got it." One of the SEALS pulled out a pressure bandage while Josh and the SEAL with the Stoner watched and listened. A tap on the shoulder told him they were ready to go.

Big Mother 40

Thai was looking at a map, trying to visualize the pattern of attacks. Men were running around the command center, the phones were ringing, and as usual, the reports were confusing and inaccurate. In the background, he could tell the difference between the AK-47s used by his men and the weapons fired by the Americans.

Inside, it looked like chaos, and to an outsider, it probably was. These men had never been in a battle before and while they understood what to do intellectually, this was the first time they'd see that nothing ever really goes according to plan.

He forced himself to remain in the command cave where he hoped to communicate by radio and telephone with each of the four company commanders until he knew what was happening, so he could give directions to his companies scattered all over the base. The one thing that was clear was that there was a firefight going on around the launchers, so he directed D company to commit all its platoons to engage and pursue any intruders. He guessed the missile launchers were the raiding party's primary targets. He didn't know how many were in the attacking force, but at this point numbers didn't matter. Contact and forcing the Americans to use ammunition did. His men knew the terrain, so they could move around and trap the raiders.

There was another fight down the road, near the cave complex. He was sure that this was a diversion by the Americans, who were trying to keep troops in that area from getting into the field. Thai ordered A Company's reserve platoon to push them back into the woods and pursue aggressively. Same orders—maintain contact, press the Americans and force them to use ammunition.

Then the D company commander committed his forces piecemeal: the first platoon rushed headlong into a firefight and got chewed up. By the time the second platoon arrived, the Americans had disengaged and were moving through the jungle.

Thai was standing by the radio in the command center, which was his only link to the company commanders, and it was tenuous due to the short range and unreliability of the early sixties vintage radio sets he was given. "What direction are the Americans going?"

"I'm not sure. We're trying to regain contact," was the only answer the D company commander could provide. He directed his men forward, knowing that they were walking into another trap and that many would die when they regained contact the hard way.

Thai grabbed the radio handset and spat out a stream of orders to each company, pausing only to make sure that the recipient understood his intentions. He'd already mentally played out how a battle like this would unfold and he believed he had the advantage because the Americans were on his base. So far, it was close to what he imagined, for the Americans were fleeing up the ridge opposite the cave complex along one of the four logical escape routes.

His next objective was to regain contact with both groups of Americans. Once he had that, he could keep the pressure on them until he could overwhelm them by numbers and/or run them out of ammunition. Right now, the American's had the initiative and he had to get it back.

Satisfied that the companies knew what he wanted them to do, he motioned to his orderly—who was now his radioman—and together, along with an eight-man squad for security, Thai left the command cave, confident that the two lieutenants on duty would feed him information by radio.

Tuesday, 9 minutes later, September 5, 1972, 0111 Local Time, Venom Base

Josh's Team 1 was taking a five minute break as they headed toward the rendezvous when two men from Chief Jenkins' Team Three appeared out of the jungle. "Where're the other two?"

"The chief sent us ahead after the skipper's team helped us finish off a platoon of NVA. One of our guys is KIA and they're carrying him out."

"Got it."

"Who's that?"

"A Russian colonel by the name of Koniev. He is either defecting or our prisoner. Take your pick, but we're bringing him back in one piece."

The SEAL rolled his eyes. "Yes, sir. Are you ready to move?"

"We are. Move out. You two take the point. We've got one walking wounded who will be number three in the line. The Stoner will be number four. I'll watch Koniev and one of my team will bring up the rear."

"Got it. Good plan, sir. You've been paying attention."

Josh flipped him the bird. The SEAL smiled and started moving toward the rally point. As Josh stood up, he spoke into the mike. Again, no answer, but he wasn't going to worry about whether the radio was working or not.

Big Mother 40

Thai spread the map out on the jungle floor; one of the lieutenants from C Company held a cloth over the group so the colonel could use a flashlight to light the map and show what he wanted them to do next. His orderly handed him the handset halfway through the discussion.

"Thai." He listened and then keyed the mike. "Maintain contact, force them to expend ammunition and use the tactics you were taught." He turned back to his group. "A Company is trailing the group that was by the caves and are about a hundred meters or less behind them. They are trying to move one platoon around them and the next time the Americans stop, they are going to attack. That confirms we are chasing two groups, which means we have to catch the one in front of us and prevent them from joining up. Captain, I want to move up the ridge in two platoons with three squads roughly abreast and one in reserve. Push your men. We have to move fast but make sure they stay in contact with the squads on their left and right. We don't want the Americans to slip through. When, not if, we find the Americans, we are to engage as soon as we make contact and then try to get on their flank and force them to fight us in two directions. Most important, we cannot let them escape. Do not worry about ammunition. We have plenty stored around the base and we'll get it when we need it. Understood?"

Team 4 stopped for a moment to make sure the wounded SEAL was no longer bleeding.

"Give me man's weapon and I help, no?" Koniev said to Josh.

"Not on your life, Colonel. We just met and I don't trust you yet."

A SEAL tapped Josh on the shoulder and pointed to their left. The seven SEALs readied their weapons. Rather than continuing in the direction they were going, Josh pointed in the new direction they would go, which was at an angle up the ridgeline toward the center of the base. His plan was that after they broke contact, they'd zig-zag back in the direction of the rally point. Josh figured the NVA would try to keep them confined to this area on the ridgeline within the base and were probably moving to get on one of his flanks in order to surround his team.

Josh noticed, while lying the on the cool, damp ground, that the jungle had become as quiet and almost as dark as a tomb. Only his stomach was churning and it wasn't from hunger. He hoped his mind wasn't foretelling his immediate future by its symbolic reference to closed-in burial grounds and the thought that the four-legged and slithering jungle predators that hunted during the night were watching the two legged ones and staying out of the way.

He could hear sporadic gunfire in the distance, but couldn't gauge how far away it was. When they were training, he had been surprised at how the jungle distorted sounds that were not nearby. Yet Josh could tell the difference between the disciplined short bursts from the Stoner, the ripping of an AK being fired on full automatic, and the rapid cycling of MP-5s firing three-round bursts. He guessed they were about fifteen hundred meters from the rally point and he needed to give their pursuers a very bloody nose to get them to back off.

At about fifty feet, Josh could see the silhouettes of about a dozen men and the unmistakable shape of the AK-47, which confirmed the identity of the owner. Josh pushed Koniev's face down and peered through a notch in a thick tree that he hoped would stop the AK-47's 7.62mm x 59mm round. The red tracers and the sound of the Stoner and other MP-5s told him to start shooting. The drill was simple. Knock down the targets you could see, then move in the planned sequence that took you diagonally away from the threat, and do it again.

Each time, the two men closest to the enemy moved back past Josh, he fired, then shouted he was moving. When he did, Josh tapped Koniev on the shoulder as he stood up to run, and they ran about twenty yards. The second time he grabbed Koniev's collar as a signal to get up and move, Koniev was already on the move. It took three attempts in the darkness that was punctuated by muzzle flashes, but soon, the jungle was again deathly quiet. He tried to control his breathing to keep from hyperventilating, since breath control was one of the secrets to accurate shooting.

Now he really knew what Churchill meant when he said, "Nothing is as exhilarating as being shot at without result." He wasn't sure it was exhilarating; exciting, maybe, scary absolutely. It was worse than being in a helicopter, because in the air you could move in multiple dimensions and make it harder for the shooter. Right now, he just wanted to make sure that whoever was shooting at him never got the desired result.

TUESDAY, 33 MINUTES LATER, SEPTEMBER 5, 1972, 0159 LOCAL TIME, VENOM BASE

Thai heard the radio call. After telling the radioman to turn down the volume, he pressed the handset to his ear and keyed the mike. "Thai."

He flipped open the map as he listened. After repeating their location and jotting it down on the map, he turned to the C Company captain.

"A Company has lost contact and taken many casualties. The Americans attacked them and killed the company commander, but they are pressing on as we are. We need to pick up the pace and catch up so we can overwhelm the Americans."

As they pushed into the jungle Thai's instincts screamed, *Cabot is leading the Americans!* And this time, he was sure he, not Cabot, was going to win.

TUESDAY, 42 MINUTES LATER, SEPTEMBER 5, 1972, 0241 LOCAL TIME, VENOM BASE

Josh pulled out a map when the group stopped in the jungle near the junction of two trails. "My guess is that based on the firing we heard, Lieutenant Cabot and the rest are moving up the ridge through here, and if we are lucky, we should meet about here as planned." He stabbed the map at just below a high point on the ridge. "We can be there in ten to fifteen minutes, so let's get moving. Once there, we can decide what to do next." They pressed on and reached the ridge without coming under any more fire.

Looking around the rally point, Josh understood why Marty picked it. There was a small clearing under the jungle canopy in front of the cluster of large boulders that gave them protection, so anyone approaching would be out in the open. The senior SEAL, a petty officer second class, suggested the six of them deploy in an arc, facing where he thought the threat would come, with Koniev in the middle and the Stoner in the back and high up where it would have a wide field of fire.

"Good idea. We're here early." Josh's voice was hushed but clear to all. "It is oh two-fifty. We'll wait to oh four-thirty and then decide whether or not to head to the helicopter." Despite the time of night, there was enough ambient light to see the shapes of the other men. Josh keyed the mike. "Team One plus two at Aspen." Silence. He repeated it a second time; again, no response.

"Ammo status?" He didn't know what else to say.

"Stoner could use some belts. I'm down to my last two."

Josh tapped the man next to him, who reached into his pack and took out the plastic magazine carrying 150 rounds, and then he did the same. Like the remaining SEALs, he'd shot off about half of what he'd started with; he had three, not including the magazine in his MP-5 left. Ammo, or the lack of it, was now a concern. They had enough for two, at most three, short engagements.

Each member took the time to gulp down a D ration bar along with at least half a bottle of water. Despite the material he'd collected, Josh was amazed at how much lighter his load had become without a Claymore, one grenade, four thirty-round magazines and a quart of water. He dug a small pit into the soft earth, buried the wrapper, and covered the disturbed dirt with a broad dead leaf. A faint sound made him hold up his hand and each man slid his weapon into a firing position.

"Surfboard." The word came out of the jungle on the left side of the clearing.

"Ski area." Josh hoped he wasn't too loud.

"Teams 1, 2 and 3, minus two." It was Marty. "Kitcher is wounded and we need a few minutes to keep him from bleeding to death. Chief, get two guys to make a stretcher. Johnson bought it." He lay the corpse carefully down on the ground. "We have two guys trailing us to watch for the NVA. They're about a hundred meters behind us and will come up in a few minutes. We think we're thirty minutes ahead of the company-sized force of NVA chasing us. They're moving in platoon-sized groups with two out front and one in reserve."

After Marty counted noses, he realized they were now a band of seventeen. "Who's he?"

"I am Colonel Alexei Koniev of Soviet Anti-Aircraft Artillery Forces. I am defecting."

TUESDAY, 22 MINUTES LATER, SEPTEMBER 5, 1972,
0343 LOCAL TIME, VENOM BASE

"Newport Beach." The whispered words froze the men in the small perimeter bounded in the back by large boulders along the edge of a clearing for a second.

"Come in." Marty's' voice was a hoarse whisper.

Petty Officer Second Class Mike Norris led another grime-covered SEAL as they crossed the clearing in a crouch to the front of Marty, who was wedged into a firing position between two waist-high rocks that would let him fire from behind cover while lying flat on the ground or kneeling.

"Skipper, we're facing about two companies." Norris took a deep breath. "One is about a hundred meters away. They don't know we're here. There is another one about a thousand meters behind them and to the east. Both are moving just like the others: two platoons abreast, one in reserve, and as soon as they make contact, they'll try to get us into a clamshell. They tried that earlier tonight down in the valley. They walked right past us about an hour ago."

"I saw those tactics in Cambodia. I wonder if they've adopted them or if it's the same guy leading them."

"Yup, I remember, skipper."

"Benton, where's their command element?"

"Back near the third platoon and between the two companies. Looks like two officers and about ten other men, including a radio operator."

Marty took a deep breath and then slowly released it. It gave him time to think as well as help get oxygen to his muscles. "Okay, here's what we're going to do. It's a change in the plan because we can't move as fast as they can with the two litters, so we're going to give them a reason to stop. Lieutenant Haman and Chief Jenkins, you take the colonel and your teammates and head out and make sure the helo is safe. If it's not, then backtrack with the guys there and we'll go to plan B. Also, give us your Claymores and as much ammo as you can spare and we'll set up some booby traps as we slow the bad guys down behind us."

Marty took another deep breath and then pointed at two SEALs, "Whitlock and Norris, you two plus Benton and me will stay here for the initial delaying action and then follow to the helo and provide rear security. Whitlock, you and Norris have done this plenty of other times on ops with me, so you know what to do. My guess is that when you bug out of here, you'll be about thirty minutes or so behind when you leave here, but you will be able to move faster than the guys carrying the litters. We've got to buy enough time for the group led by Lieutenant Haman and Chief Jenkins to get to the helo without being caught. Chief, how long do you think it will take you to get to the helo?"

"From here, we'll be there between oh six hundred and oh six-thirty, assuming we don't have to make a big detour or get engaged in a long firefight."

"That'll be around dawn." Marty thought for a few seconds. "My guess is we can buy you a half hour or more. There's always a chance that there's a blocking force up there, so just be careful. That's a chance we have to take. Avoid a fight if you can."

Both Josh and the chief nodded before Josh said, "Got it."

"Okay, then back to the delaying action that will get you out of here." Marty paused to make sure that everything he had said before was now the plan. "Now for the hard part. Sometime during the firefight, I'm going to yell for Whitlock and Norris to bug out, at which point you two take off and follow Lieutenant Haman and his guys. When I yell, you move. Don't ask questions, don't hesitate, just get out and provide rear security for Lieutenant Haman. You should get to the clearing about ten to fifteen minutes after them."

Marty looked at the two SEALs, who started to say something but then hesitated, wanting to hear more. "Now we get to the really ugly part.

Marc Liebman

Sorry Benton, but that's you, your Stoner and me. You and I will attack the gap between the two platoons. This'll cause a hell of a lot of confusion, I hope, because to shoot at us, they'll have to shoot at each other if we're in between. If we find the command element, we'll kill as many as we can and keep moving away from the helo, so they'll have to pause and re-group and decide who they're going to chase: us, who they will have just engaged, or you guys who are moving away from them. That should buy you guys some more time. With a bit of luck, we'll escape to the other side and head for a new pick-up point. Assuming the NVA are about here—" Marty pointed to the map "—we'll make a beeline to this clearing, where by then Josh the Helo Pilot Extraordinaire will be there to haul our asses out a little after first light. If you don't hear from us by radio when you get airborne, don't wait for us because it means we didn't make it. Or, we're still alive and we go to Plan C, which will become plan A, if and when we get there. Questions?"

Josh handed Marty a pencil flare gun and a plastic holder with six flares, along with the survival radio he'd forgotten he was carrying; he'd discovered it as he was rummaging through his pack looking for his D-rations. The olive-drab radio had a spare battery duct-taped to the back. He twirled the dial, turned it on, keyed the mike, and heard a side tone, which told him the radio was transmitting, and then turned it off. "Here, flip this on when you hear the helo or at oh six-thirty and give us a shout. I'll find you. Use the D rings on your harnesses to hook up so we can hoist you through the trees. It'll be a wild ride 'cause you'll be hanging below the helo for a maybe thirty seconds to a minute until we can get you on board."

"Sounds like fun."

"Marty," Josh pointed at his friend, "I'm not leaving you here, so you better get on the radio, disappear into the jungle, and let me know where to come get you if it's someplace else. I'm not going to see M'ai in San Diego and have to answer the question of why I had to leave you behind, or how you died or got captured. That, my friend, is an order."

"I'm counting on that, and I will do my level best to carry it out, sir!"

Josh held out is hand and the two of them shook and then hugged. "Good luck."

All Marty could see in the rocks above him was the tip of the barrel of the Stoner sticking out between two rocks. He was lying next to a large tree and listening to the jungle get quiet, which meant the animals sensed there would be more shooting. Since arriving at the rally point,

307

the noise had begun rising to its normal crescendo as the firing died down. Now, for some reason, it was getting quiet again.

He saw one shape in the thinning vegetation in front of him and then, using the corner of his eyes to maximize his night vision, he saw another. For the umpteenth time, he made sure the selector switch on the MP-5 was in the three-round-burst position to give him maximum knockdown power and still conserve ammunition. When he saw the third figure emerge about thirty meters away, he squeezed the trigger on his MP-5 and stitched three holes in the NVA soldier's chest.

Two grenades burst about ten yards in front of him and he felt the burning sting of a piece of shrapnel bite into his right bicep. Ignoring the pain and sure his arm was still working, he fired another burst and then rolled to the tree about a meter away when two of their Claymores went off.

Red tracers were going in the enemy's direction from the two Stoners, and several streams of green ones, probably from PKMs, were coming in his. All were high and either banging into the rocks behind him or whining past into the trees and beyond.

Among the screams of the wounded and dying he heard a whistle, and then more men than he could count began charging his position. He began knocking down one after another, changing clips as fast as he could. During one reload, he rolled on his side when the charge seemed to have slacked off a bit. "Benton, when I yell 'cover us,' lay down covering fire, then we'll we toss one grenade and go through their line."

"Got it, boss."

He was down to his last three magazines when he saw what he wanted and keyed the throat mike. "Cover us!"

Once the Stoner in the rocks began its deadly work and after the grenades exploded, Marty swallowed his fear and charged forward, shooting. In less than a minute, the jungle went from erupting flashes of gunfire to dead quiet. Marty and Jason Benton guessed they'd covered about fifty yards when they kneeled back-to-back against a tree to take a deep breath.

"Ammo." Marty's heart was pounding from exertion, exhilaration, adrenaline, and fear.

"About one fresh magazine in the gun and one spare left, plus a loaded .45 and three magazines and a big Bolo knife."

"I've got two for the MP-5 left beside a half-empty one, my Gurkha knife and the .45, plus three." Josh reached back behind his neck and was reassured that the handle of the knife was where it was supposed to be. "Jason, are you ready to move?"

"Yes, sir."

They began to move toward the clearing for pick up when Marty held up his hand and pointed to his ear and then to the side. They could hear voices moving toward them and then they heard the crackling of a radio. Marty mouthed "Command element," followed by "Let them come to us and then we'll attack," to Benton, who nodded before he rolled about ten feet away and rested the barrel of the Stoner on the bipod. Both of them were aiming across a tree-covered gap in the woods that was about twenty yards wide.

Marty could see eight silhouettes move cautiously out of the darkness and into the clearing and then one on each end moved into the shadows along the edge of the trees. By the time they were halfway across, three more men emerged in the center and Marty could make out the radio antenna sticking up above the grass.

"Officers," Marty mouthed.

Both SEALs knew they didn't have the ammo for an extended firefight, so they planned to end it quickly by finishing off the enemy with a quick flurry of fire or, on Marty's command, withdraw. Marty decided to work from the center out and hope the muzzle flashes from the guys in the trees gave away their position.

He opened fire at ten yards, dropping the first three men with well-aimed bursts. Benton made mincemeat of his initial set of targets with the Stoner, and then cut down the ones on the edge of the woods before killing the radio operator and one of the officers. Marty got up and charged toward the middle, firing at muzzle flashes when bullets started winging over his head. He dove for the earth while 7.62mm slugs chewed clumps out of the ground.

The distinctive ripping sound of the Stoner firing bursts sang over Marty's head. Then there was silence. After waiting for a few seconds, he started moving toward where he suspected the officers were located. He rose to a crouch to get a better view, when he saw a Vietnamese officer rise up and fire a Makarov pistol in his direction. The first bullet went way wide and the second smacked into his pack.

Marty pulled the trigger on the MP-5—only one round came out and the bolt clanged back. Empty! He grabbed his .45 as he saw the man trying to reload the Makarov and pulled the trigger. Nothing happened. In a series of practiced steps, he tapped the magazine to make sure it was seated, racked the slide to put a new round in the chamber, rolled the pistol to make sure the bullet was out of the pistol, and released the slide. Again, he pulled the trigger. Nothing. *Shit! It's jammed and there's no time to clear it.* The charging Vietnamese was less than twenty feet away, waving what looked like a six-foot-long machete. He reached behind his neck, flipped off the snap and pulled the Gurkha knife out from its sheath and prepared for the knife-fight dance as he shrugged out of his pack, slipping the useless .45 into his left hand.

At about five feet, Cabot could see the Vietnamese soldier was wearing officer shoulder boards. As he got close, the officer screamed, "Cabot, I am going to kill you!"

The use of his name stunned Marty for a second and he moved just in time to avoid a slicing blow from Thai's machete. He circled warily, still holding the jammed .45 and the Gurkha knife. In the background, he could hear the Stoner doing its deadly work after an AK-47 barked and a couple of rounds went past him, almost unnoticed.

Marty feigned a lunge and Thai backed off, then came forward again, slicing the air with the long machete. The heavy blade clanged off the raised .45's barrel before sliding down and hitting the bone in a glancing blow on the fleshy part of Marty's left forearm. Despite the searing pain, Marty jumped back and glanced down at his arm, where he could see the blood soaking the sliced fabric.

"Cabot, I am going to slice you up like a butcher, and you are going to die a slow, painful death." Thai stepped back, panting from the exertion as he swung the machete in a series of rhythmic, menacing arcs.

Marty moved sideways away from the long, swinging machete, trying to decide if he should try one more time to clear the .45. For a second, he wondered how the Vietnamese Colonel knew his name, but then decided that killing the man and staying alive was more important than wasting energy talking. Then he wondered how long it would be before he'd start losing strength from blood loss and tried flexing his fingers; he was surprised his hand still worked just fine, other than the movement changed the pain from dull and throbbing to intense.

Again Thai came forward; this time he had both hands on the machete that Marty was convinced was so long that it could be considered a small sword. He needed to get inside the weapon where he could use his superior size to gain the advantage. This time he caught the machete under the bent blade of the Gurkha knife and the hand guard stopped the motion of the machete long enough for him to slam the barrel of the .45 on the side of his attacker's head.

Thai staggered backward, stunned by the unexpected blow. The machete hung loosely in one hand. Marty watched and then started to advance before he realized he'd waited too long. Thai started waving the machete again and Marty had to jump back to get out of the way of the slicing blade that hissed through the air. The move created enough distance so Thai could use his sleeve to wipe some of the blood streaming down his face from the wound gouged out of his head by the trigger guard of the .45.

I've got to end this quickly before his help arrives. In a knife fight, both guys get cut and the winner is just cut less. Marty looked at his opponent as he circled to the side away from the menacing machete slicing the space between them.

"Cabot, you will not get away. If I don't kill you, my men will."

"Fuck you. You haven't managed to kill me yet and you won't do it today." It was all Marty could think of saying to make the man angrier. If it gave him an edge, that was fine; he needed all the help could get. Knife fighting was not one of his strengths.

"Oh, yes, I will!" Thai charged like an enraged bull and Marty let the Vietnamese officer close on him while he crouched slightly, balancing on the balls of his feet. As the machete came down, his Gurkha knife came up, catching the machete in the crook of the blade, stopping the downward movement of the long blade. Marty lashed out in a kick that landed first on the inside of the Vietnamese officer's thigh and stopped in his crotch.

Thai doubled over in pain as he staggered back, struggling to keep downward pressure with his machete. The movement gave Marty the chance he needed as he spun away from the blade and delivered a downward kick with the sole of his boot on the side of the Vietnamese officer's knee. The man screamed in pain as his knee shattered and struggled to stay on his feet. Marty brought the unique oval head of the Gurkha knife's blade down at the base of Thai's neck. The force of the blow went deep into the Vietnamese officer's spinal column and cut the cord.

Thai groaned as warm blood warm spurted out his neck's severed carotid arteries, spraying Marty on the chest and arm. This close, Marty could see the scarring on the man's face and wondered how that had happened. He yanked up to get the blade out of the Thai's limp body and shoved him clear. "Take that, you son of a bitch."

The colonel didn't respond as he fell in a heap.

Seeing his adversary was dead, he held his left forearm and slumped down on a knee, exhausted.

A few seconds later, Benton grabbed his leader. "Let's get out of here. I've got both officers' map cases. You killed an NVA colonel and we shot a captain."

Benton pulled the slide back on the .45 so the jammed round popped out and handed the pistol back to Marty, who stuffed it back into the holster before they jogged out of the clearing, pulling on their packs. A couple of hundred yards away, in relative safety, Benton wrapped Marty's wound with a bandage and fastened it with duct tape from a roll taken from his back.

"Ammo?"

"Not much, about half a belt plus the .45."

"All I got is the .45 and three magazines. I dropped the MP-5 back at the clearing. I was out of ammo for it anyway."

"Let's hope the helo can find us. Do you want me to go back and get a couple of AKs and ammo?"

"No, let's move out and get to the clearing so we can get picked up. Josh will be there. I'll give him a call at oh six-hundred, or if we hear the helo take off." He pulled the radio out of the pouch pocket on his chest and inspected it to make sure it was undamaged.

Chapter 17
IT'S BETTER TO BE LUCKY THAN GOOD

"Is the second battery rigged?" Josh asked Van der Jagt.

"Yes, sir, but we have a problem."

"What?"

"We're pretty sure the spare battery is dead. We charged it before we left, but it didn't hold its charge."

"Shit. We'll just have to get it started on one." Battery starts of the H-3s engines were iffy because a fully charged NiCad battery barely had enough juice for one, sometimes two attempts, but never three.

"Sir, we're working on a fix. I keep a spare battery to power the mini-gun just in case we lose electrical power. I can hook it up in about thirty seconds and be back in action. It'll run the gun long enough for me to fire whatever ammo we have."

"Why aren't you working on it now?"

"We are. Kostas is modifying the harness as we speak."

Josh turned to the radioman. "Have we heard from Marty yet?"

"No, sir. We're maintaining a listening watch. I've got two fire teams on the other side of the clearing where we came from. Should we try to raise him on the radio?"

"Not yet. He'll call at oh six hundred. If we don't hear from him, we give Marty a shout by oh six oh five. It'll almost be daylight about then and I want to be out of here as soon as we can. Jack, do you have a daylight route out of here yet?"

"It is the same one we planned before. We've only got one good option and that's west the way we came in. It has the fewest known defenses. Whether we keep going southwest to Udorn or NKP is TBD. Going south to Firebase X-Ray is also an option but we'd really be tight on fuel. I don't want to go east to the Gulf."

The faint sound of gunfire stopped the conversation. Several bursts were followed by the distinctive bangs of grenades.

"Lieutenant." Chief Jenkins handed Josh the handset.

"Sir, its Whitlock and Norris. We're about fifty yards from the edge of the clearing and they're about two hundred yards behind us trying another flanking maneuver."

"We'll get the sewing machine going and use it for fire suppression," Josh replied into the radio before turning. "Okay, everyone listen up." Josh's yell stopped everyone. "As soon as I get one engine started, I want everyone aboard. The bad guys will hear the engine start and know the helo is near and come at us with everything they have. Van der Jagt, make sure the mini-gun is ready to shoot."

"What are you going to do?" Jack was strapped in before Josh settled into his seat after making a quick jog around the helo to make sure it was clear.

"We turn nothing on until number one engine is started."

Vance twirled his finger over his head. Josh nodded, made sure the switches were in the emergency start position, and pushed the starter button on the speed selector. "Pray we have enough juice."

The starter motor whined faintly and they both willed the engine RPM gauge to increase. As soon as the gas generator speed passed seventeen on the gauge that showed the speed of the gas turbine section in percent rpm, Josh slid the engine control lever into the start position and took a deep breath. They could hear the igniters clicking; the engine hung up at nineteen percent for what seemed to be an eternity before they heard a whoosh and the engine accelerated to eighty percent rpm.

With the first engine and its generator on line, number two started normally, and as soon as it was up to speed Josh released the rotor brake while Jack's hands flew around the cockpit, moving switches into the right position for flight.

"All set in the back. Kostas has the grenade launcher and the SEALs are ready to provide covering fire. Spare battery is in place and we're ready to rock and roll with the mini-gun," Van der Jagt reported in.

"Take-off checklist complete."

"Big Mother, Sierra Six-dash-two is in position."

"Dash-two, we'll be there in less than a minute with the cavalry. Come around the front and use the passenger door."

Two clicks answered as Josh pulled the big helicopter into a ten-foot hover.

"Are you about to do what I think you're going to do?" Jack was speaking as his hands were handing the M-79 grenade launcher to Kostas who was grabbing grenades out of the box in the center console.

"Yup. Watch and learn. The NVA is about to meet the mini-gun, up close and personal."

The HH-3A groaned as the blades bit into the humid air and rose to a ten-foot hover. Once clear of the two-foot-high grass, Josh air-taxied sideways so that the helicopter was about seventy-five feet from the end of the clearing. Muzzle flashes were visible and several rounds pinged through the fuselage before the humming of the mini-gun began as Josh set the H-3 down on its wheels.

Each subsequent muzzle flash was greeted by a short burst from the mini-gun and a 40mm grenade from Kostas. Then Van der Jagt began hosing the tree line with 7.62 bullets that spat out of the GAU-2A at 1200 per minute. Explosions from the grenades Kostas was pumping out of the M-79 punctuated the firestorm coming from the mini-gun.

First to emerge from the jungle was a man carrying another. As soon as they were pulled into the helicopter, the last two, Jenkins and Vance, dashed for the helicopter, ducking underneath a steady stream of three- and four-second bursts from the mini-gun as Van Der Jagt swept the tree line, and fire from the SEALs in the helicopter.

"Go, go, go!" Chief Jenkins yelled after he counted noses. He almost fell as he stumbled forward through the cabin to tap Josh on the shoulder, who was pulling power and dumping the nose to get the HH-3A to accelerate away.

"Anyone hurt?"

"We're okay in the back," Van der Jagt reported on his security check. "Helo has a bunch of extra holes from the AKs, but no fuel or hydraulic leaks. Whitlock has got a leg wound. He'll be fine."

Josh took a deep breath; so far so good. "How much fuel do we have?"

"About twenty-eight-hundred pounds. About two hours and fifteen minutes until flame out," Jack said.

"Options?"

"After we pick up Marty, Nakhom Phenom is still the only choice. Udorn may be too far. X-Ray means we have to fly near the trail in broad daylight and we'd arrive on fumes. Not a good idea. If we head to NKP, we can climb to about four or five thousand feet to get out of small arms range and save some fuel and cross the Ho Chi Minh Trail at its northern end. Suggest you head two-four-eight, which is the direction of the

Big Mother 40

clearing as well as on the way to Nahkom Phenom. After we get Marty, fly one-eight-oh if you want to go to X-Ray."

The HH-3A was up to ninety knots in seconds and fifty feet above the trees while he hugged the ridge line on the north side of Venom. Pillars of smoke from the base's fuel supply and missile storage sheds were visible behind them in the clearing sky. As soon as they passed the end of the ridge line, Josh headed the helicopter west southwest.

"Let the good guys know we're airborne, and while you're at it, have them call in an airstrike. There should be some A-6s around waiting for this opportunity." Josh's mind was racing with potential options. First order of business, get out of North Vietnam. Then they'd worry about crossing Laos.

Jack flipped the IFF to the ON position, selected both Mode 3 and 4 and pushed the IDENT button to send a signal to any U.S. aircraft carrying air-to-air surveillance radar. Seeing the yellow light blink twice, he knew that someone had them on their radar. "Eagle Eye, or Red Crown, or Billiard Ball, Anyone, Big Mother 40. Do you copy?" Jack already had the planned UHF frequency selected.

"Big Mother, this is Billiard Ball SixFour, authenticate, over."

Jack checked a pad, found the right sequence and scribbled two letters on the windscreen so Josh could see it.

Josh keyed the intercom, "I hope they don't get too inquisitive," before rocking the switch to the radio transmit position. "Roger, Billiard Ball. Authentication for Big Mother 40 is Zulu Foxtrot, repeat, Zulu Foxtrot."

Thirty seconds or more passed while the radar operators looked at their code cards. "Big Mother 40, squawk Five-Zero-Six-One and say intentions."

"Billiard Ball Six-Four, need you to pass a message to Red Crown. Do you have radio contact with them?"

"Big Mother 40, we do. Ready to copy message?"

"This will wake Mancuso up." Using his forefinger, he rotated the rocker position to the radio transmit position with his forefinger. "Billiard Ball Six-Four, ask Red Crown to pass to our home plate that Big Mother 40 is about to exit Indian country with good news and has eighteen, that is one eight souls on board and will call when we arrive November Kilo Papa. Break, break, need an immediate air strike at ..." He hesitated and then Jack keyed the mike and gave the grid coordinates of the missile base that was about two kilometers from their position.

Over a minute passed. "Big Mother 40, Billiard Ball Six-Four, Red Crown copies and says wait three hours before calling home plate. Steel

316

Tigers Five Oh Nine and Five One Oh on the way. Should be on target in ten mikes. Copy?"

"Roger."

"Big Mother 40, do you need assistance?"

"We will need medical assistance when we arrive and November Kilo Papa."

"Break right and climb!" Van der Jagt interrupted and by the time he finished speaking the HH-3A was groaning through a sixty-degree angle bank turn and struggling to climb. "Tracers, probably 23mm, at our six. Now at our four. Turn left, now, now, now!" The volume for each call *now* increased and Josh reversed the turn on the third *now*.

"I've got two sites tracking us on the right side and one on the left."

There was a loud thump followed by a loud bang. Even with the windows open, they could smell the smoke in the back from the exploding shell. Josh kept jinking the helicopter erratically by cross-controlling the stick and rudder pedals as calls from the crew leaning out the doors kept him informed when he couldn't see the gunfire. He tried to keep the helicopter close to its base course of 248, but survival was more important than covering ground. For the first time he was worried that they would be shot down, and the thought pissed him off.

Two more thumps followed by another bang. More smoke and the pungent smell of spent explosives.

"No lights, gauges normal." Jack switched between looking outside for tracers and checking the instrument panel because the helicopter was vibrating more than usual. He wasn't sure if it was because Josh was alternating flying the lumbering helicopter in coordinated flight with cross controlled jinks to make it harder to hit.

The shooting stopped as abruptly as it started.

"Boss, we've got a couple of minor shrapnel wounds here. We took one 23mm round in the armor plate. Another hit the hoist and it's fucked. It sprayed splinters all over the place. We're getting patched up and no one is seriously hurt. That, plus the radio rack in the back took a hit. Not sure what is out of action, but one of the boxes is blown all to hell. We have a couple of large holes on both sides in the aft fuselage."

Josh looked at the clock on the instrument panel. It was 0601 and keyed the mike. "Van der Jagt, ask the Norris if they know what happened to Marty."

"Norris here, Sir ... I believe the Lieutenant and Petty Officer Benton got through their lines. That's when we bugged out as per the plan. What happened after that, I don't know, but I think the lieutenant's plan worked."

Big Mother 40

"Thanks. Break, break. Jack, call Marty."

"Sierra Six, this is Big Mother 40, over."

"Sierra Six is up. Standing by."

"Big Mother is airborne. We have a problem. Hoist is out of action." He looked at the chart. "How long will it take you to get to LZ Atomic?"

"Stand by."

Josh kept jinking the helo at varying altitudes and angles of bank.

"Six hours, give or take a couple. We'll be way away when the steel rain begins."

"Good. Get there and we'll be back in about eight. Listen for me."

"Will do."

"Shit." It was all Josh could say.

Tuesday, 44 minutes later, September 5, 1972, 0607 local time, Venom Base

In the dim dawn light, Major Loi studied the black HH-3A as it made a circle over a point in the northwest corner of the base from the observation platform near the command cave. His first thought was, *That is what a ghost's helicopter looks like.* His second was, *That's interesting,* and his third turned into, *Why is he circling instead of running for home?*

Loi had climbed up to the platform with the hopes of being able to see the battle better if it evolved after daylight broke. He brought with him a chart showing him where A and C companies were pursuing the attackers. D company was no longer an effective force, and B company had taken some casualties in the fight around the caves but was essentially intact. The fire from the diesel fuel was burning off to his right, sending a black pall of smoke high into the air. He could see a second pillar of dense smoke about a half a mile away where the spare missiles were kept, sending flames and smoke above the trees.

The net had collapsed in the middle of the valley and the burning missiles on the two launchers and one of the trucks had burned large holes in the camouflage netting. From his perch, almost a thousand feet above the valley floor, the collapsed net gave the central part of Venom base a pockmarked appearance.

When he picked up the handset, Major Loi assumed, since it had been well over an hour since he had heard from Colonel Thai, that the regimental commander was either dead or out of radio contact. If Thai were dead or seriously wounded, he would have to take command. "Have you heard from Colonel Thai?"

"No, sir." One of the captains in the command center answered the radio.

"This is Major Loi; are you in radio contact with A and C companies?"

"Yes, sir. Major, they have suffered heavy casualties and have lost about half of their men. Both are at the clearing where the American helicopter took off. They also found the bodies of the team that was watching the clearing. Our men think the American helicopter spent the night because they left behind camouflage netting and what looks like some kind of battery."

"Tell them to head southeast and look for Americans. Also, tell B Company to stop trying to put out the fire and move into the same area. I think the Americans may have left someone behind."

"Major Loi, sir, A and C companies are running low on ammunition and have many dead and wounded. Both company commanders are either dead or wounded."

"I understand; they have been in a battle. Leave a few men behind to care for the wounded, take their ammunition and to get moving immediately. The Americans won't be coming back there and I think we may have a chance to capture an American SEAL or two."

TUESDAY, 1 HR, 6 MINUTES LATER, SEPTEMBER 5, 1972, 0712 LOCAL TIME, ON BOARD BIG MOTHER 40

No one spoke while they exited the valley and headed for Thailand. Josh ran the cost of the raid through his mind. One of the SEALs was dead, two wounded pretty badly, one with a shoulder wound, and almost everyone else has shrapnel wounds.

"By my estimate, we're almost into Laos. You fly. Heading is about two-five-oh. No ASE." As soon as he finished, Josh pointed to Jack who took the controls and continued climbing. They reached about two thousand feet when the number two engine started to unwind. "What the fuck? No additional lights on the caution panel. Fuel pump warning lights are still out." Josh touched each item as he spoke. "Let's go through the in-flight engine shut-down procedures, and then let's see if we can figure out what happened. Am pushing both engine speed selectors full forward."

Jack leveled off while Josh read off the check list from the pocket NATOPS manual for a number-two engine failure, then gestured as if to ask, "Do you want control?"

Josh shook his head. "Number two engine is shut down and the shut-down checklist is complete. Still no secondary indications … See if she'll maintain ninety knots at this altitude. If not, hold anything you can above seventy and maintain altitude. Break break, Van der Jagt, do we have any fuel leaking into the cabin?"

"Negative. We can smell it, but nothing is coming in. I can see fuel on the side of the helicopter and it is coming out of the engine bay. My guess is we took a hit in a fuel line or the fuel control. If the round went through the armor, it would have caused the engine to grenade. We'll keep an eye on it, but I think as long as it doesn't start to burn, we should be OK."

By now the pungent odor of JP-5, the Navy's version of jet fuel had reached the cockpit. "Okay, I want you to prepare everyone in the back so that if we have to go down, we can get out fast and with enough gear so we can walk out."

"We're ready. Just get us on the ground in one piece."

"No problem. That's why they pay me the big bucks." Josh paused for a few seconds. "Jack, my guess, since we now don't have any fuel pressure for the number one engine, is that we have a pump failure of some kind or a break in the fuel line. So, I'm going to shut the firewall valve to the number two engine and wait a minute or so before I open the valve that will let us pump fuel from the aft tank into the forward one so we can use all the fuel we have. I'll monitor the quantity gauges to make sure we don't overfill the forward tank."

"Got it."

"Just keep us close to two thousand. If you're a bit erratic with no ASE, don't worry. Just try to minimize the power changes. If you get tired, we'll swap flying every ten to fifteen minutes or so." Josh keyed the UHF radio. "Billiard Ball Six-Four, Big Mother 40, over."

"Billiard Ball Six-Four, over."

"Billiard Ball Six-Four, Big Mother 40 just took some 23mm hits and have had to shut down an engine. If possible, could you send some Jolly's out from NKP to pick us up if we have to crash land?" He looked down at the dense jungle; he could see the leaves that topped very large trees. Any autorotation would be dicey, and some, if not all of them, would be injured or killed. There weren't any clearings or rice paddies in sight.

"Big Mother 40, Billiard Ball Six-Four, Jolly Greens Zero-Six and One-One will be airborne in less than five minutes, along with four Sandys. Pigeons to November-Kilo-Papa are two-five-zero at seventy-five. Copy?"

"Big Mother 40 copies." Josh rolled the switch to the intercom after watching the fuel totalizer stabilize. "With any luck, we'll land with about two hundred to three hundred pounds of fuel."

"When do you want the helicopter back?" Jack had been hand flying the HH-3A maintaining about eight-five knots at two thousand feet.

"Are you getting tired?"

"No."

"Well, then, you've got it unless you can't handle a single-engine landing with no stabilization equipment in a heavily loaded, battle-damaged helicopter with limited fuel in VFR conditions on an nine-thousand by three-hundred-foot runway."

Jack mouthed, "Fuck you."

Josh keyed the intercom, "I didn't hear that, say again."

"Someone just removed the training wheels." The voice on the intercom was anonymous and Jack held up his middle finger for everyone in the cabin to see.

TUESDAY, 90 MINUTES LATER, SEPTEMBER 5, 1972,
0834 LOCAL TIME, NAKHOM PHENOM AIR BASE

After the two wounded SEALs were put in an ambulance along with the body, Josh ran over to the Air Force Rescue and Recovery Squadron's command center to find the officer on duty. This proved to be a young looking major wearing silver Command Pilot wings. He looked shocked at the sudden appearance of a dirty, grimy, blood-stained Naval Aviator who needed a shower so bad his BO spilled over the counter.

"Sir, I need a private office with access to a TS line, right now"

"Lieutenant, you can call from any phone here in the command center."

"Major, if I were to do that, I would have to ask every man to leave, which would shut down the command center. I realize that they all have clearances, but not for this op, sir."

"I understand, Lieutenant. That's what the watch officer at Commac-V said when we called to tell them that you were inbound. Apparently, congratulations are in order. For what, I don't know, but apparently, a job well done."

"Thank you, sir, but I hope if they told you anything about what we've done, you keep it to yourself until it's released."

"They didn't say anything other than give you whatever you need. Use my office; it has a direct secure line and just dial the number. There's a speaker connected to the phone if you two want to use it. You need to get that arm looked at by a doctor."

Josh looked down at his arm, which had fresh blood oozing through his flight suit. "Thank you, Major, I will do that after I make the call." He closed the door and wearily sat down and dialed.

"Mancuso. This is a secure line."

"We're at NKP," Josh said.

"So I heard. Who's the extra SOB?"

"Are you sitting down?"

"Yeah."

"Colonel Alexei Koniev of the Soviet Anti-Aircraft Artillery Forces. He was the brains behind the tactics they were using at the secret base to shoot our planes down. Koniev wants to defect and has some interesting documents he's brought along that prove we have a communications leak. When they are translated, the intel folks are going to wet their pants. Plus, I got some Soviet code books."

"Anyone else know he is with you?"

"No, sir. One of my guys had a spare flight suit in his bag and that's what he's wearing. I've got a SEAL babysitting him and he's not allowed to speak to anyone. His English is sort of okay, but he has a heavy accent."

"Good, keep him isolated." At his end, Mancuso took a sip from his coffee mug. "Where's Marty?"

"We had to leave Marty and Petty Officer Benton behind. Long story, but the hoist took a hit. He's on his way to LZ Atomic and should be there in four to six hours. I'm going to take a nap and go back and get him."

"How'd you get separated?"

"We were being pressed pretty hard by what Marty thought were at least two companies. We were able to disengage, but each time they caught up to us we had to give them a bloody nose. They followed right to the LZ and we had to shoot our way out. To give us more time, Marty and Petty Officer Benton created a diversion and went through their lines, shooting. The idea was to confuse them and allow the rest of us to get to the helo and get out. The plan was that once we took off, I would fly to a small clearing and haul the two of them out. That was before we took a hit in the hoist along with a few others places."

"How many did we lose?"

"One. Petty Officer Kitcher.I thought Johnson was the dead guy...? Four more are going to be in the hospital for a while. The rest of us have minor shrapnel wounds, which can be treated in the dispensary, and then we'll be released."

"Braxton should arrive at NKP any minute."

"Yeah, base ops told me. We're going to get some sleep and then hope to get the helo flyable this afternoon, assuming we get everything fixed. And then we'll go back and get Marty and Jason Benton. If I have to, I'll take Braxton's helo. The worst hit we took was a 23mm shell that went through one of the pockets in a main rotor blade, and the Air Force is going to help us check the spar. We don't think it was damaged, but we want to make sure. Worse comes to worse, we can borrow one of their rotor blades. A 7.62 round nicked one of the armored fuel lines and it failed, but we should have that fixed pretty soon. We also took another 23mm shell in the forward avionics compartment and another in the aft fuselage. Bad news is that we don't have an HF, stabilization equipment, or a secure radio, and the radar altimeter is dead. But, the good news is that we can still fly the helo without them, although without the ASE we don't have an autopilot. The guys think the box is what's screwed up, not the wiring."

"Is Marty or Petty Officer Benton hurt?"

"I don't know; he didn't say they were."

"What do you think the chances are of getting him out before the bad guys get him?"

"At least fifty-fifty. As long as they don't stumble into a big patrol, they should be okay. My guess is that they don't have a whole lot of ammo left so they are going to play hide-and-seek."

"You're more optimistic than I am." Mancuso paused before he changed the subject. "The others?"

"Baxter took a round in the thigh. Just missed his femoral artery. He's in surgery now. Francis has a shoulder wound, Whitlock got hit in the thigh and it broke the bone and Wilson took a shot in the side. They think Wilson, Whitlock and Baxter will be out of action for a few months and they'll send them back to us as soon as they can be moved. Francis should be able to travel in a few days."

Josh took a sip of his Coke. "Chief Jenkins said they took out the control van, a Fan Song radar van, four SA-2 launchers, the fuel and missile storage area, the generators too, as well as killing or wounding a bunch of NVA, at least sixty, maybe more. Plus, I know we killed at least a half dozen Russians. And an A-6 hit two 57mm guns and a missile control van."

"Let me know what you need to get Marty out before you take off. I want you to think about letting Braxton go get Marty. I won't order you not to go, but my guess is that you're running on fumes. Don't push it."

"Yes, sir, understand. I'll think about it, but my first priority is to get him out of North Vietnam. I've never left anyone behind before and am not going to start now."

"I understand. Do you have a plan?"

"Not yet, but I will have one in a bit."

"Look, you're near your limit and may make a dumb decision just because you're tired."

"Sir, I'll get Braxton and his guys involved when they get here. I left one of my best friends back there and I am going to bring him out. Count on it."

"Just don't die trying and kill a bunch of people unnecessarily because your ego got in the way of common sense."

"Yes, sir, I won't."

"Okay. Is Marty out of the valley?"

"Yes, sir, he should be. We know what LZ he's heading for."

"Good. Now that you're in Thailand, we're going to paste that valley tonight. I won't tell anyone you have Koniev, but if you need anything, call General Cruz or me."

Chapter 18
ELATION AND FRUSTRATION

Marty grimaced when Benton ripped the duct tape off his arm. With more time to work, he used an antibiotic cream on the wound before he pressed a better wrapped bandage over the gash to press the skin together and used another strip of duct tape to hold it in place. Marty swallowed a handful of aspirin to dull the throbbing pain.

"Sir, if I have to, I can sew the wound up with fishing line if I get a chance to get it good and clean."

"Leave alone for the time being." Marty pointed to the two packs on the ground. "Besides the weapons, what else do we have?"

"Two grenades, six D ration bars, two quarts of water, the PRC 90 and a spare battery, one complete first aid kit and one partially used one. The usual survival gear. Oh, and two bottles of halazone tablets. We're traveling light, sir."

"Yup, I've got the compass and the map." He laid it out on ground. "Here's about where we are. We need to continue moving southwest toward this clearing, which is designated LZ Atomic. When we make contact with Big Mother 40, we'll use the usual emergency authentication calls."

"You're sure he's coming back."

"Yes. If his helo is broke, he'll either beg, borrow or steal another one from the Air Force, so yes, he'll be there at LZ Atomic tonight if he's not incapacitated or dead. So will we." Marty didn't doubt that Josh and his crew would do everything, including dying, if it meant getting them out. That thought alone was enough to keep him going and quell the fear in his gut.

Big Mother 40

Back in the command center, Major Loi had been issuing a stream of orders to return the chaos in the cave to some kind of order so it could function again as a command center. In the absence of any direction from Colonel Thai, he wanted to give the regiment its best chance to capture the Americans who were still inside Venom. If they did, it would be a feather in the regiment's cap and good for his career. He was studying the map of the base, trying to visualize which clearing the helicopter had been circling when he was handed a telephone.

"Major Loi." He listened for a few minutes and jotted some notes down on piece of paper. "Thank you, Lieutenant. Good luck. Keep pushing your men and you'll capture the Americans. They can't be too far ahead of you."

Major Loi put down the handset and realized his eyes were moist. "Attention in the command center." Within seconds, conversations stopped and all eyes turned to him. "Colonel Thai is dead. We believe that two Americans are on the run. Both A and C companies are in pursuit. I want D Company to reorganize into one reinforced platoon and take up a blocking position just inside the tree line at the ravine at the entrance to the base and then spread out to prevent the Americans from escaping to the south and into open country where they can be easily picked up."

He studied the recently plotted positions and directions of movement on the large chart in the center of the cave, when a private came to attention next to him. "Major, you have a call from Hanoi." The young soldier pointed to a secure phone in the corner of the cave.

"Major Loi here."

"Major Loi, this is General Chung. I understand that Venom was attacked this morning."

"Yes, sir. An American commando team infiltrated the base early this morning and destroyed all four of our launchers, our spare missiles, as well as our primary generator. We are running on our spare generator and only have about six hours of diesel fuel left. Most of the Americans escaped, but we are sure that at least two are still on the base and we are pursuing them. We believe their helicopter was damaged, but we don't know how badly."

"Casualties?"

"Many, sir. We don't know the exact number, but A and C companies reported that they lost about one-third of their strength. B Company was already at half strength and D Company was cut to pieces in a firefight around the missile launchers. I don't have an accurate count yet, but we probably more than one hundred dead or wounded. Colonel Thai is among the dead."

"I am sorry to hear that. Colonel Thai was a good man."

"Yes, sir. One of the best."

"Any Russians killed?"

"Yes, sir." Loi wondered why he asked the question. "We don't know how many. Colonel Koniev is missing, but his cave is on fire so he could be in there. There are four bodies down by one of the control vans and two in their communication center."

"Find the Americans."

"Yes, sir. We are searching for them now."

"Very good." General Chung paused. "We have two companies of reinforcements on the way from Ha Giang by truck. They should be at the base in about an hour. Report back to me when you have more information."

TUESDAY, 1 HR, 26 MINUTES LATER, SEPTEMBER 5, 1972, 1034 LOCAL TIME, VENOM BASE

Both SEALs lay flat and motionless on the ground, listening to North Vietnamese soldiers creep through the jungle all around them. They waited a full ten minutes after the last soldier passed before they got slowly to their feet. Marty motioned diagonally to the west and they moved out, hoping the sounds of the jungle would mask any noise they made. They tried to step only in places where they would not leave footprints, but that was not always possible. After another twenty minutes of walking, they stopped to listen while they munched on D ration bars washed down by about a quart of water.

Marty sat cross-legged with the map spread in his lap as he figured out where they most likely were. Adrenline was still flowing but Marty knew that fatigue would be coming soon to pay a visit. Both had been counting steps, and Marty had tried to keep them on a compass bearing that would take them to LZ Atomic. What he needed was a place he could see the sky so he could take a proper bearing to get a more accurate fix.

"Jason, you look like shit." Marty was looking at the petty officer whose fatigues were covered with a mixture of sweat and dirt. His floppy boonie hat was dark with sweat.

"Yes sir, with all due respect, sir, you look worse than I do!"

"Yeah... You may be right. OK here's the sitrep...." Marty had to force himself to be the optimist even though his gut was churning. This was the first time his whole team wasn't extracted as a unit and now he was on the run with almost no ammo, very little food, and deep inside North Vietnam. He caught himself smiling, thinking that most people would think the situation was hopeless and they should just surrender. That was *not* what they were going to do, not while they had a chance to get out. There was a saying in the SEAL community about the only easy day.

"Boss, what's so funny sir?"

"Just thinking that the only easy day was yesterday and that if this job was easy, anybody could do it!"

"Amen, sir."

"You ready to move?"

"You bet."

"Then let's get going. We've got to catch a helo ride."

"

They hadn't moved more than about a hundred yards when Marty froze. Not ten feet away were two NVA soldiers looking right at him, raising their rifles. As Benton was getting his Stoner in a firing position, Marty pulled out his .45 and fired one shot at each soldier. The first one dropped, but the second pulled the trigger as he fell backward, dying as he emptied the thirty-round magazine into the sky. Bullets started flying everywhere as both SEALs started crawling backward as fast as they could. After about five minutes, the firing died down; they had retreated to what they thought was a safe distance and had started traveling laterally when they almost bumped into another patrol. The two SEALs hid in a stand of elephant grass as a patrol passed a few feet away and when the jungle sounds started increasing, they felt safe to continue moving.

It was about noon when they came on a small stream. Marty could see the ridges on both sides of the valley from a rock on the top of the large pool. While he took bearings from several distinguishable geographic features, Benton filled both water bottles and then dropped a halazone tablet in each before capping and shaking them, though nothing would change the nasty chemical taste the pills gave to the water.

"The good news is that we're closer than we thought to LZ Atomic. The bad news is that the bad guys are all around us and know we are somewhere in the area. That means we have to be even more careful. Maybe they won't have LZ Atomic staked out. If they're smart, though, they'll have a platoon on each large clearing just waiting for us to show up, because they are betting that we are not planning on walking out!"

"Sir, the reinforcements have arrived. One company is unloading at the entrance to the base and the other is on the way up here."

"Excellent. Designate the company by the road X Company and the one up here as Y. Have the Y Company commander report to me immediately."

"Yes, Major Loi. Any other orders?"

"Not yet. Do you have any more news from A Company?"

"No, sir, other than they were in a brief firefight with the Americans and lost four more soldiers killed and two wounded. They are very low on ammunition. Two of the men were killed by our own gunfire, but we confirmed that it was the Americans because we found two .45 shell casings at the scene of the firefight—"

"Forty-five?"

"Yes, sir, .45. Why?"

"That means they are down to pistols and must have run out of rifle ammunition. That is good news. Do we know what direction the Americans are going?"

"We believe southwest. A and C Companies are in position to stop them from escaping in that direction."

"Good, do we have men at all the clearings?"

The lieutenant gave Major Loi a quizzical look. "We don't have enough men to chase the Americans and put men at all the clearings where a helicopter could land in that area of the base."

"How many clearings are in the direction the Americans are heading?"

The lieutenant looked at the map. "I believe six, sir. They are located in this area."

Loi looked at the area of the map the lieutenant circled for a few seconds. "Get X Company to move two squads into position at each one of these clearings as fast as they can get there. They are not to fire until either an American helicopter lands or they see the American soldiers."

Big Mother 40

"Van der Jagt, you look exhausted," Josh said, staring at his senior air crewman.

"It's been a long day, sir, but we're almost done. Big Mother 40 will have a new rotor blade installed in about thirty minutes and be ready for a test turn. The Air Force has been very helpful with tools and people. Not sure about the ASE and won't know until we start it up and try it out, but right now, when we powered up the electrical system, Vance said it tested okay. We'll see when we start the engines and engage the rotors."

"Is Big Mother 16 up?"

"Yes, sir. She is ready to go."

"How long would it take to swap the hoists?"

"About an hour, give or take a few minutes. Why?"

"If we want to use Big Mother 40, it needs a hoist."

"Sorry sir, I didn't think of that. I was too focused on getting a new rotor blade. I'll see if the Air Force has a spare. They have at least three of everything else."

"Don't beat yourself up about it. We're all very tired." Josh put his hand on the second class petty officer's shoulder. "We're leaving to go get Marty and petty officer Benton no later than sixteen forty-five, and I'm either going to take this helo or Lieutenant Braxton's. Where's Chief Jenkins?"

"They're all over there with Koniev." Van der Jagt pointed to a small building at the end of the flight line.

Everyone stood up when Josh entered the building, which consisted of two large rooms and a bathroom. Weapons in various stages of disassembly or assembly were in piles in front of each SEAL as they cleaned their weapons. "Where's Chief Jenkins?"

"Sir, both he and Lieutenant D'Onofrio are off getting us some more ammo. They should be back any minute."

"Okay, listen up, we're going to man-up at sixteen-thirty to get Lieutenant Cabot and Petty Officer Benton. I need four volunteers, plus my crew."

Everyone in the room raised their hands. As Josh was looking at the men in front of him, a small pick-up truck pulled up in front of the building.

"Howdy." It was Jack D'Onofrio. "I understand Big Mother 40 will need a test flight in less than half an hour before you take it into the wild blue yonder over North Vietnam. I presume you'll need a co-pilot for both evolutions."

"Sir, if I may add, all the SEALs in here are going to get on the helo with you whether you want them on board or not. So plan on it, sir." The last word sounded as if it was added as an afterthought.

Josh blinked and smiled. "OK." He was sure he was just given an order in the form of a statement by a chief petty officer. He didn't take it as insubordination, but merely a statement of fact.

"You also need me." Koniev walked up to Josh. "I know all gaps in radar coverage, and where all anti-aircraft guns are."

TUESDAY, 1 HR, 22 MINUTES LATER, SEPTEMBER 5, 1972, 1553 LOCAL TIME, LZ ATOMIC

Machinist Mate Second Class Jason Benton set up his Stoner in a rock pile that gave him a clear field of fire across the grass that covered the large boulders and clumps of grass in the clearing. While Benton was improving his position, Marty worked his way around the clearing, which was large enough to allow two H-3s to land. Now he understood why his friend listed this clearing as their third choice; the rocks must have been clear in the photos.

Marty slid back into their hideaway. "It looks like we have company. There're twelve NVA at the far end of the clearing, setting up an ambush. I don't know if they're the lead element or all there is. If the leader is curious about this LZ and scouts it, he'll find our little nest and realize it's a perfect place to set up an ambush for the helo. If they come our way, we'll have to fade into the woods and work around to the opposite end. The next LZ is a full day away; it will be a long slow, tough walk with all the NVA around. We'll alert Josh when he's inbound, and knowing him, he'll have some air support to help because where there's some NVA, there's a lot more. And this time, they are really pissed after what we did to their missile base."

TUESDAY, 5 MINUTES LATER, SEPTEMBER 5, 1972, 1558 LOCAL TIME, LZ ATOMIC

The NVA lieutenant stood back inside the tree line, scanning the clearing to the west with his binoculars. Behind him, resting prone on the jungle floor, were four twelve-man squads, plus two PKM teams. Satisfied he now knew the ground, he motioned for his platoon sergeant and four squad leaders to come forward.

"It looks like there's a group of large rocks at the far end of the clearing where we can cover the entire clearing with machine guns. We will put our two PKMs there and then deploy two squads on the north side so we can get any American helicopter in a cross fire. My guess is that if the Americans come here, they will do so either at dusk or during the night. That will give us time to dig in and camouflage our positions. To scout the clearing, we'll move two squads up the right side and two up the left. If you should find the Americans, engage at once and the other two squads will move to their flank. Headquarters says there are two, maybe four of them, and they have very little ammunition so we should be able to overwhelm them. I'll move with the radioman up the right side between the two squads. When we are in position, we will report to headquarters. We move in five minutes."

The NVA lieutenant, who just two months ago graduated from training, thought this was very similar to an ambush exercise they'd practiced several times at the school northeast of Haiphong. The affirmative nod from the senior platoon sergeant, who was a veteran of many battles in the south, gave him confidence that he had made the right decision.

TUESDAY, 3 MINUTES LATER, SEPTEMBER 5, 1972, 1601 LOCAL TIME, LZ ATOMIC

At the opposite end of the clearing, Marty tapped Benton the back of the calf. The SEAL slid back slowly. "What's up?"

"I just saw a flash that could only be from an officer using binoculars. That means they've got at least a platoon here." He looked at his watch. "We've got about two hours, so if they move in our direction, we'll just exchange sides of the clearing as we play hide and seek. Let's pull out of here now and go into the jungle far enough so we can see what they do before the helo get here. We'll go about halfway down the left side and stop."

TUESDAY, 1 HOUR, 45 MINUTES LATER, TUESDAY, SEPTEMBER 5TH, 1972, 1746 LOCAL TIME, LZ ATOMIC

From their new position, the SEALs counted twenty-eight North Vietnamese soldiers, backlit by the light from the clearing. They waited ten minutes before moving again and then stopped between two large trees. They could see the entire clearing, as well as anyone who was moving inside the tree line in either direction, from their vantage point that was almost to the southeastern corner of the LZ.

Marc Liebman

Marty pulled the PRC-90 out of his pack and placed it on a leaf. He gulped down the last of the aspirin he had, noting that the pills did nothing to ease the pain in his left forearm or where Benton had popped out a grenade fragment with his survival knife from his bicep. He'd put some ointment on it, bandaged it, and then again used a duct tape wrap to keep it in place. Now, there was nothing to do but wait, hope and most of all, pray.

TUESDAY, 9 MINUTES LATER, TUESDAY, SEPTEMBER 5TH, 1972, 1755 LOCAL TIME, LZ ATOMIC

"Lieutenant." The senior sergeant walked up to the officer who was sitting about ten yards behind the tree line. "They were here."

"Are you sure, Platoon Sergeant?"

"Yes, sir. We found fresh boot tracks that were made by American boots. The footprints are much larger than any of my men would make. Some go down the right side and some the left of the clearing. Some go back into the jungle. There's not enough to know what direction they went, but we are pretty sure they were here today."

"Can you tell how long ago the footprints were made or how many soldiers?"

"No, sir. We cannot."

"Platoon Sergeant, our orders from Major Loi are to ambush any American helicopters that land in this clearing and that is what we will do." The lieutenant paused for a few seconds. "Are you suggesting that we try to track them?"

"No, sir. Our men couldn't tell you which direction they went, but they are confident that they were here in the past day or so."

"Thank you, Sergeant. That tells me the Americans are going to try to pick up their friends here and we will kill them. Are the men ready?"

"Yes, sir." The veteran sergeant didn't think it was appropriate to tell the lieutenant that it would take more than AK-47s and two PKMs to bring down an American helicopter unless they killed the pilots, and when the Americans came to rescue their comrades, they turned the battlefield into a hell none of his green soldiers had ever seen.

TUESDAY, 1 HOUR AND 10 MINUTES LATER, SEPTEMBER 5, 1972, 1905 LOCAL TIME, LZ ATOMIC

Marty awoke with a start, upset with himself that he'd dozed off. Next to him, Benton's head was on the ground, fast asleep.

Big Mother 40

"Sierra Six, Big Mother 40, over." The crackling of the radio, despite Marty having the volume almost at its lowest setting and pressed hard against his ear woke Benton, who mouthed the words "Sorry, boss."

The sound of Josh's voice on the radio lifted his mood. "Big Mother 40, Sierra Six , over."

"Sierra Six, Big Mother 40 authenticate."

"Surf's up. One board has minor damage. But it is a party."

Jack looked at Josh. "That means they're okay but one of them is hurt but not bad, and there are bad guys around."

"Where's the party?" Josh asked Marty.

"Northwest corner. Figure at least fifty attending."

"Where's your table?"

"Middle, east side."

Josh clicked the mike twice, thought for a few seconds, and then pulled it back to transmit on UHF. "Sandys Oh-One and Two-Five, bad guys on the northwest corner of the LZ. Need you to do your magic. Sandys Five One and Three Four, stand by. Pick up in the middle, east side. Jollys, orbit as planned."

Josh waited until everyone acknowledged his radio call, including Billiard Ball, who was monitoring the rescue effort and then keyed the mike again. "Sierra Six, we're about fifteen, that is one five mikes out, with the cavalry and the kitchen sink. Keep your heads down."

"Sierra Six, roger."

The North Vietnamese soldiers heard the rumble on the other side of the clearing and sensed the concussion of the double-row eighteen-cylinder supercharged 2,700-horsepower R-3350 radial engines that powered the A-1 Skyraiders long before they saw them. And then the planes were on top of them, and the earth and trees erupted from the explosions from the lead aircraft's four 20mm cannons.

The lieutenant heard what he feared most as they passed overhead: the pops of napalm canisters opening. In seconds, the northwestern end of the clearing was ablaze from the jellied gasoline, and the lieutenant remembered the face of a burned Vietnamese colonel by the name of Thai who taught at the school when he'd first got there. He hoped he'd be lucky enough to survive, but that hope ended when the 4,000-degree heat sucked the air from his lungs and began to set off the ammunition in his harness. In the fireball, second platoon, X Company ceased to exist.

The old sergeant, who was with his squad farthest from the rocks, could feel the intense heat as he kept his men from running. The rising smoke told him that the American helicopters would land heading in their direction and would pass overhead as they took off, which would let his squad fill the helos' bellies with rounds from their AK-47s.

"Wait until the helicopter is almost on the ground before you start shooting. Then keep firing until it is out of sight. It should take off over our heads." The thirty-three-year-old sergeant was old by NVA army standards and had survived three tours in the south. He ran up and down the ragged line of twenty men in his command, yelling instructions and encouragement.

"Sierra Six Actual, Big Mother 40, where did this helo's HAC go to school and what kind of car does he drive?"

"Norwich, and a Porsche convertible. Now will you come get us out of this shit hole?" Marty wasn't pissed or annoyed; he knew the drill.

"Roger that." Josh pulled the nose up and flared the helicopter. "Get in the passenger door."

Jack saw two figures emerge from the tree line on his side of the helicopter. "They're coming out!"

"Big Mother 16 is in hot."

Out of in front, Josh could see the other HH-3A moving at about fifty knots and tracer streams coming out of the mini-gun and the M-60. Josh watched it slow to hose down the tree line, when Big Mother 40's instrument panel erupted in a shower of glass and metal shards. One of them stuck in his tinted visor like a mini-spear.

"Shit piss and corruption, I'm hit!"

"Who's hit?"

"Me, D'Onofrio, your co-pilot. Let's get the fuck out of here before I bleed to death. They're on board."

Josh pulled power with the collective as his looked at Jack, who was pressing his left side with his left hand and holding the throttles forward of the circuit breaker panel with his right. In the background, Josh could feel and hear the helicopter taking hits from the gun flashes on the tree line in front of them and wondered if he was the next to get hit.

As they passed 1,500 feet, Koniev came from the back and helped Jack unstrap before lifting him out of the bloody seat by the armpits and carrying him to the back of the cabin, where Van der Jagt and the SEALs put a compress on the wound in his side. Koniev then returned and climbed into the copilot's seat. He plugged in his helmet and yelled across the cockpit.

"Tell me what to do. I follow orders well, even if they are stupid!"

Big Mother 40

Rokossovsky got up much earlier than usual after only a few hours of sexually satiated sleep before the hotel concierge called. He got up, cursing the early wake-up. Today, despite the bad weather, the flight was supposed to depart at 0900 because the Aeroflot flight crew refused to leave if the Americans were anywhere near Kep Airfield. Why the commercial flight landed at a MiG base northwest of Hanoi was still a mystery to him despite his pointed questions. Now he had to arrange transportation for the thirty-odd passengers, who were a mix of embassy workers, Soviet army and air force advisors going home, and Laotians, Cambodians, and Vietnamese going to the Soviet Union for training.

Usually, the four-engine AN-12 was painted bright white with a blue band down the side of the fuselage. But for some reason, this one was unpainted aluminum, which glistened in the dim lights and the reflections from the large puddles. The civil registration in six foot blue letters on the side of the aft fuselage appeared to be black.

He spread the documents out on the table in the customs office one last time to make sure they were all in order and hoped the Vietnamese customs and immigration officers would not be late or thorough. The special pallet was one large, three meter wide by four meter long and a meter and a half high wooden box held tightly together with steel bands and already loaded on the plane. It had seals from Laotian customs that had not been broken and he was confident that the Vietnamese would accept the work of their neighbors and not open the container with Soviet Ministry of Medicine markings. If they wanted a look, he had several thousand Dong handy with which to dissuade a thorough inspection.

Satisfied everything was in order, Rokossovsky decided to stretch his legs in the cool damp air, and just as he was thinking that the Americans wouldn't attack Kep in this lousy weather he heard the distant whine of a jet that turned into a roar as the distinctive delta shape of an F-111 passed overhead. Its bombs landed with bright orange flashes in the fuel dump, whose yellow flames cast a billowing, flickering shadow over the parking ramp.

Thirty seconds later, the same sound, but much louder, surprised Rokossovsky, who looked over his shoulder. He'd never seen a bomb in flight before and now he was seeing two. He watched the first enter the fuselage of the AN-12 before the second slammed into the concrete less than fifty feet away. He saw the blast from the first, but not the second.

Marc Liebman

"You look bright and cheerful today." Marty was sitting with his arm in a sling at the desk they shared at the SEAL compound. "How's Jack doing?"

"He was lucky. The bullet went through the fleshy part of his side and didn't hit anything vital. I told him that if he worked out more, he'd be trimmer and wouldn't have gotten hit. He was so dopey from the anesthesia that all he could do is flip me the bird. He'll be back here in a day or so and we'll have to listen to him whine about how his side hurts and it is all my fault." Josh paused for a second. "How many stitches?"

"I didn't count. Probably thirty or so, but they say other than the scar, I should be fine."

"That's good news. How are you really doing? That was pretty ugly."

"Yeah. Benton got hit as we were climbing in the helo. He grunted when the bullet hit him and I pulled him the rest of the way in. When I asked him how he was doing, he said 'I'm good,' and then died. I spent most of the flight holding him and feeling the warmth go out of his body." Marty paused and Josh could see the tears starting to well in his eyes. "This is the first op in which I've lost anybody; and we lost two, with four, including Jack, in the hospital."

Josh hugged his friend for a while before speaking. "Yeah, but they wouldn't have had it any other way. We went in, kicked ass, blew up the target, and made a second trip in to get you out."

"I still would like to think we could have done something that would have prevented the guys from getting killed. How's the helo?"

"Shot up. It'll be down for a while. We probably shouldn't have flown it back here, but there wasn't anything major wrong, at least mechanically. I figured if we left it at NKP, it would take much longer to fix. I know this sounds mystical and maybe stupid, but Big Mother 40 is a tough old bird that's gotten us in and out lots of tight places without letting us down, so I couldn't leave her in Thailand. Getting her ready for the next mission is more about parts and sheet metal work than anything serious. It'll take us some time, but the trusty old machine should be fine." Josh had just come from the flight line where his crew was making a list of the parts they would need to get the helicopter fully mission ready again. The heat had already created sweat stains around his armpits, even though he hadn't done anything other than stand around listening to his maintenance crew. Now it was just a matter of fixing the sheet metal while waiting until the parts arrived.

"On the good side, our spook thinks we've got a nice big fish who's saying things that scare the shit out of me," Marty said.

"I talked with Koniev a lot at NKP, and he told me that they knew we were coming, but not when. We were very, very lucky we didn't get our asses kicked; everyone could have ended up dead, wounded, or in the Hanoi Hilton." Josh paused for a second. "How long have you been here?"

"About nine-ish. Took a quick nap, cleaned up, and got back over here to spend some time with the good colonel. We've just started the after-action report and we'll need your input on the ground action as well as the flight in and out. CINCPAC is sending a debriefing team for Koniev and us."

"Good." Josh poured a cup of cold water. "By now the Russians must know he's missing. From what my guy said, Koniev emptied his safes and then set off thermite grenades in them and a fuse that set off a couple of kilos of plastic explosive. Who knows, the fire in the cave may still be burning. At best they think he may be dead; at worst, the Russians may have figured out that Colonel Alexei Koniev of the Soviet Air Defense Forces has been captured."

"What do you make of him and his material?" Marty knew Josh had started looking through some of the folders Koniev carried out of North Vietnam and was finding the Russian harder to read that he would have thought.

"I think it proves what we've been saying all along. We've got a serious leak, which explains a hell of a lot. Now they just have to go find out where it is or who it is. Where is Koniev?" Josh hadn't seen the Russian since they got back to Cam Ranh Bay.

"In the officers' quarters, under guard. We have a gentleman's agreement. If he tries to escape, he's dead." Marty smiled at his gallows humor.

"Gentlemen, I hate to interrupt this séance, but I have a suggestion for the two of you." Neither lieutenant had noticed Mancuso walk into the room before he spoke.

"Yes, sir." Both officers started to stand up.

"Stay seated." Mancuso plunked his coffee mug down on the table and pulled up a chair. "I want you guys to get in a room with Koniev and get everything out of him you can before the spooks show from CINCPAC. It is up to you whether you tell him that he's going to go through this twice. What I want you to find out is everything he knew about that base and the messages he was getting. My guess is that you have about forty-eight hours before you lose him. I'm expecting messages from CINCPAC to start arriving any minute, telling me what they're going to do, who is coming, what their clearances are, et cetera, et cetera, ad nauseum." Mancuso took a sip. "I'd start with how he got there, what he did, and his career. Then fill in with questions."

"Yes, sir, we will."

"I know you have a tape recorder. Do you have two?" Mancuso looked at Josh. "Do you have enough tape cassettes? If not, I'll send someone to raid the exchange. Make two copies, just in case the guys from Honolulu want one. That will leave us with one of our very own."

"Yes, sir. We have Marty's reel machine, as well as Josh's cassette. We have plenty of tape and cassettes. I'll make sure that we have back-up copies."

"So why are you sitting here talking to me?"

Koniev was wearing clean olive-drab fatigues with a name tag with someone else's name sewn above the left pocket. The Russian was several inches wider at the shoulders than Josh, the former ski racer. Koniev looked to Josh, to use a Texas expression that one of his friends from the training command used to use all the time, "run hard and put away wet." But now it was clear why he could carry fifty pounds of files through the jungle: the man was fit.

"Good morning, Colonel."

"Good morning, Lieutenants. Thank you for getting me out of shit hole." Although his English was good, his pronunciation of some of his words reminded Josh of Natalie's father and made him smile.

Marty sat on the other side of the metal cruise box that served as a coffee table and pushed the record button on the two tape recorders. "Lieutenant Haman and I would like to ask you some questions and we're going to record the session."

"Of course. What do you want to know?" The Russian leaned back against the wall using his pillow as a cushion.

"First, tell me how often you got those decoded messages."

"Three, four times week. Each time they get a, how do you say?"

"A batch?" Josh prompted him. "That's many or a group of them."

"Yes, yes. That good description. Each time they get batch, they send them via special secure line. When they come, one of four GRU cryptographic officers on duty decode messages. They only ones had access to codes or equipment. Usually, I get call from colonel at embassy, intelligence type, name Rokossovsky. Rokossovky was at one time infantry then changed to intelligence. He alert me that messages coming.

I was not to show messages to North Vietnamese. I don't think Rokossovsky was GRU, but he knew what was happening. This was his last posting; he was planning to retire. I wasn't to keep copies, but I did. I needed them to compare what we saw. They were perfect match."

"Who was Rokossovky's boss?"

"General Arkady Nikishev. World War Two tank officer, and many times Hero of Soviet Union. Nikishev was in charge of all Russians in Vietnam. He never told me how many, but I think over three thousand. He did say more than one thousand Russians died."

"Did Rokossovsky or Nikishev ever come out to this base?"

"Base name was Venom. Like poison from snake." Koniev paused for a second. "Once. They stay whole day; only safe time to travel was night."

"What was in the messages?"

"Each message gave Air Force's time on target, route, call signs, IFF codes, weapons loads, and information I didn't understand … We knew when and where planes were going to bomb, along with route they fly. It was like shooting gallery. If I had full regiment of missiles launchers, I could take out two squadrons each time they flew by."

"What about radio frequencies?" Josh asked.

"*Da.* We had settings for your secure radios also. The Vietnamese captured many from downed helicopters and gave us working set; we could enter settings from messages and hear talk on radio. I didn't hear all conversations. If we wanted them, their air defense center would give us copies of tapes." He paused for a second to gather his thoughts. "We would use messages to plan how to fire our missiles. We knew where your planes would be so was easy to shoot one or two down. Then we would be silent until we decide to shoot again."

"What about helicopters?" Josh paused. "Did you shoot down any helicopters?"

"You mean ones carrying your Spetznaz?"

"Yes," Marty said, guessing where Josh was going with the question.

"Ahhhh, special interest. Colonel Thai—the base commander—was very interested. I don't know word, but he had pictures of you two in his office."

"The English word is obsessed," Josh said.

The Soviet colonel gave him a quizzical look. "Do not understand, obsessed."

"It means that a person is totally absorbed in something, almost to the exclusion of everything else. The absorption consumes a person's thoughts and affects his actions."

"Ahhh, that was Colonel Thai. He was *obsessed* with you," Koniev pointed at Marty. "I don't know what happened to him."

"Did he have burn scars on his face?"

"Yes, and on arm and side of body."

"I killed him." Marty said, remembering the fight with the stranger who'd called him by his name.

Koniev nodded slowly. "Colonel Thai was a good man. Served country well."

"Why was he obsessed with me?"

"Both of you. You killed his men in Cambodia and were difficult to catch. He called you ghosts. He knew you were around, but he could never capture you."

"How did he get burned?"

"In Vietnam. One of your fighter bombers dropped napalm and killed most of his company. He was out front and was burned on side, arm and face. It took many months to recover and he was lucky to survive."

"Oh." Marty had no idea which fight that could have been.

"I know one Navy helicopter was shot down over base and one Air Force one a few kilometers away. Thai took me to see wreck. Colonel Thai told me base got one before I got there. We would wait for them when they come near us, Thai would order the S-60s 57mm guns to shoot at helicopter. They were high value; North Vietnamese hate your SEALs and Green Berets. We get message some days before you come that detail four options. So I know you are coming and made ready to defect if I didn't get killed."

"What was in the log of what you shot down?"

"Extra notes from every missile engagement and same information that is on note cards. I am sorry we didn't bring chart. I can re-create and show you how we operate. Bad news. It is in Russian."

Josh switched to Russian. "That's okay; I speak and read Russian and we have many intelligence officers who can as well."

"Where did you learn my language?"

"In school."

"Navy school?"

"No, Norwich University, a private university that is a military college."

"Ahhhhh. What did you study?"

"Engineering."

"You're accent is very good."

"Thank you. My fiancée's father is from what you now call Moldavia." Josh switched back to English. "I think our intelligence officers will want you to go through each missile engagement in detail when you get to Hawaii."

"I can do that easy." Koniev paused for a second. "Moldavia. Used to be Bessarabia. They know how to cook there. Very independent, like Ukranians. Do not like government from Moscow."

Josh smiled at the Soviet colonel's comment and then went back to business. "Colonel, do you have a report in there for a shoot down of two Navy helos, one with the call sign Big Mother 22 and the other with the call sign Big Mother 12?"

Marty handed him a pile of folders and it took Koniev only a few seconds to pull one out. "This has information you want. I know about Big Mother 22, not Big Mother 12. After we knew we had shot down plane or helicopter, we match it against what we thought was mission number and call sign from decoded message." Koniev handed the gray-green folder to Josh.

Josh looked at it and made some notes before putting it on the floor next to him.

"These people in the helos, they were friends, no?" Koniev looked each of them in the eye.

"Yes," they answered, almost in synch.

"I am sorry. It is war. I am doing my job."

"We understand. We are furious at the bastard who is giving you the codes."

"Furious. I not understand?"

"Angry. Mad."

"Ahhhh. Mad. Yes. Spies and traitors are scum." Koniev tapped the mattress with his forefinger to emphasize his point.

"What do you think about defectors?" Marty's voice was flat.

"Defection is not betrayal of country. Is not spying. Is want of a better life. Freedom in Soviet Union is joke. There is none. Soviet leaders betray us."

"Yes." Marty's tone told both Josh and the Russian that the session was over. The click of the tape shutting down confirmed his point. "Colonel, how about some lunch?"

"*Da*! Food here better than at Venom."

WEDNESDAY, SAME DAY, SEPTEMBER 6, 1972,
1550 LOCAL TIME, CAM RANH BAY

"Lieutenants, the captain would like to see both of you. I'll have your mail when you come out. And congratulations to both of you on a very good op despite the losses." Master Chief Tannenbaum stopped for a second. "Lieutenant Haman, sir, you need to call Commander Nagano. He left a message, and we'll get a secure line any time you are ready. Suggest you see the boss before you call him."

"Thank you, Master Chief." Despite the heat Tannenbaum always wore a set of utilities, and on this uniform he was also wearing a UDT badge under his SEAL insignia. He was one of the few former "frogmen" left in the SEAL community.

Mancuso, already stripped down to a brown T-shirt, waved them to the two chairs in front of his desk. His fatigue top, still damp from sweat, was hanging on a nail.

"How's the interrogation of Koniev going?"

"Good, sir." Marty looked at his friend and then his boss. "He is telling us stuff that will make the hair stand up on the collective necks of people back in Hawaii and DC. We're losing guys because the bastards know what we are doing and are ready for us."

"I was afraid of that. Unfortunately, there's been a change in plans. We—actually, you—don't have much time," Mancuso said, employing his style for getting right to the point. "We've got guys burning up the copier so we have our own set of what you brought back. Once it goes to CINCPAC, who knows what they'll do with it. We've got enough guys around here who speak Russian so we'll get our own translation." He sipped his coffee. "CINCPAC's messenger boys—and I don't know who they're sending—will arrive here in about twenty-four hours. In the meantime, you keep getting whatever you can from Koniev."

"We can send recon aircraft and strike aircraft to check out his info." Josh's mind raced. "General Cruz can have them tasked because Koniev has given us locations of two additional missile launchers and another two storage areas. If we move fast, a few bombs and a recon pass ought to tell us whether or not he's telling the truth."

"They're going to want some justification for going after a target."

"They fly road reconnaissance missions all the time. This time, we'll give them the coordinates; a couple of A-6s or A-7s can do their thing and the RA-5s can take the post-strike photos. They just have to make it look like it was a random find."

"Okay, I'll call get General Cruz to make it happen today."

Big Mother 40

"Sir, I need at least a couple more hours with Koniev to get him to lay out what he knows of the Vietnamese air defense network on a map and make some detailed notes for future missions."

"He's all yours. Spend as much time with him as you need. Once the honchos from CINCPAC get here, we'll be squeezed out because we're just lowly operators."

Master Chief Tannenbaum stuck his head in the door. "Captain, the HC-7 squadron CO is on the line. He *really* wants to talk to Lieutenant Haman."

"You want to take it in here?"

"Thank you, sir, but I probably won't be doing most of the talking."

"Why not?"

"He's not happy that Big Mother 40 got shot up and will be doubly unhappy because I parked one of his helicopters on the ground overnight in North Vietnam. That's number one. Number two is that I have been very tardy in reporting back to him. All I send him is aircraft status, hours flown, flight purpose codes and maintenance records. He doesn't know much about what we do here, much less the Sunset Sam mission, and I am reluctant to tell him because, despite what he thinks, Nagano doesn't have a need to know and is not in my operational chain of command."

"He hasn't learned his lesson yet, even though is retiring at the end of the month." Mancuso knew exactly what Josh was implying. "Well, for what it's worth, you can always work with us. I'll see what I can do to cover your skinny ass."

He and Cabot walked out of Mancuso's office.

"Lieutenant Haman." It was all he could think of saying when he picked up the phone to talk to Nagano.

"Haman, where *the fuck* have you been? I have been waiting for a call back to get a verbal SITREP or an aircraft status report and all I get is excuses that you are not available!"

"Sir, I can't give you a lot of details, but we just completed a very successful operation."

"What operation? How come I haven't seen a mission plan or report? All I've seen are copies of messages requesting parts and maintenance support for *another* damaged helicopter that's in *my* squadron. From what I gathered, you got another one of my helos shot up, borrowed a blade and a hoist from the Air Force without the proper paperwork, got it shot up *again*, and flew it back without the proper maintenance work, much less the quality inspections, even though you, as a maintenance test pilot, *knew* that the helicopter was down and should not have been flown. *And,* the notes on the parts requests simply say the helicopter was involved in a classified mission. What kind of classified mission? I need to know that for the squadron's records and my reports. Haven't you heard of sending classified messages?"

Josh imagined the Nisei sitting in his office. He was so heavy that he could barely climb up on the platforms to preflight the engines, transmission, and rotor head on an H-3 so he had the co-pilot do it. "I can't tell you. There's a problem with that method of communication, sir."

"What do you mean, you can't tell me? The problem is you're not keeping me informed. Answer my fucking questions! That's a fucking order. I assume you know what that means. I'm your fucking commanding officer."

"You don't have a need to know, sir." Josh winced as he said the words.

"That's bullshit and you know it."

Josh held the handset away from his ear and Nagano's voice could be heard ten feet away. "No, sir, it isn't." He looked up and saw Mancuso standing in the doorway pointing at his chest. "Sir, if you wish, I can have Captain Mancuso, whose SEALs I am tasked to support operationally, speak with you. He reports directly to the Commander, Military Assistance Command, Vietnam."

"Did you or did you not shut down one of my helos inside North Vietnam? Answer that *fucking* question."

"Yes, we shut it down. We did so because it minimized our exposure, as well as risk to the SEALs, the helicopter, and my crew." *As usual, Nagano was more interested in keeping his record clean than mission accomplishment.*

"So it *is* true. That's the stupidest fucking thing I ever heard. You're goddamn lucky that you got it started again! Do you have a death wish, or want to spend the rest of the war in the Hanoi Hilton? You dumb shit, I warned you to keep your nose clean. I'm going to put you on report and it will be written so your next stop is in front of a general court-martial on your way to Leavenworth."

Josh forced himself to maintain an even tone of voice, knowing the facts would just aggravate Nagano more. "Which would you rather have us do, make two round trips into the same heavily defended area, or one? We thought one with the landing several hours from the take-off was not as dangerous. We had two spare batteries in case we needed them. And, sir, we got shot at on the way out because it was broad daylight."

"Haman, I'm going to have your ass for this before I turn over my command. Consider yourself on report, in hack, and relieved. I'll have a replacement sent down as soon as I can find a suitable one." Nagano's tone suggested he was pleased with his decision.

"Sir, to do that, I believe you will have to check with Captain Mancuso first. If you remember, I report to him operationally. He'll need to approve any change." Josh wanted to make sure the fat commander knew his fitness report for this TAD deployment to Vietnam was going to be written by the SEAL captain, not by the CO of HC-7. That was part of the deal he made with Captain Mancuso and General Cruz.

"Haman, don't give me any of your fucking sea-lawyer shit. You're relieved, do you understand me? YOU ARE FUCKING RELIEVED!"

"Lieutenant, you're not relieved until I say you're relieved." Captain Mancuso spoke loudly as he took the phone from Josh's hands. "Commander Nagano, this is Captain Mancuso." His tone was formal and firm, but pleasant. "I understand you have a problem with how Lieutenant Haman has executed a combat mission that was personally approved by my boss, Commander, Military Assistance Command, Vietnam, his boss: CINCPAC, and up through the chain of command, i.e., the Joint Chiefs of Staff, the Secretary of Defense, and the President of the United States. The operation was an outstanding success and every day Lieutenant Haman proves to me what a fine officer he is."

Captain Mancuso paused to sip his coffee and grin at Josh. "Commander, may I suggest that if you have a problem with the performance of any of the officers or enlisted men under my command that you convey your displeasure to me first so I can take prompt disciplinary action. If I remember correctly, the crews of Lieutenants Haman and Braxton and the twelve enlisted men who provide excellent maintenance support have been detached from HC-7 and assigned to my command. HC-7 is therefore a supporting command providing administrative and logistic support when and where it is needed."

Mancuso paused for a few seconds. Josh could imagine the frustration smoking Nagano's brain. "So, Commander Nagano, may I ask one more time, what is your problem with Lieutenant Haman?"

FRIDAY, 3 DAYS LATER, SEPTEMBER 8, 1972, 1000 LOCAL TIME, PEOPLES' ARMY HEADQUARTERS, HANOI

"Good morning, General Chung. Thank you for coming. Tea?"

General Nikishev thought he knew the main topic for this meeting. Over the past few days, Nikishev had spoken at length with all the surviving Soviet officers and men who were now either in hospitals in the Hanoi area or quartered at the embassy.

Along with Koniev, there had been two Spetznaz officers, seventeen enlisted men, four cryptographic officers, and eight anti-aircraft artillery officers on the base at the time of the attack. Besides Koniev and Rokossovsky, four Spetznaz were killed in firefights. By the time he'd walked into the NVA headquarters, the bodies of four anti-aircraft artillery officers and three cryptographers had been identified. Nikishev had been told by the Spetznaz captain that the North Vietnamese admitted they lost at least seventy-five men killed, including Colonel Thai, and another thirty wounded in the initial raid, but he also said that he thought that the real number killed was closer to two hundred and fifty with about sixty or so wounded.

The surviving Soviet officers had found pieces of three bodies in Koniev's charred cave, and it was presumed that Koniev and a cryptographic officer, along with one of the Spetznaz, died in his cave, because the officer was on his way to deliver another message when the attack occurred.

When Nikishev saw that General Chung was alone, he nodded to the senior surviving anti-aircraft artillery officer, who stepped outside the room.

"I presume your wounded are being well cared for?"

"Yes, thank you for asking."

Nikishev was not going to tell him that they were going to be airlifted out as soon as possible because the Vietnamese hospitals were places men went to die, not recover. The planes were already on the way.

"General, I do not look at this as a defeat or a setback."

True, it had been successful in the beginning. But Nikishev wondered how Chung could say that, now that the base was pulverized.

"We have seen the American SEALs before. They are very good. They provided accurate targeting and the Americans bombed one of our bases. That happens quite frequently."

Nikishev sipped the warm tea, enjoying its strong taste and aroma. *What about the missiles and the trained men? You lost a lot more than we did.* The storage facility near the base had held more than a hundred missiles, and they were all gone.

"The loss of Venom and the extra missiles is a setback, nothing more."

"General Chung, let us be candid, you lost many men and much equipment. It is more than a setback."

"The loss of men is regrettable. The missiles can be replaced. We have more coming on ships from your country. Remember, Venom shot down sixty-two airplanes, two helicopters, and twelve drones in its short life. Its loss is a setback. In this war, we have had many disappointments and tactical defeats; but in the end, the Americans, just like the French, will leave because they want to stop bleeding, and they will leave their allies out on a limb. Then, we will win."

Nikishev decided saying nothing was better than saying something that he would regret. The Vietnamese general would eventually get to the real subject of the meeting and why they were alone.

"It is my understanding the late Colonels Koniev and Thai had a close working relationship. In fact, several of our officers said it was an excellent one."

"Colonel Koniev was an outstanding officer and one of our best." Nikishev wanted a cigarette, but seeing no ashtray in the room, he fought the urge to light up.

"Yes, so I was told several times." The slight general made a tent of his hands with his elbows along his side in an un-Vietnamese position. "I was told by one of my officers that he thought Colonel Koniev may have had warning of the attack? Is that true?"

Ah. Nikishev now knew the real reason for the meeting and struggled to conceal his growing unease. The messages! How could General Chung know of the messages, unless he'd read one, the NVA had been able to decode them, or Koniev had kept files and the NVA had found them? He'd have to find out if Koniev's men followed proper security procedures.

"I don't think he had warning. We passed him some analysis from the GRU and told him he could share it. Our people in Moscow felt that the Americans were planning some kind of attack but did not know when or how." That's what Rokossovsky had told him he'd told Koniev. Rokossovsky wasn't here to defend himself, either. Nikishev really needed a cigarette.

"Do you know if he shared that analysis with Colonel Thai?"

"No, Comrade General, I do not know if he did or he did not."

"I don't think he did. If he trusted Colonel Thai, wouldn't he tell him?"

Nikishev had read the message and had been skeptical—a land attack was the most risky option. Why would the Americans go for it? "I don't know what he said. Colonel Koniev may have thought the analysis was inaccurate. He was an anti-aircraft artillery officer, not an infantry or intelligence specialist. He was told what he shared was his decision."

"But it was based on a top secret U.S. message from CINCPAC."

How the hell did he know that? "He and—" Nikishev stopped before he included himself, "may have thought it was disinformation."

Chung crossed his hands so that his forearms were resting on the table. "General, your government has been very generous with its intelligence and we are very grateful because it will help us win the war. But we, too, have intelligence. I believe that if Colonel Koniev shared everything he received with Colonel Thai, the two officers would, as the Americans like to say, put two and two together and the battle would have had a different result."

What does he know that he is not telling me, other than the Vietnamese had access to every message we sent to Venom? Nikishev decided to be direct. "How?"

"Ah, my good General. You are not as arrogant as many of your fellow officers. Let me share with you what we know." Chung spun around and pulled a thick, red folder off his desk and pulled several pictures off the top and arranged them in a row. "We are convinced this man, a Lieutenant Martin Cabot, a Navy SEAL, led the attack." Chung slid the photo toward the Russian general. "He was flown in by this man, a Naval Aviator by the name of Joshua Haman." He slid that photo next to the first one. "Both are highly decorated and very capable military fighting men. In planning the mission, they work for this man, a Navy captain by the name of Mancuso, who is a Korean War veteran and also a Navy SEAL." The third photo was in the row close to the Russian.

Nikishev picked up each one of the pictures and studied the young men's faces. They looked like his sons, both of whom were career officers, one in the Air Force, and the other in the Navy.

Chung waited until Nikishev put the picture down. "Colonel Thai trained special battalions who specialized in hunting U.S. Special Forces teams. We are convinced that Cabot and Thai fought each other several times in Cambodia. Each time Cabot's team escaped and Thai's unit suffered many casualties. They were the only ones to get away from Thai. We believe Thai would be prepared and very motivated to react to an attack by Cabot if he knew when it was coming."

"Why are you telling me this?"

"Because I am sure that Koniev, for whatever reason, withheld the information and now he is missing."

"He died in the fire in his cave." Nikishev really wanted to light up, so much so he had to put his hands under the table to keep the Vietnamese general from seeing them tremble.

"We are not so sure, because our dentist from Venom, who filled a cavity in Koniev's mouth, examined the bodies in the cave and said those were not his teeth. Yes, there were three bodies in Koniev's cave, but not one of them was his. So my question to you, General, is, where is Colonel Koniev?"

Nikishev's hands stilled. *If this is true, how am I going to avoid a bullet in the back of my head?*

SUNDAY, 2 DAYS LATER, SEPTEMBER 11, 1972, 1742 LOCAL TIME, CAM RANH BAY, 180 MILES NORTH OF SAIGON, SOUTH VIETNAM

Mancuso had four pieces of paper in a neat row on the front of his desk, which was usually a collection of messy stacks with a clear spot where he could work next to a message pad. In front of him were Josh, Marty, Jack, and Chief Jenkins.

"Okay, listen up. There is good news and better news." Mancuso put his finger on the first line of a yellow pad.

"First, CINCPAC's boys are convinced that Koniev is the genuine article. Second, they want you four to fly back to Honolulu and be debriefed along with Koniev. That is, assuming of course, that you're able to travel." Mancuso chuckled at his rhetorical question. "They will have a special plane here sometime tomorrow, and the guys who came from NICPAC and helped plan this will go back with you." They all smiled at each other, knowing that they were going to spend more time in Hawaii.

"Calm down. Third, along with khakis, you need to have full sets of both summer and full dress whites, so plan on an expensive trip to the Navy Exchange Uniform Shop as soon as you land in Hawaii; anything you have here will look like crap compared to the others around you."

Mancuso held up his coffee mug as a way of saluting them and also to get their attention. "I have saved the best for last. You two," he pointed at Marty and Josh, "are through with combat operations unless they are personally approved by CINCPAC. Specifically, Lieutenant Haman, this is your New Year's present and the Navy's attempt to ensure that the good Lord inscribes you in the book of life next week on Yom Kippur." Mancuso looked at Josh's surprised expression before looking down at his pad. Mancuso chuckled. "Not bad for a Catholic who grew up in Boston. I do occasionally look at the calendar. Cabot, you are to return to me as my operations officer, in a training role. Haman, you will be commuting between Cubi Point and here as part of your new job, which is to teach what you have learned to your fellow pilots. You will also be my new air ops officer. Between the two of you, you are going to

Marc Liebman

document all the lessons learned in your pointy heads, come up with a realistic training program and then train everyone coming in country on how to do what you do so well so they can maximize their chances of living through a tour in this jungle paradise. Don't either one of you object, because it's already in your orders from CINCPAC."

Jack looked pleased, but he clearly wondered what he was doing in the meeting.

"Oh, D'Onofrio, you get Big Mother 40 as its new HAC and its motley crew. Haman or Braxton can give you the necessary check ride. You'll need to see if you can control your crew better than your predecessor did, and you get to pick a co-pilot, whom our new air ops officer will have to approve. Lieutenant Braxton will be the new HC-7 Det 117 O-in-C and will report to me operationally. Chief Jenkins, you are now Senior Chief Jenkins as soon as my other chiefs report back to me that you have satisfactorily completed a proper senior chief's initiation. Master Chief Tannenbaum's tour with us ends in December and he is going to rotate back to the States and, unfortunately for the Navy, retire shortly thereafter, having served his country for thirty-five years. I would like you to be his replacement, which means you'll have to extend a bit; or, if you want, you can go back to the States to a BUDS training billet. Your choice."

"Any questions on the new arrangements?" Before anyone could speak, Mancuso waved his coffee mug. "One last item. General Cruz is coming up here to pin a Navy Cross on Roy Vance for that rescue near Vinh. Vance is not to know about it."

"Out-fucking standing, he deserves it." Josh flashed a thumbs-up.

"I can't agree more. And last, two good deals and two sort of screw jobs. First, the screw jobs. Soon-to-be Senior Chief Jenkins and Lieutenant (junior grade) D'Onofrio are to return here as soon as the debriefing at CINCPAC is completed. Lieutenants Cabot and Haman are on basket leave after their work at CINCPAC is completed and are to return via their scheduled Magic Carpet return flights, which I believe departs Hickam on the morning of October eighth. Now get the fuck out of my office, I have a unit to run."

WEDNESDAY, TWO DAYS LATER, SEPTEMBER 13, 1972, 1346 LOCAL TIME, HALEKOA HOTEL, HONOLULU

"Sir, we have two urgent messages for you. Both are from a Natalie, uh…" The clerk struggled with the last name.

"Vishinski, and it is a San Diego number." Josh had just shown his ID card to the clerk at the reception desk and was checking for some messages. Next to him were several bags with new uniforms.

351

Big Mother 40

"Yes, sir. I took the last call and she really wanted to speak with you. Is there something wrong?"

"I don't think so."

"Sir, just dial the operator from your room when you're ready and they will make the call. And we don't need a copy of your orders, CINCPAC has already sent them over. Enjoy your stay."

Josh looked at the times on the two pink slips of paper. The last one was just over an hour ago. He had been late arriving because the P-3 had diverted to Midway to pick up a sailor going on emergency leave. He picked up the receiver and dialed the numbers.

"Hi." It was all he could think to say.

"Josh, I'm so glad to hear from you. I didn't know what to do. First, I get a call from a captain by the name of Rand claiming to be CINCPAC's aide asking me what flight to Honolulu is most convenient for me. At first I thought it was a joke and asked why, and he said to come meet you. I tried to tell him that I wasn't coming until September thirtieth, and he said he knew that, but this was special and the Navy was paying for the one-way ticket. Then Ma'i called and asked me what flight I was on and said the same guy called her. So what's going on?"

"It's all okay. I'm calling you from Hawaii while I am waiting for you to get your beautiful body here so I can make love to you. What flight are you on?"

"The first American flight out of LA leaves on Wednesday. It's the same one I took the last time, and it gets there about ten in the morning. I have classes I can't skip on Monday and Tuesday. Then when I told that to the captain, he asked for the names of all my professors and said he would personally call them and have CINCPAC send them a personal letter to make sure that my absence for the next few weeks wouldn't affect my grades."

"Wonderful. I'll be at CINCPAC when you land, so take a cab to the Halekoa and they'll be expecting you. I'll also speak to the chaplain on CINCPAC's staff to find a synagogue for Yom Kippur. We'll go to Kol Nidre on Saturday and then services on Sunday. Anyway, I'm sure no one at CINCPAC will mind that we take the days off and in reality, nothing will go on over the weekend. I think a little praying for sparing me is in order."

"Okay, sounds good, but the captain said I need to bring a cocktail dress or two. I don't have one. What's that all about?"

"My guess is that we will be asked to go to some kind of reception so you'll have to go shopping."

"Okay."

Marc Liebman

"You sound unhappy." There was quiet at the other end of the line. "Look, don't worry. You're so beautiful, they won't care."

"I was hoping to surprise you and come on two legs."

"I don't care how you come as long as you get here." Josh paused to think of a way to offer the love of his life encouragement. "Look, if there was ever a crowd who understood amputees, it would be this one. My God, how many men have come home from wars missing arms and legs?"

"I know that. I was planning to surprise you because I had a leg made, but it is sooooo heavy and uncomfortable. When I wear it, I need a cane for balance because of the way I have to lift the leg and sort of toss it forward with my hip. I wanted more time to work on what they call 'my gait' because I'm so awkward and clumsy. Anyway, I can keep it on for just three to four hours at a time. To pee, I have to unbuckle the damn thing and take it off. It is such a pain in the ass to use, I just feel guilty having been back and forth to the prosthetist at least a dozen times. And, even though I am not paying for it, it is not cheap."

"So don't wear it. I think you are very graceful and sexy on crutches. Anyway, I've never known you with two legs."

Natalie giggled. "That's true. Call me after dinner tonight. I've got to go shopping and study."

"I will, and I love you."

"I love you, too. See you on Wednesday."

TUESDAY, 6 DAYS LATER, SEPTEMBER 19, 1972,
1533 LOCAL TIME, HALEKOA HOTEL

"How do I look?" Natalie twisted left and right, showing off a knee-length cocktail dress with a subdued flower print. The wide shoulder straps dipped down to show the top of her breasts as well as highlight the triple string of eight millimeter diameter white pearls. "Beautiful." Josh was struggling to get the snaps closed on the blouse known as "service dress white." To those who have worn them, the garment is simply called the "choker."

"Let me do it." Natalie let her crutches hang from her forearms. "We're supposed to meet Marty and Ma'i at the entrance and then we're going to sit together while you guys get to stand in some formation. At least that was how it was explained to me. Right?"

"That's it. We get to listen to a couple of speeches because Admiral Hastings is getting his third star before going to Washington."

353

"But you're not on the CINCPAC staff, so you shouldn't have to go to this ceremony."

"All four of us were asked to attend, and when a three-star admiral asks a lieutenant to do something, it behooves the lieutenant to do it. Anyway, after the ceremony, there will be cake and booze and then a formal reception at the O Club. We can leave after an appropriate time, come back here, change, and go out to dinner."

"Okay, but I'm still nervous, and I don't know anyone except Ma'i, Marty, and Jack."

"You'll do fine. You'll like Senior Chief Jenkins."

"I'm afraid I'll say something stupid or do something wrong that will hurt your career."

"I'm not worried. I do enough by myself to put my career at risk." Josh hugged his lover. "Let's go."

Admiral Hastings waited patiently while CINCPAC and his wife snapped the new gold shoulder boards with three white stars onto his uniform. He then strode to the podium and waited a few seconds. "Ladies and gentlemen, we are going to dispense with the usual speech in which I tell everyone how delighted I am to be promoted, what a wonderful command I am leaving to take on new challenges, and to thank those who have helped me during my career."

He smiled at the ranks of officers and enlisted men who were anticipating a long speech and now were being told that there wouldn't be one. Admiral Hastings waited a few seconds, and started again. "Instead, along with CINCPAC, I have the honor to decorate four men whose dedication, bravery, and leadership are in the highest and greatest traditions of the United States Navy. This is the greatest reward one can enjoy as a commander." The admiral paused for about ten seconds. "Lieutenants Martin Cabot and Joshua Haman, Lieutenant Junior Grade Jack D'Onofrio, and Senior Chief Machinist Mate Christopher Jenkins, front and center."

The admiral waited until the four men were arrayed in a line in the order called in front of the podium on the flower-draped dais.

"I am not going to read each citation, but suffice it to say these men are being decorated for their leadership and bravery under fire during a highly classified mission that involved them penetrating deep into enemy territory, attacking and destroying an enemy missile base, and bringing everyone home. In addition to the individual medals, which I will be presenting, each man was wounded, and I am awarding them all the Purple Heart."

The admiral moved his reading glasses off to one side of the podium. "Lieutenants Cabot and Haman planned and executed this audacious— the perfect word to describe it—mission. For their efforts, both are being awarded the nation's second highest award for bravery, the Navy Cross."

While the audience applauded, Admiral Hastings pinned the medals on the two officers. Returning to the podium, he said, "Lieutenant Junior Grade D'Onofrio, even though he had been in-theater only four months, coordinated and developed the intelligence that they used to plan the mission and was Lieutenant Haman's co-pilot on the mission.

"Senior Chief Jenkins helped Lieutenant Cabot plan and carry out the actual attack on the ground, as well as the routes through the jungle that the assault teams would take to and from the target. The ingress was so well planned that the sixteen-man assault team was able to arrive undetected in the midst of a major North Vietnamese base and destroy it. In the firefight, in which all these men were engaged, they managed to kill well over a hundred of the enemy. They are being awarded the nation's third highest award for bravery, the Silver Star."

When he was finished pinning on the Silver Stars, Admiral Hastings returned to the podium. "For those who have not met these men, I suggest you take the time to do so during the reception and wetting down. After these brave men join me in a brief review of the assembled men and woman of the CINCPAC staff, I will return to the podium and dismiss the command so we can enjoy each other's company in a more informal manner, share a formal toast to our great nation and Navy, and enjoy some refreshments." He waited a few seconds. "Gentlemen, please honor me by joining me as we troop the line."

"Congratulations! I'm proud of you." Natalie kissed Josh gently on the lips. "Did you know it was coming?"

"Thank you. No, it was a total surprise."

"They told me when they called me in San Diego. I was sworn to secrecy. Do you think it was a test?"

"No."

"You didn't tell me you were wounded. So that is what the fresh scar on your arm is from?"

"Yes."

"Next time tell me." Natalie tapped an angry finger on Josh's chest and then changed her tone. "By the way, Jeanie Hastings came over to Ma'i and me right after you joined the formation. She was so happy we came, and we talked for almost ten minutes. She said being awarded the Navy Cross is a really big deal."

"It is."

"What's next?"

"I get to show off my future wife while we smile, shake hands, eat and drink."

"Do you think you'll ever make admiral?"

"Are you kidding? I spend most of my time trying to avoid being dragged in front of a court-martial! I'll be lucky to be allowed to stay in the Navy and make lieutenant commander."

"That's not what Jeanie Hastings said. Her husband told her that officers like Marty, Jack, and you come along very rarely. She said Admiral Hastings and CINCPAC's job was to nurture your careers and make sure no one orders you to do something stupid so you survive the war. That's something I want to see."

"Well, did she tell you about my new job?"

"No."

"My days flying combat missions in Vietnam are over. I'm being sent back to finish my tour to train pilots and work with Marty to share what we have learned with others. But no combat missions for either of us."

"So I am going to collect on your IOU."

"Only after you officially say yes."

Natalie put her arms around his neck and crushed her lips to his as her crutches clattered to the floor. "Does that answer your question?

FOOTNOTE
COLONEL GUS THOMES

When the list of POWs was finally released in January, 1973, Gus Thomes' status was changed from MIA to POW. He arrived at the Hanoi Hilton the day after his dinner at Venom Base at a time when the North Vietnamese were improving the conditions of the Americans held there.

Thomes was beaten and aggressively interrogated at the Hanoi Hilton for about two weeks and then tossed into solitary confinement for what he believed was thirty days. When he emerged, he met many of his pilots from the 355th Tactical Fighter Wing as well as others he'd known in his Air Force career.

In the few times he was allowed to socialize with other prisoners, he was careful not to say anything about the treatment he got from Colonels Thai and Koniev, because it was so dramatically different from what the others experienced when they were captured. So, rather than cast doubt upon himself, he kept quiet other than to say he evaded for five days before being caught and then cleaned up and brought to Hanoi.

During the debriefing sessions when he got back to the U.S., he provided as much detail as he could about the base from the evening's discussions. When alone with both the Vietnamese and Russian colonels, they were quite open about Venom and what its mission was, knowing that he was going to the Hanoi Hilton and would not be able to pass any information to his fellow pilots.

At first, the Air Force debriefers, who were not trained intelligence officers, thought it was a tall tale and questioned him closely. One thought it was made up as part of a defense mechanism to cope with being shot down, captured, and tortured. Since many of the debriefers heard stories about how planes were shot down by this mysterious Vietnamese base, one of the Air Force officers had a conversation over a beer with one of his Navy counterparts from the Naval Intelligence Center, Pacific, asking if he had heard similar stories about this mysterious base. When the stories were confirmed, the debriefer's had a different and improved attitude and respect for the wing commander.

Thomes, whose debriefing was taking place at Nellis Air Force Base, was staying at the BOQ when the phone rang. It was his debriefer, who asked him if he were free for lunch.

When the two officers arrived at the officers' club, he was led to a table in the back of the dining room. Alexei Koniev got up and warmly shook his hand. Since that conversation, the two men have become close friends and see each other often. Koniev is an advisor to the Department of the Navy and works in San Diego and Gus Thomes is a corporate pilot flying for a Fortune 500 company based in Los Angeles.

POST SCRIPT

The Navy did not find out until 1986, a full thirteen years after the Vietnam War ended, that it was Jerry Whitworth and his mentor, John Walker, who were providing the Soviet Union with the encryption keys to our codes. The Navy got lucky because they were tipped off by John Walker's disgruntled ex-wife, who called the FBI to tell them that her husband was a spy; the first time she did, no one took her seriously. They did on her second call.

Among the first documents he gave the Soviets were code keys to U.S. cipher machines, primarily the KL-7/KL47 and KW-37. After several deliveries, the Soviets realized they could not de-code U.S. messages without the cryptographic gear for which they were designed.

This is where the waters get a bit muddy, because in January, 1968, the North Koreans seize the USS *Pueblo* and gain complete access to fully functional KW-37s that can code and decode messages using the code keys given to them by Walker. Whether or not the Soviets encouraged the North Koreans to seize the *Pueblo* or not can be debated for days on end and we will probably never know the truth in our lifetimes.

However, the seizure enabled the Soviets to figure out how the equipment worked and possibly/probably reverse engineer them so that they could decode U.S. messages from the comfort of their own facilities in Moscow. My assumption is that's what they did, because without the encoding/decoding machines, the keys that Walker, then his partner, Jerry Whitworth, were passing to them would have been useless. If the Soviets thought they were worthless, they wouldn't have kept paying them until the very end.

Based on this, I believe the Soviets have been reading our mail since shortly after the capture of our equipment on the USS *Pueblo* in 1968 until Whitworth and Walker stopped providing the codes. If one assumes the Soviets were reading our messages, it enabled them to understand how the U.S. Navy was able to detect their submarines and aircraft as well as how we operate. The codes gave them the ability to read encrypted messages that gave them information on air tasking orders, carrier air plans, and mission and equipment status reports. Descriptions of what they could have learned would fill a book of its own.

In addition, the North Vietnamese captured a KL-7. There is no indication that they were given access to any additional key lists after the device was captured, but there is a possibility that the Soviets could have provided them with keys acquired through Walker's treachery.

At a strategic level, this is the equivalent of the advantage the Allies had during World War II. In the European theater, the British were decoding German messages almost as fast as they were sent using captured German equipment and an early computer. In the Pacific, our ability to read Japanese messages, even just snippets, led to major victories such as what happened at Midway.

It is probably clear to those who delved deeply into the damage from Walker and Whitworth's treason that if we had gone to war with the Soviet Union before they were caught, the U.S. Navy might not have prevailed. Yet what is surprising to me is that the cost of their treason is discussed primarily in material terms, i.e., dollars that funded improvement programs that quieted our submarines, made our communications even more secure, and improved our surveillance capabilities and ships and aircraft.

Very little has been written about the possible cost in terms of lives lost during the Vietnam War, in peacetime covert operations, as well as in many of the other shadow conflicts during which members of the U.S. military were advisors and were injured or killed. Every day during the time Walker was passing encryption keys and Naval Aviators took off from carriers in the Gulf of Tonkin, the Soviet intelligence gathering ship or AGI was someplace near the carriers. One can assume its crew was noting the aircraft type, take off time, and monitoring radio and radar transmissions. While that information is tactically useful, it is far more valuable if you combined it with details about:

Where the airplanes were going;

What their targets were;

What route they were taking'

What time they would arrive in the target areas;

What weapons they were carrying, etc.

That is just some of the information that Walker's treason may have given the Soviets on a silver platter. Other critical information he gave away was our underwater sensor capabilities and how we tracked their submarines, which led to a new generation of Soviet subs that were quieter and much harder to find.

Marc Liebman

And I can't help but wonder how many Naval Aviators and Flight Officers, as well as our brethren in the Air Force, Army, and Marine Corps, perished because the Russians and their Vietnamese allies knew when we were coming and where we were going to attack. This question in my mind is one of the reasons the plot of *Big Mother 40* has so many references to leaks in the communication system and the Russians reading our messages. Theoretically, after the capture of the *Pueblo* in 1968 and until 1986, when the ring was shut down with the arrest of Walker's son, Michael, the Soviets could decode and read our messages just as we did. *Big Mother 40* is my tribute to those we lost because of a traitor in our midst who put us all at risk.

Marc Liebman
July, 2012

WAY BACK IN 1972

It was a different world then. Back in 1972, smart phones, GPS, personal computers, and laptops didn't exist. Bill Gates didn't launch Microsoft until April, 1975; Steve Wozniak and Steve Jobs founded Apple Computer in January, 1976. The men of Apollo 17 were the last to walk on the moon in December, 1972.

The United States and its allies have been involved in a never-ending series of hot proxy wars since the end of World War Two:

Greek Civil War (1946-1949)

Korea (1950-to this day)

Arab-Israeli (1948, 1956, 1967, 1973, and to this day)

Guatemala (1960-1995)

Malaysia (1948-1960)

Malaysia(1964-1968)

the Congo (1960-1965)

Yemen (1962-1970)

to name a few.

One of the biggest conflicts took place in Southeast Asia and involved Cambodia, Laos, North and South Vietnam, and Thailand, where the U.S. was locked into Act III of a long-running war in the divided country we now know as Vietnam and long-running civil wars in Laos and Cambodia.

Act I began in 1940 when the French colonial rulers in Vietnam swore allegiance to Vichy France (the side that fought with the Axis powers against the Allies in WW II) and allowed the Japanese to occupy Vietnam. The Communist Viet Minh, led by Ho Chi Minh, began a retaliatory guerilla war against both the Japanese and the French occupiers. After the war, Ho Chi Minh entered Hanoi and declared independence, only to be ousted in 1946 by the returning French, who wanted Vietnam back under French colonial rule, not only for the status as a world power, but for access to cheap raw materials—primarily rubber—to support French industry.

The Viet Minh, now armed, supplied, and supported by a victorious Mao Tse Tung and his Chinese Communists, began Act II: a war to expel the French. To increase the pressure on the French, Ho Chi Minh expanded the war throughout the rest of French Indochina, which we

363

Big Mother 40

now know as Cambodia and Laos, while the United States helped the French with equipment, munitions, and aircraft, often flown by U.S. citizens. The French loss at Dien Bien Phu led to a peace treaty signed in 1954 that divided the country along a ten-mile-wide demilitarized zone that more or less followed the 17th parallel into the Communist Democratic Peoples Republic of Vietnam in the north and the Republic of Vietnam in the south.

Between five and ten thousand Viet Cong stayed behind in the south and began Act III in 1960 with a guerilla war to overthrow the government. President Kennedy responded by sending advisors to help the fledgling South Vietnamese military. As it became clear to the White House that the South Vietnamese were not capable of defeating the Viet Cong, President Johnson decided to escalate by increasing the number of Americans in-country and changed their role from advisors to active combatants.

One event led to another, and by 1965 the number of U.S. troops in-country passed two hundred thousand and the U.S. had begun bombing North Vietnam. The 1968 Tet Offensive was a military defeat for the Viet Cong, because it decimated their ranks and forced the North Vietnamese to commit even more troops to the war. However, Tet was a shock to both the Pentagon and the White House, neither of which thought the Viet Cong or the NVA were capable of such an attack. Furthermore, for the White House, Tet was a strategic defeat because the retaking of Hue and the attack on the embassy in Saigon were seen on TV in living color. This led to the perception that the U.S. was losing and public pressure limited President Johnson's options which made it harder for him to prosecute the war.

Fast forward to 1972: the ground and air wars were in full swing, even though the U.S. was beginning to reduce the number of troops in South Vietnam. At the peak of the build up, there were more than 500,000 U.S. service men and women, along with soldiers from Australia, Nationalist China, New Zealand, the Philippines, South Korea, and Thailand, in action in South Vietnam or off its coast. The U.S. had fighter bombers, tankers, electronic warfare, rescue aircraft and helicopters stationed at bases in Thailand, Guam, and South Vietnam. The Navy was maintaining two or three aircraft carriers on Yankee Station, about one hundred miles south east of Hanoi in the Gulf of Tonkin, and Dixie Station off the coast east of Hue.

Outside of the political and social ramifications of the Vietnam War, Act III was militarily significant for three reasons. First, the helicopter as a battlefield weapon came of age. Introduced in the later stages of World War II and used in the Korean War, the lighter, more powerful and reliable jet-engine-based, turbo-shaft engine revolutionized the helicopter's capabilities by enabling greater payload, longer range, better high-altitude performance and faster cruising speeds.

Second, it was the first war the U.S. had fought since the Philippine Insurrection in 1902 where divisions and armies didn't maneuver as combat units on a battlefield contesting large swaths of the countryside. Regiments and divisions were deployed to Southeast Asia as whole units, but didn't fight that way. Instead, it was a small unit war on the ground where platoon or company-sized units were airlifted into position or walked into the jungle to hunt an elusive enemy. Once found, artillery and air strikes were called in as reinforcements to contest a piece of ground.

A few battles involved whole regiments, but most were small unit actions in which the U.S. used its superior mobility and firepower to make up for a lack of numbers. The enemy, on the other hand, tried to close with the U.S. forces—or, to use the NVA term, "grab them by the belt buckle"—to make it difficult for the U.S. commanders to take advantage of close air support or artillery.

Third, U.S. special forces—Army Green Berets, Navy SEALs, Marine Force Recon—were deployed all over the country, displaying their unique skills to the public at large for the first time.

The U.S. Navy entered the Vietnam War prepared to fight either a conventional, or God forbid, a nuclear war with the Soviet Union. U.S. carrier battle groups would ensure the sea lanes were open to its European and Asian allies and the Soviet bases along its coastline could not support significant military actions. In the mid-'sixties, as the Vietnam War escalated, the U.S. found itself without a significant aviation capability to support special operations or combat search and rescue CSAR (pronounced sea-sar).

At the start of the war, the CSAR mission was first given to two West Coast squadrons: Helicopter Combat Support One (HC-1), flying Kaman UH-2A/Bs Sea Sprites, and anti-submarine warfare squadrons equipped with Sikorsky anti-submarine helicopters (SH-3A) called Sea Kings. Despite the fact that neither helicopter was designed to survive hits by small- and medium-caliber rounds, both machines were modified as the war went on, the crew training syllabus changed, and successful tactics were developed based on lessons learned.

To support SEAL operations in the Mekong Delta, the Navy created Helicopter Combat Attack Squadron Light Three (HAL-3) flying UH-1 Huey gunships the Navy got from the Army. Helicopter Combat Support Squadron Seven (HC-7) emerged from a 1967 reorganization that split HC-1 into four squadrons and was tasked with CSAR and special operations missions. Its official call sign was the Sea Devils, but over time the matte-black helicopters became known as the Big Mothers.

Cast of Characters

Americans

LT (Lieutenant) Big Tom Bridges—helicopter aircraft commander of downed Big Mother 12

LT (Lieutenant) Bill Braxton—HC-7 helicopter aircraft commander and former co-pilot for Josh Haman

LCDR (Lieutenant Commander) Greg Winston—electronic warfare specialist

COL (Colonel) Gus Thomes—Commanding Officer 355th Tactical Fighter Wing, United States Air Force

Carla Growacki—friend of Natalie Vishinski

CGM (Chief Gunners Mate) Chris Jenkins—CGM with Marty Cabot's SEAL team.

AMS2 (Aviation Machinist, Sheet Metal and Petty Officer Second Class) Derek Van der Jagt—senior enlisted crew-member on Josh Hama's Big Mother 40

MGEN (Major General) Hector Cruz—U.S. Marine Corps and chief of staff for operations for Commander, Military Assistance Command, Vietnam (COMMACV)

LTjg (Lieutenant Junior Grade) Jack D'Onofrio—Haman's friend and co-pilot on Big Mother 40

Jeanie Hastings—RADM Hastings wife

MCBM (Master Chief Petty Officer, Boatswain Mate) Jeffery Tannenbaum—Senior enlisted man under Captain Mancuso

LT (Lieutenant) Josh Haman—helicopter aircraft commander, Big Mother 40.

Ma'i Cabot—Marty Cabot's wife

LT (Lieutenant) Marty Cabot—team leader of SEAL Team Sierra Six

Natalie Vishinski—Josh Haman's girl-friend

Big Mother 40

AE3 (Aviation Electrician and Petty Officer Third Class) Nicholas Kostas—crew-member on Josh Haman's Big Mother 40

AT3 (Avionics Technician and Petty Officer Third Class) Roy Vance—crew-member on Josh Haman's Big Mother 40

CAPT (Captain) Tony Mancuso—Commander Navy Special Warfare Vietnam under COMMACV

RADM (Rear Admiral) Allen Hastings—deputy chief of staff for operations, Commander-in-Chief, Pacific Command (CINCPAC)

CAPT (Captain) Martin Ruppert—Chief of Staff, Task Force 77

CDR (Commander) Kaito Nagano—Commanding Officer, HC-7

MGEN (Major General) Mike Jameson—Deputy Commander, 13th Air Force

COL (Colonel) Nathan Becker—Commander, Firebase X-Ray, Vietnam

MM2 (Machinist Mate and Petty Officer Second Class) Jason Benton—member of SEAL Team Sierra Six

PT2 (Photo Interpreter and Petty Officer Second Class) Elliot French—photographer and intelligence specialist

GM3 (Gunners Mate and Petty Officer Third Class) Harvey Thomas—member of SEAL Team Sierra Six

LCDR (Lieutenant Commander) Jesus Montemayor—HC-7 Cubi Point detachment officer-in-charge (OinC)

CAPT (Captain) Marcus Johnson—7th Seventh Air Force Intelligence Officer

SSGT (Staff Sergeant) Ben Grayson—7th Seventh Air Force photo interpreter

GM3 (Gunners Mate and Petty Officer Third Class) Elliot Whitlock—member of SEAL Team Sierra Six

GM2 (Gunners Mate and Petty Officer Second Class) Michael Norris—member of SEAL Team Sierra Six

In the U.S., enlisted men have "rates" rather than ranks. In describing an enlisted man's rate, one can use Petty Officer Second Class Jones which would mean he is an E-5. Or, you can refer to him by his job specialty, i.e. Machinist Mate Second Class Jones. Either is correct. U.S. Navy enlisted rates are:

E-1—Seaman Recruit

E-2—Seaman Apprentice

E-3—Seaman

E-4—Petty Officer Third Class

E-5—Petty Officer Second Class

E-6—Petty officer First Class

E-7—Chief Petty Officer

E-8—Senior Chief Petty Officer

E-9—Master Chief Petty Officer

U.S. Navy Officer Ranks (U.S. Army, Marine Corps, and Air Force equivalent ranks)

O-1—Ensign (second lieutenant)

O-2—Lieutenant junior grade (first lieutenant)

O-3—Lieutenant (captain)

O-4—Lieutenant Commander (major)

O-5—Commander (lieutenant colonel)

O-6—Captain (colonel)

O-7—Rear Admiral (lower half) (brigadier general)

O-8—Rear Admiral (upper half) (major general)

O-9—Vice Admiral (lieutenant general)

O-10—Admiral (general)

Big Mother 40

<u>North Vietnamese Army</u>

Captain Dai—administrative officer and adjutant of the 133rd Special Operations Regiment

Captain Nguyen Binh—leader of assault team that attacked the SEAL base at Cam Ranh Bay in So. Vietnam.

Colonel Nguyen Thai, commander of the NVA 133rd Special Operations Regiment

General Chung—Thai's former battalion and regimental commander, now head of personnel assignments for the NVA

General Tran Van Dong—head of the NVA's air defense system

Major Chinh Loi—Thai's executive officer/deputy

Major Trung—political officer of the 133rd Special Operations Regiment

<u>North Korean Peoples Army</u>

Lieutenant Colonel Kim—head of the North Korean engineer unit that helped build Venom

<u>Russians</u>

Colonel Alexei Koniev— Soviet Air Defense Artillery

General Dimitri Polikov—Head of the Zhukov Command Academy of Air Defense

Colonel Boris Rokossovsky—deputy head of the Russian military mission to North Vietnam

General Arkady Nikishev—Head of the Russian military mission to North Vietnam

Captain Pavel Prokiev—one of the missile officers that came with Koniev

Colonel Valentin Grushkin—Shadowy Soviet officer who is also a member of the Mafya, which is a criminal organization similar to the Italian Mafia.

GLOSSARY

2P—Pronounced "two P." Designates a copilot. The term came from the patrol and transport aircraft communities which often had crews with three pilots on long missions or transits.

AGI—U.S./Nato designation for a Soviet electronic intelligence gathering ship

"Alive in 65" medal—Also known as the National Defense Medal which was awarded to any service member who has spent 181 days or more on active duty.

Alpha and Bravo—Designation of the two crew-members which were preceded by the aircraft's call sign. For example, the pilot of Swordsman 505 is "505 Alpha" while the bombardier/navigator is "505 Bravo."

Angels—Term used to describe altitude in thousands of feet, i.e., "Angels ten" means that the aircraft is at ten thousand feet.

AN/PRC-90—See PRC-90.

ATO—Air Tasking Order.

AUTOVON—Acronym for Automated Voice Network which is the military's "private" global telephone network.

ASW—Anti-submarine Warfare.

Bar Lock—NATO designation of the surveillance radar normally associated with the Divina (NATO code name SA-2 Guideline). It was normally paired with a target tracking radar with the NATO code name of Fan Song that guided the missile to its target.

BDA—Bomb Damage Assessment.

BEQ—Bachelor Enlisted Quarters.

Big Mother—Call sign of the HH-3As flown by Helicopter Combat Support Squadron 7 crews.

Billiard Ball—Call sign for Air Force EC-121 signal intelligence gathering aircraft which flew orbits up and down the Ho Chi Minh trail and west of North Vietnam. Also performed the radio relay function for special operations teams who were deployed behind enemy lines.

BOQ—Bachelor Officer Quarters.

BN—Short for bombardier/navigator who was the second crewman in the A-6. While the pilot flew the aircraft, the BN operated the radar and other navigation instruments, as well as the aircraft's sensor package.

Buster—Fly as fast as the airplane or helicopter will go.

Bullseye—An arbitrary reference point in space used by U.S. Air Force and Navy to disguise actual bearing and distance information. Bearing and distance calls are made referencing the "bullseye" which makes it difficult for the enemy to understand the strike package's intentions or the location of the aircraft. The location of "bullseye" changes for each strike.

CDO—Command Duty Officer is the CO's representative and acts in his stead during the command's off hours.

Cherubs—Navy term to describe altitudes less than one thousand feet, i.e.: "Cherubs two" means that the airplane or helicopter is at two hundred feet.

CINCPAC—Commander in Chief, Pacific.

COD—Carrier on-board delivery, an acronym for the cargo airplane that delivers cargo and passengers from the beach to the carrier.

DCOS—Deputy Chief of Staff. Also known in the Navy as an "N head" because the deputies are numbered on Navy staffs, N1 thru N6. In the 1970s, department heads were:
- N1 – Administration
- N2 – Intelligence
- N3 – Operations
- N4 – Logistics
- N5 – Communications
- N6 – Plans

Marc Liebman

COMMACV—Commander, Military Assistance Command, Vietnam. Responsible for all U.S. forces operating within the boundaries of South Vietnam.

COMNAVFORVN—Commander, Naval Forces Vietnam. Responsible for in-country Naval forces. Reported to COMMACV.

CSAR—Combat Search and Rescue.

CTF-77—Commander, Task Force. Navy provided close air and naval gunfire support from the Gulf of Tonkin. Its aircraft flew strikes into North and South Vietnam

DET—Short for "detachment."

ELINT—Electronic Intelligence.

FAC—Forward Air Controller.

Feet Dry—Term naval aviators use when crossing from a body of water to flying over land. Opposite of "Feet Dry" is "Feet Wet."

"Frag"—Section of an Air Tasking Order that details all aspects of the mission, i.e., ordnance load, transponder codes, route, call signs, and other information.

GAZ 53 Truck—It is a 3.5 ton 4x2 truck from GAZ, introduced first as GAZ-53F in 1961. The original models were powered by an old 75 hp straight 6-cylinder engine from the GAZ-51. In 1964, a new variant the GAZ-53 and then the GAZ53A appeared which was manufactured until 1993. It featured a brand-new 4254 cc light-alloy V8 ZMZ-53 engine producing 120 hp at 3200 rpm giving a top speed of 90 km/h (56 mph). Payload was increased to 4 tons. All variants use four-speed gearboxes, synchronized on third and fourth gears.

GRU—GRU is the foreign military intelligence directorate for the the Soviet Army General Staff of the Soviet Union. GRU loosely translates to Main Intelligence Directorate. It much larger than the KGB and like the KGB, has its own military units.

HAC—Helicopter Aircraft Commander. The Naval Aviator responsible for completion of the mission and the safety of the helicopter and crew.

Big Mother 40

Hack—Unofficial disciplinary action in which the officer is restricted to quarters and may or may not be permitted to perform all of his normal duties. Being placed "in hack" is a temporary situation which may or may not result in a formal disciplinary action such as a letter of reprimand, unsatisfactory fitness report, or a court-martial. In most cases, it is used as a "time out" to send a message to an officer who otherwise performs his duties competently or exceptionally well.

HAL-3—Stands for Helicopter Attack Squadron. Light Three, a unit created during the Vietnam War to provide close air support using Huey (UH-1) gunships to Navy operations in the Mekong River Delta. It operated off several land bases and modified World War II-vintage LSTs anchored out in the delta that had a helicopter pad built over the main well deck.

HS-10—Helicopter Anti-Submarine Squadron Ten. This squadron was the Fleet Replacement Squadron (FRS) or RAG for the H-3 Sea Kings. Its mission was to transition pilots and crew members to the H-3.

IFF—Identification Friend or Foe. In U.S. military aircraft there are four modes. Mode 3 is a four-digit code that provides a unique aircraft ID along with speed and altitude information to the Mode-3-equipped radar. Mode 4 is a different, encrypted code which provides aircraft and weapon specific data used only by the U.S. and its allies.

JEST—Jungle Escape and Survival Training. This was a two-week course conducted during the height of the Vietnam War that selected Navy aircrews and others attended. The course included two or three days of practical "classroom" training followed by living and working at a captive camp and then five days of being chased through the jungle by Filipinos. The last five days were spent in a simulated POW camp in which the "instructors" accurately portrayed NVA and Russian interrogators.

Jolly Green—Call sign of the HH-3C and HH-3Es that the Air Force flew as CSAR helicopters. The name came from the dark green-and-brown camouflage paint scheme used by the helicopters. Later in the war, when the HH-3Cs and Es were augmented by HH-53s, the call sign continued regardless of the type helicopter.

LPA—Life Preserver, Model A. This vest had two bladders around the waist and another one that went up the back and around the neck. When inflated, it kept the pilot upright and his head out of the water.

MAC—Military Airlift Command.

Mustang—Slang term for a Naval officer with prior enlisted experience.

NATOPS—The Naval Air Training and Operating Procedures Standardization program prescribes general flight and operating instructions and procedures applicable to the operation of all U.S. naval aircraft and related activities. This also includes instrument flying where separate annual check rides are also given to each aviator. In addition, there are check rides for qualifications such as flight leader and helicopter aircraft commander and tactics. Open and closed book as well as oral exams are all part of the NATOPS check. In the '70s, the check rides were given in the aircraft, versus today, where they are often administered in a simulator.

Nisei—According to the Miram-Webster dictionary, a Nisei is "a son or daughter of Japanese immigrants who is born and educated in America, especially in the United States."

NKPA—North Korean Peoples Army.

NICPAC—Naval Intelligence Center Pacific.

NOFORN—Stands for "No foreign dissemination" and is term used to designate classified material that was not for foreign dissemination, i.e., could not be shown to members of friendly armed forces unless they were cleared for the information. For example, material in this category with a secret classification is designated SECRET NOFORN.

NVA—North Vietnamese Army.

O Club—Officers' Club.

O-in-C—Officer in charge.

USS *Oklahoma City* (CLG-5)—The *Oklahoma City* started out as a Cleveland class light cruiser designated CL-91 when the keel was laid in December, 1942. The 11,800 ton ship was launched in 1944 with a main armament of twelve six-inch guns in four armored turrets with three guns apiece, twelve five-inch guns and twelve 40mm guns. It could reach 32 knots, and in World War II its primary mission was to provide anti-aircraft defenses for the carriers. After being decommissioned in 1947, the ship was re-activated in 1957 and converted to a guided missile cruiser as part of what was renamed as the Galveston class and given the designation CLG, for Cruiser, Light, Guided Missile. The modifications reduced the displacement to about 10,000 tons by removing both of the aft six-inch turrets and seaplane handling equipment, which were replaced with a single dual Talos missile launcher and magazine. All the 40mm and five-inch turrets along its main deck were removed, along with the upper forward six-inch turret, and replaced with smaller, lighter turrets housing two five-inch guns.

Ops Oh—Short for Operations Officer.

PACAF—Abbreviation for Pacific Air Forces. When used as a name, the speaker is referring to the Commander of the Pacific Air Forces to whom all the Air Force units in the Pacific Theater report. He is also responsible for providing those units with logistic support. Air Force units that he is supporting may report to other commanders, such as Commander-in-Chief, U.N Forces in Korea; or, as in Big Mother 40, Commander, Military Assistance Command, Vietnam for operational tasking.

PI—Philippine Islands.

PI—Photo Interpreter.

Pigeons—The term for bearing and distance to a specific destination given from a radar controller to an airplane. The normal reference from the aircraft or helicopter's present position to the destination.

PRC-90—Survival radios for in-country teams. Enemy could pick up these transmissions with ease.

RAG—Replacement Air Group, a holdover from WW II and a term/acronym for the squadron that transitions Naval Aviators from what they had flown before to a new aircraft; or, if one has been on shore duty, back to the airplane. RAG or Replacement Air Group is still used today as a Navy term for Fleet Replacement Squadrons whose mission is to transition pilots just out of the training command or leaving desk/non-flying jobs to fly an aircraft or helicopter. Going "through the RAG" is required even if the aviator had flown the airplane or helicopter before.

RAWS—Radar Warning System. Sensor and display that shows an airplane that it has been targeted by a surveillance or fire control radar or the terminal seeker in a surface-to-air missile. On the cockpit display, it

Marc Liebman

shows the direction from which the missile is coming, and tones in the pilot's head set will tell the pilot whether or not the missile is in tracking or terminal (i.e., about to explode) mode.

Red Crown—Call sign for ships: guided-missile cruisers (CLGs) or large guided-missile destroyers (DLGs) stationed in the northern part of the Gulf of Tonkin. Ship's mission was to monitor North Vietnamese air and communications activities and provide radar vectors for intercepts and coordination for search and rescue operations. When it was operational, a data link between the ship's combat information center and the airborne E-2 gave them a shared and accurate radar picture of what was happening over North Vietnam.

REMF—Rear Echelon Mother-Fucker. Abbreviation is a derogatory term used to describe anyone who gets in the way of providing maximum effort in support of those at the pointy edge of the sword.

RHIP—Rank Has Its Privileges.

Ring-knocker—Slang term for a U.S. Naval Academy graduate. Term came about because during boards of inquiry, the accused would turn his ring around and gently tap the green covered table as a subtle reminder that he was an Annapolis graduate in the hopes that the board would find in his favor or assess minimal punishment.

RPV—Remotely piloted vehicle, aka: drone.

Route Packs—To prosecute the air war against North Vietnam, strike planners divided the country into six "Route Packages." Route Packs 5 and 6 encompassed Hanoi and Haiphong, while Route Pack 1 was the southern panhandle of North Vietnam from just south of Vinh to the DMZ. Route Packs 2, 3, and 4 encompassed the remainder of the country. The Air Force was assigned primary responsibility for Packs 1 and 5, while the U.S. Navy was assigned Packs 2, 3, 4 and 6. Route Pack 6 was later divided into Packs 6A and 6B with the Air Force being given 6A and the Navy 6B.

SARCAP—Search and Rescue Combat Air Patrol. Refers to the aircraft designated either ad hoc or as part of a pre-briefed and planned operation to a CSAR mission to provide close air support.

SERE—Acronym refers to the Survival, Escape, Resistance and Evasion course which is mandatory for all Naval Aviators and other designated war fighters. The curriculum includes classroom and field training in survival and evasion techniques. It culminates when students spend at least three to four days in a "simulated" POW camp where they are subject to many of the methods of interrogation and torture used by our enemies.

Shitty Kitty—Derogatory nick name for the USS *Kitty Hawk* (CV-64). Other ships got similar names such as "Forrest Fire" for the USS *Forrestal* (CV-59) after its disastrous fire, "Toasted O" for the USS *Oriskany* (CV-34) for a similar event, "Foul, Dank, and Rusty" for the USS *Franklin D. Roosevelt* (CV-42) due to its age, and the "Shitty Shang" for the USS *Shangri-La* (CV-38) due to its age and other habitability issues.

SIGINT—Signal Intelligence.

SLJO—pronounced "Slo Joe" and stands for "Shitty Little Jobs Officer." The Slo Joe in a unit is typically the most junior officer and he/she gets the jobs no one else wants, or those that come up that everyone else is too busy to do but need to be done.

SOB—Souls on Board. This term was borrowed from ship operations to designate the number of people on a particular aircraft.

Spetznaz—Soviet Special Forces.

Spooks—Pre-political correctness Navy term for those involved in the intelligence business.

Spoon Rest—NATO designation of the long-range surveillance radar normally associated with the Divina (NATO code name SA-2 Guideline) that could detect a high-flying targets out to about 250 nautical miles. It was normally mounted on either a truck or a trailer for portability. It was normally paired with a target tracking radar with the NATO code name of Fan Song that guided the missile to its target.

TACAN—Tactical Air Navigation system. Unique to the military, system provides bearing and slant range from the ground (or sea-based station) to the aircraft.

TAD—Temporary Additional Duty.

Thud—Slang name for the F-105.

Wetting Down—Traditional celebratory gathering during which the Naval officer getting promoted or receiving his warfare designator buys appetizers and adult beverages for his peers in his unit and invited guests.

Wild Weasel—Name came from a classified program during which the Air Force developed the capability to electronically hunt the radar used to control surface-to-air missiles. The term was given to the F-100s and then the F-105s that were tasked with the mission of finding, suppressing, and destroying North Vietnamese surface-to-air-missile launchers, radars sites, and control vans. The two-seat F-105Ds carried both bombs and missiles that homed in on radar that were tracking aircraft. Since the Vietnam War, the term refers to both the aircraft tasked with the SAM suppression mission and the missions themselves.

Winchester—Term used in Naval Aviation to indicate that they were out of weapons.

XO—Short for Executive Officer or the second in command of a Navy unit.

U.S. Aircraft Type Designations
A Attack
B Bomber
C Transport
E Special Electronic Installation
F Fighter
G Glider
H Helicopter
L Laser
O Observation
P Patrol
Q Unmanned Aerial Vehicle
R Reconnaissance
S Antisubmarine
T Trainer
U Utility
V Vertical take off and landing: VTOL; Short take off and landing: STOL
X Research
Z Lighter-than-air

Big Mother 40

Designations for Specific Mission Modifications
A Attack
C Transport
D Director (formerly G)
E Special Electronics Installation
F Fighter
H Search and Rescue (formerly S)
K Tanker
L Cold weather
M Missile carrier or Multi-mission
O Observation
P Patrol
Q Drone
R Reconnaissance
S Antisubmarine
T Trainer
U Utility
V Staff
W Weather reconnaissance

A-1C/Es—Piston engine dive bomber designed for the Navy in the mid-1940s and used to support rescue aircraft. Call sign for the A-1s flown by the U.S. Air Force during the Vietnam War to support search and rescue missions was Sandy.

BQM-34L—This was the L-model of the Firebee series of drone vehicles designed in 1961; they were taken out of service after the Vietnam War. The jet-powered drone was about 29 feet long and had a wingspan of about nineteen feet. Range and speed varied based on the model, but the L could fly at about 580 knots and fly about 750 miles and weighed just over 3,000 pounds with full fuel. Over four hundred of the L models were built.

EC-121—Military version of the Constellation transport designed in the 1940s. In this book, Billiard Ball is the call sign of an electronic intelligence gathering/command and control aircraft.

F-105—Thunderchief Fighter bomber.

HH-3C/E—Rescue helicopter with the call sign Jolly Green Giant. The HH-3C/E flown by the AF has the same rotor system, engines and cockpit as the Navy version. The helo has a different cabin with a ramp in the back instead of the boat hull of the Navy versions. It is a derivative of the Navy's SH-3A.

RF-101 Voodoo—Reconnaissance aircraft based on F-101 fighter

A-3—The A-3 Sky Warrior was, at the time, the largest aircraft to operate from an aircraft carrier. The A-3D was also known as "All Three Dead" because there were no ejection seats and the crew had to bail out through a slide from the cockpit. It was also known as the "Whale" and the gyrations during an arrested landing were the source of amusement among those who didn't fly it. By the Vietnam War, the A-3s were no longer used as bombers and all the ones in the fleet had been converted into either EA-3Bs, which had five electronic warfare officers or linguists in the belly where the bomb bay was, or made into tankers and called KA-3s.

A-4 Skyhawk—Small single-engine attack aircraft designed in the early 1950s. Over three thousand were produced and used by ten different countries.

A-6E Intruder—Twin-engine, all-weather attack aircraft. Grumman-built, carrier-based medium attack aircraft designed for low-level, all-weather strike operations. The A-6 carried a crew of two, a pilot and a bombardier/navigator, who sat side by side. The A-6E model was introduced late in the Vietnam War.

A-7E Corsair—Single engine, light attack aircraft.

E-2A Hawkeye—carrier-borne airborne early warning and control aircraft. The radar was optimized for over-the-water operations. Carried a pilot and co-pilot, four Naval Flight Officers, and an enlisted air controller in the cabin.

H-3 Sea King—During the Vietnam War, the Navy used both the ASW version, the SH-3A and the version modified for combat search and rescue, the HH-3A. Big Mother 40 was the call sign of an HH-3A in Helicopter Combat Support Squadron 7

H-53—Large, single-rotor, heavy-lift helicopter flown by the U.S Marine Corps and Air Force.

RA-5C Vigilante—(a.k.a. Viggie) Twin engine, supersonic reconnaissance aircraft that started as a bomber. Squadrons who flew them were designated RVAH for Reconnaissance Helicopter, Heavy Attack.

North Vietnamese Aircraft
MiG 21—Jet interceptor. NATO code name Fishbed.

Russian Aircraft
AN-12—four engine transport aircraft, also known by its NATO code name of Coot

Bear—NATO code name for the Tu-94, which is a four-engine turboprop. The Bear comes in several flavors: bomber, cruise missile shooter, electronic surveillance, radar, and anti-submarine versions. Designed and built in the '50s as a strategic bomber, the versatile aircraft is still in use in the 21st century.

Weapons
AAA—Spoken as "Triple A" and is a generic term that refers to any country's anti-aircraft artillery.

AK-47—7.62mm assault rifle.

AZP S-60—A Soviet-towed, road-transportable, short-to-medium-range, single-barrel anti-aircraft gun from the 1950s. It was used extensively by the North Vietnamese.

DshK—12.7mm heavy machine gun designed by the Russians to give it an equivalent weapon to the U.S. military's M-2 heavy machine gun, which is another classic John Browning design.

52-K 85mm Anti-Aircraft Gun—Gun originally designed in 1939 to shoot down airplanes as high as 34,000 feet. Weapon was widely used by the Soviet Union in World War II and has been exported to many countries. It required a crew of seven and could fire 10-12 rounds per minute. It was the primary heavy anti-aircraft gun used by the North Vietnamese to shoot at high flying U.S. jets.

Hush puppy—Smith and Wesson Model 39 9mm caliber semi-automatic pistol used with a silencer for use in killing people and not giving away one's position with the sound of gunfire.

GAU-2B/A Mini Gun: Six-barreled, electrically powered gun designed and built by General Electric that was capable of firing up to

6,000 7.62mm rounds per minute. Modeled after the Civil War era Gatling Gun. Other versions were built in 20mm and 30mm.

Model 1911: .45 caliber semi-automatic pistol designed by John Browning

MP-5: 9mm assault rifle. Designed by the German company Heckler & Koch and widely used by free world special operations teams.

LAW: designated the Mk. 72 Light Anti-tank Weapon. Designed to destroy tanks and armored personnel carriers. Used in Vietnam to take out bunkers.

M-2: .50-caliber machine gun.

M-16: U.S. Army standard rifle in 5.56mm.

M-60: Standard U.S. military 7.62mm light machine gun.

M-61 Vulcan: Six barreled 20mm cannon carried in the F-105 that is loosely based on the Civil War Gatling Gun.

M-79: Single-shot, breach-loading grenade launcher that fires a 40mm grenade about 300-400 feet.

PKM: A Soviet light machine gun that fired the same cartridge used in the AK-47. It fires at about 650-850 rounds per minute from box magazines that contain 100, 150 or 200 round belts.

S-75 Divina: (also known by its NATO code name of SA-2 Guideline) Divina is the Soviet name for a surface-to-air missile that is what they call "command, line of sight." When the missile gets near the targeted aircraft, the missile explodes based on its proximity fuse or by a command from the operator.

Stoner: Light machine gun designed by Eugene Stoner, who also designed the AR-15, which is now the M-16 family of weapons. The Stoner, designated the M63A1, was used by SEALs in Southeast Asia as a light machine gun. It could fire from standard 20 and 30 round M-16/AR-15 magazines as well as special 100 and 150 box magazines and belts of the standard 5.56mm ammo. The weapon was replaced by the M-249 squad automatic weapon

ABOUT THE AUTHOR

MARC LIEBMAN

Marc Liebman is an experienced writer as well as a Naval Aviator combat veteran of both Vietnam and Desert Shield/Desert Storm. He retired as a Captain after twenty-four years in the Navy and a career that took him all over the world. He has just under 6,000 hours of pilot-in-command/co-pilot flight time in a variety of tactical military, civilian-fixed and rotary-wing aircraft. In the business world, he has been the CEO of an aerospace and defense manufacturing firm, an associate editor of a national magazine and a copywriter for an advertising agency. Marc lives in North Texas with his wife of 42+ years, Betty, and two dogs. He spends a lot of time visiting his four grandchildren.

Marc Liebman

THE SEA
WAS ALWAYS THERE

"Admiral Callo takes you to sea...with the perspective of a naval leader with more than thirty years of experience as reserve officer and a seaman, with far-ranging experience under sail, including three hurricanes at sea."

Peter Stanford, President Emeritus, National Maritime Historical Society

"Callo's book is thus comprehensive. He finds in the sea and seamanship an education in virtues as fine as those that apply to family life and as broad as those that shape the fortunes of empires. In between is his experience as a naval officer and his consistent effort to understand from experience.

Fireship Press
www.FireshipPress.com

Sales@ Fireshippress.com

Found in all leading Booksellers and on line eBook distributers

387

**For the Finest in
Nautical and Historical
Fiction and Nonfiction**

WWW.FIRESHIPPRESS.COM

Interesting • Informative • Authoritative